The Bookshop
of
Second Chances

The Bookshop
of
Second Chances

A Novel

JACKIE FRASER

BALLANTINE BOOKS

NEW YORK

A Ballantine Books Trade Paperback Original

Copyright © 2021 by Jackie Fraser
Book club guide copyright © 2021 by Penguin Random House LLC.

Published in the United States by Ballantine Books,
an imprint of Random House, a division of
Penguin Random House LLC, New York.

BALLANTINE and the HOUSE colophon are registered
trademarks of Penguin Random House LLC.
RANDOM HOUSE BOOK CLUB and colophon are
trademarks of Penguin Random House LLC.

Originally published in the United Kingdom by Simon & Schuster
UK Ltd in 2020. This edition published by arrangement
with Simon & Schuster UK Ltd.

ISBN 978-0-593-35565-7
Ebook ISBN 978-0-593-35566-4

Printed in the United States of America on acid-free paper

randomhousebooks.com
randomhousebookclub.com

Title-page image: © iStockphoto.com

Book design by Dana Leigh Blanchette

For

KAY NELDRETT

5/28/46—2/14/01

AND

ANNEMARIE FRASER

11/8/45—12/17/10

The Bookshop
of
Second Chances

One

Yesterday was Valentine's Day. Three weeks since I lost my job—made redundant and turned out of my office with no notice—and ten days since my husband, Chris, henceforth known as "that bastard," left me. Or did I leave him? Maybe I did, since I'm the one who had to, you know, leave.

I spent the day lying on the ugly uncomfortable sofa bed in my horrible new flat and cried ugly uncomfortable tears. And I drank a lot of gin. I watched *Black Narcissus* and *Mary Poppins,* randomly, and wept throughout both. Today I have a headache and it's hard to say if it's a hangover or a surfeit of emotion. My eyelids are swollen. I'm only dressed because Xanthe—best friend, confidante and primary support system—shouted at me when she rang earlier. We're now sitting at the tiny table in the kitchen half of the flat, writing lists. Soon, in half an hour or an hour, we'll go to my old house and pack up my things and that will be the next step on this god-awful "journey."

"Do you want me to go?" Xanthe asks. "I could do it for you. If you wanted."

It's odd to see her so serious. She usually laughs all the time, endlessly amused by everything. Hard to find anything funny about this.

"No, don't be . . . You can't, can you? You won't know what everything is. I know I've got to do it."

"I'll come with you, though." She looks at me, clearly trying to judge whether I'm in any fit state to do this.

"That would be . . . Yes. Thank you."

Crying all the time is so *boring*. It's been a long time since I've had a broken heart and I'd forgotten how tediously dull it is. I blink at her and blow my nose for the billionth time. The original plan was to do this task yesterday, but I couldn't see him on Valentine's Day, could I?

This time last year we went away. We stayed in a tiny cottage near Rye. Our eighteenth Valentine's. We drank champagne and sat in front of an open fire and said things like, "Still here, then!" and told each other we loved each other. I think one of us may have been lying.

Because people who love their wives don't tend to sleep with their wives' friends, do they? And that's what my husband—sorry, I mean "that bastard"—has been doing, with my so-called friend, Susanna Howich-Price (also known as "that bastard") for the last . . . Well, they wouldn't tell me how long. But does it even matter? Not really. Five years or five months, the result's the same.

I've hired a van. Chris and I have already had not an argument, but a debate, about some mid-century modern occasional tables we bought last year. I'm not sure how we're going to deal with the things we both actually want.

"Put anything you can't agree on in one room and then go through it at the end. You'll just have to compromise," says Xanthe, sensibly.

She's right, but I feel sick with anxiety. I don't want him to . . . win. But it's not about that, is it? It's not a battle, or a competition. And I don't want to fight; I'm exhausted. Some of it I don't care about, so he can keep the sofa, the sideboard, and the dining room table and chairs. I've never liked those chairs. So that's something for the bright side, along with never having to listen to his dad and brother talk about Formula One ever again. I'm trying to be positive.

"Don't tell him you don't care, though. Go with the assumption you want everything. You're already ahead with the compromise, aren't you?" she says. And I am. Because he's keeping the house. And Susanna's already living there, some of the time at least, although she won't be there when we go round. I made him promise. I don't want to see her. The idea of her living in my house, using my plates, eating food I probably bought, sleeping with my husband . . . Ah. It's not surprising, is it, that it makes me feel sick?

. . .

I don't know what to say to him when he opens the door and steps back awkwardly to let me in. I had to knock, on my own front door. But it's no good thinking things like that. As soon as I start thinking about the carpet in the hall, which is new, or the mirror in the dining room, which belonged to his grandmother, whom I loved, I'll get upset. It's just stuff. But all this stuff is shorthand for our relationship. Everything chosen or placed by both of us. A thousand decisions, the background to love. No. Think about something else; think about the practicalities.

The easy things first. Up into the attic for the box of schoolbooks and the other boxes I moved to this house from the last house, and to there from the flat and to the flat from my parents'. I'm a bit of a hoarder, so there are Sindy dolls and Lego pieces and all sorts of junk. I should probably get rid of some of it, but now is not the time. I bought boxes from the storage place and we work quickly. Who gets the Christmas decorations? We should split them, shouldn't we? D'you know what? I don't care.

"Screw all this," I say. "They can have it. Whatever."

"Okay," says Xanthe. "I think you should leave yourself an open door, though. In case you change your mind."

"Ugh. Let's just . . . get on with it."

I shovel random things from the bathroom cabinet into a box. I'd already taken all the things I use regularly, but there's Halloween makeup and occasional-use false eyelashes and—will I ever need any of this?

"Just pack it," Xanthe says patiently. "You can decide if you want it when you unpack in your new house."

"Ha. Whenever that will be."

I pack three winter coats I haven't worn for ten years and my leather jacket. I fill a box with fabric. Chris and Susanna are sleeping in the spare room—some kind of moral thing, I assume. It would be a bit much, wouldn't it, for them to sleep in our bed? I don't like to think about whether they've been doing that for all these weeks or months or years, anyway.

But I guess this means I can have the big bed. That's mine—or at least, I bought it, with the money from a bonus. The mattress cost nearly a grand. All the king-size sheets go in a box and we fold the duvet into one of those vacuum-pack bag things. Four pillows, half the pillowcases. Three tablecloths. The second best towels—they can have the new ones, a gift last Christmas from Chris's sister. How magnanimous of me. Xanthe empties my clothes from the wardrobe into a suitcase and tips the contents of drawers on top of the clothes. Stockings, socks, slips, and nightdresses; my fancier underwear, none of which I'm likely to need ever again, let's face it. Scarves and jewelry, hair slides and curling irons, and T-shirts.

"So much stuff," I moan weakly.

"Come on. Half done," she says.

We take the bed apart, exposing acres of dusty carpet, an earring. Xanthe stoops quickly to pick something up, but not so quickly I don't see it: the torn half of a condom packet. She pushes it casually into the pocket of her jeans and neither of us says anything.

We wrestle the mattress downstairs.

"I'm going to take the little bedside cabinet," I tell Chris, who is sitting tensely in the dining room. He nods, silent.

That's everything from upstairs except books. I'm exhausted. At least being busy stops me from crying.

He's put all the photographs of us in a box.

"Don't you want any of these, then?" I'm upset about that, to be honest. But he looks haunted, and says, "I just can't—I'm not in the right place to do photos, Thea, I'm sorry."

"Okay. Shall I leave them? We could do them later. I mean, please don't throw them away—"

"I'll put the box in the wardrobe," he says. "Take what you want, though."

"I'm not sure I can look at them either." It's easy to pack my photo albums from before I met him, but who gets the wedding album? This is awful. I'm almost inclined to say it's the worst day of my life, but I think that happened already.

We come to an agreement about the occasional tables. I pack my great-aunt's china but leave our wedding-present saucepans and the champagne glasses we only bought in December. I take my records—yes, I still have my records—and my CDs. The books are overwhelming.

Xanthe makes tea, and we all sit, slightly awkward, at the kitchen table to drink it. There's a vase I've never seen before on the table, full of daffodils from the garden. My daffodils, that I planted.

"I'm not sure I can do any more today." I look down at my jeans, which are furred grey-brown with dust.

"You don't have to," says Chris. "I mean, it's mostly books now, isn't it? You can do the books whenever you like. Or I could do them. If you wanted."

"I expect I should just get on with it. I don't want it hanging over me."

"Give me a box, then, and I'll do some."

He wants me gone, and who can blame him?

I'm thinking, trying to remember what else needs to be packed. "Sewing machine. And my bike."

"Okay," says Xanthe. "I'll get your bike, shall I? Garage keys," she adds, holding her hand out to Chris. He gets up and lifts them off the hook by the back door. We bought that in Cornwall; it's shaped like a mushroom. The house is full of things that remind me of other, better times, but I can't take them all with me; it's not possible. And would it help? Probably not. I take a pair of fused glass hearts from a nail by the fridge and put them in my pocket. I open the cutlery drawer and say, "You'll need to get a new garlic press. I'm taking this one because it used to belong to Polly Watson's granny."

I shared a house with Polly Watson twenty-five years ago, and I never met her granny. However, the garlic press is part of my life, and I want it.

By the time we've finished, I feel like I've run a marathon, or walked the length of the country or something. The thought of unpacking all of this into a storage unit and then one day packing it all back into the van and on to a mysterious and unknown home makes me want to cry and never stop.

"If you think of anything else," says Chris, "just let me know. And I'll give you some money, for the sofa and the dining room furniture, and—"

"Good," says Xanthe. "Maybe you should write that down? It will save any hassle later. When my dad left, my folks didn't sort anything out. They still moan about it now. You know, someone else"—we all know who she means—"might tell you you're being overgenerous. I don't think you are; I think you're being very reasonable, which is great, but stuff changes. You'll forget what Thea's like. You might get resentful."

He frowns at her. "I don't think—"

"I know. But seriously. Just write it down."

"All right," he says, and goes to find some paper.

I agree to make a payment to Thea to cover the cost of half the sofa and the tables, etc., he writes. "Okay?"

"Thanks," I say.

"Yeah, look, I don't want to be a dick about this."

"More of a dick," says Xanthe, and laughs at his expression.

"You know I didn't plan for any of this to happen," he says. Not to her, to me.

I can't look at him, or not full-on. I keep glancing side-ways, just catching glimpses. Our eyes never meet.

"Yes. It's all right. Or . . . no, it isn't, it's . . . but I know you didn't exactly do it on purpose."

"No. I really didn't." He looks knackered, almost as bad as I feel.

"Anyway, I'd better go."

He nods, and then says, "Oh, wait. There's a letter."

"A letter?"

"It only came yesterday. I thought, as I was going to see you . . . Hang on," he says, and disappears for a moment into the study. "Here. A solicitor's letter, I think. Have you—"

"Not my solicitors," I say, taking the envelope from him. I hesitate and then tear it open, rapidly scanning the con-tents. "Oh, weird."

"What is it?" says Xanthe.

"It's Uncle Andrew." I look at Chris. "Great-Uncle An-drew I should say."

"The one who died?"

I nod. Great-Uncle Andrew died last year. I didn't go to the funeral, he lives—lived—in Scotland, and I'd only met him a few times. My grandfather's eldest brother, he'd out-lived Grandad by a good fifteen years and made it to ninety-three.

"And?"

"He's left me his house," I say, rather stunned.

"Ooh, really? Where is it?" asks Xanthe. "Somewhere glamorous?"

"It's about an hour west of Dumfries," I tell her, and laugh at her disappointed expression. "I've never been there. It's the arse end of nowhere."

"That's useful," says Chris. "I mean, so you'll be able to sell it, hopefully, and buy somewhere better . . . than if you just had the money for this."

I can see he's relieved; it will make him feel better, and look better, if I can afford something reasonable. "I suppose so," I say. The letter mentions some money as well, but I don't say anything about that. It's quite a substantial sum. I'm suddenly aware that the mostly low-level but occasionally serious anxiety I've been feeling about my job, or lack of, has dropped away. It's not enough to live on forever or anything, but it's certainly a relief.

"How come he's left it to you? No kids?" asks Xanthe.

"He had a daughter. Dad's cousin. But she died, years and years ago." I try to remember what happened. "I think she drowned? Or something. It's weird he didn't leave it to Dad, though, or Auntie Claire."

"How exciting," she says. "So do you have to go and pack all his stuff? I guess you're in the right mood to sort through more boxes."

This makes us all laugh, a release of tension.

"I hadn't thought of that. I suppose so." I look at the letter again. "Apparently it's all gone through and everything, so this bloke"—I turn the letter over—"Alistair Gordon, of Smith, Gordon and Macleod, has the keys for me and some paperwork. 'Let me know when is convenient for you to take possession of the property. I'll be delighted to take you to the house' and etcetera. And yes, it says 'contents' and it says . . ." I continue, reading again more carefully, "He collected books, and the library—ha, library—was valued a couple of years ago, but should probably be reappraised. The collection should be sold through a reputable dealer if I decide I don't want it."

"Wow," says Xanthe. "Does the house have an actual library?"

"I don't think so. I don't think it's very big. West Lodge, it's called. Anyway, we can look it up later. Poor Uncle Andrew. I feel bad now that I didn't go to the funeral."

"Is that the will?" asks Chris, as I unfold a fat photocopy.

"Yeah. Oh look, he explains—'and to my great-niece Althea Lucy Mottram née Hamilton' blah blah 'whom I have only met on four occasions, but who each time was intent on reading rather than talking, which has always been my own preference.' Oh bless. Well there you go, Mother, so much for saying no good will come of it."

Two

It takes me almost six weeks to organize myself sufficiently to take a trip to Scotland. I don't know why; I'm not busy unless you count lying in bed and crying as busy.

I have several telephone conversations with Alistair Gordon, who has a delightful accent and sounds rather lovely. He says the lodge is "perfectly habitable," although it will need airing if I want to sleep there. The electricity is still connected, and the phone, so it won't be like camping, which is lucky as it's still March for another four days. We discuss how long I might stay, and he offers to go over and check how everything is, which I suspect is above and beyond, but I shan't complain. I ask if this favor will cost me three hundred pounds an hour and he sounds shocked when reassuring me. He and Great-Uncle Andrew were good friends, he tells me. I admit this is rather disappointing, as it must mean he's at least sixty-five. Even that would make him thirty-odd years younger than Andrew.

Not that it matters how old he is, I just quite liked the idea of meeting a charming Scottish lawyer. He's probably married. Most people are, aren't they?

...

"I'll come with you," offers Xanthe. "How long you going for?"

We're in our favorite coffee shop, downstairs among the secondhand books and bits and pieces. It's always quieter downstairs, because the staircase is an unhelpful cast-iron spiral, off-putting to young mums and old people alike. Outside, the rain is relentless, disguising the signs of spring.

"I dunno, I thought maybe two weeks. It shouldn't take too long to sort out his stuff. And then I can put the house on the market and do a bit of sightseeing. If it's warm enough."

"What's to see?" Xanthe looks unconvinced.

"Castles. And beaches. It looks quite pretty, a bit like Cumbria. Not so dramatic as the Lakes. Or as touristy."

"Cool. I don't think I can come for a fortnight," she says, "but I could come up for a week?"

"That would be brilliant. It might even be fun if you're there."

I've been a bit worried about going on my own. It's a long way to go by yourself if you don't know anyone. I know that's a silly thing to think; I'm an adult, and from now on I'll be doing everything on my own, but it's still nicer to have company.

I wonder if I should hire a van. I might want some of the furniture, perhaps; and there are bound to be things that will need to be brought down and added to my storage unit. Or maybe I should wait until I get up there. I don't want to drive a van to Scotland on the off chance. And I suppose it doesn't matter, I've got plenty of time and there is, rather excitingly, forty thousand pounds in my current account. I've divvied up a further forty-five grand into various savings accounts

and fought the temptation to buy something completely ridiculous. I did get some new clothes, though, even though
I'm unlikely to need summer dresses in Scotland in April.
Especially if I'm mostly going to be driving to the charity
shop or the dump.

I've never had to make so many decisions all at once. I
can't even remember if I've ever had to make any on my own
before. I must have, but this all seems . . . almost overwhelming. But not quite. It's good to have things to think about
that have nothing to do with Chris.

. . .

The night before we leave for Scotland, my friend Angela
phones to tell me she's been invited to dinner by Chris and
Susanna, and to ask if I mind if she goes.

"It seems so odd that it'll be at your house," she says. "I
don't want to upset you. I think it's awful, Thea, but I feel
like I should go. Should I? I like Chris." She tuts. "I thought
I liked Susanna, as well, but now I'm not sure."

I'm faintly amused by this. I feel she should have asked
Xanthe's opinion, rather than mine, but Angela isn't tactful.
"You must go if you'd like to. Don't think about me."

"But it's so *awful*. I can't believe she—"

"It is awful. But it's . . ." I thought I was going to be able
to say this without that light-headed feeling of misery and
the pricking tears, but apparently not. I clear my throat. "But
the thing is, she did, they have, it's—that's how it is. It's not
my house anymore. It's their house." I wonder if I'll ever
truly believe this.

"I'd be so *angry,* though, Thea. If it were me."

I laugh. "I am quite angry. And I'll probably be angrier yet, before I feel better. But there's nothing I can do, is there? And it makes no difference whether I'm angry or miserable or whatever. If you want to be friends with them, you know, it's fine. Go to their house and eat their food and . . . just don't tell me about what they're up to." I pause for a moment, thinking about this. "Unless I ask."

"Well, okay."

"And even if I do, you probably shouldn't, to be honest."

• • •

I'm packed and ready. I just have to collect Xanthe, who is doubtless frantically rushing about, preparing Rob for a week alone with the kids, and then we're off. It's a Sunday, so I'm hoping the roads will be empty. We should be in Gretna by half past four.

Six hours in the car. It rains the whole way. We eat sweets and sing along to an exhaustive playlist that Xanthe has compiled, tracks picked deliberately from before I met Chris, songs from our youth. It's always fun to go on a road trip with a girlfriend. As long as no one gets shot and you don't have to drive off a cliff, it's all win, right?

At Gretna, we're staying in the nicest hotel I could find— sick as I am of efficiently bland budget hotel chains. I demand cocktails (although maybe not too many), a super king-size bed and fancy chenille sofas. It's glamorous in a low-key modern way. We toast each other in the bar and make up stories about the other guests. We go to bed early because we're old and exhausted. I lie awake for a while, listening to Xanthe's gentle snores. I try to calculate how many different beds we've shared but I get muddled around the mid-1990s and fall asleep to dream the sort of oddly complex and anxiety-driven dream that's not much more relaxing than being awake.

· · ·

We're due in Baldochrie for eleven o'clock, which seems quite a civilized time to meet a lawyer. I'm not sure why I'm nervous about it, but I am. It's an odd thing to be anxious about. It's not like he can decide I'm not a suitable person to inherit Uncle Andrew's house. It takes me ages to realize that perhaps I'm not anxious at all, but excited.

Dumfries and Galloway is one of those large, amalgamated counties. It's not astonishingly beautiful, or wild, not like the west coast farther north. It's quite rural: cattle country and sheep. The towns are small, and the A75 bypasses most of the ones I've heard of. We drive past Dumfries itself, Castle Douglas and Kirkcudbright. Sometimes we get a brief view of the sea. It's still raining, though, grey and wet, a sharp wind. There are lots of lorries, heading to or from Stranraer. Maybe it would be pretty, if it wasn't raining; it's hard to say. We drive past little cottages and large Victorian villas and untidy farmhouses and caravan parks. There are castles, in various states of ruin. It looks cold out there, and some of it is definitely windswept. It's strange to arrive somewhere knowing parts of it might become familiar, but you don't know which bits. I always feel like this on holiday, wondering which road I'll drive along most frequently, which shops I'll go into, where I'll buy petrol.

And then here we are in Baldochrie, finding somewhere to park outside the rather grand Victorian town hall in a little square of neat stone houses. There's a church, a war memorial with a kilted soldier, and proper shops—a Co-op, an antiques shop, two cafés, a chemist. Daffodils, long over at home, are still dancing in the churchyard. It's quite nice, old-fashioned. Nothing exciting, obviously, but I've seen some sad little towns where everything's boarded up or for sale and it's not like that. There's a butcher's and a baker's and everything.

"Bloody hell," says Xanthe. She gazes through the raindrops on the car window. "Imagine living here."

"It's not so bad," I say. "Although I can't think there'd be much to do if you were a teenager."

"Jesus. Nearest nightclub fifty miles away, probably." We both shudder. "And I'll be bringing some much-needed diversity to the scene," she adds. "There'll be people here who've only seen black women on the telly."

"Oh, come on."

"Betcha."

"Anyway," I say, "there's the solicitor's." It was a large square Georgian building, originally a house, with three steps up from the pavement, statutory brass plaque and a boot scraper.

"Exciting. Are you excited?"

"I'm not sure. I suppose so. It's odd."

"I'll go and have a coffee. You don't need me to come in with you, do you?"

I hesitate. "I guess not."

"It's nearly eleven," she says. "Come on."

It's windy, a bit of drizzle blatting against the windshield. I pull on my jacket and smooth my skirt, crumpled from two hours in the car.

"You look very smart and responsible," she says. "Text me when you're done. I'll be in"—she looks across the road—"that one. The Lemon Tree."

...

A terribly pleasant middle-aged lady looks up as I close the door behind me.

"Good morning," she says. "Now, you'll be Mrs. Mottram?"

I nod in agreement. A little sign on her desk says she's Mrs. McCain. I look around at the room I'm standing in, a large entrance hall, black and white marble tiles. Perhaps a little chilly for Mrs. McCain. I can smell an electric heater of some kind, and suspect it's under her desk, keeping her legs warm. An impressive staircase of polished dark wood curves upward, the desk tucked in beside it. On the wall next to her there's a large and rather gloomy portrait of a young woman in white satin, draped on a sofa.

There are three doors, one to my left, and two on the right. White-painted, elegant. A large vase of daffodils sits on the desk, along with a telephone and computer. Between the two doors on the right, a cushioned but backless bench, long enough for two or three people to sit on. Above it, a huge mottled mirror, which has probably been there since the house was built.

Mrs. McCain smiles at me. "I'll let him know you're here. Have a seat."

I haven't time to, though, as the door on my left is opening and here's Alistair Gordon, hand out in greeting. "Mrs. Mottram. It's good to finally meet you."

He's much younger than I was expecting. In fact, I suspect he's rather younger than I am. And he's reminded me that I might have to change my name. Should I? I'm not going to be Mrs. Mottram for much longer. How does that work? How do you decide?

As we shake hands, I'm confused and tongue-tied. I follow him into his office, and accidentally say, "I thought you'd be older. I mean—I'm sorry—you said you were friends with Uncle Andrew."

"We weren't at school together or anything," he says, amused.

"No, I . . . Even if you were older," I say, "you couldn't be as old as he was and still be working. I was just expecting you to be older. Not that it matters. Oh God, now I'm just . . . Do excuse me." I laugh. "Everything's rather unexpected."

"Have a seat," he says. He offers me a drink, asks about the journey. We talk about the traffic and the roadworks and he opens his office door and asks Mrs. McCain to make some tea. I've always wondered what it would be like to have a PA. I doubt I'll ever find out. I almost ask him but, really, I need to control this urge to just say whatever comes into my mind.

I feel a bit awkward, partly because Xanthe spent quite a lot of the journey wondering about Mr. Gordon, and we laughed a lot at her imaginings, mostly because he was bound—guaranteed, in fact—to be very different from her daydreaming. And he is, I suppose, as we thought he'd be dark but he's blond. He is quite good-looking, if you like people who look posh, which I always pretend I don't. They have good bones, usually, and tend to be attractive; it's centuries of breeding. He's probably only thirty-five or something, though.

He comes back to his desk and sits down. "My father was Andrew's solicitor before I was," he says. "I'd known him since I was a child. I gather you didn't know him that well yourself?"

I shake my head. "Hardly at all. The whole thing was rather a shock."

I look around, surreptitiously searching for the obligatory photograph of wife and children. I can't see any but, then again, these days people have their kids as wallpaper on their computer screen, don't they, rather than a framed photograph on their desk. There's a small painting of a dog on the wall by the door. A golden retriever. The room has a fireplace and beautiful plaster cornices, and shelves in the alcoves on the fireplace wall filled with boxes neatly labeled with surnames. One of these, with *HAMILTON, A F & M G* written in beautiful handwriting, sits on the desk between us. There's another painting over the mantel, of mountains and moorland, and a watercolor between the windows, which I think is of the town square. It's amusing to have a painting more or less of the view outside.

"So, have you been to Baldochrie before?" he asks, leaning back in his chair.

"No, I never have." I tell him I feel terrible about never

visiting, about not coming to the funeral. I ask him to tell me what Uncle Andrew was like, and begin to form a picture of him: self-reliant, a gardener and a lover of books, always smartly dressed, and funny; very sharp, says Alistair Gordon. "He made me laugh a lot. I miss him."

Three

I pull off the road behind Alistair's BMW, onto the wide graveled drive that curves round beside West Lodge. I'm excited to see it in the flesh, although I've looked at it on Google Street View many times. It's a neat one-story grey stone building with a slate roof. The lawn in front is beginning to be shaggy, there are tulips and primroses, and some sort of climbing plant, still very naked, so possibly wisteria, curling round the bright red front door. Xanthe and I get out of the car and crunch across to where Alistair waits. It's stopped raining, and there's a hint of sunshine away to the south. Water drips from the eaves. He hands me two sets of keys and gestures toward the gate and the road that passes through it, onward toward the house for which the lodge was built. I've looked at that on Street View too, a large and imposing Georgian building that might be a hotel or a school. There's no sign, though, no car park full of cars—so perhaps not. Although surely no one lives in such a big house these days.

"So that's the Drive," he says. "It's private—as much as one has private land in Scotland. That's all the road up from the turning, and through the gates. You and your visitors and tradesmen and so forth are allowed free access. As I say, that's just a polite technicality."

The gates are elaborate wrought-iron things easily twice my height. I don't think they've been closed for a long time.

"Your uncle bought the lodge in the late fifties, from the present laird's grandfather. So Lord Hollinshaw would be your closest neighbor. The house—Hollinshaw House—is about a mile further on up the drive."

"An actual lord?" asks Xanthe, disbelieving.

Alistair nods. "I'm afraid so. Quite a lot of the estate buildings were sold—not just West Lodge. The postwar period was tough for the gentry," he says, slightly sarcastically. "They had to sell various things to pay for the upkeep on the house, which is an unnecessarily grand building. The tenth Lord Hollinshaw sold almost all the estate buildings. East Lodge, this one, some cottages built for gardeners and game-keepers, and the home farm. And then his son sold off all the land that wasn't directly associated with the house, so they just had the park."

I step backward, looking up at the roof of the lodge. It looks fine from here. My dad said I ought to have a survey done, like I would if I were buying it. I suppose he's right.

"Dreadful for them," I say.

"Yes. Anyway, since Charles took over in the midnineties, he's been buying things back. West Lodge is the only estate building still belonging to someone else. I can assure you that, should you decide to sell, he'll bite your hand off."

"Oh really?"

Alistair has stepped up to the front door. He turns to look over his shoulder at me. "Very keen to get it all back. He rents them as holiday lets, mostly. His first wife was an interior designer; the properties are very stylishly done. They were in all the magazines when he finished East Lodge and the cottages. And the newest one was in *The Telegraph* magazine just last year. Andrew was holding out, but I don't think you should let that affect your decision."

"How many wives has he had?" asks Xanthe, always eager to know the details.

"Oh, only two. I mean, he's been married twice. And divorced twice," adds Alistair.

"Really?" Xanthe raises her eyebrow at me and I try not to laugh. She's decided that being with the same person for twenty years is "horribly boring" and I've had a "lucky escape" from the tedium of long-term monogamy. This is all an elaborate joke to make me feel better, of course. It's not exactly working, but I appreciate the attempt.

I clear my throat. "He didn't want to sell? Or he didn't want to sell to Lord Whatsit?"

"Hollinshaw. They didn't get on, it's true. Ironic, really, because . . . Well, it's a long story," he says, "and it's not my story to tell."

"Oh, go on," says Xanthe, "you can't just leave us hanging."

He unlocks the front door with a third set of keys, which he then hands to me, and ushers us inside. There's a long passageway with a flagstone floor and various white-painted doors opening off it on both sides. It smells slightly stale, but not damp. There's a twirly Edwardian hallstand with a mirror and hooks for coats, with walking sticks and a multicolored golf umbrella leaning against the central drawer. A pair of Wellington boots, a waterproof jacket. These objects, evidence of the life lived here, make me feel slightly melancholy. I shiver, wishing again that I'd visited Uncle Andrew before he died.

I open the first door on the left and glimpse a pale-carpeted sitting room with lots of furniture. We stand in the hall, though, while Alistair continues, "Your uncle didn't get on with Charles's father at all. James. I'm not exactly sure what caused that, to be honest. But anyway, when Charles . . . It's rather complicated. Charles is the younger brother, you see; Edward renounced the title."

"Gosh," I say, "like Tony Benn?"

"I should think Tony Benn was a pretty big inspiration, yes. So he—Edward—didn't get on with his father either. He and your uncle were good friends, actually. Because of the books."

"Oh yes, the books. We should look at the books."

"Through here." He leads the way down the corridor and opens the third door on the right. The room's in darkness, blackout blinds at the window. Alistair pauses on the threshold and continues. "Yes—Edward's a dealer. A book dealer, I mean," he adds hurriedly, which makes Xanthe snort with laughter. "He has a shop, in town—you might have noticed it? It's across the square from my office. His father hated it. Anyway, when James died, Edward . . . Well, as I say, he renounced the title, which passed to Charles. Charles is more business-minded, I suppose. Made a lot of money from property development in Edinburgh and Glasgow. He was determined to buy back the estate houses at least, although all the farmland is another matter. He got the home farm back about five years ago, but there's a lot more land that was bought up piecemeal by various people in the fifties and sixties. And, like I say, he bought East Lodge and the lower farm cottages and so on." He taps his fingers on the door and changes the subject. "But these are the books. Edward appraised this lot for Andrew the back end of . . . not last year, the year before. The appraisal probably still stands, but you might want to ask him to take a look for you."

He flicks the lights on.

"Bloody hell," says Xanthe.

The room is lined with bookshelves, and the shelves are full of books. Most of them are leather-bound with gold-blocked titles. Like a mini, stately home library with busts of Milton, Shakespeare and Newton, and a very faint musty smell overlaid with leather.

"Shit," I say, and then apologize.

"Yes, so, these"—he waves a vague hand—"are all first editions, I think, Scott and so forth, and there's quite a large Burns collection. And, anyway, I don't know if you'll want to keep them, but they are worth quite a lot of money. Edward has said he'd be interested, of course . . ."

"So I could sell the house to Charles and the books to Edward?"

"If you wanted, I should think so, yes."

"Handy."

"Yes. Or you might want to give the books to someone, I don't know; the Burns people might be interested. Anyway, you should probably talk to Edward about that. Although I warn you, he's not easy to get on with. My fiancée"—Xanthe pulls a disappointed face at me; hopefully Alistair doesn't notice—"prefers Charles; she says 'at least he's charming.'" He laughs. "But perhaps I'm being unfair."

I can see he doesn't think it's unfair at all.

"Yes, and as I say, they don't get on. Did I say that? Hate each other."

"It's like a soap," says Xanthe, delighted.

"Why don't they get on?"

"Oh, heavens. Very complicated. Um. Something to do with Charles's wife," he says, embarrassed. We both turn to look at him. "Ex-wife, I should say. Or at least that's the rumor. Or one of the rumors; look, I'm being indiscreet, I should stop. Anyway, you might prefer to take the books home, and sell them in London or something. Edward knows his stuff, but he can be . . . difficult."

...

After four days, Xanthe and I are doing well, sorting out Uncle Andrew's belongings. It's been quite a lot of work, but I feel like we're getting somewhere. I've been through all his clothes, and the everyday shirts and trousers and sweaters are in bin bags ready for another trip to the charity shop. I've kept some things—there are four splendid tweed suits with waistcoats, and a kilt with all the trimmings. A pile of beautifully pressed handkerchiefs. Several brimmed hats that I suppose are trilbies. I don't know what I'll do with any of it, but I couldn't quite bring myself to get rid of it all.

In the wardrobe in the spare bedroom there's a box of things that belonged to my dad's cousin Fiona, Andrew's daughter. A sad teddy bear, baby shoes, some school prize, children's classics, photographs. She was only fourteen or something when she died. So long ago. I'm still not sure what happened; I must remember to ask next time I speak to my parents. I put the lid back on the box and return it to the shelf. There's enough going on without upsetting myself by thinking about the young woman who never really got to be, who should be the one doing this, who has been dead for such a long time.

Also in the wardrobe, and folded into the chest of drawers, are some of Aunt Mary's clothes: the clothes of her youth, beautiful full-skirted dresses from the 1950s; some lovely knitwear, cashmere; and smartly tailored tweed skirts. I don't think any of it will fit me, but I should be able to sell it, along with the handbags and shoes and scarves. There's a fur coat too, which I personally wouldn't wear, but I know people do.

We've packed up the duller, less interesting kitchen stuff, and various ornaments that don't appeal, and some fishing-themed prints and drawings that I don't care for. It's difficult to make decisions about the rest of it, since I don't know what I'm going to do with the house.

"You could let it," says Xanthe. "I mean as a holiday cottage. It's just the right size."

"I could. In which case I should definitely keep some of the kitchen stuff. Although I guess people will prefer mugs, won't they? And plates from IKEA. New things." I stand, hands on hips, and look at the contents of the cupboards laid out before me on the table and the counters.

She shrugs. "You could buy some new stuff as well. You'd need to get the bathroom done, if you're going to rent it."

The bathroom is fine, but she's probably right. It must

have been done in the seventies; the suite is pale green, avocado I suppose, with angular taps, and it doesn't have a proper shower.

"Might need to get a dishwasher if I was going to rent it out."

"I'd certainly never stay anywhere that didn't have a dishwasher. I mean, imagine washing up on your holiday?" She pulls a horrified face.

"I don't know where you'd put one. So that might mean a new kitchen, and then if I spend ten grand or something on doing it up . . . I don't know. And Wi-Fi."

"Oh my God, yes."

There's barely a signal out here, no 4G, and of course Uncle Andrew didn't have a computer. There's a landline, a cream-colored dial telephone that sits on a little table by the window in the sitting room, and a second one, in green, in the master bedroom. We spend a lot of time writing notes of things we need to look up when we're next in town, using the free Wi-Fi in one of the cafés, or sitting in the car outside the town hall, piggybacking.

"You'd have an income, though, which might be handy. I suppose it depends on what you're going to do when you go home. And when you get the money from Chris."

"Ugh. Yes. I don't know what I'm going to do, I can't even think about it."

"We'll just get rid of the stuff you definitely don't need. It'll be fine."

Clothes, then, and nonessential/nonpleasing kitchenware. There are some ugly glasses, and some cups and saucers that don't match anything else, and some elderly pans, which probably need to go to the dump, although I'll try to offload them at the charity shop.

We're filling the trunk of the car with stuff when the clip-clopping sound of a horse on the drive grows louder and louder. We both look up and watch as someone trots along the road toward us, coming from the direction of what I like to call the Big House, aka Hollinshaw.

"Blimey," says Xanthe, "a man on a horse."

The horse stops at the entrance to the driveway, where the gravel begins, and the man touches his hand to the brim of his riding hat.

"Good afternoon," he says.

"Good afternoon," I respond, interested. This must be him, surely, the twice-divorced lord, the brother of the bookshop man, whom I have yet to meet. Although his hat hides his hair, I can see he's dark, with firm eyebrows and a square jaw. Quite handsome, in fact. Not young, probably about the same age as us. Tweed jacket, biscuit-colored jodhpurs, shiny black boots.

He swings himself down from the horse, which is large and brown. Bay, is that what they call it? It's that bright, almost ginger color with a black mane and tail, and a white blaze on its nose. Everything I know about horses comes from reading pony books as a child, so I'm no expert. It pricks its ears toward us. The man loops the rein loosely over the gatepost, and walks up the drive, unbuckling his black riding hat as he does so. He takes it off as he reaches us, runs his hand through his curls, and looks from one of us to the other. I wonder if he's trying to decide if it would be racist to assume it's me he needs to speak to.

He avoids choosing which of us is Mrs. Mottram née Hamilton by saying, "My name's Maltravers, Charles Maltravers. We're neighbors. I live up at Hollinshaw. Thought I should pop down and say hello."

Perhaps it's not him, then? Or do they have different surnames to their titles? I try to remember. Nancy Mitford's father was a lord, but he wasn't called Lord Mitford, was he?

I step toward him and hold out my hand. "How kind. I'm Thea Mottram, this is my friend Xanthe Cooper, she's come up to help me get organized."

He shakes my hand, then Xanthe's, and then looks at the car stuffed with boxes and bin bags.

"Sorting out Andrew's belongings?"

"Yes, quite a job," I say. "I'm not sure he ever threw anything away."

"Always difficult when there's a whole life to deal with. He lived there for a long time."

I nod, and we all stand and look at one another for a moment. Then he says, "He was your uncle?"

"Great-uncle. My grandfather's eldest brother."

"Ah, so you're a Hamilton," he says, smiling at me. His eyes crinkle attractively. "I think we're very distantly connected. And what are your plans? Are you going to sell?"

Xanthe snorts with laughter but manages, perhaps convincingly, to turn it into a cough. I smile winningly. "I'm not sure. I haven't decided yet. I thought I might keep it, at least for a while. I've heard you let some of the houses on the estate as holiday rentals?"

"Yes, that's right. Just working on a conversion of some outbuildings, actually. When those are finished, we'll have six holiday rentals and two long-term. You won't be living here yourself?"

"I'm not sure it's practical," I say. "I live in Sussex."

"Ah!" He laughs. "No, perhaps not. Well, you might hear from others that I'm keen to buy back the properties my father and grandfather sold off. If you do decide to sell, let me know. I'll make you an offer. Market value of course."

"Oh," I say, pretending ignorance, "really? That's interesting. I'll keep it in mind."

"And do come up to the house, if you'd like," he says. "We'll give you the tour. Have you seen it?"

I admit that we've sneaked a look from the road that crosses the park.

"Just follow the Drive up," he says. "I'm usually about the place." He shakes my hand again. "Good to have met you."

He shakes hands with Xanthe, puts his hat back on and untethers the horse, swinging himself smoothly up into the saddle. Once again, he touches the brim of the hat to us, and trots off in the direction from which he came.

"Who's 'we'?" I wonder. "I thought he was divorced."

"Must have a girlfriend, though, surely. I mean, phew, etcetera."

I look at her.

"Well? Didn't you think?" She laughs.

I laugh too. "I don't know, I suppose he was quite handsome. You can't fancy lords, though, Xan, you have to resent them and their privileged nonsense."

"He must be rich if he's buying back houses. What did Alistair say he did? Property development?"

"Slum landlord, more like."

She snorts. "Cynic. You won't be able to say stuff like that

to people up here, will you? They'll all be in thrall to his centuries of oppression." She chuckles to herself. "My mum is
gonna freak when I tell her I've met an actual lord."

"It's a bit mad, isn't it? Anyway, come on, let's get this lot
to town."

Four

It's Xanthe's last day. I left her drinking coffee in the Old Mill, which is, we've decided after some experimentation, the best coffee shop. It has a little gallery selling artwork by local potters and painters, and a courtyard garden full of flowers. Jilly and Cerys, the women who run it, are incredibly friendly and helpful, recommending the best places for a bigger shopping trip than you can manage in the Co-op, but without driving to Dumfries for the giant Tesco. They've introduced me to a builder, and a plumber as well; and they do very good bacon sandwiches.

Xanthe's stayed longer than she should have—a week and a half—but she can't stay forever; she has a job and children and dogs to think about. As we ate our breakfast in the sunny kitchen this morning I told her I'd been thinking, vaguely, about perhaps staying up for a bit. I could spend the summer here. I feel comfortable and at home in the lodge, surrounded by Uncle Andrew's belongings, some of which were once my great-grandparents'. (I know this because there's a note in with the paperwork Alistair gave me. *Dear Thea, I thought you might be interested to know that the table in the sitting room belonged to my parents, your great-grandparents. It was a wedding present from my mother's father, your great-great-grandfather, and was purchased in Dumfries in 1896.)*

Now that the sun's out, it's tempting. It's too late to do much in the garden, but we looked in the fruit cage and I did briefly fantasize about living here permanently. A fruit cage is a good thing to own, after all. Plus, it's wonderfully quiet, being so far from any other houses, and the trees are fantastic. I'm looking forward to being here by myself, although I didn't say that to Xanthe. I expect it's pretty miserable in the winter, though. And what would I do? I doubt there's much work. And although that's not urgent, even selling the books won't keep me forever.

Selling the books—that's why I'm here, outside the bookshop. The dark green sign says FORTESCUE'S BOOKS in elegantly curled writing, and ANTIQUARIAN AND SECONDHAND BOOKS is painted in gold across the large plate-glass windows. I push the door open and a bell jangles above me. The shop is, I think, converted from a house, a large square Georgian house, like Alistair's office, which is across the street. There aren't steps at the bookshop, though; the wide, recessed, half-glazed front door is at pavement level and opens into a broad sunny space, perhaps knocked through from two smaller rooms. There are what might loosely be described as window displays, although, to be honest, they're just piles of books. I think someone should be paying more attention. My suspicion, unfounded of course, is that whoever is in charge thinks such things are beneath them.

The floor is slightly uneven, with large worn flagstones, the walls are probably twelve feet high and lined with bookshelves. The fireplace has been boarded over, but a large green majolica jardinière full of tulips sits on the hearth.

There are stacks of orange Penguins on the mantelpiece, and above them, a framed print of the town hall. A bookcase beside the door holds crime novels from the seventies and eighties and shields the counter from the doorway. There are two middle-aged men browsing, a pair of wooden step-ladders to access the higher shelves, and signs everywhere. PLEASE ASK FOR ASSISTANCE IF YOU WANT SOMETHING YOU CANNOT REACH, says the one closest to me. There's a rack of vintage postcards of the local area in fantastically saturated colors, and a list of QUESTIONS TO WHICH THE ANSWER IS NO, all of which are quite obnoxious. I can tell Edward Mal-travers (or someone who works for him) adds to these as they occur to him, since halfway down it says, DO YOU HAVE OR WANT TO BUY *FIFTY SHADES OF GREY*? Another one says, ARE PEOPLE MORE IMPORTANT THAN BOOKS? and, MY CHILD DOES NOT READ, WILL THEY BE OKAY?

Curmudgeonly, I decide.

Here on the more dimly lit right-hand side, clearly visible from the counter, are the antiquarian books, quarto and folio: a whole shelf of Shakespeare, Victorian and older, and many other things, some titled in Latin. PLEASE DON'T TOUCH THESE BOOKS UNLESS YOU ARE SERIOUSLY THINKING OF BUYING, says a sign, BUT FEEL FREE TO ASK FOR HELP.

I like books, but I'm no expert. Uncle Andrew owned a lot of books, many of them by people I've never heard of. I have the most recent appraisal, done the September before last, a year before he died, and the total is rather unexpectedly high. Now I want to know how much the Scotts are worth. I don't get on with Scott, and I imagine that they might fetch more up here, or in Edinburgh, perhaps, than if I took them home. I'm not sure whether to sell the entire library or not, but I definitely don't want to keep them all, or even most of them, because of the responsibility as much as anything. And because think of the *other* books I could buy with the money. I had a dream last night that Uncle Andrew's library was filled with my own books. It was quite satisfying.

...

A door at the back of the first room of books leads into a passage that widens into a hallway where a wide, elegant staircase climbs upward. There are more shelves in the passage, and even some leading up the stairs to the half landing. It's hard to get a feel for what the building would be like without the books, but it's well proportioned and there are so many period details it's hard to concentrate. The books and shelves make it feel quite dark, but there are lamps everywhere and natural light falls down from the stairwell, filling the hallway with golden sunshine. There are battered Persian rugs on the flagstones, and each nook and cranny is neatly filled with shelves and books, each section labeled: Children's (Collectible), Children's (Just for Fun), Military History, Ancient History, etcetera and so on. There are three rooms: the main one at the front; another, beyond the staircase, which is Poetry/Plays/Lit Crit and looks very cozy with two sofas and a coffee table spread with poetry mags; and a much larger one at the back, with stripped oak floorboards, its window obscured by shelving. A door leads out to a garden, I presume, although you can't see much. There's a large shed or workshop in the way, allowing just a glimpse of trees and shrubs. The whole place smells of beeswax and old paper and is, I have to admit, rather lovely.

Having explored, I return to the first room and approach the counter. I think it's an old sideboard or console table, slightly Arts & Crafts, with doors at the front and three drawers in beautiful honey-colored wood. Topped by a vast slab of marble and quite high, it's certainly above waist height to most people standing on the customer side. There's an old-fashioned wooden box till sitting on the top, a couple of books propped up in Perspex stands and a desk bell, like in a hotel. Thick dark curtains hang down, blocking the light from the window. Behind the counter, up a step, there's an unraveling armchair and a little desk with a laptop. Sitting in the armchair, hunched and crowlike, is a dark-haired man. It's shadowy, and he has a green-shaded desk lamp to light his little corner. He's looking at something on the screen and is surrounded by more books piled around him, lots of them with pieces of paper sticking out, marking his place or maybe just particularly fascinating parts. I stand by the counter for a minute or two, but he doesn't look around or acknowledge me at all. I'm not exactly surprised; it's not like I haven't been warned.

I'm tempted to ring the bell, but that seems even ruder than being ignored.

"Hello," I say eventually.

He looks up. He doesn't actually sigh, but he may as well have.

"Yes?" he says.

"I was wondering if you could help me," I say, refusing to be discouraged.

"I doubt it."

For some reason, this amuses me. "You probably can. It's a book-related question."

This time he does sigh. "Whatever makes you think I know anything about books?"

"It's just a hunch. Are you Edward?" I can see him wondering whether to deny it. "I've inherited some books," I continue. "And I probably need to sell some of them. Or all of them."

He stands up, or rather unfolds, and comes to lean on the marble countertop. He has good bones, a strong jaw, and eyebrows clearly made for scowling. He scowls. I know he's older than the other one, the lord. Charles. He might be five years older than I am, perhaps. Approaching fifty. There's not much grey in his hair, which is wildly curly like his brother's, but rather longer and more unkempt. He's wearing a dark blue sweater with a small hole (moths?) in one shoulder, a dark patterned shirt underneath, vaguely floral. He has dark eyes, a wide mouth, and the straight teeth of the well-bred. And he's tall, much taller than I am, he might be six four, even allowing for the fact that he's standing on a raised platform. He looks down at me, and I look up. It's quite intimidating.

"What kind of books? I'm not interested in your granny's Mills and Boon." He pauses, thinking. "Unless you have any from the early sixties or before."

"I don't think either of my grannies ever read any Mills and Boon," I say. "They were *Jane Eyre* and *Rebecca* all the way. But anyway, no. I think you've seen them. The books, I mean. If you *are* Edward. I want to know how much my Scotts are worth, and whether I should sell them up here or at home."

"You think I've seen them?"

"Yes, apparently. First editions. Uncle Andrew's books."

He frowns at me. "Uncle . . . Well, but you can't be Andrew Hamilton's niece, surely."

"Why can't I? Oh, but I'm not. I'm his great-niece."

This is apparently more acceptable. He nods. "Char-
lotte," he says. "Or Emily, or something."

"Thea Mottram," I say, slightly irritated. "Hello."

"Yeah, hi." He looks at me for a moment and then walks
to the edge of the counter and down the step, coming out
into the room toward me. I step back, involuntarily, which he
seems to find amusing. He grins at me and sticks out his
hand. "Hello. I'm Edward Maltravers."

We shake. I like shaking hands, much prefer it to kissing
people. His hands are very large. I'm not a remotely small
person—I'm five eleven, more with my shoes on—and I
rarely feel short, but he really is tall, a good four or five
inches taller than I am.

"The Scotts," he says. "All of them?"

I nod.

"About eight hundred quid for the lot. Maybe a bit more.
I'd have to look at them. A couple of them are in worse condition than the others. But some are very good."

"And should I sell them here? Or in Edinburgh?"

"You should certainly sell them to me."

"Yes, I can see that would be good for you, but would that
be the best thing for me to do? If you don't think you can give
me an objective answer," I add kindly, "I'll ask someone
else."

"My prices are fair," he says abruptly.

"I'm sure they are. But if I'm going to sell them, I want
the best price I can get, naturally."

"Why don't you want them?" He frowns at me.

"I've tried and failed to read *Ivanhoe* about five times," I say, "and *Waverley* twice. And if I were going to read them, an ordinary Penguin Classics edition with notes would be more my thing. I mean they're lovely, but wasted on me, I'm afraid."

"Huh. Are you going to sell the lot? I mean, all the books?"

"I'm not sure."

"The Burns stuff is probably worth more. Those Dickenses. The twentieth-century first editions. And the Newton." He says "Newton" with particular intensity.

"Is it? You see, I've no way of knowing. Alistair suggested I might want to give the Burns stuff to the Burns people. I can't imagine I've got anything they don't have, though."

"Alistair Gordon?"

I nod.

"Hm. There are American universities who'd snap them up. Buy them off you, probably. Or if you want to be Lady Bountiful . . ." he says sarcastically.

"I don't know what I want to do with them."

He looks at me, pulling at his lower lip. "Are you going to live there? At the lodge?"

I shrug. "I doubt it, it's not practical. It's a long way from home."

"Which is where?"

"Sussex."

"Going to sell it, then?"

"Probably."

"Don't sell it to my brother," he says.

"If I put it on the market, I don't think I really get to choose who buys it." I smile my glossiest, most society smile at him.

He snorts. "You won't have to put it on the market. He'll just turn up and offer you money. How long have you been here? I'm amazed he hasn't been round already."

"We've been here ten days," I say. "Came up last Monday."

"Who's we? You and Mr. Mottram?"

I decide to ignore this, since it's none of his business. "But actually, you're right, he did come and introduce himself the other day. He said he'd buy it if I wanted to sell. He didn't make me an offer, though."

He nods, clearly pleased to be proved right. "Not yet. He will. I'd prefer if he was foiled."

"It's so nice to see family feeling," I say, brightly.

•••

After arranging a time for Edward to come and look at the Scotts, I collect Xanthe from the Old Mill and drive her to Dumfries station, an hour and twenty minutes away. It'll take her seven hours, more or less, to get home. Rather her than me.

We're pretty much the only people at the tiny station. "Let me know how it's going," she says, "message me when you're having a coffee."

"I will."

"And you can phone me. From your actual telephone." She mimes dialing a number.

"I know."

"If you feel sad, or lonely."

"Yes. Thanks, Xan. You've been brilliant." I'm almost anxious, now that she's leaving.

"It's been fun. It's nice here. I'm really not sure if you should sell it."

"Maybe I'll move up." I look around at the more or less empty car park. "There's probably room for me."

"Don't go crazy." We hug. "Oh now, look, I'm crying," she says, wiping her eyes. "What an idiot."

"You are an idiot," I agree. "But I love you. Have a . . . Well, I won't say have a great journey. Have a journey that's not too awful. Give my love to Rob and the kids. I'll see you when I get home."

"All right, my love. I'd better go." We hug again, then she picks up her rucksack and heads to the barriers, turning to wave before she goes through. I wave back, and stay for as long as she's visible moving through the station. There are only two platforms, up to Glasgow, down to Carlisle.

Then I'm alone. It's an odd feeling. I'm three hundred miles away from everyone I know. Well, technically of course I'm not three hundred miles away from Xanthe. And I'm not three hundred miles away from Bobby and Sheena, who live in Newcastle, or various second cousins who are scattered round the Lowlands; not that I really know any of them. But the point is, for all intents and purposes, I'm alone. No one to please but myself. No one to talk to, unless I make an effort. I'm both thrilled and terrified by this feeling.

I drive back to the lodge. The weather is mixed today—quite grey this morning, and raining a light mist in Dumfries. But on the drive back the sun comes out and I'm feeling quite . . . positive. I wonder if I *could* live up here. Not forever, that doesn't seem realistic. But I could definitely stay up for the summer, couldn't I? Go home if I get bored, or when the weather gets bad. Although that will mean paying rent for a flat I'm not living in. But does that matter? I can afford to do it, and Xanthe or Angela can water the plants and send on my mail. It's rather tempting. I can find out about holiday rentals, and see what the lodge is worth if I wanted to sell it, or have a new bathroom put in, and just . . . not be at home. I can pretend everything's all right. I can maybe get to a point where everything *is* all right. That must be possible, surely?

Five

This morning Edward Maltravers is coming to look at my books. He'll be my first visitor—I don't think Xanthe counts. I hoovered for the first time and decided I'll need to buy a new vacuum cleaner since this one is ancient and inefficient. I ought to buy it locally and contribute to the economy—and since I can't immediately go online and order one, I might even manage to do this. I'll ask Edward if he can recommend somewhere. I tidy up and dust in the library. I expect he'd disapprove if it was dusty in there. I expect he'll disapprove anyway. I line up two cups in the kitchen and get the biscuit tin out. I'm almost nervous.

He's due at ten-thirty and it's absolutely on the dot when he knocks.

I open the door and am surprised again by how tall he is. I rarely have to look up when I speak to anyone. Today he's wearing dark jeans and a purpley blue jacket over a dark shirt.

He frowns at me, as though faintly confused by my presence. "Hello," he says. "You asked me to come and look at your books."

I'm amused he might think I've forgotten why he's here. "I did. Come in. Thanks for coming out."

"No problem." He looks around. "Bit strange to be here without Andrew."

"I haven't changed much," I reassure him as I usher him into the sitting room and gesture at the sofa. "Have a seat. Would you like a drink?"

He nods. "Tea, no sugar. Thanks."

"Won't be a moment," I say, and hurry out to the kitchen. When I come back with cups and saucers (note to self again: buy mugs) on a tray with the biscuit tin, he's standing by the window with his hands in his pockets, looking out at the garden.

"Always liked it in here," he says, "nice sunny room. Although that fire surround is an abomination."

We both look at the fireplace, which is brick, with a horrible copper sort of hood thing and niches for ornaments.

I laugh. "I suppose Andrew must have done it? Looks fifties or early sixties maybe."

"Yeah, I expect it's more efficient than what was there before. You could probably open it up, though," he says, coming over to sit down. "The original one will be behind it."

"It's not old enough to be an inglenook or anything thrilling, though, is it? I mean the lodges would have been built at the same time as the house. When was that? Eighteenth century? I can't picture what would be behind it."

"It probably is bigger. You could ask Charles"—he says the name with a twist of dislike—"to dig out the plans for you. They'll be up at the house."

His legs angle upward from the sofa, making him look as though he might be a different scale to the furniture, half a size larger, perhaps.

"Really?" I stare at him, although it makes perfect sense, of course.

He nods. "Whole archive full of that stuff."

"When was the house built?"

"They started work in 1770. The lodges were built after the house was finished, so probably around 1775."

"It's odd; it doesn't feel as old as that. I suppose there's been so much done to it."

"They tried to modernize it. Make it more appealing to the tenants. In the 1911 census there were twelve people living here," he adds. "Nine children. A granny. And the lodge-keeper and his wife."

"Bloody hell." I can't imagine it. "Nine children? I suppose the library was another bedroom. Bloody hell."

"I think so. It was pretty spacious I should think, for working people at the time. I've got some pictures at the shop. I should have brought them to show you."

"Of the lodge?"

"Yes, some early prints, and some old photos as well. There are loads more up at Hollinshaw. Actually, there's probably stuff here. I'm sure Andrew had some drawings and prints."

"Oh, I'd love to see what it used to look like. Not much different?"

"All veg out the front, and a pig," he says, smiling. "No wisteria."

"Oh, so it is wisteria. I wasn't sure."

"It'll look amazing in about two weeks. You have to prune it hard twice a year. February and August."

"Oh, okay, so I've missed one lot. I'll have to look it up. I don't know anything about wisteria." I open the biscuit tin. "Two ends of the spectrum. Rich tea or Tunnock's caramel wafer?"

"Oh," he says, "you've learned my weakness." He takes a wafer from the tin and grins at me. "Thanks."

"So you appraised the books before?"

"I did, yes. Must be eighteen months ago, two years maybe. Probably won't be much different, although he did buy more."

"I just want to know about the Scotts, and then if there are other, like, sections. I think I'll keep some of them, but mostly, like I said, they're wasted on me. But I do like them. I'm a bit conflicted."

"If you're not going to read them . . ."

"I know, and I probably won't. I looked at the Dickens, but I just think . . . I've got some already, you know, and although mine aren't worth anything, that's a good thing in some ways. I don't know. And I was thinking maybe I should turn the library back into a bedroom. Or a dining room or something. I just need some advice, really."

"Okay." He takes a bite of his wafer and chews thoughtfully. "The Newton's probably worth the most. You might get forty grand for it. I don't know what he paid; he'd had it for fifty years or something."

"Forty grand? For one book? Shit." I'm horrified. "Should it be locked away somewhere?"

He shrugs. "Two volumes. It's probably in the safe, isn't it? And it's unlikely it'd get stolen. Unless someone knew it was here. I won't tell anyone," he adds.

"Is there a safe? I haven't seen one. Alistair never mentioned a safe."

"I'll show you. Anyway, Newton. They're quite rare. And he's very famous."

"Well, I know, but—"

"Second edition, 1713," he says. He sips his tea.

"Oh my God." I think for a moment. I read a biography of Isaac Newton quite recently. "Is it maths or optics?"

"Maths . . . well. The *Principia. Opticks* you can get for about three grand. I've got one, if you want one."

"Wow. No. Forty grand?"

"Yeah, I can't buy that from you, sadly, but I could sell it for you."

"Shit."

He drains his cup. "Let's go and have a look, then, shall we?"

I follow him out to the library. "Hope you're keeping the blinds drawn," he says.

"Oh, yeah. For the bindings? Yeah. I only opened them this morning to dust and because you were coming."

He stands in the middle of the room, looks about and sighs. "It's a shame to break it up."

"I know, don't make me feel worse than I do already. But, you know, I'll probably sell the house and I don't have room for a library. Oh and now I'm so anxious about the Newton," I say, wringing my hands.

He laughs. "Don't be."

"Easy to say."

He walks across to the desk by the window. There's a cupboard beside it, supporting the bust of Shakespeare.

"There's no key for that," I tell him. "Or at least I haven't found one."

"It's got a catch," he says, and leans round behind it to

press something. The cupboard door springs open to reveal the green-painted door of an old-fashioned safe.

"Oh!"

"Yeah, the lock on the door is fake," he says. "The safe came from one of the banks in town. He had the cupboard made to fit round it."

"How clever. But how do we get it open? I don't have the combination."

"Fifteen, ten, twenty-eight," he says, twirling the knob. "Mary's birthday. Unless he changed it. Ah, no, there we are." He opens the door and we peer inside. The books lie on the top shelf. There doesn't seem to be anything else in there, no jewels or piles of cash, sadly. He pulls a pair of white cotton gloves from his jacket pocket and puts them on. "I'll take them out."

I watch as he places the first volume carefully on the desk. It's remarkable to own such a thing; in fact, I'm not convinced I really do. It should be in a museum or something, surely. He turns some pages. There are diagrams and equations, and the text is in Latin.

"Oh lord, it's all so intimidating."

"It's just a book. No need to be intimidated." From the way he runs a finger down the edge of the pages, though, I'm not sure he thinks it's "just a book."

"There," he says, "I'll leave it out for you to look at. Make sure you put it away later." He takes off his gloves and hands them to me. "Try not to touch it without them."

"Okay, thanks." I'm not sure I want to touch it at all, the whole thing is overwhelming.

He clears his throat and turns away from the desk. "Anyway," he says, "the Scotts. I had a look online this morning,

I could give you five hundred pounds for the matching 1871 set—those aren't first editions. Retail is about six hundred. This *Ivanhoe* is a first edition, and in lovely condition. Six grand. I forgot he'd bought that."

"Wow."

"The other first editions aren't in such good shape. Two hundred quid each for *Guy Mannering* and *Heart of Midlothian*. Five hundred for the rest."

"Okay." It's terrifying, frankly.

"Your Burns collection's worth about eight grand. I doubt there's anything amazing there that the Burns people would want."

"Would you buy them?"

He pulls at his lip. "Yeah, probably. I can usually shift Burns. The Trollopes are good; the matching bindings mean they were put together as a collection, probably in the twenties. Three and a half thousand."

"Gosh."

"I mean the whole lot"—he waves his arms—"you're probably looking at eighty to a hundred grand. I can't afford to buy them all. Or not all at once, anyway."

"Shit, no. No, okay. But you could sell them for me? I mean I guess there'd be commission on that?"

"Fifteen percent."

"Yes. Fine," I say. "Yes."

"You look frightened." He smiles at me.

"I am frightened. Also, I'm a bit concerned you may have undervalued them before."

"We talked about the tax," he says, "Andrew and I."

"Oh God, of course. Well, I don't know if I—"

"You can declare it if you want. No skin off my nose."

"I do believe in tax," I say, doubtful.

He grins at me. "So do I. But we thought it would be useful to give you the option."

I stare around at the books. A lifetime of love, of seeking out, collecting. "Did Uncle Andrew know he was going to die?"

"We all die," he says. I look at him. He raises his eyebrows.

"I know, but—"

"He was ninety-one when we did the appraisal. That's pretty old."

"Yes."

"So. I'll take the Scotts, shall I? And the Trollopes? Do you want me to write you a check, or shall I transfer the money?"

"Oh, well, I guess a transfer is easier. As I'd have to drive to Newton Stewart to put the check in. Take the Burnses as well."

"Okay. I'll write you a receipt. And then I'll transfer anything that comes in if I sell them."

"What if you don't? Sell them, I mean?"

"I'm confident I will. How about, anything I haven't sold in six months I'll buy myself."

"Okay. Um. We should write that down or I'll forget. And what about the rest?"

"Newton?"

"I . . . I'll have to think about that."

"I can come back and take some other stuff another time. We can look at early twentieth century. The Fitzgerald and the Waugh are worth a bit. Got a first edition of *1984* as well; that's worth at least fifteen."

"Fifteen grand?"

"Mm. If it was signed," he says, "it'd be worth fifty. He didn't sign many. I've got a signed *Down and Out* that cost me twenty-three."

"Bloody hell." Twenty-three thousand pounds for a book? One that isn't even a hundred years old? That's . . . I don't know what it is, really. Absurd.

"Yes. I'd buy it all," he says, looking around the room, "but I don't have a hundred-odd grand floating about."

"No, I'm sure you don't. Bloody hell."

"If you need to shift it quicker, just let me know. I do know other dealers who have more cash flow than I do."

"I don't think there's a desperate rush. Gosh. Thank you so much, this has been really useful. And an eye-opener. Blimey."

"Still some money in printed books," he says, grinning at me.

Six

It's the middle of May. I've been here for six weeks, puttering about. I'm enjoying myself, exploring, going through more of Andrew's belongings, and tidying up the garden. I've had people round to give me quotes for a new bathroom, and discussed where I could put a dishwasher with Angus, the plumber. His sister Jenny is the local vet, and also Alistair Gordon's fiancée. It's a very small town. Cerys, who owns the Old Mill with her girlfriend, Jilly, tells me to be careful what I say, and to whom.

"Because everyone's related," she says, "and you never find out until after you've said something awful. I was always putting my foot in it when I first moved here. If they're not related, they went to school together. It's a nightmare."

I believe her, and am suitably circumspect. I'm cautiously constructing a social life, which thus far has involved attending a talk about Kirkcudbright artists at the town hall, and the opening night (or private view, I suppose?) of an exhibition of quilts at the Old Mill. Alistair was there and he introduced me to Jenny. He was rather surprised, I think, that I hadn't yet put the lodge on the market and headed back to England. Jenny has dark hair, cropped into a pixie cut, and fiercely bright blue eyes. She's forthright and efficient; I like her a lot. I talked to them for ages about art and crafting; it was an unexpectedly fun evening.

I've made quilts in the past, most recently for Jasmine, Xanthe's daughter, who had a "bedroom redesign" for her tenth birthday; and I discover that Aunt Mary must have made them too. There aren't any at the lodge, but one of the drawers under the bed in the spare room is full of neat piles of fabric, fat quarters ready to be turned into patchwork. I wonder who she gave them to once she'd made them. I don't know much about Mary, who died about ten years ago, and I know nothing about her family. Her sewing machine is much better than the one languishing in my storage unit, though, so I'll be keeping that. I think she probably made all the curtains at the lodge; they're certainly handmade and much better than I could ever manage myself.

I'm mostly going through paperwork now. It's all quite tidy, nothing like the nightmare I helped Angela deal with when her dad died. He'd really never thrown anything out and we grew quite hysterical over bank statements from the sixties and receipts for long-discarded appliances and the unsteady stacks of *Razzle* and *Men Only*. Fortunately, there's nothing like that at the lodge. I could probably have done it all by now if I'd focused, but I've decided not to rush. Most of it's pretty straightforward; I'm putting anything interesting to one side, and not being too strict about what counts as interesting. He did keep a lot of things that were probably unnecessary, but of course the older something is—especially if it's ephemera—the more interesting it becomes. I arrange all kinds of bills and receipts neatly on the table and take photographs for my Instagram. They prove popular with the font-obsessed and lovers of what you might call "local de-sign," from back when everything in your town was owned by some chap you went to school with, or his father. Back in the days when phone numbers had three digits, and every-thing was typed on a typewriter by a lady employed for the purpose.

Andrew also wrote notes—I suppose it's a memoir, really, although it's quite scrappy. Some of it's handwritten and some of it's typed (and he must have done that at work, I suppose, or dictated it; there's no typewriter at the lodge). There are a couple of notebooks and a pile of loose pieces of paper. There are stories about his parents and grandparents (and I have to remind myself that I too am descended from these people, with their almost unimaginable lives), child-hood tales of poaching and general japes, and a whole list of dinners and dances, along with dance cards and menus. It's not exactly scintillating, but whose life is? I like his gentle stories. And it's not like nothing ever happened to him; after all, he and Mary suffered the worst a parent can imagine when they lost their daughter. I don't know if he wrote about that—if he did, I haven't got to that bit yet. I might be avoid-ing it. You know that feeling where you might start crying and never stop? I'm trying not to get myself into a place where that might happen. I'd rather read about nineteenth-century furniture from Dumfries, and Baldochrie during the war.

...

As time passes, I've been wondering if I should get a job. Nothing too strenuous. Making sandwiches or serving in the baker's or something. Just something so I meet people and have something to occupy myself.

I ask Cerys to let me know if she hears of anything, making it clear I don't expect her to employ me. I don't think I'd be very good in a café, to be honest; I'm not sure I could sustain that level of cheery service.

"Did Jenny find a new receptionist?" asks Jilly. "Since Pam's working at the school now?"

"Kirsty Macdonald took it, didn't she?"

"Oh, aye, of course she did." They both look at me, considering. "I heard they were looking for someone at the farm shop." Jilly straightens the labels on the cake stands by the register.

"That's a ways out, mind," says Cerys.

"It's not that far really. Maybe I should give them a ring." I like the farm shop, with its neat shelves of fancy jams and chutneys, beautiful displays of locally grown and reared produce, and excellent bread.

"You're staying up, then?"

"Oh, just for the summer. Or I might not, if I can't find anything."

"Och, there'll be something," Jilly says, reassuring. "If it's not a career you're after."

"I find I don't much care about having a career. Or not at the moment, anyway."

. . .

This morning I'm walking on the beach with Jenny and the dogs. Mags is an enthusiastic golden retriever, great-granddaughter of the dog in the painting in Alistair's office, and Rollo is a collie cross, needle-nosed and wiggly. It's sunny, but there's a cold wind. The beach is quite exposed, a wide sandy strand, and the dogs bound away into the distance before dashing back again, zig-zagging ahead of us, noses to the ground, tails wagging. There's no one else here, even though it's a fine expanse of sand and shingle; no picnicking families, no other dog walkers, no children. Perhaps it's too early—we were out by eight-thirty to make the forty-minute drive, and it's probably not even ten o'clock yet.

Jenny's been talking about the plans for her wedding. She and Alistair are getting married in December and everything, more or less, is arranged. She doesn't seem to be looking forward to it, though.

"I want to be married," she says, "but I wish we didn't have to have a wedding."

It seems like a very long time since my own wedding, memories of which are pin-sharp in places and a blur of confusion in others.

"I usually advise people to run away," I tell her. "It's much easier. And cheaper. Unless you really want a dress and all that stuff." I stoop to pick up a bright orange periwinkle shell and put it in my pocket. There are huge swaths of shells here, in every shade, and rolling banks of those narrow spirals, the ones like miniature unicorn horns.

"I wish I'd thought of that. We could have just gone somewhere the weekend after we got engaged or something, and now it would all be a distant memory."

"I'm sure it will be lovely, though," I say. Both families live locally. She's known Alistair since she was at school, despite the five-year age difference; he was the same year as her eldest brother. They didn't get together until quite recently, though—a couple of years ago. They're getting married at the church in town, and the reception's at the town hall, making best use of the municipal Christmas decorations.

"I suppose so."

"Anyway, it's all over in a flash," I tell her, "and then you're off. You don't even have to stay to the end if you don't want to."

"Aye, that's true. But still." She pokes with her toe at a piece of driftwood. The high-tide mark wobbles away from us, crispy black seaweed and plastic bottles, gull feathers, twists of pale blue-and-orange rope. My eyes are busy, searching for treasure.

They're going to Skye for their honeymoon, which I found amusing when she told me. I might prefer somewhere warmer, myself, than the Highlands in December. Dinner at the Three Chimneys, though, and a beautiful cottage by a loch. It's a seven-hour drive, which seems incredible, so their first night as husband and wife will be spent in a hotel near Newton Stewart.

We pause, looking out to sea. The breeze is whipping up white horses farther out, and pale clouds are scudding rapidly across the sky.

"So," she says, "is it very insensitive to be talking to you about my wedding?"

I laugh. "No, not at all. Why would it be?"

"Totally none of my business. I like to pretend I'm not nosy," she says, "but of course I am."

"Isn't everyone? It's fine. You can ask me," I tell her, "but I might need you to not talk to anyone else about it."

"Did something happen, with your husband? Are you separated?"

"I suppose we are, yes. I mean, yes, we definitely are." It's the first time I've said this since I came up here. I'm quite surprised by how much easier it is than when I had to tell all my friends back in January.

"Are you getting divorced, then?" she asks as we move on up the beach.

"Not yet. If you leave it," I say, "and you're separated for two years, that makes it easier, and no one has to go to court. At least, that's my understanding. I haven't really looked into it. Maybe I should."

"Are you selling your home?"

I laugh. "God, no. No, he lives there with his, er, girl-friend." I think it's the first time I've called her that, out loud at least.

"Oh. But what about you? That's not right, is it? Is it his house? How does that work?"

"No, it's ours. He's buying me out. Eventually."

She hesitates. "Did he leave you for her, then, aye?"

"Aye. I mean, yes." I tell her a bit about Chris and Su-sanna, just enough to explain how I came to be here, alone.

"He sounds like a wee prick," she says disapprovingly, which makes me laugh.

...

Cerys and I are at Bookers wholesalers in Dumfries. I think she was quite surprised when I said I'd like to go with her, but that's because I love a cash-and-carry and you never get to go to them unless you run the sort of business that uses them. We've filled a trolley with enormous bottles of olive and sunflower oils, and sacks of rice, couscous and quinoa.

Everything's giant, I love it. Lumps of cheese the size of your head, huge jars of herbs and spices. Tins of tomatoes like barrels. (She doesn't buy those, disappointingly; they get their vast tins of tomatoes delivered.) I can never decide what I like best: tiny things like dollhouse furniture, or giant things like those comical deck chairs you get at the seaside that make you look like a doll yourself.

"You're easily entertained," Cerys says, amused by my rapture.

"I really am, though. I think it's a blessing. I never get bored."

"I'll send you by yourself next time. I can't say I exactly love coming up here."

"It is quite a long way." I help her sling various bags of beans and lentils into her car. "I always wonder how you work out how much you'll need of everything."

"I leave all that to Jilly; she's the brains of the operation. And the one who went to catering college. I just do as I'm told. Buy what's on the list, try not to get distracted by chocolate."

"That seems unfair."

"Tell me about it. Anyway," she says, slamming the trunk closed and waiting while I return the trolley. "I thought we could stop on the way back and have lunch in Kirkcudbright. There's a new place we've been meaning to check out."

"Ooh, a rival establishment?" We get into the car, and she turns on the wipers to clear the drizzle from the windshield.

"I guess they're not *direct* rivals, but yeah. Like to keep an eye on the competition."

"Industrial espionage," I say happily, as I do up my seat-belt. "Plus lunch. Sounds great."

Kirkcudbright is probably the most touristy of all the little towns west of Dumfries. It's got a fancy ruined castle, and a thriving arts scene, lots of charming eighteenth- and nineteenth-century buildings, and a very unusual 1920s concrete bridge that is (in my opinion) both ugly and beautiful. In addition to all this, it's a proper, though tiny, fishing port. We park by the castle just as the rain begins in earnest.

"It's not far," says Cerys, and we hurry along, holding our hoods up as a sharp breeze blows down St. Cuthbert Street. Cerys turns a corner, and another, and then we're standing outside what was clearly once quite a grand shop, a draper's perhaps, or a chemist. It has tall, beautifully curved windows, and the mosaic tiles in front of the door spell out BRISTOW's in splendidly assertive curly letters. There are large, moss-filled pots of red and white tulips arranged in the windows, and a chalked A-frame sign on the pavement reads, CAKE! COFFEE! AND MORE!

"Hm," says Cerys, and pushes open the door. Inside, it's all original wooden shop fittings and mismatched furniture, a wide selection of lunching ladies, and a very impressive glass-fronted cake display, along with a menu chalked on the wall, and a very shiny coffee machine. There are two women behind the counter, one about my age and a teenager. They smile at us. Cerys is too busy looking about to respond, so I ask if we should order at the counter and they present us with menus and send us off to find a table.

"Where do you want to sit?" I ask her. "At the window?"

"No, let's go down the back so I can see everything," she

says, and I follow her past a staircase leading down to the loos and kitchen.

"That's annoying for them," she says. "Up and down the stairs all day."

"Think of their calves, though, Cerys—like iron." She splutters with laughter and we find ourselves a table with a long, dark grey velvet banquette against the back wall and a pair of unmatched dining room chairs. I unwind my scarf, struggle out of my jacket and finally sit down with my back to the room. She's already poking at the little blue glass bottle in the center of the table with its single tulip, and picking up the salt and pepper grinders to see who they're made by. The walls are covered with vintage advertising for corsets and things, so I'm inclined to think the shop must have been a draper's or a dress shop. It has high ceilings and fashionable light fittings.

"What do you think?" she asks me. I get my phone out to take some pictures of the tulip. The blue of the glass makes the orange of the petals sing. I lean awkwardly to get a different angle with some of the white anemones on the next table.

"Good florals," I say, scrolling back through my photos and deleting the rubbish ones. "Most Insta. I like the furniture too. I quite like that it's dark, but not gloomy."

"Hm," she says, turning her attention to the menu. She wrinkles her nose.

"Anything good?" I ask, picking up my own menu—printed on brown paper, naturally.

"Actually it all looks annoyingly good," she says. "The cakes looked ace, didn't they?"

"Your cakes are very good. I don't think they looked better than yours." Jilly's mum, Kate, makes their cakes; she's a marvel.

Thinking of Jilly's mum reminds me of something. "Kate's always lived in Baldochrie, hasn't she?"

"Yes," says Cerys, turning the menu over to consider the drinks. "The whole family's proper local."

"I should ask her about Fiona."

"Who's Fiona?"

"My cousin. Well, no—my father's cousin. Uncle Andrew's daughter."

"Oh yes, what about her?" She frowns at me. "Why didn't she get the house? Is she dead?"

"Yes, she died when she was young. Fourteen."

"Oh my God, really? That's awful. What happened?"

"I know. And I'm not sure, I keep forgetting to ask my mum. But she'd be around Kate's age, I suppose. I think she was born in the early fifties."

"Kate's sixty-three," says Cerys. "So that sounds about right."

"I'll try and remember to ask. It must have been a big deal at the time."

"God, yes, I should think so. Her poor parents."

Seven

I pop into Baldochrie to buy bread and milk. I park up by the bookshop, thinking I might go in and see if Edward has managed to sell any of my books. There's a sign in the window: SALES ASSISTANT URGENTLY REQUIRED. APPLY WITHIN.

I pause and study the sign. I've always quite fancied working in a bookshop. And working in town would help me meet people. If I'm going to be here for a couple of months, I'll need to know more people than I do now; I can't expect Jilly and Cerys, or indeed Alistair and Jenny, to take up all the slack. I've already been on several beach walks with Jenny and the dogs and to dinner at theirs twice. I like Jenny a lot, but you can't swamp someone with friendship, can you? And you can't expect someone to share all their mates with you.

I'm not sure whether Edward would be a great person to work for. But that doesn't much matter, if I'm not staying forever. Anyway, we got on fine when he came out to the lodge. I even made him laugh.

I mention the job to Jenny when we're drinking tea in the Old Mill later that day. She puts her cup down and stares at me.

"Oh my *God*," she says, "you can't work there. He's such a dick."

"Is he, though? He seemed okay when he came around to value my books. We had quite a nice time. Anyway, I can deal with that. My old boss was a complete wanker. And it's not like it'll be permanent."

"Ach, I suppose not. I wonder if Rory's leaving. Oh, he must be off to uni in the fall. He'll be studying for his exams."

"Rory's the boy who works in there?" I saw him the day I visited the shop, putting things on shelves in the distance.

"Aye, bless him. Before that, Tom worked there—Rory's brother."

"They get on all right with Edward, then?"

"Oh, he's only a dick with women. Mostly." She rolls her eyes.

"What sort of a dick? I can handle moody and bad-tempered; I can't be doing with wandering hands."

Jenny laughs. "No, I've never heard that about him. The opposite even—I've friends who've made quite an effort in that direction."

"Really?"

"Aye. To no avail. He's a miserable git."

. . .

A couple of days later, I'm in the shop again, leaning on the counter. Edward is in his chair, turned toward me. We've already talked about when he might come out again and look at the twentieth-century first editions. They'll be harder for me to give up.

"Oh, by the way. I saw your advert," I say. "I thought I'd apply."

"Advert?"

"In the window. For an assistant?"

"Oh, shit, no," he says. Even for Edward, that seems quite rude. I blink at him.

"'Oh, shit no?' You could just say I'm clearly overqualified or something, no need to be offensive. Or more offensive than usual."

He rummages in the drawer of his desk and pulls out a laminated notice, much like the others dotted around the shop. It says, REMEMBER, NO GIRLS.

"This is my staffing policy," he says.

I laugh, and then try to disguise it with a cough. "I think that's probably discriminatory. And illegal. But never mind, I haven't been a girl for decades."

He looks at me, his mouth twisted. "Should I change it to say, 'No Women'? I could get Rory to do that before he leaves. Anyway, it's all the same. No female staff. Unless I'm desperate."

"I heard you *were* pretty desperate. When's he off?"

He looks hunted. "Next Saturday's his last day."

"A week today? Studying and then Interrailing, is it? That's what I heard."

"Yes, does his exams and then it's four weeks on a bloody train with his so-called mates, and then he's off to uni. *Ingrate!*" he yells in the direction of the fireplace, where Rory is shelving books from a large box. He turns his head and grins at us.

"So anyway. No girls?"

"Too much trouble."

I shake my head, disbelieving. "It's not your *tree house*."

"Yes, it is. It's totally my tree house." Edward nods, firmly.

"What kind of trouble, anyway? Weeping? Menstruating?"

"Jesus Christ."

This makes me laugh. "Well?"

He lifts a shoulder, irritable. "They fall in love with me. Or I fall in love with them. It's stupid and annoying."

I laugh again. "Oh, come on. You're not serious."

"No, it's true."

"Well, you needn't worry. I'm not in a position to fall in love with you and I can't imagine you're likely to fall in love with me, are you? Don't answer that," I add. "Let's just assume it goes without saying."

Rory puts the final book on the shelf and comes over. "You n-need someone, Edward. I'm only here this week."

"There, you see? Anyway, you can keep looking. I'll only be here for the summer."

"How come you're staying up? I thought you were only here for two weeks? You've already been here for a lot longer than that." He folds his arms and looks at me suspiciously.

"I like it. And it's not like I've got a job at home. I told you, I was made redundant. So I can stay, for the moment."

"What about Mr. Mottram? Doesn't he mind you staying away all summer? Or is he coming up too?"

"I don't see why you're so interested in my husband. He'd be very surprised."

He glowers at me. "I'm not interested. I just wondered."

"That s-sounds like you're interested," says Rory. He grins at me. Edward makes a sound of disgust, and Rory and I laugh.

"Oh, for God's sake. Can you work a till?"

We all look at the wooden box on the counter. I suck air in through my teeth. "Looks pretty technical. But I expect if someone teaches me how, I'll be okay. I worked at HMV when I was at college," I add, "but I can see things have moved on a lot since those days."

Rory laughs again. Edward frowns at me for a moment. "All right, then. You"—he points at Rory—"can train her. Can you start now? Today?"

I blink, surprised. "I suppose so. Yeah, why not."

"I'm going to Glasgow for the sale, then, now that there's two of you. I'll be back on Friday. Don't let her do anything stupid. You"—he points at me—"it's minimum wage for the first month. Then we'll discuss it. You"—he points at Rory again—"teach her how the catalogue works. And there's a delivery from Murchison coming later—so you can show her how to shelve."

"I reckon I can work that out myself."

He glares at me. "Do as Rory tells you. Don't do anything stupid."

"I'll try not to. All right, then. Thanks." I salute smartly. "You won't regret this, Mr. Maltravers, sir."

"I'd better not," he says.

. . .

Rory and I have quite a laugh. He's shy, almost as tall as Edward, with pale strawberry-blond hair and a rash of unfortunate spots. He's off to St Andrews to do English in September, assuming he gets his grades. I love his accent.

Edward's one of those annoyingly posh Scottish people who don't really have a Scottish accent, which I think is a shame.

Rory introduces me to Holly Hunter, the shop cat, an ancient half-Persian who leaves clumps of pale fur around the place and sleeps on a pile of towels on top of the radiator in the hall. He shows me how to work the till—both of us pretending it's complex and technical—and explains how the catalogue works. This feeds through to the website so the listings are up to date. Most of the sales, especially of the antiquarian books, come through the internet, so carefully making parcels and going to the post office is also part of the job.

Rory's already on study leave, so he brings his books and study notes into the shop every day, although he ought to be at home. In term time during the week he usually only works from four-thirty until six. I ask him lots of nosy questions whenever we stop for coffee, which he mostly answers.

I quite like being middle-aged; if I were his age I wouldn't know what to say to him, but it's easy enough to ask him questions, and he's willing to talk to me, probably because I'm a stranger. I talk about my own university adventures, without expecting him to pay much attention, and he tells me about Chloe, his girlfriend, who's off to Edinburgh in September. He's worried about what will happen when they're both away meeting new people, and I don't blame him.

"Everything expands when you go to university. It's hard not to let it go to your head. And it's hard not to take it personally, the stuff that happens. But everyone's selfish when they're your age. That's not a criticism."

"I love her, though." He picks at a price sticker that some-one has stuck on the marble countertop.

"I know, and I'm sure she loves you. It's not really about that."

He looks at me, serious. "Is this one of those horrible things that adults take for granted, aye?"

"Sort of. I know I was furious when someone told my boyfriend that we'd split up when I went to university."

"B-but you did?"

"In the end." I sigh. "And in the end, it didn't even matter that much."

"It makes me s-s-s-sad," he says, his face flushed, "to think the things that seem important to me now might n-not in the future."

"Yes. It is sad. But—and this won't help much—I think if you always lived as intensely as you do between, I don't know, sixteen and twenty-four, you'd be dead by the time you were twenty-five. I was relieved when everything calmed down."

"Is that when you got married?"

"I met my husband when I was twenty-five, yes."

"You d-didn't want to talk to Edward about him the other day. Your husband."

Perceptive, young Rory. I think for a moment before reply-ing. "No, I didn't. He's a bit obnoxious, isn't he? I don't par-ticularly want to talk about myself to him."

"Why n-not?"

I wrinkle my nose. "I'm not sure. I don't want to give him ammunition."

"Is your husband ammunition?"

I laugh. "Sort of. We split up in January."

"Oh. I'm s-sorry to hear that," he says. "B-but why's it a secret?"

"I'm not sure." I hesitate. "It isn't, really. But I'd rather you didn't mention it to anyone. Sometimes it's better to appear to be a married person. Easier."

I don't expect him to understand, but he nods. "That makes s-sense. And Edward's weird. About women."

"I thought he might be. Although I expect I'm too old for him to be weird about."

"Yeah, I dunno," says Rory.

. . .

So now I have a job. I quite like it. Although the hours are long, it's not taxing. The shop never gets too busy, and it is, of course, endlessly interesting. I don't think Edward expected me to be interested, but when he returns from Glasgow and Rory's left to concentrate on his studies, we have lunch at the Old Mill and talk business.

We sit in the conservatory, which is a beautiful, light-filled room even on a grey day like today. Cerys brings us our food—their cheese toasties are amazing—and then retreats to the counter. Every now and then I look around and see her watching us; wondering, I suppose, why on earth I'd want to work with Edward. For a while we eat in silence, and then I say, "If you don't mind, I'd like to learn things, about books or bookselling or whatever. So don't think I won't care if there's anything you'd tell someone who might be staying longer."

He looks at me for a long time, chewing thoughtfully, and then nods. "Okay, I can teach you stuff. Are you handy?"

"Handy?"

"I mean, are you neat, with an eye for detail and a steady hand? I fix things sometimes."

"Ooh, with clamps, and glue made from rabbits? I know you shouldn't mend books with Sellotape."

He shudders. "No, you shouldn't."

"Yeah, I was a librarian at primary school. We had special tape for fixing the books." I think fondly of the shady classroom, always quiet, where I learned about the Dewey decimal system and spent break times by myself twice a week, fixing books for Mr. Thompson.

"Okay, good. Yeah, I can show you how to do that, and what to look for online and in sale catalogues and so on. If you're sure." He returns his attention to his plate, eating two final slices of tomato.

"Yes please. I like to get involved. You must tell me if that's annoying."

"Why would it be annoying?" He pours water into his glass and, after a questioning look, into mine too.

"Well, it's your shop, isn't it? I wouldn't want you to think I was interfering."

He looks amused. "Do you want to interfere?"

I see this as an opportunity, and say, "No, I just . . . I wondered about the window displays."

He sighs heavily. "Go on, then. We can discuss it."

"We could have—I mean, you could have—a different theme every month. Like 'international month of' whatever, maybe? I'll come up with some ideas for you to look at. And Rory says there's a Facebook page?"

He shakes his head. "I never post anything."

"I know. I could look after that. I'm quite good at social media. I used to run the Twitter account at the last place I worked. We had fifteen thousand followers."

He sighs again. "I run a bookshop to avoid all this."

"I know. But you can still avoid it; let me look after it. Do you do events?"

Now he looks wary. "Like what?"

"Well, I know there's a New Books section. So do you ever have people for signings? Or readings?"

"I never have. I'm not good with people. You may have noticed."

I ignore this. "No, but would you? I mean, say we could get Amy Liptrot or someone."

"I'd very much like to meet her," he says, briefly animated.

"Yes, she's nice and tall, isn't she?" I nod approvingly. "And she sounds really interesting. But anyway, say she was doing stuff at Wigtown, for the festival, or something, we could ask." I get my phone out. "The shop definitely needs a Twitter account. Can I set one up? And Instagram?"

"What, and take photos of our sandwiches every day?" he says, amused.

"It's not just for lunch pics." I tut, although I think that could be a cool gimmick. Booksellers' lunches. "I could take pictures of beautiful or rare books. And if we do any mending or whatever."

"I didn't expect you to be so keen." He frowns at me. "It's disconcerting."

"Young people are great, but you can't expect Rory to have a marketing brain, can you? However tech savvy he might be. But I've done a bit of marketing and there's loads you can do nowadays that doesn't cost anything. I suppose you don't have a budget for marketing?"

"You suppose correctly."

"Okay, I bet I can still make a difference. Increase turnover. I'm not saying by loads. But a bit."

He's amused, a half smile curving. "We'll see."

Eight

When I'm not at work, I'm exploring. Every Sunday, even if it's raining, I determinedly go out for the day, or half the day. I've been to Whithorn Priory and Caerlaverock Castle and poked around Castle Douglas and Newton Stewart. I've looked at ruined tower houses and stone circles and driven up the narrow track to Cairn Holy, a famously dramatic burial chamber. There's no point being up here if I don't see the sights, is there?

One unusually sunny day I drive to Drumtroddan Farm to look at the cup-and-ring marks, carved into slabs of rock five thousand years ago.

It's quiet. Farms are strange places, either furiously busy or not, and during the day even on a big farm you'll often see no one, and no animals, just empty buildings and rusty collections of stuff: mud and whitewash, complex arrangements of gates and fences, great bales of mysterious wire, looping twirls of pipes. As I follow the signs through the farmyard I wonder whether they're annoyed or pleased to have these famous carvings on their land.

I park by the big NO DOGS sign and put fifty pence in the box on the wall with its painted message—DONATIONS WELCOME. I don't imagine they make much from the visitors, even if everyone pays, which they probably don't. I wonder if they get a grant for taking care of the stones. Or is it just an annoyance, wear and tear on their tracks and footpaths, a whole field you can't use for cows unless they're friendly? I wonder all of this, but there's no one to ask. I open a five-bar gate and close it carefully behind me, and then another, and finally a third lets me into the field. The ground is rough and uneven beneath a shaggy coat of lush green grass. The stones are at the far end, enclosed in black-painted iron railings, rusty in places, with creaking kissing gates. They don't surround the slabs of rock generously—they're rather tightly arranged to corral as many carvings into one place as possible. Inside the enclosure, the grass is shorter, nibbled by rabbits; there are daisies and buttercups and harebells.

The breeze has dropped and the view back to the farm is all green grass, blue sky, and the red mass of the new barn and the old farm buildings huddled on the horizon. I can hear a distant tractor and rooks calling in the stand of trees to the east. The outcrop surfaces in three or four places, exposing wide expanses of lichened grey rock carved with a startling array of rings and spirals and the scooped dishes of the cup marks. I sit down on a natural shelf and lean to trace the whirls and dips with my fingers. It's rather impressive and pleasing. No one knows what they mean, these markings, but they must have taken some effort—they're not just the scrawl of a moment.

...

At work the following day I browse Local History and ask Edward if I can scan some lovely line drawings of the rock art.

"Have the book," he says, looking up to see what I'm doing.

"It says it's a tenner," I object.

He waves his hand. "Whatever. You can have it. There are lots of inscribed rocks round here. Have you seen any?"

"I went to Drumtroddan yesterday."

"Oh, yes, those are the best known ones. There are some at Hollinshaw," he adds. "In the park."

"Are there?"

"Mm. I could show you on a map, hang on. If you're interested?"

"That would be cool."

He comes round from behind the desk and begins to look through the maps in the Cartography section. We have dozens of pink Ordnance Survey Landranger sheet maps for all over the country in various editions, and orange Explorers. He wrestles with number eighty-three and then leans to pore over it. "Here," he says, jabbing with his finger. "This is your house—"

"I'll never get tired of seeing my actual house on a map."

"And this is the Drive, see the old castle was here—"

"Was there a castle? Gosh."

"At Hollinshaw? Yeah. There are ruins in the woods, not much left now. They—we—lived there until the beginning of the seventeenth century. Then we built on the site where the house is now, but you can't see much of the original building. Anyway, if you skirt the edge of the woods here, the inscribed rocks are just off the track. There's an outcrop here, but you need to look for the flat bit to the left of that. Not as impressive as Drumtroddan, but you can see it all quite clearly. There's a cairn west of there and a standing stone too. I think it's on the map . . . yes, there you go. On the higher ground above the river."

"Wow, nice. I shall have to have a look. I saw your brother the other week and he said I could go anywhere on the estate." I glance sidelong at him to see how he'll react to this.

"Did he?"

"Yes, so at least I won't feel like I'm trespassing."

"We don't have trespassing here anyway." He shakes his head at me.

"I know, but it seems odd and I couldn't just wander about willy-nilly; I'd feel guilty."

He laughs. "Well, you can rest easy if Charles says it's okay."

"Yes. Thank you. I'll get my maps out when I get home. And can I really have this?" I wave the book at him.

"Sure. Are you going to read up about it?"

I nod. "I like to learn things. It's all very different from Sussex. I want to make the most of it. Otherwise when I go back I'll be sorry."

He looks at me for a moment, his expression hard to read. "You're not going back immediately, though?"

"Oh God, no. No, I'll stay until September, at least."

"Good," he says, and goes back to what he was doing.

• • •

Today it's my birthday. I'm forty-four. Cards arrive at the lodge from Xanthe and Angela and my cousin Sarah and my parents. They're in Shanghai. They've sent something, but my mother doesn't know when it will get here. There's a card from two of the women I used to work with as well. When I get somewhere with a signal, there will be Facebook messages, I expect. I've had nothing from Chris. I tell myself I didn't expect anything. I open my cards and put them on the mantelpiece. Last year we were away for my birthday. I don't think about that. And it's no good complaining you've got no cards if you never mention your birthday. No one up here knows, and I'm not planning on telling anyone. It's just a day like any other.

Maybe I'll buy myself a steak or drive to Newton Stewart and have dinner in a pub. A strange pub by oneself, though, isn't much more enticing than cooking one's own dinner. I don't mind, really; I'd rather be by myself than pretending to have fun somewhere. I wonder what I'll be doing on my birthday next year. Perhaps I should plan something. Plenty of time for that.

I'm parking in my usual spot outside the town hall when my phone rings. I don't know the number, but when I answer I recognize Chris's voice, of course. I wonder if there'll ever be a time when I don't. This is the first time we've spoken since I came up here—we communicate via email usually, and that's rare enough.

"Happy birthday," he says. "Thought I'd ring. I've failed to send you a card."

"That's okay." I watch the swallows swooping over the town hall and try to distance myself from the conversation.

"Failed everyone's birthdays," he adds.

"Oh, Chris, really? They're all on the calendar."

"I know."

"Well, you'll have to make an effort. You didn't miss your dad's, did you?" That was last week, six days before mine. I didn't send him a card, rather childishly.

"No, we—I went round there."

I try not to think about this. Did they all go, I wonder? Susanna's kids as well? I can't picture it. Probably for the best. "Oh, well. Good. Just . . . you should look at the calendar at the beginning of the month. There are cards in the sideboard."

"Oh, is that where they are? I thought there must be some. But anyway, yeah, happy birthday, Thea. Are you doing anything?"

I get out of the car and close the door. There's a sharp breeze and I shiver. "No, nothing planned." I nearly tell him I've no one to do anything with, but that seems pathetic, so I don't.

"Well, okay. Have a good day. Er . . ."

I can tell he doesn't know what else to say. It makes me sad that we've nothing to say to each other. "I'd better go," I tell him. "I'm just going to buy cake."

"Oh, for work?"

"Yeah." Not that I've told Edward it's my birthday, and I'm not going to. But if Chris wants to think of a jolly office birthday, let him.

"All right, then. Take care."

"Yes, and you."

He says goodbye and we hang up. I lean against the car for a moment and bite my lip hard. I think I'd have preferred a card, or nothing. It's easier when I don't have to speak to him. Such a tiny, meaningless conversation. I push open the door to the baker's and consider the cake selection. Buns, I think.

· · ·

When I get home, there are flowers in a box on the doorstep. For a wild moment, I think they might be from Chris, but of course they're not; they're from Xanthe and Rob. Which is fine. I let myself in and take the flowers to the kitchen, digging through the cupboard under the sink for something to put them in. Hot pink and yellow gerberas; they look very modern in the old-fashioned pressed glass vase, but I like them, and I leave them on the kitchen table so I can look at them while I eat my birthday steak.

I haven't had a bad day, actually; the sun was shining and we sold quite a lot of books, which put Edward in a good mood. All in all, it could have been a lot worse.

I try to fill my evening by phoning Xanthe and watching *Monty Python and the Holy Grail*. At this time of year it doesn't get dark until nearly eleven up here, and on my way to bed I sit on the windowsill in my bedroom and look out at the garden for ages, watching the blue twilight grow deeper. I feel strange and nostalgic, not necessarily for all the birthdays of my marriage, but for the years before that: my teens and early twenties when I didn't know who I was or what I wanted. There's a certain feeling in the air this time of year that always reminds me of studying for my GCSEs. Not that those evenings were as long and light as they are up here, but even at home it doesn't get dark until nine, and we spent a lot of time in the park near the school, in the gathering dusk, drinking illegally obtained cider and smoking.

Something about the quality of the light triggers memories, and for all the Junes since then, it's that one that feels strongest in my memory, or perhaps the run of five or so when "summer" meant "preparing for exams" or at least attempting to. I think of evenings spent at Mark Woodley's, the first year of my A Levels, his parents out or away, and the things we found to do instead of studying. It seems unimaginable that it's twenty-seven years since I lost my virginity. What would seventeen-year-old me say if she could see me sitting here, my arm cold against the glass, wearing a pair of pajamas that belonged to Uncle Andrew, with no real plans or dreams for the future?

Nine

A Thursday, late June. Edward in his green armchair and me perched on the counter. I don't have a chair, there's not room for two, so I climb up a step stool and sit on the counter when we're not busy. He says it adds an air of youthful informality, to which I usually roll my eyes.

We're eating our sandwiches, bought by me from the Old Mill. As I chew, I remember something.

"Your brother's invited me to a party," I tell him.

"What?" I don't answer, assuming he heard me perfectly well. "What sort of party? Jesus."

"I don't know. A cocktail party? I've never been to a cocktail party."

"Did you get a written invitation?"

"No, he sent me a text. I admit I was a bit disappointed." A vision of a printed invitation with curly writing and gold edges floats in the air before me.

"A text? Good grief. How vulgar. And how does my brother have your phone number?" He glowers at me. The disapproval in his voice makes me chuckle.

"He asked for it, last time I saw him."

"When was that? Why did you give it to him?"

"Last week, he called round. He's softening me up, I

think. To sell him the lodge." At least, I assume that's what he was doing. He's been round a couple of times recently. Never for long, always polite chitchat about generalities. Last week we talked about the barn conversion his team of builders is working on. He did ask me about Chris twice, but I was noncommittal. I'm not sure who knows about my situation. Presumably not Charles; I think he was trying to find out if we were separated. I didn't tell him, though. We sat in the garden and drank tea; it was reasonably pleasant. No need to mention any of this to Edward.

"I told you. He's desperate to get his hands on it."

"He hasn't asked directly, not since I first got here. He wanted to know if I'd decided what I was going to do and blah blah. You know what he's like, terribly charming."

"He's a bastard." This is more or less what Edward says whenever Charles is mentioned, although he still hasn't said why he thinks so, and I'm not going to ask him.

"Whatever. Anyway, what should I wear for a cocktail party? I can't help but picture something a bit eighties."

"A dress."

I snort. "Yes, thanks, Anna Wintour."

"Who else is going? Are you sure it's a party?"

"He said it was a party." I laugh. "You think he's trying to get me there on my own? Oh lordy. Alistair and Jenny are going. And Richard and Catriona, and the Callows, apparently. I asked him; I don't like going to things where I don't know anyone, and being single—" I stop myself, remembering that Edward doesn't know I'm single, and I don't want him to know either. "I mean—being by yourself where everyone else is in a couple is awkward."

"Can't you get Mr. Mottram up for the weekend? Is he ever going to visit you?"

I'm annoyed with myself for bringing it up. "Too busy," I say. "Work's a nightmare at the moment."

"Well, Charles will be by himself, won't he?" He rolls his eyes.

"Will he? I wasn't sure. I saw him out riding with a blonde." I remember Charles saying "we" when he invited me to go and see the house, although he hasn't done that again since, I've noticed.

"Oh, Miranda, probably. I don't think they're . . . although they might be." Edward shrugs, implying a complete lack of interest.

"But anyway, he'll be busy being the host and everything; and even if he wasn't, you know, I wouldn't want to spend all evening hanging out with your brother."

He looks at me for a long moment. "Wouldn't you? Why not?"

"I don't think we've got much in common, to be honest."

"No," he agrees, "probably not."

"Anyway, he said there'd be some single people as well. Before you ask, no, I don't know who. What sort of dress? Not full length, right?"

"No, that's evening dress."

I sigh. "I'm pretty sure I don't have anything suitable. Unless there's something in the spare room." I keep meaning to go through Aunt Mary's frocks and take pictures so I can put them on eBay. Vintage extravaganza. "There might be some amazing fifties thing I could wear. Although vintage looks a bit sad on someone my age."

"Don't be absurd."

"It does, though. It's not like her fifties stuff was for a middle-aged woman; she was like twenty, with an eighteen-inch waist probably. Which I don't have. And didn't have even when I was twenty."

"Buy something?"

"From where? I can't be bothered to go to Dumfries." I drum my heels against the counter.

"They sell clothes in Kirkcudbright. And Castle Douglas. Or so I believe."

"Boutiques," I say. "I dunno. I suppose I should look on the internet. I'll have to do that today."

I still don't have broadband at the lodge, because it's not as though I actually live there, even though I sort of do. Perhaps I should get that sorted; it's quite inconvenient.

"Edinburgh. Or Glasgow."

"I'm not driving to bloody Glasgow, it's two hours away."

He shakes his head. "Lots of shops, though. When's the party?"

"Saturday." There's a pause. I finish my sandwich and drink half a pint of water. Holly Hunter stalks in from the hallway, looks at us both and wails at Edward, demanding to be picked up. He settles her on his knee, where she purrs like a chainsaw. She still won't sit on my lap, no matter how much I try to entice her. I assume the conversation is over and get my phone out to check for messages.

"Do you have to go?" he asks eventually.

"To the party? Seems rude not to. And I'd like to see the house. I still haven't been inside. I'm nosy. I'd like to go to a proper big house as a guest rather than a visitor. See where you grew up."

"Huh. It's not interesting."

"Don't be stupid, it's fascinating."

He looks vaguely appalled. "Not really."

"*Pfft.* Yeah, you can try, Edward, but you'll never be normal. Because a normal person would know that a giant stately home where someone you know grew up is always going to be interesting."

· · ·

After some anguished shopping, I have a new dress. It's rather a bold shade of kingfisher blue, and shiny. It looked okay in the shop. Jenny says it looks okay now, but I can't say I'm totally convinced. It's a good color, though; and it's a good shape for me, with a high waist. No sleeves, but I've got a little black shrug thing so that's all right. I arrived with Alistair and Jenny, and now I'm inside the house, at last, being ushered across an echoing hallway that's all marble and stags' heads. There are candles, walls of paneling, and dark paintings of flowers and fruit. Then we're in a brighter room, with sofas and mirrors and a huge carved fireplace. There are lots of people—more than I was expecting—and a painted ceiling with fat cherubs. It's not dark outside, and the two enormous windows draped with huge swagged curtains and pelmets three feet deep look out over the lawns in front of the house. It looks much as I'd pictured it, I suppose, but still very odd. I try to imagine what it would be like to grow up somewhere like this, and fail utterly.

Alistair and Jenny have been swept away from me, but Gavin McPherson, who owns a bathroom supplies company and who I met when I went to look at showers, comes over to say hello, and then introduces me to a horribly attractive woman called Miranda before disappearing again. I try not to feel abandoned, and instead turn my attention to Miranda. I assume she's the blonde I saw out riding with Charles, since there can't be that many people called Miranda, surely.

"Charles says you're friends with Eddie," she says. I sip my kir royale and try not to feel flustered, although I do feel flustered. Her dress definitely cost more than the fifty quid I spent on mine. I should think her haircut probably cost more than my frock, shoes, and shrug combined.

Eddie? Christ.

"Yes, I work for him," I tell her. "In the bookshop."

There's another, equally attractive woman sort of standing with us in that way you do at these things. I think her name is Sophie. She turns to stare at me, wide-eyed and curious. "Oh, really? Gosh. Is he a good boss? He's got a terrible temper."

"I just ignore him when he's cross," I tell her, shrugging. I look from one of them to the other. "How do you know him?"

Miranda says, "Our parents were friends. I've known the family since we were children."

I nod and look at Sophie. She laughs. "Oh, I've known both of them"—her eyes slide across to Charles, who is talking to yet another attractive woman by the French windows—"for years and years. Although, not as long as Miranda, thank goodness. I should think they were horrible little boys."

Miranda laughs. "Charles especially, yes."

"Awkward that they don't speak to each other," I suggest.

I still don't know why and, I admit, this fascinates me. Sophie's drifted away, collected by a much older man with crisp white hair—her husband, I guess.

Miranda agrees. "God yes. I mean it was quite funny for a while, but honestly. So difficult. You can't invite them both to the same thing. It's hard to get Eddie to come out at all. Such a waste." She sighs. "Although I do mostly blame Carolyn, for that."

"Who's Carolyn?"

She puts her head to one side, an unspoken question. I suppose they assume everyone knows all this background. Well, not me, lady. I know nothing. She steps slightly closer and lowers her voice. "Charles's wife. Ex-wife, rather. I mean, Julia and Charles were already separated when . . . But Carolyn . . . You know, I've never liked any of those people— all *dreadfully* badly behaved, and in such an old-fashioned way."

I have no idea what she's talking about, but nod anyway.

She shakes her head, sighing, and rather annoyingly changes the subject. "Have you lived here long?"

"I don't really live here," I say. "Just up for the summer. My uncle died and left me his house."

"Oh, are you the lodge woman?"

I blink at her. "I suppose I am."

"Charles told me about you. But I didn't realize you were the one who knew Eddie." She laughs. "How strange."

"I didn't know him before I got here," I say, irritated. I don't like the idea of people talking about me. I'm not interesting, after all. What do they say, these awful people with their beautiful bone structures and total lack of Scottish accent? I suppose she comes from a house just like this one.

The house is doing my head in. It's fun to be somewhere like this without teasels or holly leaves on the furniture to stop you from sitting down and rope to keep you away from the trinkets. I could touch anything in this room, and although it might look odd, it wouldn't set off an alarm. But the portraits of pretty young women from the last three centuries and a series of wigged and uniformed young men who look increasingly like Charles and Edward as they work their way forward in time is just too strange.

"Are you going to sell him your house? Charles, I mean?" Miranda asks, interrupting my thoughts.

"I'm not sure yet."

"He's very keen. Oh, I probably shouldn't have said that." She laughs. "In case you ask for more money!"

"I'm aware of his interest," I say, and then I'm embarrassed for some reason, partly because I think it might have sounded abrupt and partly because it sounds like I think he's interested in me, which isn't what I meant.

"I expect you are," she says blandly. The doors from the hall open and some more people arrive. "Ailsa, darling!" says Miranda, her attention diverted. "How lovely." Then she's air-kissing a small round woman wearing a pair of earrings so sparkly they can only be real diamonds, and I wander away absently.

I wish now that I'd turned the invitation down. I don't like small talk with strangers and I sometimes find myself wondering what all these people are really thinking at events like this (not that I've ever been to an event like this). I'm sure none of them are thinking any of the things I am. I catch Jenny's eye across the room and she pulls a face briefly before turning back to the man she's speaking to.

I feel overly large and—I try to identify the sensation—coarse. As though my feet are too big and my clothes too cheap, and my entire being just not quite well-bred enough. Is it the people or the environment making me feel like this? Or my own attitude? Everyone's charming, but I wish I was at home or that I had someone with me, so I wouldn't have to stand here beside a console table by myself, trying to look self-contained and relaxed. I drift slowly about and am offered canapés by a smart young woman in a vaguely military-style white jacket. I take a tiny mozzarella ball smeared with pea purée and avoid making eye contact with Johnny, a balding man of about fifty to whom I was introduced earlier. We're the four singletons: him, Charles, Miranda and me. I can't help thinking poorly of Charles's choice for me, assuming he put any thought into it. Although he and Johnny seem to be great pals, so perhaps he didn't choose him to entertain me at all.

I wish Edward were here; it would be amusing to see him hating it. Perhaps he wouldn't hate it, though—after all, he must know all these people, even if he doesn't like them.

. . .

"Thea! Enjoying yourself?" Charles leans his shoulder against the ornately carved mantelpiece and smiles at me. "Is that glass empty? We can't have that." He looks around for a waiter.

"Oh, I only just finished it. I'll get some more in a moment, don't worry." I clear my throat. "More to the point, since it's your party, are you enjoying yourself?"

"Always nice to have people in the house," he says.

"It's quite big, isn't it, for one person?" The understatement amuses me, and I smile to myself.

"I'm not completely on my own *all* the time. The children are here quite often, and I have a housekeeper, but she's not exactly company."

He has two children, Jenny told me, by his first wife Julia, the interior designer. They're in their early teens, a boy and a girl. They're away at school most of the time, and spend half their holidays with Charles and the other half with their mother, who has a house up near Dumfries. He and second wife, Carolyn, weren't married long, or so I gather. No kids, anyway. I wonder what his housekeeper's like. A solid woman in tweed is what I imagine, but who knows? She can't be glam, though, or she'd be at the party, surely? I don't really know how these things work in the twenty-first century.

"Do you have one of those enormous kitchens with a million copper pans?" This has been on my mind for some reason.

"Well, yes, but we don't use that for cooking these days. Got a smaller, more sensible kitchen in my part of the house. Luckily it's reasonably manageable, but there are some rooms we keep shut up most of the year, unless I have a lot of people stay. And in the winter, we stick in the east wing because it's easier to heat."

"Wouldn't it be easier to sell it and live somewhere more convenient?" I ask, curious.

"I suppose it depends on your definition of 'easier.' In some ways, perhaps. But we've always lived here. Since the fourteenth century, anyway."

"Yes, I know. Not that I can imagine it." I wonder what

my ancestors were doing in the fourteenth century. Dying of plague, I expect.

"You must come up sometime so I can give you the tour," he says. "I suppose it would be rude of me to abandon everyone else this evening."

I laugh. "I should think so."

He sips his drink and looks around the room at his guests, all of whom are eating and drinking and chatting merrily. I expect him to murmur something and glide off to talk to someone else, but instead he says, "I heard you've been talking to Gavin McPherson about your bathroom."

"Oh, yes. Well. It's a bit of a pain not having a proper shower, and if I decided to let it—or even sell, to be honest—having a new bathroom wouldn't hurt, would it? I'm not . . . I wouldn't be trying to get more money from you," I add. "I mean, if I decided to sell it. You're just one of my options."

"Yes," he says, "I suppose I am." He smiles, and I think—although I couldn't one hundred percent swear to it—that he winks at me.

That's weird. Maybe he has a twitch. I ignore it, anyway, and continue to blather on about bathrooms. I mention the hideous fireplace in my sitting room, and remember that Edward told me about Charles's archive and that he might have pictures of the lodge.

"Oh, of course," he says. "There's a whole room full of plans and photographs." He looks around the room at his guests. "I'll show you, come on." He nods toward a door, not the one we came in through. "There's lots of interesting stuff in there. You'll like it."

I follow him. He's probably right. "Yes," I say, "but what about your guests?"

"They're fine. Look, everyone's talking, they won't even notice." He holds the door open for me and I hesitate for a moment and then go out into the corridor. He shuts the door behind us, and it's suddenly rather quiet. The corridor stretches away in both directions, and we turn right, away from the entrance hall. There are various doors on each side, more paneling, more paintings lit by pools of light from lamps on side tables.

"Charles," I say, "you really don't have to show me now."

"In here," he says, and opens a door. He turns on the light. The room we're in is small, lined with shelves and drawers, a large desk in the middle with a chair on either side. There's no window, so perhaps it's more like a giant cupboard.

"It's all labeled," he says, gesturing. "Estate records, invoices, wills; you know, all that sort of thing. The plans of the house are in here. And all the estate buildings."

There's a big plan chest against the far wall. He walks over to it and peers at the labels. "Haven't had these out for ages, not since we did the work on East Lodge."

I look around the room, fascinated. It's mad, isn't it, owning all this stuff, things your family has owned for centuries. My great-grandparents' dining table can't really compete.

"Here," he says, pulling a large cardboard file out of a drawer. "I think this is photos. And the plans . . ." He bends and opens a lower drawer. "Yes, here we are." He spreads them out on the tabletop and I move closer to peer at the paper.

"Let's shed some light . . ." he says, flicking the button on an orange Anglepoise lamp. "There."

It's rather splendid to look at a plan of my house, drawn up in the eighteenth century.

"Cool," I say.

He opens the file. "Yes, look, these pictures were taken just before your uncle bought it. And these are from"—he turns one over—"the twenties. That's the lodgekeeper—Dougie MacNeil. My father used to talk about him. It was when he died that they sold the lodge."

I look at the man in the photo, in his shirtsleeves and waistcoat, smiling awkwardly at the camera. A black-and-white cat sits on the doorstep behind him. There's no wisteria, which makes the front of the building look strangely naked.

"Been meaning to say . . ." Charles pulls out another picture, older, with a woman in a hat standing beside a girl sitting on a kitchen chair. They look pre–First World War, maybe 1910.

"Hm?" I prompt him.

"That dress really suits you. Great color."

"Oh," I say, embarrassed and slightly concerned. "That's kind of you. I chose it because of the color."

"Yes, it's very striking."

I look down at myself. "I'm not sure 'striking' is what I was going for, but thank you. It's a bit too shiny I think."

"No, it's . . . it looks . . . You look great."

"Well, thanks. I'm not used to going out anywhere that requires dressing up." I clear my throat, still embarrassed. It's very warm in here, or is that just me? I don't much want to be alone with Charles if he's going to talk about my outfit. "And thanks for showing me these. But people are probably wondering where you are; we should get back."

He looks at me for a long time without saying anything. Then he looks down at the photos.

"Come up any time if you want to look at this lot properly," he says. "I can get Lynda to scan some of them if you like."

"Who's Lynda?"

"Oh—housekeeper."

"Does she do your admin?" I'm surprised by this.

"She does most things." He smiles at me. "Like having a wife—without any of the . . ." He pauses. "Um, trouble."

I snort—very elegant—but I don't respond to this. Instead I repeat, "We should get back," and he clicks off the lamp and steps away, leaving the contents of the files spread over the chest. I follow him to the door, which he holds open for me, putting his other hand lightly on my back. I speed up slightly, not wanting to look like I'm running away, but equally not wanting to encourage anything. If there's anything to encourage. God, I hate this stuff. I'd forgotten how much having a husband removes all this crap from any equation.

. . .

Back in the sitting room, I hope no one noticed our absence. Easily long enough for all kinds of bad behavior. When Jenny walks past, I say, "Oh, there's Jenny, I was going to ask her about . . . Excuse me." And I hurry after her.

"Hey," she says. "I saw you come back in. What have you two been up to?" She grins at me. "Nothing untoward I hope."

"Good grief. No. He wanted to show me the old plans of the lodge."

"Oh, aye," she says, raising her eyebrows. "Never heard it called that before."

"Jenny."

She's laughing now. "Ah. Now everyone will be wondering about the pair of you."

"I'm pretty sure they will not."

Grinning, she says, "But apart from that, how're you bearing up? It's a terrible strain, isn't it?"

"Exhausting. Talking to strangers is tough. And these people are so fancy."

She laughs again. "Aye, they are a bit. Come and talk to me—Alistair's gone to the loo. I was just pursuing the canapé girl. Have you had one of the wee prawn things?" I shake my head, relieved to be talking to someone more straightforward.

"How's work?" she asks me after we've both deftly swiped two canapés each (half a fig with goat cheese, and the aforementioned prawn coated in spicy panko breadcrumbs) from the tray.

"Oh, yeah," I say, trying to shove half a fig into my mouth elegantly. "Going well, I think. I like it."

"Do you?"

"Mm. Yeah, it's interesting, and Edward's quite funny."

"You like him." That's not a question, it's a statement. She's looking at me, curious.

"I do like him, yes. I guess I've never seen him being really obnoxious; I can't quite see why you all hate him so much."

"I don't hate him," she says. "I just . . . He's so spiky, I can't be arsed with it. And it doesn't matter how hard you try—we've invited him to dinner a million times—it makes no difference. I think he enjoys being miserable."

"I don't think he is miserable, though," I object. "He

seems happy enough on his own. And I think he likes pretending to be grumpy."

"You've said before you think he's pretending."

"You can make him really laugh, so I just don't think he can be truly grumpy."

"I've never seen him really laughing," she says. "You must be hilarious."

I test the idea that this might be the reason. "God, I don't think it's that. Maybe I just don't . . . I don't know. Because I'm new, so he's got no history with me. Whereas for all the rest of you . . ."

"Aye, that's true. We're used to him."

"Yes. Anyway, luckily for me, we get on okay. It would be a bit rubbish otherwise; after all, he's basically the person I see most."

. . .

On Monday, when I arrive at the shop, Edward's unpacking boxes of new books. He glances up as the bell jangles.

"How was the party?"

"Oh God, awful."

He looks amused, as well he might. "Was it? How come?"

"I'm no good at that sort of thing. I hardly knew anyone; they were all really posh." I put my bag behind the counter, sighing.

"You must have expected that, though, surely?"

"I know it's my own fault for going."

"Curiosity killed the cat."

I glare at him. "Well, fortunately I wasn't killed."

"What were you, then?"

I tick off on my fingers. "Self-conscious. Anxious. Bored."

He laughs. "Anxious? Why were you anxious?"

I lift a shoulder in a half shrug. "I don't like that sort of thing. I had to talk to strangers. I felt . . ."

"You felt what?" He's focused on me, intent.

"I don't suppose you'd understand." I sit down in the green chair and shake the mouse to wake the laptop.

"Try me."

"Fat, and old, and . . . common." He blinks at me. I laugh. "I know. Ridiculous. I mean, to feel common. The rest of it . . . Anyway, it's my chip; I forget about it sometimes but it's flipping massive." I laugh again.

"The chip on your shoulder? Can't say I've noticed." He looks perfectly serious, but I'm suspicious.

"Are you making fun of me?"

He grins at me. "Not really. A bit. Anyway, you're not fat, or old. And you're certainly not common."

"I am, though. I mean your brother's a *lord*. Not that I care if he is, or if I am. But it's hard not to think about how all the women in my mum's family were domestic servants. For the last two hundred years or something." I stand up and stretch, my elbows cracking. "Probably longer. It's like a race memory. I'd have been scrubbing things, not flouncing about eating canapés." I deliberately don't pronounce the accent. "A hundred years ago, neither of you'd have been speaking to me, would you, except to give orders, or . . ." I can't quite express what I mean. "It made me uncomfortable."

"A hundred years ago we'd have been drowning in mud at the Somme," he says. "Too busy to shout at the staff."

"Oh. Well. Perhaps. But you're a bit old, aren't you? I know you're doing the same thing as me," I add, "thinking of yourself as a young man. Like I see myself as a kitchen maid, whereas I'd hope I'd have been a cook or housekeeper by the time I got to my age, and you'd be a general, or too old to fight."

He frowns at me. "I suppose so," he says. "You're right, I'm always twenty in my head."

"I know. Depressing, isn't it?"

Ten

It's the beginning of July and I've been working at the bookshop for nearly two months. I've taken over the window displays, which have improved one hundred percent, if I do say so myself. The Twitter account, much to Edward's horror, is a resounding success and I've been Instagramming pictures of books, and actually posting things on the Facebook page Rory's brother set up five years ago.

"I don't know why you bother," Edward says. "I won't do any of this when you've gone."

"Make it part of my replacement's role. E-marketing."

"Jesus."

"We've got more than five hundred Twitter followers already," I say. "I think that's pretty good. And loads of them are actual people, not just other bookshops." I'm opening boxes, three of which arrived this morning, and unpacking the contents. I stack books on the floor by the counter.

"Ugh."

"If you get another young person they'll be happy to do it. It's not difficult. And I sold that Austen box set from the Folio Society because of Twitter."

"I know," he says grudgingly. "I suppose you're quite good at it."

"I don't know if I am, but it's hardly difficult. Interaction, Edward, that's what it's all about." I open a 1970s travel guide to the Lowlands and flick through the pages. Some great oversaturated photographs, my favorite kind of municipal flower beds, scenery with suspiciously blue sky and lochs. It's the things you never think about, like bins and bus shelters, the typeface on shop fronts, that make you nostalgic. There are some shops in Castle Douglas that still have their 1960s shop signs; I've been photographing them for my own Instagram. One got nearly eight hundred likes; I'm a social media maven. Ha.

I look back at my boss, who is huffing to himself.

"I didn't open an antiquarian bookshop in order to *interact* with people," he says with loathing. I laugh at him. I sincerely believe almost all this miserable grumpiness is a pose. Sometimes a pose he believes himself, perhaps. But mostly a pose, a concealment. I'm not sure why he wants to hide away like this, because although we often spend all day together, and sometimes go for a drink in the evening, we still don't talk about ourselves much, being too busy talking about books.

"Have you seen the forecast?" he asks me, looking up from his phone.

"No," I say, slicing open another box. "Ooh. Local history."

"Is that what's in there? It's taken him long enough. Anyway, look, it's supposed to be seventy-three degrees later, maybe seventy-five tomorrow. What sweltering heat; we'll never recover."

"That's properly warm," I say, surprised. "I didn't realize it ever got that hot up here."

"*Tsk.* Of course it does. About every five years, for two days. I'll tell you what we should do."

I put a final pile of books on the counter and begin to disassemble the box. "Oh yes? What should we do?"

"Close the shop and go to the beach."

This seems so out of character that I laugh. "No. Seriously?"

"We should go to the Shed."

"What's the Shed? And don't tell me it's a shed, please."

"It is, though. Although that's . . . It's a bit grander than a shed. But not grand in any way. They call them beach huts, but it's not like the beach huts you get at Southwold or Brighton. It's more like a shack. No electricity. But there's a loo. It's primitive, but more comfortable than camping."

"At the beach?"

"Mm-hm. About ten miles away. A wee bay. There's a burn—a stream—and rocks and a bit of sand. Used to go there a lot when we were kids."

"Oh really?" A snippet of family information.

"Go home and get your swimsuit," he says.

I laugh. "I didn't bring a bathing suit with me. I only came to empty the house. I wasn't planning on staying."

"Buy one, then."

"Oh, if only it were that easy. I doubt I'd get a swimsuit here. Which shop would you suggest? The Co-op? Have to go to Dumfries I should think."

He pulls at his lower lip. "Hm. You might be right. But anyway, go and get some beach clothes and a towel. And your book. And maybe a sweater for tonight. I'll sort out the food."

I look at him. He's excited by the idea, I can see that.

"Tonight?"

"Oh, well, it's good to have a fire on the beach and look at the stars," he says.

Slightly doubtful, I ask, "Would we sleep there?" I'm not sure about sharing accommodation with Edward. Not that I think . . . but it's intimate, isn't it, even if you're not intimate.

"Oh, there is a bedroom, but I never sleep in there. It's one big room mostly, but it's comfortable. The sofa folds out, and . . . But I wasn't thinking we'd stay over, just go for the day."

"Oh, okay, that sounds . . . okay." I'm relieved not to have to worry about spending the night with him. Or not "with him," you know, but in the same building.

"Go and get your stuff together. I'll come and get you." He looks at his watch. "In about half an hour? Pointless to take two cars. Go on. Do you ever drink beer?"

"Not really."

"A bottle of wine, then, to have with lunch. I'll pop to Rabbie's and see what fish he's got."

"Really close the shop?"

"Ach, we don't get weather this good very often. I'll change the answering machine message and put a sign on the door. Go on, away with you. I'll be across to collect you, say at ten-fifteen."

. . .

Edward drives a Land Rover Defender that has seen better days. It's filthy, and there's a terrible scrape down the driver's side. The backseats are piled with stuff, including a battered wicker hamper and a big red cooler. He jams my bag of odds and ends in as well and stands in the road, thinking.

"Sun hat," he says.

"Check."

"Sunscreen."

"Check."

"Got your book? There's no signal, so don't expect to be able to get online."

"No problem."

"Okay. Come on, then."

I climb up into the passenger seat and admire the view from the dizzy heights of the 4x4.

"Off-roading?"

"We do actually have to, yes. There is a road, but it's shit."

I put on my sunglasses. "How thrilling," I say, "like going on holiday."

"I've only been down a couple of times this summer. I don't mind going when it's wet or windy—storms are great when you're right on the beach—but it's blissful in hot weather."

I turn to look at him. I've never known him to be in such a good mood. "So is it, like, a family place? If you used to go when you were a kid?"

He's silent for a while, thinking. "Yeah. My grandfather built it, just before the war."

"I thought you gave up all your family stuff," I say cautiously.

"Yeah, well. I wanted to keep the Shed. I guess I'm a hypocrite."

He's as scathing about himself as he is about everyone else, I suppose.

"Oh, I think you're being harsh," I say.

"Am I? I don't know that I am. Anyway, I kept the Shed. It's probably not worth much, I don't know."

"If there's no electricity . . ."

"Yeah, the other beach houses down there have it. I could get it hooked up, but I prefer it without. My father got the plumbing sorted. For which I'm grateful, obviously—"

"Look at the sky," I interrupt. "Isn't it amazing? I mean it's not like it's rained all the time since I arrived, but bloody hell it hasn't been like this."

He laughs. "No, it isn't often this hot. Although there are plenty of fine days. The weather moves quickly up here, it's unusual for it to rain all day."

We're driving through farmland mostly: fields of cows, fields of sheep. I'm still surprised by how rural it is. The road runs along the coast, so it's salt marsh on one side and fields on the other.

...

Eventually we turn off the main road, and then turn off again onto a track between brambly hedges, and then onto another, rougher track. I glimpse the sea across a field. I'm genuinely excited.

"All caravans down there," he gestures. "They have a shop, so you can get milk if you need to."

"Don't they ruin your ambience?"

"Can't see 'em from the Shed, and the holiday people don't come down here; it's quite a walk, and they've got their own beach. Get some dog walkers. Sometimes you catch people peering through the windows, or they sit on the bench; I don't care, as long as they don't make a mess. Sorry," he adds as we bounce over a particularly rough patch and I grab at the dashboard. "Here we go, this is us. Would you be a darling and open the gate for me?"

I climb out of the car and cross the track to the mossy five-bar gate to my right. There's a piece of painted slate attached to it that just says MALTRAVERS, as though that's the name of the house. I slide the bolt and push the gate open. There are trees, short and twisty, windblown; on the boundary, a lichened, ferny drystone wall. I step out of the way so he can bring the car through, and look over toward the Shed. It's made of black creosoted wood, single story, the front door on this side is neatly painted in a sunny yellow. It opens onto the wide swath of weedy shingle where he's parking the car. There's a window on this side too, covered with a wire grille. So far I can't see the sea, although I can hear it. Another, smaller shed with double doors, newer looking, stands over to the left.

Edward's out of the car and heading toward me. "I'll unlock and show you round. It'll be dark because I need to take the shutters down." He fiddles with the door, leaning his shoulder into it. "And it sticks—oh, there we are. Come in."

I follow him into a shadowy hallway. The still air feels dry, and it smells of warm wood, dust, and wood smoke. The smell of a hot shed reminds me of the summer holidays spent at my friend Tara's house. Playing in the garden shed was forbidden for some reason, but we'd creep in there while her dad was at work, unfolding the lounge chairs, pretending the shed was our house, ignoring the lawnmower and the spades and forks.

"Careful," he warns, opening another door, "there's a step down. Wait here a moment."

He disappears behind me and I peer around, stranded in the half dark. Light creeps round the edges of the shutters, so I can just about see some sofas and a chair, a table against one wall, a wood burner. I hear the whoosh of something sliding, and then the room is full of light.

"Oh, wow," I say feebly. Most of the front wall is glass, half of it sliding open when he unlocks it. Outside, brilliant green lawn, rocks, ocean. I can't see the beach because it's lower than the grass, but I can see the rocks that curve around, forming the bay, and the sea itself. The sky and the sea are equally blue; there's not a cloud to be seen. The wood-walled room has pine tongue and groove, like a chalet. There are pictures, a bookcase. The chair I noticed is the mate of the one in the shop that Edward sits in. One of the sofas is a tiny mid-century two-seater with skinny angled legs, upholstered in nubby blue fabric, while the other is a huge, fat four-seater that probably cost a fortune when it was new. It's covered with tartan blankets. There's a sink on the same wall as the burner, and an old sideboard with a marble top, similar to the counter in the shop. On the wall above the sink there's a cupboard, and three open shelves with plates and cups and bowls. Pans hang from the wall.

"Bathroom—I use the term loosely—is back through the hall and off to the left. There's a bedroom as well, but I always sleep in here or out on the grass," he says. He watches me as I look at everything. "And that's all there is to it." He shrugs. "Obviously, it's all about the beach."

"Oh yes! The beach!" I hurry out onto the lawn and across

the grass. It falls away to a tight curve of yellow-brown sand, alexanders and sea kale, great slabs of rock, washed up piles of kelp and bladder wrack, patches of shell and pebble. A pair of gulls watch me from a silvery pale branch of driftwood. In the bay a solitary orange buoy bobs in the waves. It's pretty much perfect, like something from the Famous Five children's books. I turn back to the Shed, where Edward watches me, grinning.

"It's beautiful. How splendid."

He's pleased, I think, that I like it. He nods, smiling. "Let's get things sorted before it gets too hot. Tea?"

"It's much too warm, surely," I say, surprised. "Won't the burner make it unbearable in there? Are you going to cook inside?"

"No, I'll cook out here. I could boil a kettle on the Primus stove. Need a cuppa."

"That might be better. Although it's up to you," I add. "I'm not trying to boss you."

"Are you not?" He grins at me. I wonder if it's being outdoors that makes him less . . . combative, or our skipping work today.

I widen my eyes and shake my head. "I never boss anyone."

"No, no, of course not."

I watch as he carries the shutters away one at a time, back round the side of the house to the smaller shed. He returns with a beautiful Indian parasol, bright purple, with glittering beads hanging from it. He leans it against the wall and goes back for the stand.

"It gets stupidly hot out here, and there's no shade," he

explains, putting the parasol up and going off again, returning this time with a wheelbarrow full of wood.

"If I get all this done now," he says, "we won't have to do it later when it's really warm."

"Let me help," I say, and he asks me to unpack the hamper in the Shed.

"It's a bit early for booze, d'you think?" he says.

I nod. "It is for me, yes."

"So bring the wine out here and I'll show you the fridge."

"Fridge? But there's no electric."

"All will be revealed."

I go inside and unbuckle the lid of the elderly Fortnum's hamper he's put on the countertop. Inside I find two bottles of white wine and four bottles of sparkling water, as well as various ingredients for lunch and dinner. I load up with bottles. I'm no expert, but the wine looks expensive. I trot outside again.

"Did you buy this specially? I should give you some money."

"Oh no, don't be ridiculous. Okay, so look—this is the shady side, because of the trees. And under here . . ." He rolls a rock, much like the other rocks piled around the place, to one side. Under it is a piece of tarpaulin, and under that, rather thrillingly, a trapdoor. He pulls this up and shows me a square hole in the earth, neatly lined with slate, creating a cool place just tall enough for a large wine bottle. There's something in there, wrapped in a shopping bag.

"Huh," he says, "I forgot about that."

"What is it?"

"Champagne." He pulls it out and unwraps a bottle of Perrier-Jouët.

"Get you," I say, amused. "Abandoning bottles of champagne."

"Profligate."

"Just a bit. Anyway, that's clever, the fridge. Did you make it?"

"Yeah, I built it when I was fourteen." He grins at me. "I'm pretty proud of it to be honest."

"It's very cunning."

"Yeah, it used to drive my mother mad that you had to put the milk in a bucket of cold water. And no ice for her G&Ts. Still no ice, but you can keep your tonic cold, especially if you put the ice packs from the cooler in here. Right, then. What's next? I think I'm going to go for a swim. Did you get a swimsuit?"

"Of course not. But it's okay, if I go in the sea I'll just get my feet wet."

"You're missing out. Could skinny dip? It's very quiet—"

"Yeah, d'you know what, I don't think so. I'm afraid I require quite substantial support and buttressing."

This makes him laugh. "Fair enough. I'll go and get changed, anyway," he says, and heads back indoors. I stand outside on the grass and close my eyes. Apart from the sound of the waves, it's totally silent. The sun on my face is heavenly. I stretch out my arms and soak up the warmth. I should probably put on some sunscreen before I'm burnt to a crisp.

Should I lie on the grass and read while he's swimming, or walk on the beach? If I was even five years younger, I'd have been on the beach already. I smear myself with factor thirty, remembering this time to do the back of my neck. Then I put my hat on and stuff an empty linen tote bag into the pocket of my skirt. I'm pleased with myself for remembering this, so I won't have to try and hold any results of beachcombing in my hands. I look back toward the door into the hallway. Edward is still inside; I'm not sure whether to wait for him.

It suddenly seems a bit odd that we're out here together. It's not as though we're . . . Are we friends? Not exactly. I mean he's my boss, isn't he? Would he have brought Rory with him? Maybe he would have. Maybe he did. He doesn't seem to have any proper friends, although I'm not sure why.

I walk to the edge of the lawn and look down at the sand, and then clamber over the rocks until I'm standing among the pebbles. I stoop to take off my sandals and leave them on a rock, and then begin to walk slowly along the beach, heading to the left, where a long spur of rock juts out into the bay.

I love a beach. A beach with shells and driftwood, sand and rock pools. I like things to look at, and things to collect. A good beach has beach glass, worn smooth, in unusual colors; and pieces of patterned Victorian china; interesting shells. There are certainly lots of shells here. As my eyes adjust, I'm amazed. Different from the ones at the beach where Jenny walks the dogs, here there are huge heaping swaths of limpets and mussels and, caught up among them, the same bright yellow and orange periwinkles, deepening to maroon. I'm farther down the beach now, the intertidal zone, on firm sand that was underwater earlier. I look back at the faint impressions of my footsteps. There's a slight breeze and the endless whisper of the waves.

What a gorgeous day. I feel my spirits lift further. You could almost say I was happy. I don't like to address this thought head-on, though, because if you look at happiness it usually disappears, a shy creature. And also—it's just a layer, isn't it? A moment's joy that's come from nature, sunshine, and seaside, overlaying everything else.

Since I've been up here I haven't ever been as unhappy as I was in the first month or so after Chris and I split up. It would be impossible, I think, to sustain that level of misery. It's a slow journey but things will improve, have improved— but I also know that in some ways I'm avoiding having to deal with my feelings. It's easy not to think about it because I've come somewhere else. That "change of scene" they talk about. Being busy in a new place allows you to avoid looking at things you should maybe look at. There are things I need to work on and I worry that this is merely displacement. That when I go home to my horrible flat, which is costing me money despite its emptiness, I'll be back where I was when I left; none of it addressed or fixed at all. I shiver, as though the sun has passed behind a cloud, although there are no clouds, the sky a dense and brazen blue in every direction.

· · ·

I'm lying on the beach peering at shells when Edward runs past me, leaping over patches of pebbles, dropping a towel on an exposed rock and wading out into the water. He doesn't edge cautiously in but flings himself carelessly into the waves. I should think the water's still cold, even if it is July. I sit up and watch him as he front crawls, splashing, in the bay. I'm jealous, I can't remember the last time I swam in the sea.

Holding my now-heavy bag, into which I have gathered interestingly striped stones, limpet shells worn away to narrow loops and rings and some pale blue-green sea glass, I walk down toward the water. There are three-toed gull foot-prints on the sand. And smaller ones—oystercatchers? Lacy wavelets ripple toward me and I look out to sea and the distant swimmer, and step into the water, which is, as anticipated, freezing. At first it seems too cold, but I'm quickly accustomed and walk out, jumping over the wavelets the way I did as a child. Soon the water's halfway up my calves and a larger wave slaps against my knees, making me gasp and laugh. My toes dig into the sand, my ears are full of the sound of the waves and again I am conscious of a precise moment of happiness.

···

Back at the Shed, I empty my finds into the sink to wash the sand off them, and then arrange them on a plate that I put on the lawn in the sun. I poke about in the hot silence, opening the bathroom door. There is the smell of sun-warmed wood, a view through the top half of the window, which is clear glass, contrasting with the bottom half, which is frosted, of the trees on the edge of the property. A large old-fashioned basin, a toilet. Clean but basic. There's no actual bath, just a shower pan with a curtain in the corner. The shower itself is just one of those rubber tubes that you attach to bath taps. There's only one tap—I assume because there's no hot water. A cold shower in Scotland seems unnecessarily harsh, but I suppose it's good enough for rinsing salt out of your hair. There's an old white-painted medicine cabinet on the wall, and above the sink a rectangular mirror with angled edges on a chain, vaguely deco. Perhaps it's been hanging there since the Shed was built. Etched with flowers, it reminds me of the one my Hamilton grandparents had in their bedroom. It amuses me to think that, just possibly, it might have been bought in the same shop.

Opposite the bathroom, another door, which I open. The room is dark, the window still shuttered. I open the door wider to allow as much light in as possible. There are faded curtains in a splashy seventies flower print. The bed is larger than a single, but not as big as a double. Did Edward's parents sleep in here? With the boys in the main room? It's hard to imagine Lord and Lady Whatsit in here. There's a small, slightly wonky wardrobe, a bookcase stuffed with paperbacks, and a chest of drawers, all in smooth, yellowy wood on stumpy legs. On top of the chest of drawers, a selection of shells and rocks, and something that, as I peer at it, I decide might be a whale's vertebra. There's an old Kilner jar half-full of beach glass. Folded on the neatly made bed are towels and blankets. The room smells of dust and pillows. On the back of the door, a bright orange waterproof jacket. A mirror that matches the one in the bathroom, and hanging beside it a framed photograph of a woman, sitting outside the Shed, shading her eyes against the sun. Her hair and outfit—loose-fitting white dress but still with shoes and stockings—put her somewhere in the twenties or thirties. Edward's grandmother, is my guess; wife of the man who built the Shed.

I love how quiet it is. The silence, the smell of warm wood. The distant waves. Uncle Andrew's is quiet—in fact, probably quieter since there's no ocean—but this feels more isolated and empty. I know Edward said there are more holiday homes around, but you can't see them from here. And I've a theory that when you go to a place with somebody else, and that person leaves, it's quieter than a place you've gone to alone.

I go back outside and shade my eyes, looking out to see if I can spot Edward. I can't see him anywhere and am just about to feel slightly anxious when his head appears above the rocks as he climbs back into the garden.

"Hey. Good swim?"

"Fantastic, thanks. I feel suitably invigorated. And I'm starving. Ready for lunch?"

"Oh, yeah, sure. Let me help."

"Okay," he says, "you can fetch things if you like. Plates. Frying pan. Some sort of"—he gestures—"implement. I was going to make a tomato salad, so you could chop up tomatoes. I usually drag the table over to the barbecue. I'll go and get dressed; won't be a minute."

He rubs his head briskly with the towel as he moves away. The dark hair on his legs and belly is uncurled by the water, pulled dead straight. It's odd to see someone mostly naked, difficult to know where to look. Previously I've never seen his feet, or even his forearms. He has swimmers' shoulders, broad and muscular in an understated way, and an unexpected scatter of freckles across his arms and chest. I try not to look at him, feeling embarrassed. I'd be deeply resentful if I was in a bathing suit myself and thought someone was thinking anything at all about my body. Jesus.

Eleven

Later, as we sit on the bench looking out over the bay, eating pan-fried mackerel and tomato salad, I ask him if he often brings people here in the summer.

"People? No, hardly ever. Usually come by myself. Brought Rory and one of his mates down last year. We got very drunk."

"Gosh, really?"

"Yes, tragic, isn't it? They could be my kids." He slices his fish into pieces and avoids my eyes.

"Well—"

"Mm. Pretty tragic. Wasn't the plan, but they brought some beer, and . . ."

I consider this. "Rory doesn't seem like a drinker."

"Oh, he's young, though, isn't he? Even if you're not a drinker, you can still drink a lot at eighteen. Or seventeen. More than I can, anyway. I was sick as a dog."

"So no drunken parties down here this year?"

"I'm a solitary creature," he says. "Mostly."

• • •

After lunch, we lie on blankets on the grass, shaded by the parasol. It's unbelievably hot, and I'm drowsy. I feel my eyes close and my head nod.

"Sleepy?"

"Looks like it."

"Have a nap. I'll wake you in an hour. If you like."

"Seems a waste," I object, but I'm drifting.

. . .

When I wake up I feel quite odd, uncertain of where I am, self-conscious in case I snored. My neck's stiff and I blink unsteadily at the distant sea. Edward's not beside me any longer. I sit up awkwardly and look around for him.

He comes out of the Shed. "Ah," he says, "there you are. Champagne?" He hands me a tumbler. "Sorry, those are the only glasses I've got. Except pint glasses."

"I do usually drink champagne by the pint."

He laughs. "Oh yeah?"

I stretch, shifting on the blanket. "Thanks. God, it's warm." I raise my glass to him and then sip my champagne. "This is the life, though."

He grins at me. "Isn't it?"

"It's just lovely; you're very lucky."

"Hm. Am I? I suppose I am." He looks away, closed off again; I wish he wasn't so touchy. Never quite himself, always . . . It isn't that he's awkward, exactly, or I don't think it's that. There's just something strange about him, an indefinable tension.

He sighs. "We used to come down most weekends in the

summer when I was a kid. I always thought my father was most able to be himself down here. At the house it's a bit more formal."

I raise my eyebrows, amused. "A bit."

"And it was worse, of course, in those days. My grand-father was a formal sort of chap. He died when I was eight. I imagine he ran things the way his father had and so on, or tried to, although we were down to three staff by then. My father was more of a free spirit, I suppose. He was drinking a lot then. They used to fight."

I watch him. This is a lot more than he's ever told me.

"Once my father inherited the title, it was as though he'd been taken over by the"—he pauses, pulling up grass—"weight of history, or something. He stopped drinking, but by the time I was fifteen we were having almost exactly the same fights I'd listened to as a child."

"That's quite depressing."

"Yeah. Yeah, it was."

"And, um—how old were you, then, when he died?"

"Twenty-five."

"And you—"

"I'd already decided I was going to give it up, when I was still at university. He went predictably nuts when I told him."

"But surely," I say, "I mean, it's not like you don't have a brother—"

"I can't imagine how much more furious he'd have been if I was an only child. Or, God forbid, Charles had been a girl. It would probably have killed him."

I think about this. "Well, but Charles isn't a girl, and you weren't an only child, and it didn't kill him."

"No. And I know it was the right thing to do. But he wouldn't even try to understand it. Never forgave me."

"Does that . . . is that a thing that worries you?"

He flicks grass off the blanket. "No. Sort of. Sometimes. Mostly not."

"I suppose it's only to be expected, that you might feel ambivalent about it. But you don't miss the house? Or regret not being, you know, Lord Thing?"

"Jesus, no. No."

"There you are, then. You can't please everyone, and parents are weird. And even parents without any history are peculiar, so . . ."

He frowns at me. "What are your parents like?"

"Oh, well, they're okay. They putter, you know; retired. Although they're not puttering at the moment, the mad bastards. They're halfway through a trip round the world. I think they're in Cambodia. Or Laos." I shake my head at the idea of it.

"Are they? Shit, you never tell me anything, do you?"

I grin at him. "Sorry, boss. Anyway. I don't think they ever had any particular expectations of me, so I haven't been able to let them down too much." I smile to show I'm joking, although I don't know if I am, really.

"There's just you? Or have you got brothers and sisters?"

"No, there's just me."

"And your dad's from up here?"

"Not really. Grandad moved to Birmingham before the war, and then down to Chichester, that's where he met my grandmother. He was an engineer," I add. "He didn't fight. Reserved occupation."

"Is that where you live? Chichester?"

"It's where I grew up." I'm not sure where I live now. I don't say this, though.

. . .

"Another glass?"

"Oh, go on, then. I don't usually drink during the day, I should be careful."

"Careful?" He raises an eyebrow, almost flirty.

"I don't want to be hungover at half seven. Ghastly feeling."

"Always a risk." He gets up to fetch the champagne from the slate-lined hole in the ground and tops up my glass.

"Cheers. Do you really sleep outside when you stay here?"

"Sometimes, depends on the weather."

"Isn't there, like, dew?"

He laughs at me. "Yes, but I can handle it. And the sofa's very comfortable, if I'm feeling delicate."

"It's just the ground seems to be getting harder and harder," I say, "or it feels like it."

"I'll get you more cushions if you like?"

I shuffle about and stand up to stretch. "Maybe I should go for a walk. But then my drink would get warm. Oh, it's difficult."

"Take your drink with you," he suggests. "If you walk for about fifteen minutes, there's another bay."

"Fifteen minutes? I'm not sure I can be arsed with that. Anyway, I'll finish my drink before I get there and be tempted to throw the glass in a bush so I don't have to carry it."

This makes him laugh a lot. "You could put it on a wall and pick it up on the way back."

"Don't enable my laziness," I tell him. "I'll just walk on the beach."

. . .

When I get back to the garden, slightly cooler from wading and with my empty glass, Edward has moved the parasol, following the sun, and is leaning on a cushion against the wall of the Shed, legs stretched out on the blanket, his book spread open on the grass beside him and a tray in his lap. He looks up and pushes his sunglasses onto the top of his head.

"Better?"

"Yes, thanks. What are you doing?" I drop my sandals on the grass. The empty champagne bottle stands on the table, an open bottle of wine beside it. I look at this, thinking; then make a decision and pour some into my glass. He holds the tray out toward me, so I can see the contents. It's what we used to refer to as "paraphernalia"—all the requirements for rolling a joint. I'm mildly surprised.

"You don't mind, do you?" he asks.

"God, no."

"There's something about a sunny afternoon," he says.

I watch him for a moment, and sniff. "Is it skunk? I hate skunk."

"No, it's just homegrown, not very strong. You'd be able to smell it, wouldn't you, if it was skunk."

"I suppose." I think of the white-painted windows of the greenhouse in the garden at the shop. "Did you grow it?"

"No. Get it off a bloke. D'you smoke?"

"Not for years."

He licks the edge of the papers and seals the joint closed. "Want some of this?"

"Dunno." I sit beside him, back against the warm wood. "Didn't have you down as a stoner."

"Jesus Christ. I'm hardly a stoner."

I laugh. "You're easy to wind up, though, aren't you? Maybe you should allow the essence of stoner into your life. You need to relax."

"I am relaxed."

I snort. "Yeah, right. Riddled with tension."

"I am not riddled with tension."

"Gosh, no, sorry, must be thinking of someone else."

"You know you're extremely cheeky."

"It's good for you," I tell him.

He lights the joint and inhales. "Is that so?" he says through a cloud of smoke.

"Everyone takes you so seriously, don't they? It can't help."

"Help?"

"Help you not be an arse." There's a pause, long enough for me to wonder if I've been horribly rude.

"Am I an arse?"

I feel sorry for him suddenly. "I don't know," I say. "I think it's a pose, isn't it? Anyway, you've been very kind to me. Today especially."

"I have, haven't I?"

"It was lovely of you to invite me."

"I suppose it was. Mind you, I'd be here on my own if I hadn't."

I watch him for a moment as he smokes. "Are you lonely?" I've wondered about this.

There's another long pause while he considers. "No. I think one has to like people more than I do to be lonely."

"I'm not sure that's true. Even if you don't like people much you can still be lonely. But you're not, so that's good." I pull my knees up and rest my wrists on them, lacing my fingers.

"What about you? Out in the middle of nowhere by yourself. Not what you're used to, surely. I didn't expect you to stay for so long."

"No, neither did I. Anyway, that's one of the reasons I decided I should get a job. I'm not used to being on my own. I wouldn't say I was lonely, though."

"And what about Mr. Mottram? Is he lonely without you? I wouldn't be happy if my wife buggered off for months at a time."

I'm not sure what to say to this. Perhaps I should just tell him; it's not like it matters. "I doubt he's lonely," I say. "He lives with someone else."

There's a brief silence. I listen to the waves and the faint crackle of the burning cigarette paper as Edward draws the air through it. He frowns at me through the smoke.

"What, as in—"

"We're, um . . . He left," I say. "Or I did."

"Recently?"

"Not that recently. January."

"God. You didn't say. Why didn't you say?"

I shrug. "That's one of the reasons I came here. Well, I'd have had to come up anyway. But that's one of the reasons I'm still here. I mean, I didn't have to go home. Because I don't live there; someone else does."

There's a pause while he thinks about this. "But why's it a secret? Is it a secret? Does anyone know?"

"Oh, well. Jenny. A couple of other people. But it's boring, telling people. And anyway, I'm not divorced, so you have to say you're separated or whatever and it's . . . tedious. I suppose once I'm actually divorced"—I take the offered joint from him—"thanks, it will be easier. I don't want to have to explain it all the time."

"You could have told me."

"Yes, I could have." I smile. "But I didn't want to."

He frowns at me. "Why not?"

"I didn't think it was any of your business. And then I thought it would be easier, since I know you didn't really want to give me a job, and you might have thought it was . . . I don't know, a reason not to."

I see he's thinking about this. "How long were you married?"

"Fifteen years. Together for nineteen."

"That's a long time."

"Yes."

"Are you . . . How do you feel? About that?"

"About my husband leaving me and shacking up with someone I thought was my friend?"

"Shit."

"Yeah, it's not great."

"But . . . I can't believe you've never mentioned it."

"I prefer not to talk about it." I smile again, amused by his shocked expression.

"How did you find out? Or did he tell you?"

It's funny he thinks I must have found out. That's exactly what happened, of course.

"No, I found out. He sent me a message by mistake."

"By mistake?"

"He meant to send it to her."

"Oh. Shit. That's—"

"Yeah, it wasn't my best day ever."

"How did you—"

"It was a picture," I tell him. "A photograph. I recognized her rings." I waggle my own fingers. "She wears lots of rings, you know, she's kind of . . ." I think about Susanna, with her mass of curly henna-red hair and her chunky silver jewelry, turquoise, amber. "She's a bit earth-motherish. Quite recognizable, even if you can't really see her face. Even if she's rather unexpectedly sucking your husband's dick."

"Jesus."

"Mm."

"Thea, I'm so sorry."

"That's okay," I say brightly, "you haven't done anything, have you? Anyway, that sort of let the cat out of the bag. I thought he might apologize and so forth, but it turned out he liked her better." I clear my throat.

"That's awful."

"It is. But it's also very dull."

"Dull?"

I look at the joint I'm holding and realize it's gone out before I've even smoked any. I ask him for a light and he drops the red plastic lighter into my hand. I fumble with the wheel, my thumb pressing against it, hear the grating spin. I inhale and see the flame crackle, wondering when I last smoked a joint. Millennium Eve? Since then, surely. Someone's thirtieth? You could still smoke in pubs then. Not drugs, obviously. I liked pubs better when you could smoke in them, or maybe I was just younger. Now pubs smell of toilets and chip fat and stale beer, where once they smelled of cigarettes. But you can go out for the evening and not have to wash all your clothes. Take the good with the bad, I suppose.

"I'm hardly the first person to wake up one morning and realize they're middle-aged and single and nothing's going to be quite as they expected. It happens all the time. It isn't interesting. That's one of the problems," I add. "One of the things that makes it hard to work around—or through. It's just so . . . It doesn't matter how shit it is, or how crappy I feel. It's impossible to have an original thought about it. It's worse than falling in love, for clichés. Honestly, so dull." I sigh. I'm reasonably impressed with my ability to talk about this without crying.

"Well, but—"

"Anyway, the only thing duller than thinking about it is talking about it." I pause, considering. "I'm going to change my name back," I say. "I've never liked Mottram much. Hamilton's much better."

"Hamilton's a good name," he agrees.

I look at him, speculative. "So, um, have you ever been married?"

"Me? God, no."

"Or similar? Have you lived with anyone, or been engaged, or—"

"No."

I wait. Will he feel he owes me some information, or not? "That's quite unusual, isn't it? Really never even lived with anyone? But you do . . . sleep with people?" I think of Jenny telling me about her friends who'd tried and failed to attract his attention; of him telling me about the assistants who used to fall in love with him, or vice versa.

"Sometimes. I try not to. Or at least—"

"You try not to?" I blink at him. "I don't think I've ever met a man who'd say that."

He looks a bit hunted. "Best not to get involved," he says.

"Blimey." I wasn't expecting that.

It's his turn to sigh. "I'll tell you a secret," he says. I look at him encouragingly. He waits, trying to decide, I suppose, whether it's a good idea to say whatever he's going to say. He takes a deep breath. "I've slept with everyone my brother's ever cared about."

I stare. "Everyone?"

"Well, not our mother. Or, you know, any other relatives. But all his girlfriends, or nearly all of them. And both his wives."

And there it is, finally, the big reveal. I've known there was something, of course, since Alistair first mentioned it months ago. But I can't really believe it. "Bloody hell."

"I know."

"Bloody *hell*."

"I mean it's not loads of people." He smiles a rather crooked smile. "Well. A reasonable number."

"I don't think," I say, carefully, "that it's the numbers that concern me."

"No."

"Can I ask . . . I don't even know what to ask. *Both* his wives?" I say. "Jesus."

"Yeah, that's the worst, isn't it? Although he'd already split up with Julia, his first wife, before I—"

"And the second one?"

"Yeah, that was . . . No. No, it was my fault that time. Carolyn. I didn't even like her much, not really. They were all his type, obviously, not mine." He smiles at me, a proper smile this time.

"Edward."

"So yeah, um . . . for a long time, sex was mostly about revenge for me, and that's why I try to avoid it."

"Revenge? Bloody hell. Way to go from nothing to the most bizarre intimacies in, like, one fell swoop. Christ."

I blow smoke at the edge of the parasol, where purple divides from the intense blue of the sky. I hear gulls and the waves, a blackbird somewhere, a tractor or something in the distance. I take another pull on the joint and hand it back to him.

"So go on," I say, "tell me why you slept with your brother's wives. Etcetera."

"Revenge," he says. "I told you."

"That's not . . . Is that a good reason? I mean, you're not in a play. What's that guy's name? Middleton. Is it Middleton?" One of the things I like about Edward is he always knows the answer to questions about books or plays or poetry. It's handy, because my memory's shockingly poor.

"Thomas Middleton? Yes. *The Revenger's Tragedy*. And God, no. No, it's a terrible reason. That's why he hates me, though, in case you were wondering."

"I'd heard something. Vaguely."

"Yeah, it was quite a scandal."

"Not surprisingly."

"No."

"So did you . . . ? Was that . . . ?"

"I did it on purpose, if that's what you're asking. It wasn't one of those things you do and then go, 'Oh shit.'" He moves so he's lying down, pushing the cushion he's been leaning against under his head. He stares up at the blue, blue sky and takes a final drag. The smoke hangs in the air. "He didn't introduce me to Carolyn until the wedding. Just in case."

"Oh my God."

"Yeah, but I still managed. Mind you"—he sits up again, leaning to put out the joint, pushing the end against a rock and placing the butt neatly on an empty plate—"I have to say, I don't think she can have given that much of a toss about him. It didn't take an awful lot of effort on my part."

"Jesus. So what were you getting revenge for? I'm properly shocked," I tell him.

"That's why everyone hates me," he says. "It was a bad thing to do, even though my brother's an arsehole."

"I don't think everyone hates you, do they? That's just being melodramatic. And what on earth did he do that was bad enough for you to . . . ?"

He sighs. I can't tell if he's relieved to be talking about it or if he wishes he'd never started this conversation. He continues anyway. "There were a number of things. I suppose it was cumulative. We've never got on. He's a . . . he's an unpleasant man and he was an unpleasant boy." He puts his hands behind his head and stares upward.

I think about Charles Maltravers, charming in his riding gear, offering me money for Uncle Andrew's house, shaking my hand and looking me in the eye, inviting me to his house, drinking tea in the garden at the lodge, flirting gently, showing me the plans of my house, complimenting my frock. He's certainly not my type, but he doesn't seem . . . "unpleasant." But that's sibling relationships for you, as complex as any other kind of relationship.

"I'm not sure we could be *mates*," I say, "but he's never

seemed particularly horrible; just overconfident, perhaps, and, you know, um, privileged."

"Hm, overconfident is a good description. He's always been much more . . . I don't know. He's got something that I've never had, and for a long time that bothered me."

" 'Something'? What do you mean?" I stare at him.

"Oh, you know. Charm, or whatever."

He's wearing his sunglasses, so I wouldn't be able to see his eyes even if he were sitting up, but I try anyway, leaning toward him, trying to read his expression. I can't, though.

"Overrated," I say. "But it doesn't bother you now?"

"Since I ruined his marriage? No."

"Jeez. What did he do, then? To make you hate him?"

He sighs. "It was a long time ago. I probably . . . I don't know. I expect a normal person, or someone with a . . . someone who had a better sense of themselves . . ." He trails off.

I look at him. He sighs again. "Okay. When I was in my late teens—Rory's age—everything seemed very . . . I was having huge rows with my parents. Immense, shuddering fights with my dad, not just about, you know, lying in bed and not shaving"—he shakes his head at the idea of his teenage self—"but proper stuff, about the inheritance and privilege and the title and the agony of history. Yes, I was a wanker, obviously, although I don't think I was wrong about any of that. I could have tried harder to see how it had consumed him, I suppose, but that was half the problem. Like I said earlier. I was terrified it would happen to me. In my teens, school was . . . I don't know. I don't have anything to compare it with. Other people had a worse time. I kept my head down and I did learn some stuff. But I was just boiling with fury the whole time. And Charles has always been such

a smug little fucker." He laughs. "He was incredibly pomp-
ous, and the worst kind of young Tory. We had a fight after
the 1987 election. An actual physical fight."

This makes me laugh. "Did you?"

"Yes, so undignified."

I snort. "Did you win?"

"He was only fifteen; of course I did."

I snort again.

"Anyway—I was in love with this girl. She was a friend's
cousin. She used to come down sometimes, during the holidays, from Edinburgh. I'd known her since we were, I don't
know, fourteen. I got very drunk once and told Charles and
her cousin Alex how I felt. I didn't mean to; I meant it to be
a secret. Anyway, once I'd told him he teased me about it,
like little brothers do. But he's not that much of a little
brother. Only a year younger. Always much better with girls
than I was. He's better looking, isn't he?"

I wrinkle my nose, unsure. I suppose he is more conven-
tionally attractive, but I think Edward's more interesting to
look at. They're both pretty good-looking, to be fair. I don't
say this, though; I just listen. He sits up again and pulls his
knees up, takes off his sunglasses.

"He said I should tell her I liked her. He'd had girlfriends,
but I never had. I think I was a late developer; I didn't think
about girls—not girls I knew—until I was in the sixth form.
I mean I had crushes on pop stars and actresses, but . . . Anyway, I did think Charles probably knew more about it than I
did. I couldn't think of anything worse, though, than telling
her. Or more wonderful, if she liked me. But she wouldn't.
But if she did. She was beautiful, golden hair and skin like
vanilla ice cream, freckles like chocolate sprinkles. God, she

was lovely." He laughs at the memory of his younger self. "Honestly. It's still embarrassing to talk about it, even now."

I've often wondered what it would be like to be beautiful; it must be an odd thing to be objectively attractive, rather than someone's personal taste.

"Anyway, he said he'd speak to her for me. I told him not to, but I guess he did. They arranged for me to be thoroughly humiliated anyhow."

"Shit, did they? What happened?"

He shrugs, mouth twisted. "Oh, it probably wasn't that bad, really. But I was a sensitive youth. I was hurt and angry. With both of them, but particularly with him because it was his idea, obviously, and because they all found it so hilarious."

"What did they do?"

He glances at me and then looks away. "He said he'd told her, and she liked me too. And she wanted to meet up. We were up in town, Edinburgh—it was the Easter holidays. He said he'd arranged everything. I was—oh, you know. Excited and nervous and all that. Bought flowers. And my favorite book to give her." He shakes his head. "Because beautiful teenage girls love metaphysical poetry, don't they? Beautiful teenage girls in the late 1980s couldn't get enough of the stuff."

"Whose poems?"

"John Donne, *obviously*."

I laugh. "I like John Donne. I probably didn't know about him in 1988, though."

"No, well, anyway. 'She'll be on the steps outside the National Gallery,' he said. She wasn't, though. I waited for half an hour, an hour, two hours. No phones in those days, no way to find out what had happened. I just waited. And waited. Then they turned up together, with a bunch of other people, mutual friends, people from school. Our peer group, I suppose. Everyone thought it was so funny that I'd been waiting, and then she and Charles were all over each other. Kissing, and . . . Like I say, it's embarrassing to think about it." He fiddles with his sunglasses and then puts them back on, turning to face me.

"I'd have killed everyone there, and myself as well, if I could have. I don't know. It was the idea that me liking someone was so ridiculous and funny. It was painful. After that I . . . It didn't fill me with kindness toward girls. Women. He could have got much the same result without involving her, but she seemed to find it all very amusing as well. That was the worst thing. That she thought it was funny. That she liked him better. That she'd rather let him kiss her, as a joke, than accept anything I had to offer."

"Oh, teenagers are horrible," I say, sympathetic. "How cruel. And then what happened?"

He shrugs. "I've barely spoken to him since, and I never spoke to her again, or anyone else who was there. I went off to university, where I was mostly aloof and sarcastic. I was surprised and not terribly impressed when that seemed more effective than being sincere and so on."

I feel so sorry for the awkward teenage Edward. Being laughed at is a horrible thing. I imagine him, earnest with his poetry and his flowers, waiting and waiting. It's the sort of thing that affects you more than it should, perhaps.

"Hm. Were you brooding?"

"I was a bit." He laughs.

"Tall and dark and mysterious."

"That was my aim. Well, mysterious was my aim, I'm naturally tall and dark." We grin at each other.

"There was a lad on my course who was much the same. James. I don't know what triggered it for him, but he was desperately brooding."

"Did it work?"

"Not on me, I've got too much of a sense of humor. Also," I tell him, "you might find this hard to believe, but I was pretty cool myself at university."

"I don't find it at all hard to believe. How did your cool manifest?"

"I took a year off, so I was older, and I'd lived away from home. I spent eight months traveling through Europe with my friend Angela. I'd been to Berlin just after the wall came down and spent six weeks in Paris." I think about my teenage self, and I smile at the memory. "I acquired a convincing veneer of sophistication. I certainly knew a lot more about life than some of the people who'd only just got their A Level results. And I had fantastic hair, which helped. Tremendously sharp Louise Brooks bob, raven black." I laugh.

"So Mr. Moody and Mysterious didn't impress you?"

"No. I used to call him Lord Byron. Which he probably liked, although honestly, was there ever a man more annoying?"

Edward laughs. "Shelley's much cooler."

"Yes, but still quite annoying. Poor Harriet Shelley. But at least there's a point to most of his poems. Mind you I'm probably being unfair; *Childe Harold* is another thing I've never been able to get through. I can't be doing with a poem that goes over the page, really."

He laughs again. "Not even *Paradise Lost*?"

"Oh, well, I rather wish it wasn't a poem."

"Philistine."

"I know, shocking."

We're silent for a moment and then I say, "But anyway, so—I'm sorry, this is all completely fascinating—then you set out to sleep with all your brother's girlfriends?"

"I suppose I did. The first time was sort of an accident, genuinely. And then I just . . . I thought, I wonder if I could—"

" 'Sort of an accident'?" I push my own sunglasses down my nose so I can look over them at him.

"Yeah. I went to a party, we all did, and Tasha was there. She'd been . . . I suppose she was his first proper girlfriend, but they split up when he went to university. He was reasonably upset about it. Anyway, we'd always got on quite well, and it was Hogmanay, and we were drunk, and you know how it is. He pretended he didn't care, but I could see he did. I enjoyed the feeling. I'm not proud of that," he says, "or of any of it. After that it was almost an obsession. I'd sleep with girls he was seeing, if I could. And I usually could. We moved in similar circles, even though we weren't really speaking to each other. It would have been better for both of us if he'd gone to university somewhere else, but there you are. He got suspicious eventually. By the time I slept with Julia—well, like I say, they were separated by then. But that's why he didn't introduce me to Carolyn until the wedding."

"To stop you from sleeping with her?"

He nods.

"But it didn't stop you."

"Ha. No. She couldn't believe we'd never met before. Three years they'd been together. 'Did he tell you why he didn't want us to meet?' I asked her, and she was surprised. 'Is there a reason?' So I told her—'I like to sleep with my brother's girlfriends.' She was pretty outraged by that, I think. 'I'm afraid you won't be able to get the full set,' she said, and I said, 'We'll have to wait and see,' which she thought was funny, I suppose. And after that she was always . . . He didn't invite me around or anything, but I did see them sometimes. She used to come into the shop. I think she was intrigued, or whatever. For some reason. I did my best 'barely interested' and in the end . . ."

"Oh my God." I laugh, but I really am rather shocked by this.

"I didn't like her that much, as I said. But we did it quite a lot. I suppose we had an affair. He caught us eventually. That was probably the plan, after all."

"Bloody hell, Edward, this is—"

"I've never been more . . . It was incredibly satisfying. That was the moment when I realized, though, that I'd screwed up my own life, as much as his. Theirs. I mean, yeah, he was unhappy and angry and all those things, but I'd never—or hardly ever—even tried to meet anyone. Anyone for me, anyone who wasn't part of the game I was playing. So that's why I avoid it, mostly."

"Mostly?"

"I do have some friends," he says, "female friends. Close friends."

"People you sleep with?"

"Sometimes. Yes."

"But you wouldn't count them as your girlfriends?"

"God, no. No."

"Gosh. How sophisticated it all is," I say. "I feel desperately provincial." I put my empty glass down on the grass. I think I might be a bit drunk.

"You disapprove."

"I don't think you should base your sex life round your brother, but apart from that you can do what you like." I blink at him. "You're a grown-up, after all. I have no problem with any unofficial arrangements you might have with your friends. That seems extremely healthy in comparison."

"I suppose it does. And what about you?"

"Me? What about me?"

"What are you going to do about your sex life?"

"Oh, good grief. Ha. Nothing."

"Ever?"

"It's way too early for me to think about having a sex life. It's twenty years since I slept with someone who wasn't Chris. I can't imagine ever meeting anyone, or wanting to." I shake my head. "Good grief."

"Are you heartbroken?" He's sort of joking, but I'm not, of course.

"I should say so."

"Really?"

"I'm . . . entirely bereft." I feel that familiar ache in my throat.

"Shit," he says, "I'm sorry. I didn't mean to—"

"It's okay. I'm sure it will be all right eventually. Or I'll get used to it. Or something. It doesn't kill you, after all. I knew that. It's just . . . it's very sad, and tiring."

I get up, slightly unsteadily, and go back inside for a glass of water. I run the tap and wonder what Chris is doing. He'll be at work. I wonder how he's finding this almost step-parenthood he's indulging in. I wonder if he likes it, children in his house. Her middle son is quite a handful. I wonder if he's always wanted that, secretly. Not a child who is a handful. Just a child, any child.

They could have one together, I suppose; she's younger than I am, only thirty-eight or something. I grip the edge of the sink. They seem a thousand miles away, another life. It's as though I might wake up and find it all a dream, all this, these months up here. I might drive home and find him waiting for me; we might pick up the threads of our life and carry on as usual.

Or maybe he comes home to her and thinks the years I lived there were the dream, the illusion, waiting for the moment when I could be pushed aside. I wonder whose idea it was, how it happened. I didn't ask and I'll probably never know, how their first kiss emerged from their friendship, how they were drawn together, how they—I don't like to even think the phrase—fell in love.

I open the cupboard and find a glass, bend to fill it, and when I straighten, I catch the side of my head on the open cupboard door, hard enough to see stars.

"Ow, fuck, shit," I say elegantly. "Bastard." I turn off the tap, put the glass down and investigate the damage cautiously. There's blood on my fingers.

"Are you okay? What's happened?" Edward calls from outside.

"Cut my head open," I tell him.

"Oh no, how've you managed that?" He's inside now, coming to see.

"Banged my head. I didn't shut the cupboard. What an idiot. Ow."

"Come here," he says, "let me see if you need stitching. Not that I can drive you to the emergency room for like, another four hours," he adds. "I think I've had too much to drink."

"I don't think it's that bad. Hope not, anyway." I stand by the door in the bright late-afternoon sunshine so he can examine my wounded scalp. "It's here," I say. "Ow."

He gently pushes my hair out of the way. "Oh yes," he says. "It's not too bad. But it is bleeding. Hold on."

I stand, leaning against the wall, and wait.

He comes back with a damp tea towel, and presses it to my head. I feel foolish, standing there while he dabs at me.

"Does it hurt?"

"It did. Not too bad now."

"I like the way your hair is silver underneath," he says. "Does the hairdresser do that?"

This makes me laugh heartily. "No, it's grey, you idiot. Or are you teasing?"

"No, it's . . . But you've hardly any grey on top, it's all underneath. And it's really not grey, is it? Definitely silver."

He's lifting up sections of my hair now and looking at it, his fingers on my scalp. No one's touched me for such a long time, it makes me tingle all over in an inappropriate way. I feel my ears burning. I'm probably very red as well. I clear my throat, embarrassed.

"That's just how it grows," I say. "It's odd, isn't it? It's been like that for a while—seven or eight years."

"Not odd," he says. "It's pretty. Or stylish, I don't know. Aren't you lucky? My grey hair comes through much coarser than the dark, and sticks out weirdly."

"You hardly have any."

"No, not yet. My grandfather didn't go grey until he was nearly seventy. I get more in my beard." He rasps a hand across his chin, and then goes back to pushing my hair about. He seems quite fascinated by it. My hair's very fine, but there's a lot of it; it's almost shoulder-length, growing out from what was quite a neat bob earlier in the year. I sort of want him to stop touching me but also sort of don't. I'm very conscious that there are other things going on and hope he hasn't noticed, after all there's no cold breeze to explain the state of my nipples. Jesus. I think I must be a lot drunker than I realized. I put a hand up to touch the cut on my head, and he seems to realize that running his fingers through my hair, which is basically what he's doing, is a bit odd.

"Shit, sorry, I forgot what I was . . . Well. Your hair is cool."

"Thanks."

"Are you hungry? I could start dinner," he says. I wonder if he means to distract me.

Twelve

For dinner, Edward has bought steak. I can't help thinking today has been quite expensive for him. When I try to say this, however, he reacts as though I'm being offensive, and won't discuss it. We drink more wine, and that bottle is empty too. We wash up the plates, have a cup of tea, smoke another joint, and walk on the beach, talking expansively, and in places hilariously, about the books we studied at university, about our fellow students, our lecturers, about the change from grunge to Brit-pop, about the enormous, world-changing power of dance music. If we were somewhere with a signal, and electricity, we'd be playing each other our favorite tunes. It's fun; proper, friendship-making, bonding fun.

Back at the Shed, we watch the sun go down behind the hill, across the bay. I've stopped drinking. I'd begun to feel hazy and unfocused, and a bit self-conscious . . . and it seems sensible not to get drunk, properly drunk, with my boss. When I had a real job, I used to avoid drinking with my colleagues. I didn't want to see them being drunk, and I could never relax. Partly because I used to worry I might tell someone the truth about what I was thinking.

Never because I was worried I might want to kiss someone inappropriate. I'm not saying I never thought about anyone else at all during my marriage, but there was never a chance that any situation would arise where something might happen.

Not that I think there's any chance here. Or even that I'd want there to be. I don't think I actually fancy Edward, but today he's been quite different from usual, and I think this is perhaps more what he's truly like, or would be if he'd let himself. I quite like the surly rude version, it's amusing, and I like to ignore the surliness, but this more relaxed version is much nicer.

I suppose I'm interested in him, and that's partly because of his past. Not the sister-in-law shagging—although that is really interesting—but the aristocratic stuff. Like a lot of lower-middle-class people from a working-class background, I have a complex attitude about posh people. Intrigued and disgusted. Horrified but fascinated. Imagine knowing the names of people in your family from the eighteenth century. Imagine if your ancestors had been able to read and write for at least five hundred years.

It's colder now, a sharper breeze from the northwest. I shiver and fetch my sweater, huddle a blanket round myself. It might be better to go inside and sit on the sofa, but that seems defeatist somehow.

Edward says, "I might open that other bottle of wine. What do you think?"

"But . . . will we be okay to get home? You said earlier you thought you'd had too much to drive."

"I was thinking maybe we could stay?" He looks unsure, frowning. I feel a slight sense of concern. Was this his plan all along? Surely not—it seems complicated and unlikely. Doesn't it?

"Stay?"

"Yes—you could sleep in the bedroom if you wanted. Or on the sofa—which is a lot better."

"But what about you?"

"I can sleep on the floor. Or outside. Like I say, I usually do. There's a—you know—a sleeping mat thing."

"I hate sleeping in my clothes." True as this is, as soon as I've said it, I wish I hadn't.

He doesn't react, however, at least only to say, "There should be some T-shirts in the bedroom. Be enormous on you; probably come down to your knees. Very modest."

"You're only like five inches taller than I am," I say, outraged by this for some reason.

"Yeah, Shorty, whatever," he says, and this strikes both of us as extremely amusing.

"I guess we don't have much choice. It's not like we can phone anyone, with no signal."

"If you want to go home, we could walk round to the caravan park and call someone from there—I'm sure Jenny would come and pick you up. Or you could get a cab."

I stare at him. "That would cost a million pounds, surely."

"Probably not a *million* pounds. But maybe forty. I'd pay for it, obviously, since it's my fault you're trapped here."

I think about this for a while. I don't really want to walk for half an hour in order to beg for a lift like a teenager.

"Oh well, sod it. It probably won't kill me not to clean my teeth for once."

He laughs, but says, "Sure? I don't want you to feel like I've kidnapped you."

"*Pfft.* I've had less to drink than you. I could probably drive your car, eventually. Maybe."

"Have you? Would you like to try?"

"Is it hard to drive?"

He looks at me, evidently considering whether or not I'd be capable of this feat. "No power steering."

"Yeah, that's what I thought. Well." I look out to sea for a bit, and then back at him. I'm fairly confident this isn't part of some kind of convoluted plan to compromise me. Ha ha, compromise—I think I'm past being compromised. "What's wrong with the bed?" I ask.

"Oh, try it if you like. I should probably get a new mattress for it. But because I never sleep in there, and rarely bring anyone else to stay, I only ever think about it when I'm actually here."

...

I head through to the bedroom. Edward follows me. It's dark.

"Hang on," he says, "there's a flashlight in . . . Here you go. T-shirts are in the second drawer." He clicks on the flashlight and hands it to me.

I open the drawer, feeling around the neat piles of fabric, and pull out a T-shirt, shaking it one-handed to unfold it.

"Okay," I say, holding it against my chest, "that's enormous."

He laughs. "Too big even for me," he agrees. "That's why it's here, I guess. All the clothes here are a bit random."

I turn it round so I can see what it says. Two stick figures and childlike writing: *Joanna*.

"Who's Joanna?"

"Oh, no one. It's a band. My friend's band. He made the T-shirts as well."

"Are they any good?"

"I wouldn't say good, exactly. They were okay."

"Good enough to buy a T-shirt?"

"Ha ha, yeah, I didn't buy it, he gave it to me."

"Well, I reckon it will fit me." I turn to look at the bed, pale in the gloom. "So what's wrong with this?"

"Try it," he says. I hand the flashlight back to him and he directs it at the headboard.

I turn back the duvet and lie down cautiously. The mattress makes an unusual *sproing*ing noise and something— probably whatever made the noise—digs into my kidneys. In addition to this, it feels very much as though my feet are higher than my head. I turn onto my side and it makes the noise again. The spring is no longer stabbing me but there's the faint sensation that it might tip me out onto the floor.

"Right," I say, sitting up, "yeah, you should buy a new mattress."

"Awful, isn't it? Luckily the sofa's really comfortable. Bring the duvet," he adds, opening the wardrobe and rummaging about. We drag bedding back through to the other room and pile it on the sofa. He goes back for his sleeping mat and pillows, and, yawning hugely, I open a packet of fancy potato chips and empty them into a bowl.

"Should I open this wine, then?" I ask him.

"Did you want some?"

"Not really."

"Can't drink the whole thing myself."

"You can take it home with you, can't you?" I unhook the corkscrew from the nail on the side of the cupboard and open the bottle. I pour a glass for him and, after some consideration, a glass of fizzy water for me. I lean against the sink and watch him as he putters about, lighting candles in the big glass storm lanterns. I'm really quite tired; it feels as though today has lasted forever. In a good way. I've definitely enjoyed myself. Lunchtime feels like weeks ago. It's almost ten o'clock, still not really dark of course. I yawn again, and eat some potato chips.

"Are you really going to sleep outside, then?" I ask him.

"I might. Or for a while at least. The moon will be behind us for ages, but eventually it will be over the sea, and that's pretty special. And it's clear." He walks to the door and steps out onto the grass, looking up at the sky. I go to stand beside him. There are stars already, even though it's not yet fully dark.

"You should stay out and look at the stars," he says, "at least for a bit. But we could get your bed ready."

Back in the Shed he fumbles with the large sofa. "It folds out," he explains, "but I can never—oh, there you go." He billows the sheet at me.

I look at the sofa bed. It's pretty big; bigger than a double bed, probably. Now that he's flung the duvet over it, I have to say it looks enticing.

"It really is pretty good," he says, and lies down, patting the space beside him. "Try it."

"Er—"

"Plenty of room, you can get two people on here easily."

Bloody hell. I have a sudden sense of vertigo, almost panic. Maybe this whole thing was a massive mistake. I wish I was at home. At Uncle Andrew's, I mean.

"I don't think . . . Look, if you'd rather, I can sleep on the floor," I say, "I mean, it's not really fair, is it? If you'd come by yourself—"

A moth flies through the doorway and flings itself into one of the candles, sizzling unpleasantly and distracting us both.

"Damn," he says. "I should put the curtain up." He gets up quickly and pulls a large rectangle of folded fabric from under the cushions on the smaller sofa. It's a fine mesh, an anti-insect screen, and he deftly hooks it up over the open space. Then he lights more candles. He doesn't say anything else about us sharing the sofa, and I think perhaps I misunderstood. I feel a flood of relief. It was silly to panic. I'm an adult, everything will be fine. He's not going to try anything. He'd have tried already, if he was going to. I calm myself. I'm just . . . It's just because I'm not used to . . . I know we're often together—in fact, I spend far more time with Edward than anyone else—but we're not usually alone. Not *this* alone. It's fine, though. I've been enjoying myself, haven't I? I don't need to think about earlier, his hands on me, or about what it would be like, if he . . . Think about something else, quickly.

"I might just get changed," I say.

"Feel free," says Edward, luckily unaware of my confusion. It seems darker outside now, with the candles lit. I slip out to the bathroom to get undressed but forget to take a candle with me and have to go back.

"It's really dark out there now," I say.

He laughs. "Yeah, isn't it? It'll be lighter later, when the moon's up. Here, take a candle. There's a shelf by the mirror."

. . .

Much later, I hear his voice from the doorway. "Come and look at the moon," he says. "Or are you asleep?"

"No, I'm not asleep." I sit up. I've been dozing, dreaming slightly uncomfortable half dreams, brought on by the booze and anxiety. I really don't think he'll get into bed and try to kiss me or anything. It's not exactly that. But it's presumably enough of a worry that I can't quite relax.

Anyway.

I get out of bed and feel about for a blanket. It's not freezing cold, but it's not warm either. I wrap the blanket round me and duck under the mesh as he holds it out of the way. He's put on a sweater but is still wearing his shorts. I see the sleeping bag on the grass where I guess he's been tucked up, watching the stars.

"Gosh it's clear. Look at that." The wide smear of the Milky Way is always startling. The moon is three quarters full or more and hangs above the bay, where the waves barely ripple, painting a wide silvery path toward us. "Wow."

"I know, it's great, isn't it? Shame it's not full."

"Still impressive, though. Do you know the constellations? That's Cassiopeia," I say, "but I don't know much else."

"The Pleiades. The really bright ones over there. The Seven Sisters. Sterope, Merope, Electra—I forget the others."

"I'd never thought about them having individual names," I say. "What a numpty."

He laughs. "And that's the Northern Cross, aka Cygnus, if you follow where I'm pointing."

I put my face as close to his shoulder as seems appropriate and squint upward along his arm.

"It's sort of diagonal, and more like a stick man with no legs waving," he describes, to help me locate it.

"Ha, get you, Professor Brian Cox."

He snorts. "If only," he says, and I make a noise of appreciation and agreement that makes him laugh. We stand looking up at the immense multitude of distant pinpricks. Apart from the gentle hushing of the waves, it's very quiet indeed. I stare upward for so long I almost lose my balance.

"Steady. Easier to lie down," he says.

"I think that's too hardcore for me. I might go back to bed."

"Oh, okay." He pauses. "I'll try not to wake you if I come in."

...

We get back to town at about half past eleven the next morning, after Edward's had a swim and we've eaten rather cold toast on the beach.

"Are we opening the shop?"

"I thought we should have lunch first," he says. "No rush is there? We'll go to the Arms. Have you eaten in there?"

I shake my head. We go to the Railway Arms for a drink after work sometimes, but I've never been in at lunchtime.

"I wouldn't go for dinner, but it's okay for lunch. Come on, I'll treat you."

I stare at him, surprised. "You're going to buy me lunch? You really needn't. You paid for everything yesterday."

"Come on," he says.

The pub is dark inside, and old-fashioned. Scottish pubs

are mostly bars in hotels. We eat pie and French fries. "I wish my boss would take me out," the waitress jokes.

"This is my review," I tell her, "when he tells me I'm doing a good job but he can't put my wages up." This makes her laugh inordinately.

When we're drinking our coffee, he pulls something out of his pocket. "Spare keys," he says, putting it on the table. A big wooden keyring the size of a postcard, with the address of the shop in marker pen.

"Spare keys? For what?" It's not the shop keys, I have a set of those already.

"For the Shed. You can keep them until you go home," he says. "So you can go by yourself, if you want. This little one's for the padlock on the boat shed. The one with the tape on it opens the glass door."

"Oh, that's . . . How kind. Thank you. Are you sure? What if you want to go?"

"I expect I can cope if you're there. I mean we just spent twenty-four hours there together, didn't we?"

"Yes, but what if you want to be by yourself? Or take someone else?"

He shrugs. "I'm sure we can work it out. I thought you might like to be able to go whenever you want."

"Thank you." I'm quite overwhelmed, blinking back tears. I hope he doesn't notice, it's pathetic. "I don't know why everyone thinks you're so awful," I joke, "you've been very kind to me."

"I have, haven't I? I'll have to watch that."

Thirteen

Another week has passed and it's nearly August. The weather's turned, alternating between sultry and uncomfortable, and cold and grey. Today has been dry so far, but it's been threatening to rain since this morning. Edward's away; I was half expecting him back this afternoon, but he never arrived. This is not uncommon; he's often away, buying books and selling them, engaged in his mysterious social life. I've cashed out and done the catalogue and am waiting patiently for one of our regulars, Mrs. Drummond, to return from whichever corner of the shop she's disappeared to, so I can lock up. Once I had to go and look for her, and she was dozing on one of the sofas, surrounded by poetry books. Not today, though, she's drifting back into the main room with a pair of green Penguin Agatha Christies. I deal with this and wish her a good evening and follow her to the door with my keys. Before I can lock up, though, an elegant blond woman turns in to the doorway and pushes through. I step back, slightly startled. It's not as though she can't see me.

"I'm sorry," I say, "we're just closing." She looks vaguely familiar, although I can't quite place her.

"Oh, that's all right," she says dismissively. "Edward's just coming."

And indeed, there he is, close behind.

"Evening, Thea," he says. "Good day?"

"It's, er, yes. Not bad. You're back, then," I say rather foolishly. "I assumed you weren't coming back today."

"Change of plan," he says.

I try not to stare at the woman. I'm pretty sure it's Sophie, who I met at Charles's party. But not one hundred percent certain. She's wearing the most ravishing dress/jacket combination—raw primrose silk, like something I might think about wearing to a garden party if I was ever invited to one, but would then decide against because it's just too pale and effortless. She'd be very pretty, even beautiful, if she didn't look so irritated.

"Hello," I say to her, "did we meet before?"

"I don't think so," she says, the implication in her tone being that it's *most* unlikely.

"You look familiar. We didn't meet at Charles's?"

"No." She glances from me to Edward.

"Oh," he says, "sorry—this is Thea. She's . . . We work together. And this is Lara," he tells me.

"Hi," we both say, equally unimpressed.

"Maybe you met Lara's sister? Sophie?"

"Ah, yes. That's right. You're very alike." She looks even more annoyed, if that's possible. "I'm just off," I add. "I'll leave you to it."

Edward ignores this and says, "What are you up to this evening?"

"Oh, nothing much, I shouldn't think." I'm uncomfortable, conscious that Lara wants me gone, and sharpish.

"You could join us for supper," he says. "I thought we'd go to Mario's."

Mario's isn't exactly a restaurant: it's only open three nights a week, and it's basically in Mario's front room. There are only five tables. The food's good, but I can't think of anything I'd like to do less. I glance at Lara. I've rarely seen a person look so pissed off. She's settled rapidly into irritability and sighs heavily as I say I hate being a third wheel—making an assumption there that he doesn't correct, so I guess I'm right—and he reassures me that I wouldn't be. I put my keys away in my bag and go to fetch my cardigan from the kitchenette.

"Are you sure?" He follows me and adds, lowering his voice, "I could use the company."

"Oh my God. Why'd you bring her here, then?" I whisper.

"Long story."

"I think you've made your bed. I don't want to get in the way."

...

For all I know, he was already spending lots of time with Lara and just never mentioned her. After we've met, however, he mentions her quite often, and I'm pretty sure that whenever he goes up to Edinburgh, he sees her. I take it she's one of these "not girlfriends" of his, with whom he has an arrangement of some kind. He doesn't bring her to the shop again, anyway; and I'm relieved about that—with no interest in exploring why.

...

A Friday morning, late August. Edward went to an estate sale this morning—somewhere around Gretna, I think—and I was expecting him back this afternoon, but yet again there's been no sign of him. I've already locked up and am taking some pictures of soft autumn light on rich leather bindings for my own amusement, and for the shop Instagram, when he calls.

"Won't be home this evening after all," he says. "I think I left the kitchen window open. Can you check? And put some food down for Holly Hunter?"

"Okay, no problem. Anything else I should do?"

"Maybe check all the windows? I can't remember if I left any open and the forecast says it's going to be windy. Is it?"

I peer out the window. "Hm. It's just started raining. And it's hellish dark for five-thirty. But doesn't look too windy yet."

"Can you check? D'you mind?"

"No problem." I want to ask him where he is, but it's none of my business. With Lara? Shut up, Thea, so what if he is? He's allowed to—

"Thanks. Want me to bring you anything from the big city?"

Ah, so it's okay for me to say, "Where are you?" in response to that.

"Edinburgh," he says. "Pretty cold here, and miserably wet."

"Did you buy anything this morning?"

"Not much. Couple of first edition Ballards, one signed."

"Well, that's cool. Did you text Malcolm?" Malcolm collects signed Ballards, which is handy.

"Not yet. You could. *Concrete Island* and *High Rise*. The signed one is *Cocaine Nights*."

"Oh, that's annoying." It's newer, and not worth as much.

"Beggars can't be choosers. Anyway, I don't know when I'll be back. Sunday probably. What shall I bring you, then?"

I laugh. "Something shiny." That's what I always used to say to my dad, when he went away for work. "Have fun."

"I shall endeavor to do so. And I'll bring you something shiny."

"Ha, you needn't really, I was joking. I'll see you when you get back."

When I've put my photos on Instagram, I go upstairs. I don't go up there often and it always feels a bit odd. I've never been invited for a cup of tea or anything like that. I'm not sure if anyone ever goes up there, except, I presume, Lara and his other "friends"—although mostly I think he goes to see them.

It's a large flat, two stories, big enough for a whole family, easily. And it's lovely. The sitting room overlooks the square and is high-ceilinged and light, with two huge south-facing sash windows, massive sofas, and a marble fireplace, and paintings. There are books, of course, everywhere. I've noticed a couple of times, on evenings when the light was right, that you get a beautiful slice of sunset across the parquet. There are rugs, and a lovely Edwardian plant stand, a fat barley-sugar twist in mahogany, with a brass pot containing a large aspidistra. I'd love to live here. I've even looked to see if there's anything similar available on the square, with a view of the rooftops, despite quite liking the lack of stairs at the lodge. I like having a garden as well, and there wouldn't be one if I lived in a flat. Edward has a garden, but that's because he owns the whole building. I asked him once where the money came from—it's not like selling books is massively lucrative—and he looked rather hunted, before admitting he and Charles had both inherited "quite a healthy amount" from their grandmother, his mother's mother. Apparently that sort of inheritance was acceptable because it didn't come with a title or acres of land. When I looked unconvinced, he just reminded me, rather sharply, that he was a hypocrite. And I suppose I am too; it's not like I've never inherited anything.

The dining room is grand, with an elaborate plaster ceiling, and a huge, circular mahogany dining table that has enormous feet. Matching sideboard, massive mirror over the dark stone fireplace. The kitchen is long and narrow with windows in two walls and a table at the back, a big chipped butler's sink and a built-in dresser. The walls are dark green, the cupboards are white, all handmade, and it's full of stuff, tons of pans and plates and jugs and things hanging up everywhere. It's untidy but comfortable. He likes cooking, I think, although he has no one to cook for. There's a whole shelf of cookery books, and piles of them open on the table.

The window is open, as he suspected, so I pull it closed. There's no sign of Holly Hunter but her dishes are empty, so I fill one with biscuits and one with fancy cat food. It looks like something you could easily eat yourself, with a bit of toast. It amuses me that he'd buy such a thing. HH is elderly—twenty at least—he's had her since he first came back from university. I refill her water bowl and then go to check the other windows.

I've never been up any farther, since the next set of stairs leads only to the bathroom and the bedrooms. I realize I'm almost tiptoeing. The stairs up to the second floor are not as wide and sweeping as the lower ones, and instead of bookshelves they're lined with framed prints and pictures.

It does seem a shame that Edward lives here by himself. Perhaps he'll ask Lara to move in, I think cynically. I can't imagine she'd like it, although I may be doing her a disservice. Apparently, she didn't like the Shed, though, when he took her there last year. She complained pretty much the whole time. No electricity or hot water, he must be mad, etcetera. "I think she's a bit glam for the Shed," I said, when he told me.

I wanted to ask about her, how long they'd been seeing each other, how "official" she was, when they met, whether he'd slept with her sister . . . but I didn't. I did ask if she was his type and he said he didn't have a type. I said, "except for people who've been out with your brother?" and he told me to fuck off. Which was fair enough.

At the top of the stairs I pause. Two closed doors and two ajar. And one open—the bathroom, all clanking but beautiful Victorian sanitary ware, with lots of plants and a heap of white towels abandoned on the floor. Clean, though, for a bathroom used only by a man. He doesn't have a cleaner or anything, or at least I've never heard him mention one. He must do his own housework. I can't picture him dusting but I guess he must.

I assume the closed doors are to the spare bedrooms— and a quick poke of my head round the doors confirms this. Neatly made beds, unusual lack of stuff. The others must be his bedroom and the study. He writes. As one would expect.

"Shit poetry," is what he said, when I asked him what he

wrote. It can't be that awful, though; he's had some published, apparently.

His bedroom's at the front, over the sitting room. It's surprisingly white, and surprisingly tidy, although there's an unsurprising pile of books neatly stacked beside the door. And the window *is* open, so at least there was a purpose in coming up here. I fight with the sash, which is open at the top. They're never easy; I wonder if they worked smoothly when they were new, but I've never used a new sash window, only ancient ones with fraying ropes and overpainted pulley wheels. I manage eventually and fasten the screw, pulling the curtains closed, which means I then have to grope my way back past the bed in the gloom.

It does feel quite odd to be in his bedroom. Bedrooms are personal, aren't they? His dressing gown, darkly tartan, hangs on the back of the door; and there's a white-painted chest of drawers with a mirror above that does for a dressing table and houses odds and ends, cards and photographs. I hesitate and then flick the light on so I can look more closely at the pictures. There's another of his grandmother, if that's who she is—the woman in the photo at the Shed. And maybe this is his mother? A faded seventies Polaroid of a very beautiful woman in a high-waisted Laura Ashley frock, laughing at the camera. He said his parents were fashionably Bohemian in the late sixties, before he was born. I should look them up; there might be pictures on the internet, and I'm curious. I never get the impression he's close to his mother, so it's unexpected that he has a photograph of her. If it's her.

Tucked into the frame of the mirror is a photo of Edward himself, fresh-faced and grinning, in a student sitting room with two other young men, all smoking, coffee table covered in beer bottles. It's a funny thing to see a young version of someone you've only known in their forties. They all look like the boys on my own degree course: the two that aren't Edward have long hair, while his is just big, cut Jesus and Mary Chain–style, short at the back and back-combed on top. Bless. Skinny black jeans, Dr. Martens propped on the table, the corner of a poster above their heads that I confidently identify as Béatrice Dalle in *Betty Blue*.

A little glass dish full of cuff links, a pocket watch on a stand, a pair of hairbrushes that look antique, battered silver with someone else's initials—*RVTM*—on them. There's a card with an Edward Hopper painting on it. I pick it up—I do feel bad for doing so but can't help myself—and open it to read the message.

> *Super weekend, darling, look forward to the next one.*
> *Yours ever, Corinne x*

Huh. Who's Corinne, then? And does Lara know about her?

On the wall by the mirror is a drawing of the Hollinshaw house, and an old print of a ruined castle, the traditional Scottish tower house type. There's a photograph of the Shed, a blue sky above the black wooden walls. Other than this and the dresser, though, there's not much else in here; it's as if there's so much in the rest of the house, there was nothing left for his bedroom.

I turn out the light and cross the landing to the final room: the study. Ah, so that's why there's not much in his bedroom—it's all in here. Crammed bookshelves, postcards of paintings on any spare bit of wall, dust, CDs, even a pile of cassette tapes. The ancient stereo is a stack of silvery minimal separates—CD player, twin cassette decks, turntable— must have cost a bomb in 1995 or something. Records too, in crates on the floor. I stoop to have a quick flick. He only ever listens to classical music in the shop, but having discussed music so extensively at the Shed, I'm not confused to see the Nick Cave and Smiths albums. They certainly fit with the boy in the photograph. Black Sabbath, Can, Prince and David Bowie, The Clash, Nirvana—I wonder how often he listens to any of this now. What's on the turntable? I lift the lid carefully. Bauhaus. Gosh.

The desk, which is a yellow Formica-topped kitchen table, sits in front of the curtainless window, which is also open. It's above the dining room and has an interesting view of rooftops and the trees in the garden. I lean across to wrestle with it, but it works much better than the one in the bedroom, and the sash slithers downward, landing with a thump. I twist the screw and turn to the desk. There's a typewriter. This makes me chuckle; he *would* have a typewriter, although I know he uses a laptop for his writing. The typewriter is pushed to the back of the desk: a totem, presumably, rather than something he uses. There's paper too, all different sizes, drifts of it, none of it typed, all covered in his unexpectedly tidy writing, in pencil mostly. A jar of pencils in varying states sits on the windowsill. At the front of the desk is a neater pile of paper, held down with a smooth white pebble.

I glance at the top sheet. I know it's rude, and I'm always

wary of other people's words, in case I read something embarrassing. It might be embarrassing because it's awful—a dreadful poem, maybe—or because it's true. Truth can be too exposing sometimes, too naked. I read something once that a flatmate had written, pinned to the wall by her desk, about "creeping through life avoiding the land mines of love," or something along those lines—I can't remember exactly—but I remember it felt so true and naked I found it hard to speak to her afterward, as though she'd told me a secret. I suppose it was a secret—after all, she didn't ask me into her room. I used to flit through all their rooms, my housemates, when they were out. I didn't pry exactly. I'd never have opened a drawer or read a diary. I just liked to stand in their rooms and look at their posters and books, and know they'd never know I'd been in there.

Won't
Can't
Mustn't
Shan't

This is what Edward has written. Feeling foolish and guilty, I roll the sleeve of my cardigan over my hand and lift the pebble, as though afraid of fingerprints. I push the top sheet aside. Underneath is a much smaller piece of paper, on which he's written:

Silver strands
Golden sun
Golden sand
Is the sand actually golden? TRY HARDER.

And sideways on the same piece of paper:

Limpet/limpid?

I turn it over.

Pewter softness
Rain-washed
Clouds and lichen

Just bits, not actual poems, only notes. I'm faintly disappointed. I look at the next sheet, where he's written:

"COMMON"

Just like that, with angry quote marks, one of which has gone through the paper. I stare at the word, feeling the blood rise in my cheeks. It's funny to be embarrassed when you're alone. Has he written that because of what I said, weeks ago, about his brother's party? Or am I making connections where none exist? It's just a word, after all.

On the next piece of paper, lined this time, torn from a notebook by the looks of it, he's written:

An empty room seems emptier
A night alone seems longer
The moon's cold thumbnail
More distant

"That's got potential," I say aloud, making myself jump. This is rude, isn't it? I should go. I restack the paper, looking again at the piece that says *"COMMON."* The trouble with snooping is you can't ask a question about anything you find that you shouldn't have looked at. I could ask about anything in this room except the writing. I eye a pile of notebooks beside the typewriter. I wonder what's written in those. Edward is . . . I suppose he's a mystery, isn't he? A faintly glamorous mystery.

Sighing, I back out of the room without touching anything else and make my way downstairs.

. . .

When he gets home, midway through Tuesday afternoon, I've just sold a Harry Potter first edition for four hundred and fifty quid and I'm quite pleased with myself.

"Hey," he says, "how are you doing, junior bookseller?"

"Selling books like a senior bookseller. Look. You may need to promote me." I spin the receipt round so he can see.

I can tell he's pleased. "Which reminds me. Here." He pulls a long flat box out of his jacket pocket and hands it to me. "Something shiny."

I'm slightly agonized at being given a gift I essentially asked for. "You didn't have to get me anything. I was joking."

"I know. But I saw it and I thought you might like it."

I open the box. Inside, there's a spoon. A large Victorian tablespoon, silver, with my initials, all three of them, *ALH*, monogrammed on the handle.

"Oh, wow." I stare at it, and then at him. "That's amazing! My initials!"

"I know, I've never found anything monogrammed with anything useful. Cool, huh?"

"Was this expensive?" I ask suspiciously.

"No. Makes 'em cheaper if they're engraved. Because who wants someone else's initials?"

"It's still silver, though." I rub my finger over the hallmark. "How old is it?"

"I think it's mid-Victorian. Look it up."

"Look it up? How?"

He tuts. "Here." He sits down at the desk and opens Google. I watch him as he looks up hallmarks.

"Let's see it, then," he says. "I think it's Glasgow. Yep, there you are, that's the Glasgow mark, the head. And this "P" is the year. 1860. And this is the maker: Kerr and Phillips. You could probably look them up too, if you wanted. Find out where their shop was."

"Wow." I stroke the bowl of the spoon, which has a gorgeous soft sheen to it. I spoon imaginary gravy onto a plate of imaginary Victorian Sunday dinner. "It's beautiful. I wonder who ALH was. Thank you so much."

"You're welcome."

"It must have been expensive, you shouldn't have. I was only joking. I just said 'shiny' because—"

"I know. I just saw it, and it seemed perfect when I remembered your name begins with an 'A'."

"I'm surprised you remembered my middle initial." I frown at him. I'm more than surprised, in fact—I'm more or less astounded.

"I did worry I might've got it wrong," he says, "but I was fairly confident. Lucy, right? Althea Lucy."

"Yes. Well, I shall treasure it," I say, and then feel the tips of my ears burning with embarrassment. He doesn't notice, though; he's turned back to the screen.

"Sell anything else?" he asks, and we're back on safer ground.

• • •

I google Victorian tablespoons as I sit in the car after work, piggybacking off the town hall Wi-Fi. Eighty to three hundred pounds.

I don't know what to think. Perhaps that's not much money to him? Even the lower estimate seems a significant amount to me. I'm puzzled. It would be silly to read too much—or indeed anything—into this. Wouldn't it? He saw it and thought of me and can afford to buy a present—whether pricey or properly expensive—without thinking too much about it. That's all.

• • •

Last night, Xanthe rang and told me about a dinner party at Chris and Susanna's, where Angela apparently had a bit too much to drink and asked about me.

Xanthe goes to these things to keep me in touch with what's going on. I don't mind if she wants to be friends with them. She's known Chris for a long time, longer than I have, in fact. And her descriptions of social events involving the new couple are always funny.

Anyway, so while they were eating dessert, Angela asked Chris if he'd heard from me lately and how I was doing and everything. (Perhaps a *little* tactless—she could have asked Xanthe at a more opportune moment, or in fact remembered what I told her myself just last week!)

Chris said, truthfully, that we hadn't spoken in a while, and Angela said it was sad that I'd felt I had to actually move away. Chris was annoyed by this and said I hadn't moved away, I was just spending time somewhere else.

"She'll stay there, though" Angela said. "I think it's a real shame. I miss her." Xanthe chimed in to say so did she, and Susanna burst into tears and ran out of the room.

The five of them all sat and looked at one another, and Rob said to Chris, "You should probably make sure she's all right, mate." Jeff, Angela's husband, said he was sorry if they'd upset Susanna, and Angela said, "You can't upset everyone's lives without people getting upset." All in all it sounded awful, but also . . . I don't know.

Xanthe says she doesn't think Susanna had ever thought about how everyone else would feel about any of it, and that includes me, rather oddly. If I was sleeping with someone else's husband, I'd expect them to be upset when they found out. But maybe thinking that would make it harder to do it? Who knows? It's easy to speculate, but when you've never been in that situation, you can't ever know. I admit I rarely try to get into Susanna's head or attempt to have any empathy for her. After all, it looks to me like it's turned out okay for her, living in my house with my husband. But I suppose I would think that. I'm the one people feel sorry for, which pleases me but probably upsets her even more. I doubt she thinks she's the bad guy; no one ever does.

I wonder how she justifies it to herself. By thinking things were, what, difficult? Between Chris and me? I can imagine that would seem like the reason, and perhaps she's right. There must have been something wrong, even if I had no idea about it, even if I resent the thought that he could have told me there was a problem and we might have been able to sort it out.

But that's all ancient history. I don't even know when it might have been fixable. Nothing seemed any different from the usual, not to me. It all seemed exactly the same as ever. If I'd noticed, maybe I'd feel better, but I must have failed on every level.

It's no good feeling bad about any of that. I've more or less stopped running over it all in my mind, wondering where I could have applied the tape. The answer is nowhere. However, none of my sensible thinking means I'm now able to empathize with Susanna, and no one would expect me to.

I don't enjoy hearing about things like the dinner party, or how Cora Thwaite's youngest told Susanna's daughter Ruby that her mother was a "housebreaker" because of something she'd heard her parents say. Housebreaker—that's cute, isn't it—a primary school misunderstanding of "home-wrecker." Hearing about it is still better than bumping into any of them, though; the horror of seeing Susanna in town, perhaps, or at the supermarket. Or maybe that would be a good thing, helping me grow a thick skin of indifference.

Fourteen

I've been on my own for most of the week. Edward's been away in Edinburgh again. Sometimes he tells me some of what he's been up to, but not always. It's half past five, and the front door's locked and the CLOSED sign up, while I sweep. Where does the dirt come from? Off people's shoes, I guess. You have to sweep pretty much every day. On Monday mornings, I hoover before the shop opens.

I've done the catalogue and thrown out some milk that was past its best. It's been warm and dry, almost a week of those days you sometimes get in September with beautiful, slow, heavy light. The Virginia creeper on the back of the shop is flaming scarlet. The dry weather means I'll have to water the garden, or at least the flowerpots on the patio. I like the shop after hours, it's so quiet and still, dust motes dancing in unexpected shafts of sunlight.

The clocks tick and there are mysterious creaking noises from the shelves and floorboards. I like to imagine the books are settling down to sleep, although that's an unusually romantic notion for me. I fiddle about on Twitter, setting up some tweets for the weekend so I don't have to think about it. I hope Edward has taken some photos while he's been out and about. People like pictures. Tweets about books are good, but pictures of books go down better. He doesn't always think about it, though, despite me texting him reminders, which he probably doesn't even read.

I've closed down the computer and am on my way down the passage to the garden when I hear the key in the door and turn back to say hello. I wasn't expecting him, but it's not like he's obliged to tell me what he's up to.

He pushes the door open and sees me. "Oh, hey, Thea, still here?" He's carrying a box, which he puts down on the counter.

"Just about to water the flowerpots— Oh. Hello, Lara."

"Yeah, hi," she says. Is it me, or does she have the most annoying face ever? I rarely dislike people, but I definitely dislike Lara. Why could that be, I definitely don't wonder.

"D'you need a hand?" Edward asks.

"God, no, no, don't worry. You carry on." I back down the corridor, stopping by the staircase. "Did you have a productive week?"

"Not bad. There are some more boxes in the car; should be okay until tomorrow. And some stuff coming next week. I bought a lovely set of George Eliot, clothbound, from the sixties, dark blue, really smart. And a signed first edition Toni Morrison—very exciting."

"Oh, really? What is it? *Beloved*? Please say yes."

He laughs. "It is."

"How much is that?"

"Tempted?"

Lara's halfway up the stairs and she turns back, sighing at this interruption to her evening.

"I'd be lying if I said I wasn't."

"I paid one-ninety, probably get two-fifty for it."

"Ugh. I'll just be looking at it, then. Anyway, I'll let you get on."

I look at Lara, who isn't rolling her eyes, but probably only because that would be vulgar.

He looks up at her. "Go on up, I won't be a moment."

"Edward . . ." she whines.

Maybe it's not whiney, that's probably just me. I glance at him; he looks slightly irritated. I just can't see why he bothers. I suppose she must be fantastic in bed. Although I can't believe it; she seems so uptight. I assume they have angry sex. Maybe he likes that; some people do. Not that I care or have any interest in what kind of sex he might like. Shit, now I'm blushing, and I haven't heard anything he's just said to me.

"Thea?"

"Sorry, what did you say?"

"I said I bought some atlases, big ones. Maybe we should put some out on the map table. A display, sort of. You're good at that."

The map table is a new purchase. I saw it advertised on Facebook and was inspired by the plan chest at Hollinshaw. I love plan chests and map tables, because drawers are great, and map table drawers are so enormous. I said we should get it and keep maps in it, obviously. Everyone loves maps. And we do have some great atlases. Edward agreed, so now we have—I mean, now he has—a map table.

"That's a good idea. Okay, I'll think about it. I better get on, so I can leave you to it."

"I'll help you do the pots."

"No, really—" But we're walking through the back rooms toward the garden. "She'll be annoyed," I suggest, glancing at him.

"Oh well. She usually is."

There's nothing I can say to this; it's got nothing to do with me. I don't approve, though—either you like someone or you don't. If you do, be nice. If you don't, what's the point?

Out in the garden he begins to fill one of the watering cans with the hose for me. The garden's quite a surprise, bigger than you'd expect. There are trees and borders and a lawn; it's comfortable, but pretty, not as neat as the garden at the lodge. Edward gardens a bit and Jilly's niece, Wendy, comes in once a week in the summer to mow the lawn and keep it tidy. There are lots of pots, filled with agapanthus and lilies, and some small trees, acers. There is a table and chairs by the house, and benches dotted about. Edward comes out here to read in the evenings, he says, and sometimes we have our lunch out here if it's not raining. I'd like to get more involved, but there's not time—the garden at the lodge keeps me busy enough and I should think the state of it would make Uncle Andrew quite gloomy. I do my best, but I'm working, after all. I had to buy some of that weed reducing membrane stuff for the vegetable garden. Next year I'll plant vegetables.

If I'm still here.

I water the flowers and Edward fills the second watering can. Then he wanders about, looking at his plants. It's a lovely evening, very still, and the sky very blue. I might eat my dinner outside, if it's still warm enough when I get home. I finish my task and begin to roll up the hose. If this were my garden I'd leave it untidily spread out ready for next time.

"Right, then," he says, "better face the music, I suppose."

I pause, one hand on the door. "Can I ask you something?"

"Sure."

"A personal question?"

"Be my guest." He looks amused. "Unlikely to be edifying."

"I just wondered—and this is horribly nosy—why you brought her here if you don't want to spend time with her?" We're in the back room now, and I lock the door behind us. It's warm and quiet in here with the Local History section. "You needn't answer; it's none of my business."

"I often wonder myself," he says.

"I mean, have you been together all week?"

"Oh, no. No, I picked her up this morning. I don't usually bring her here; she doesn't like it."

"Doesn't she?"

"Hates books, hates the ghastly provinces. Isn't that fond of me."

I stare at him. "So why—"

"No idea."

"O-kay . . ."

"I said I was coming home, she said she'd come with me. I think her usual fella's away."

"Her usual fella? I thought you were—"

"Oh, no. She lives with someone."

"Does she? Oh, okay. Okay."

"He knows about me; assume he doesn't care."

I'm gawking at him. "Goodness. Well, it's none of my business, like I said. I just wondered." We walk along the passage, past the room full of plays and poetry, toward the stairs. "She'll be cross you didn't go straight up."

"Yes, probably." He shrugs.

"Do you . . . Will you have a row?"

"Maybe. I don't usually rise to it. Which makes her even crosser." He grins suddenly. "It's quite perverse, isn't it?"

"A bit." I'm disappointed. I couldn't tell you why, though. That grin suggests he's fine with it, and maybe I was right earlier; maybe that's the whole point.

"Have a nice evening anyway," I say, pulling the curtain aside so I can collect my cardigan from the hook by the sink.

"You too, Thea. Any plans?"

"Oh, no. Just the usual. See you later."

"You'll lock up?"

I nod. He climbs the stairs away from me and I watch him for a moment. He doesn't look back but raises his hand in farewell. I go out into the front room and pick up my bag from behind the counter. I feel awful, and I've no idea why. Sometimes it comes in waves, though, being sad. I take a deep breath and try not to think about them upstairs together, bickering.

I lock the front door behind me and watch the swallows darting over the town hall. Time to go home. There's salad for dinner, and then I might watch a film. Something comforting but unsentimental.

Why would you want to spend time with someone you don't even like much? It's all a bit beyond me. I wonder about this man Lara lives with. How can he not mind about her and Edward? Perhaps I'm just not very sophisticated. I'd assumed she was single, wanting a similar thing to him, whatever that is exactly. I can see it might be useful to have a friend you can sleep with. But they're not friends, are they?

The sex must be great, though, or why would they bother?

. . .

When I get to work in the morning, I can hear them yelling. Or her, anyway. I stand motionless in the passage, half out of my jacket. I guess they didn't hear me come in. Or they don't care—that seems more likely.

". . . pay any bloody attention," Lara screams.

I can hear the rumble of his voice but not what he's saying.

"As if I give a SHIT," she yells.

I'm embarrassed. Should I hide behind the curtain? What if they come down and they're still fighting? I hear footsteps on the stairs and she's hammering down them in a fury. She nearly runs into me, but clearly doesn't care; all she does is snarl, "Is the door open?"

"Yes—" I say, and then she's gone, whisking past me. I hear his footsteps come down the stairs as he runs after her.

"Lara! For God's sake," he says. "Oh hey, Thea. Look, I'd better go after her; she can't get home unless I give her a lift to the station."

The station's in Dumfries, which, as previously established, is an hour and twenty minutes away.

"That'll be a delightful journey," I say.

"Jesus, I know. Sorry, I'll be back later."

"Okay." I watch him as he runs after her. Bloody hell.

. . .

He slams back into the shop at lunchtime, just as I'm eating my sandwiches. I had to put up my favorite sign—BACK IN FIVE MINUTES!—so I could run across to the Old Mill and pick up my food. There was actually a customer waiting when I got back as well, the first time that's ever happened. And she bought something—will miracles never cease!

"Hey," I say. "I bought you some lunch. I didn't know if you'd want it."

"Thanks. Back in a sec, desperate for a piss."

"Oh, *do* tell me more," I mutter, as he runs for the loo.

Then he's back. "Why does the hot tap take so long?"

I shrug. "I think it's because your plumbing's ancient."

"How rude. It's no older than the rest of me," he says, and laughs at my expression. "Sorry. Are these for me?"

I nod.

"Thanks very much. I'm starving. No breakfast."

"Too busy yelling at each other?"

"Hm. Yes."

He slumps into his green armchair and takes a huge bite out of his sandwich. "Be an angel and make me a coffee?" he says, indistinctly.

"I think you'll find that sentence might sound better as, 'Thea, please would you make me a coffee?'"

"I'd be terribly grateful."

"I'm sure you would. I'd rather you didn't ask me to be an angel, though."

"A darling?"

Now I'm blushing. "That's worse."

He tuts through his roast beef. After swallowing, he says, "Would you, though? Please? I'll get you one later. Or buy you dinner or something."

I sigh and push myself off the counter. In the semidarkness of the kitchenette I make two coffees and bring them back. Now he's on the phone—his phone, not the old-fashioned shop phone, which has a dial and which I try never to use because it's too echoey and peculiar.

"If you'd just stop yelling at me," he says, "I could— No. No, it's not— Jesus Christ."

I stop watching him and move away, into the hall. I'm fascinated, but I can't just sit there goggling while he has a personal conversation. I stand on one foot and then the other and pretend I'm not listening. I can hear him clearly; he's annoyed and therefore quite loud.

"Okay. I don't care. No. Whatever. No . . . It's not meant to be difficult, is it? No. But it is . . . You tell me . . . Right, well, as I said, whatever."

I think that's it. Is it? I peer through the doorway. He puts his phone on the counter and presses his fingers to his forehead. "Fuck's *sake*," he says.

I go back into the front of the shop and pick up my coffee. "Lucky for you there's no one here but us," I say. "Very unprofessional."

"*Gah.*"

"So. How was your morning?"

He groans. "God save me from self-obsessed, high-maintenance bitches."

"I don't much like her," I say, "but please don't call her a bitch." I lean on the counter, not looking at him.

"Why not?"

"Gendered insults are lazy." I pause. " 'High maintenance' is also gendered, obviously."

"She's a bastard, then," he says, after giving it some thought. "And unreasonable. Or . . . maybe not unreasonable, then. I don't know."

"What were you fighting about? If you don't mind me asking?"

"Oh, the usual. I'm distant and uninterested apparently."

"And are you?" I take a sip of coffee.

"Well, yeah. I'm not very interested in her, why would I be? It's an arrangement of"—he pauses—"mutual convenience, not a love affair."

I wince. No wonder she's angry. "Is that how she feels about it?"

He has the grace to look embarrassed. "I think so. I mean, we were both pretty honest about it in the beginning. I hope."

"So—forgive me for prying—how does that work? Did you say, 'I wouldn't mind having semi-regular no-strings sex'? Is that effective? I'd like to find out, you know, in case I ever need to . . . do anything similar."

He laughs. "You won't need to, though, will you? I mean, you'll meet someone. You won't need to make a pointless and irritating arrangement."

I'm not sure I believe this, but still. "Is it pointless and irritating?"

"For something that's supposed to be all about sex, there's a lot of shouting. And not much sex."

"Oh."

"Yeah, oh."

"How did you meet?"

He finishes his sandwich and brushes crumbs off his lap. "Through Sophie."

"Oh yeah, I forgot about her. How d'you know her?"

He turns back to his laptop and rattles the mouse to wake it up. "How d'you reckon?"

"Um, your brother used to go out with her?"

"Bingo."

"So you—"

"I've slept with both of them, yes. Sophie was a long time ago; she was Charles's girlfriend at uni, or one of 'em."

"Was she? She looks a lot younger. Than Charles, I mean." What I really mean is "than me" but no need to expose one's insecurities.

"No, she's your age. Sophie, I mean. Lara's thirty-eight or something. There's another one in the middle—Rachel."

"Slept with her?"

He looks at me for a moment and then laughs. "No."

"Oh dear. What happened?"

"God, you're rude. I've never tried."

I consider this. "Is she desperately ugly?"

"Ha. No, she's happily married, has been for years; it's very unusual."

"Rich people are awful," I say vaguely.

"You don't know the half of it."

I'm still intrigued by something he said yesterday. "So, Lara's husband—"

"No idea. Not interested. If I'm in Edinburgh, I call her, and if he's away, we meet up. Even if he's not, sometimes. If he's away I go to hers, though, which is easier than trying to make sure wherever I'm staying is acceptable." He rolls his eyes. "I don't know why you're interested in this sorry tale. You're not planning on writing a book, are you?"

I laugh. "Oh my God, it would make a good book. I shall call it *Posh People Behaving Badly*. But no. I'm just . . . it's so different from my experience of life. I can't imagine just accepting that my wife was shagging someone else."

"I'm never going to ask her to leave him, am I? I guess I'm a safe pair of hands."

This gives me a mental picture that's a little disturbing, so

I try not to think about it. "But why don't you try and find someone you like? Wouldn't that be better?"

He turns back to the screen. "What's the point? It's too late. I've fucked it all up."

"But have you? I don't understand why you think that. You're perfectly nice, aren't you? Obviously grumpy as hell, but you might cheer up a bit, you know"—I look up as the door opens—"if you were getting laid regularly. Good afternoon," I continue smoothly, ignoring his snort of amusement as I greet a couple of tourists who have pushed through into the shop. "Just let one of us know if we can help at all." A man of about my age and his teenage daughter mutter the usual embarrassed shop murmur about "just looking."

I watch them as they look around. The girl has the most spectacular hair, a perfect, glossy low beehive. I'm impressed and slightly jealous. We get two sorts of customers: people who know what they want and head straight for it or ask immediately, and browsers. With browsers you never know if they'll buy or not, it really does depend whether they see anything they fancy. This is why I keep saying we should move Local History to the front of the shop. People on holiday like to buy things related to the area. Edward's not convinced, but I bet it would make a difference.

. . .

That evening, as we're closing up, he says, "Shall we get something to eat, then?"

"Oh, I thought you were joking."

"No, I'll take you out. Where shall we go? What do you want? Fish and chips? We could go down to the harbor."

"The chippy on the corner? I've never been in there."

"Come on, then," he says. "Don't bother sweeping up, I'll do it later."

"What about the flowerpots?"

"They'll be fine."

I fetch my cardigan and duck my head through the strap of my bag, and we walk down through the square to the harbor road. It always seems odd that there's a harbor; the town isn't exactly on the coast. There are just a few boats, and lots of boatyard buildings and winches and stuff. There's no harbor wall or sea defenses, because it's more like a river than the sea, although it's tidal and they call it a bay. There's a kiosk that sells ice cream and tea and crab sandwiches, and a fish and chips shop, traditional with a Formica counter and nothing to sit on while you're waiting but the tiled windowsill. There are two picnic benches outside and a furious sign telling you not to feed "the fecking gulls."

Edward buys us both a fish supper and we take our paper parcels of fish and chips farther along, to where there's a wall just right to sit on, with a more pleasing view of the river. He empties sachets of vinegar, ketchup, and mayonnaise from his pockets and we eat hot chips with cautious greasy fingers.

"How am I going to eat fish without cutlery?" I fret, and he produces a fistful of wooden chip forks and a Swiss Army knife.

"There you go, princess," he says, and I snort with laughter.

"I know, la-di-da, eh?"

"And you say I'm the posh one."

"I suppose you ate all your food with your fingers growing up." I crunch a piece of batter. "Or gold knives and forks."

"Gold's not very practical for cutlery, too soft."

"Oh, I suppose. Silver? Like my spoon?"

"There was silver cutlery. Only for high days and holidays." He fights with a sachet of ketchup. "Damn. Oh, there we go."

"Not every day?"

"No, Sheffield's finest for the rest of the time. Grandparents' wedding cutlery, I think."

"And eating all your meals off"—I search my brain for the name of an expensive china manufacturer—"um, Sèvres?"

"There is some Sèvres, but it's not a whole set. Royal Doulton, the everyday stuff. And some Villeroy and Boch that my mum bought Dad as an anniversary present once. Hideously eighties, be fashionable again soon, I should think."

"Do you miss all that?"

He wipes his fingers on his handkerchief and opens a can of Coke, which fizzes excessively. "Bugger." I watch him slurp at it, amused. "Christ, no. Not at all. It's absurd, living in a giant house you can barely afford to heat. And twenty bedrooms mean nothing when you all hate one another."

I lick mayonnaise off my thumb. "Did you really all hate each other?"

"Well, maybe not when I was very small. Before my grandfather died. We were closer then. Or it seemed like we were. I don't know what happened. Maybe my parents fell out of love. And they thought their sons would be, you know, nicer and less frustrating. Perhaps."

"Your mum gets along okay with Charles, though?"

"Only because they rarely see each other."

"Oh."

He stares out across the bay for a moment, and then turns back to look at me. "My mother was a raving beauty, you know. Friends with all the right people, parties, holidays on yachts, dancing all night, champagne, blah blah. They lived a wild life before I was born." He pauses. "Have you ever read *Like a Pendulum Do*?"

"I have, but not for years."

"Yeah, well, you know the one who dies of an overdose? Lady Elspeth? Based on her."

"No way." I drop a chip, distracted.

"Yep. And Johnny Meltram's Mick Jagger."

"I knew *that*. So is any of it true? Obviously she didn't die of an overdose."

"Close call."

"God, really?" I stare at him.

"So they say. She never talks about that. But she can tell you fruity stories about various people if you get her in the right mood. Andrew Loog Oldham and Dusty Springfield and Lord Lucan."

"Bloody hell. So, what, pills?"

"I think so. Uppers, downers, all that sixties stuff. Yeah, all very . . . more interesting than breeding, I should think. They were quite jaded by the time I came along. Tiring business, being fashionable."

"Must be. Blimey." I think about this. *Like a Pendulum Do* was massively popular when I was at sixth form; we all read it. And there was a trashy TV adaptation as well. I loved it. I remember asking my mum how to do cat-eye makeup—I'd only ever used a kohl pencil, never heard of liquid eyeliner. You couldn't get it. I had to buy a dry, cakey thing that you mixed with water yourself. I bought my first pair of false eyelashes in the chemist by the station, inspired by—apparently—Edward's actual mother, or a simulacrum at least.

"Your mum slept with Mick Jagger." I'm slightly disbelieving.

He laughs. "Perhaps."

"Well. She does in the book."

"She does." He drains his drink and puts the empty can on the wall between us.

"Bloody hell."

"You'd never believe it if you met her," he says. "She's not cool these days."

"Isn't she? Not like Joanna Lumley?"

He laughs again. "No. She's more . . . I think she went too far in the opposite direction."

"God. My mum would flip if she thought I knew someone whose mum slept with Mick Jagger." I eat fish in silence for a while, sawing at it with the penknife. "Personally I prefer Charlie Watts. He's my favorite."

"Not Keith?"

"I like Keith, just for not being dead. But Charlie's the best."

He laughs. "Why?"

"I think he's quite handsome. He's one of those men who got better looking. Nothing much at twenty, stunning at sixty."

"Okay."

"And I like the things he says, like how he doesn't play drums in the Rolling Stones, he plays drums for Mick and

Keith. And how mostly that involves waiting for them to turn up from somewhere. And I like how he's been married to the same person since 1964 or something."

"Yeah, that's pretty admirable isn't it? For a Rolling Stone, particularly."

"I think so. I like that he's always at the back in photos looking faintly annoyed that he has to have his picture taken." I would carry on talking in this chatty unimportant way, but I've glanced up from my chips to find Edward looking at me with a really odd expression on his face.

"What?"

"What, what?"

"You're staring. Have I got ketchup all over me?"

"No, sorry. No. Fancy a drink?" He stands up, screwing his chip paper into a ball and looking around for a bin.

"A drink?"

"Yeah, let's go to the pub."

Fifteen

The pub's surprisingly busy.

"I think there's a band on later," Edward says, handing me my drink and squeezing in beside me at the only empty table. "Hence the crowd."

"I saw they have live music. Perhaps I should make an effort and come out more," I say. "I know Jilly and Cerys go to see bands sometimes."

"Expanding your social circle?"

"I probably need to, don't I? Can't just sit in all the time, or expect Jenny and Alistair to invite me to things. Or rely on you." He looks at me over the rim of his glass. "I mean, I know you're not very sociable; it's good of you to come out with me sometimes."

"Yeah, isn't it?"

"And I've begun to wonder if one day I might be interested in meeting people, you know." I turn my beer coaster over twice and then put my gin and tonic on it.

He snorts. "People. Men, you mean."

I shift my stool closer to the wall to disguise my slight embarrassment. "Well. I don't know. Not really. I'm not sure I—"

"I don't think there's much choice round here. You'd need to cast your net wider."

"I haven't got a net. And I don't think I'll need one for a bit. But you know, if I . . . if there's . . . if I were to stay up longer, I should probably make a bit more effort."

"Hm."

Our heart-to-heart, such as it is, is interrupted at this point by Jilly and Cerys, who have spotted us from the bar.

"Are you staying for the band?" says Cerys.

"Dunno," I say, just as Edward says, "No." We all laugh, of course.

"We'll sit with you," says Jilly, scanning for another stool, "and then we'll take your table when you go."

"How rude," says Edward, but he shifts up on the banquette to make room for Cerys.

"Who's playing?" I ask.

"Ah, just a local wee band. Critheann, they're called. Two fiddle players. The girl who sings is amazing," says Jilly. "We always go if they're playing. One of 'em is Cara's son. Cara at the Lemon Tree?"

"Oh, okay. I think I've seen him. With a beard?"

"Aye, that's him, right enough." She nods. "Been away in Ireland all summer, playing all the wee folk festivals. They've a CD."

"I've never seen it so busy in here."

"You need to get out more," says Cerys. "Don't base your social life on Mr. Misery."

Edward scowls at her, and we all laugh at him. I look around. "I've never seen more than two people at the bar. This is the most I've seen since I went to Tesco the week before last."

"Ha, small-town joys."

"Oh look, there's that bloke," I say, as I gaze round the crowded bar.

"What bloke?"

"He was in the shop earlier? With his daughter?" I gesture vaguely at my head.

"Oh yes, the girl with the amazing hair," says Edward. "She bought some postcards. You talked to him for ages."

"Well, not ages. He wanted a copy of *Five Red Herrings,* so we were talking about Dorothy Sayers and Gatehouse of Fleet and Kirkcudbright. I think we should do a leaflet about that."

"You think we should do a leaflet about everything."

Jilly laughs. She finds us hilarious, I know.

"No, I don't. Just some things. We should definitely do one about *The Wicker Man.*"

"We had some people in who were looking at *Wicker Man* locations last week," Cerys says helpfully.

"There you are, see?"

"Huh. I suppose I can't stop you," says Edward, which I take as a win.

I look back at where the man from earlier is now talking to a lad of twenty or so. His son? Must be. "You hardly ever seem to get men who read Dorothy Sayers. I don't know why."

Edward shrugs. "Wimsey's more attractive to women, I imagine."

"D'you think?" I say, doubtful. Not that I'm doubtful about the attractiveness of Lord Peter—I've had a literary crush on him since I was about fourteen. "But they're properly good books, aren't they? I mean it's not just . . . *you* like them."

He grins at me. "I'm very unusual, Thea; you must have noticed."

"Ha."

At this point the man from earlier turns his head and sees me looking at him, which is embarrassing. I'm not embarrassed by anything these days, though. What's the point? I smile at him, and he smiles back. I can't see his daughter anywhere, which is disappointing—I'd like to look at her hair again and see what she'd wear to something like this. Earlier she was wearing a fantastic bright orange minidress with lime-green tights. One of the only things I miss about my teenage years is my ability/willingness to wear fabulous outfits. The postcards she bought earlier were from Edward's vintage collection, suitably. I told her about the shop fronts in Castle Douglas with their sixties fonts.

I've surprised myself by how much I like talking to customers. I suppose because no one ever knows what they want in a secondhand bookshop, and no one's ever in a rush. Mostly they're quite pleasant. And I enjoy seeing myself as a helpful, friendly person, the yin, as it were, to Edward's yang. This thought amuses me, and I chuckle to myself.

"What?"

"Oh, nothing. Just thinking. Anyway, d'you want another? I'll go to the bar before it gets too hectic."

"Are you going to stay?"

"I thought I might have one more. I don't know about staying for the band."

"Okay," he says, "I'll have another pint."

I look at Jilly and Cerys, and they raise their almost-full glasses to me in unison.

"You're all right," says Jilly, "we're fine."

I'd forgotten what a crowded bar was like, and my surprise at the whole thing amuses me. I squeeze between two men in walking gear and lean forward keenly, a tenner gripped between thumb and forefinger, operation "catch the eye of the barmaid" in full effect. I'm not paying much attention to anyone else, and when the person I'm standing next to speaks, I have no idea he's talking to me.

"Excuse me," he says, "hello?"

I turn my head. It's the man from the bookshop. "Oh! Hello. We meet again," I say, and then feel weirdly self-conscious.

He grins at me. "I'm Keith," he says.

I'm amused by this, after Edward and I were talking about Keith Richards earlier. This man seems entirely unlike Keith Richards, but then, isn't everyone?

"I'm Thea. Hello."

We smile at each other. I know he's friendly, I enjoyed our chat this afternoon, but I'm still quite taken aback. He's about my height, with hair that's beginning to grey and fashionable glasses.

"Can I get you a drink?" he asks.

I literally cannot remember the last time a man in a pub offered to buy me a drink. I gawk at him. "Er, well—"

"I feel I should just check—do you . . . is the bookshop a family business? I mean, is that your husband? That you're with?"

I glance over my shoulder toward my friends. "Um, no—no, he's just my boss."

"Right, thought I should make sure. Drink?"

"Er, sure. Sure, why not, thank you. I'll just have a Coke. And I'll still need to get a pint for Edward," I add. I'm a bit flustered, but at that moment I catch the barmaid's eye and order Edward's pint.

"Just a Coke? Sure I can't get you anything else?"

"No, I'll be driving. Thanks."

"You're not local, then?"

"Well, fairly. I live about five miles away." I failed, earlier, to ask the classic shop-to-customer question in a vaguely touristy place, so I say it now. "You're up on holiday?"

"Yeah, up for a fortnight; this is our second week," he says, and leans past me to order our drinks.

"I'll just take this over," I say, picking up Edward's pint. "And then I'll come back."

I head back over to our table, feeling quite odd. I really can't remember the last time a stranger bought me a drink. Seriously, it's been decades.

Edward accepts his pint and says, "Best pals now, then, are we?"

"What?" I say, although I know exactly what he's talking about.

"The man, the guy, the bloke—you know."

"Oh, from before, yes. His name's Keith, apparently." I feel awkward, self-conscious again.

"What did he want?"

"What, just now?"

He nods. He's glaring at me, which makes me uncomfortable, and also slightly annoyed.

"Wanted to buy me a drink. I'd better go and get it," I add, looking back toward the bar "I said I'd—"

"You let him buy you a drink?"

Cerys, who's been watching this interlude with interest, says, "People can buy Thea drinks if they want to, Edward, surely?"

"It's a long time since anyone offered to buy me a drink," I confess, "anyone I didn't know, I mean. I'll be back in a moment."

I thread my way back to the bar, where Keith waits with the drinks. We shuffle off to one side now, out of the way, or as out of the way as possible. We raise our glasses to each other and smile awkwardly.

"So, I thought earlier that you didn't sound local," says Keith. "How long have you lived up here?"

"Oh, I don't exactly . . . I haven't . . . I inherited a house." I explain about Uncle Andrew. He talks about his holiday. He's from Southampton. Divorced. They saw the posters for the gig when they were in town this morning. His son's here, somewhere, but his daughter stayed at the cottage because crowds make her anxious.

"Are you here for the gig?" he asks me. "Or is this your usual watering hole?"

"We do drink in here sometimes. It's the closest pub to the shop. The other one is a whole hundred yards farther." I laugh. "But it's just a coincidence. I didn't realize there was anything on. We usually only have one—because of me driving home and everything."

"Are you going to stay this evening?"

"Oh, well. I don't know . . ." I say, distracted. I just looked across the bar and caught Edward's eye. He's still glaring at me. I shift my gaze to Cerys, who shakes her head and rolls her eyes. "Maybe I'll stay out for a bit," I say. "My friends say the band is good, and I was just saying I ought to be more sociable."

"It's hard work, isn't it, when you move somewhere new?"

"It is. Especially if you're single." I wonder if perhaps I shouldn't have mentioned this.

He nods. "Everything's set up for couples, isn't it? I found it really difficult to adjust when I got divorced. I'm sure everyone does."

"Yeah, it's odd. I don't mind the 'doing what I want' bit, but I can't imagine going on dates or anything. I don't think I've ever been on a date." I laugh. "My husband and I were friends, and then we were going out—we never went on a date."

"I took my ex-wife out to dinner," he says. "I saved up for ages. I was only nineteen." He grins at me. "And we went to the cinema. I took her to see *Sleeping with the Enemy,* which isn't a very romantic film."

I laugh. "No. But tense—so that's good, isn't it, because you can accidentally hold hands."

This makes him laugh. "Yeah, I remember she grabbed my leg at one point and I jumped a mile. After that it seemed okay to put my arm round her." We smile at each other.

"You should come over and meet the others," I say. "And is your son all right by himself?" I look around, but as I don't know what he looks like, it doesn't help.

"He was talking to some girls earlier. He's much better at that than I ever was, never seems to get nervous at all."

"The bravery of youth," I say.

"I suppose so. I wasn't like that at his age."

I lead the way over to the table in the corner. "Oh," I say, looking at the empty seat. "Where's Edward?"

"He's gone," says Jilly. She shakes her head.

"Oh. Did he . . . Oh, okay," I say.

"Jealous," says Cerys.

"Oh really?" I laugh. "Of what? Anyway, look, this is Keith, he's up on holiday." I introduce them all to one another, and we sit down. I try hard not to think about Edward going off without saying goodbye. He's not obliged to, after all. I'll see him tomorrow. And if . . . but that's nonsense. I return my attention to the others, now discussing some of the places Keith and his kids have visited while they've been up here, where his son has been fishing and his daughter's dislike of loud noisy places.

He seems very pleasant, easy to talk to, quite funny. When he goes to the bar for more drinks, Cerys turns to look at me. "So. He's up for it, I reckon. You up for it?"

I blanch. "Oh God. No, I don't think so."

"You shouldn't worry about what Edward thinks," Jilly interjects. "None of his business, is it?"

"No," I say, "it wouldn't be. And I'm not. But he can't really be annoyed, can he?"

"I told you," says Cerys, "he's jealous."

"Don't be silly." I'm even more embarrassed. "Why would he be jealous?"

They both look at me.

"Can't imagine," says Jilly.

"No idea," says Cerys. Then they laugh. I'm not sure what to say. This is the problem with people you don't know well. I like Jilly and Cerys, but it's hard to tell when they're teasing.

When Keith returns from the bar, he brings his son with

him. People are beginning to move their chairs away from the corner by the pool table where there are suddenly amps and microphones.

"I might stay for a bit," I say.

"You should, they're brilliant, honestly," says Cerys.

So I do, and they are. I have an unexpectedly jolly evening, although it's hard to talk when the music's playing. Some people even dance and it's just like one of those little documentary films you see about communities making their own entertainment. I talk to people I've never spoken to but have seen around, in the Co-op or down by the river walking their dogs. By nine-thirty I'm flagging, though.

"I'm going to head off," I say to Keith. "So nice to have met you."

"And you," he says, "it's always good to meet people who actually live in the place where I'm on holiday, makes me feel like a local."

"You'll need to work on your accent," says Jilly. "Even Thea says 'aye' sometimes."

"Not on purpose," I object. "I mean, I worry you'll think I'm making fun of you. I always pick up words when I stay somewhere for a while, it's accidental."

"Ach, don't worry, we think it's cute," says Jilly, pulling a ridiculous face at me.

I wonder for a moment if Keith might ask me for my phone number or something, but he doesn't. I think I'm relieved. I say goodbye to everyone and retrieve my bag from the windowsill where it's been hidden behind the curtain.

Outside it's surprisingly cool—or perhaps it would be more accurate to say that inside it's been very warm indeed.

I walk up the road toward the town hall in the dusk. The sound of the band is still quite loud—I wonder if Edward can hear it. As I drive past the shop I look up at the windows of the flat, but all is darkness.

...

I try to identify how I'm feeling. I have a strange edgy excited sense of something. It reminds me of going to parties when I was in my early teens. A weird sense of, I don't know, potential? Not that there was any potential, or not really. It's not like Keith asked to see me again. I screw up my face in the dark. All the ways of thinking about this sort of thing have curiously juvenile phrasing. I suppose because the last time I was bought a drink and flirted gently with a stranger, I was young. It makes me sigh, thinking about my younger self. Not that she was unhappy, or even particularly stupid; it was a long time ago and everything she did was new. Now nothing I do is new, but some of it is unusual. I don't know. I feel as though I can almost but not quite identify something quite important.

At home I make myself a cup of tea and watch a documentary about Scottish lake villages I downloaded last week. I go to bed later than usual, but not what anyone would really describe as late. I can't sleep, though. I'd forgotten that feeling, of talking to a man who likes you. Or . . . that's not quite right. I often talk to men who like me. I mean, that thing where someone's bought you a drink and made an effort and been perfectly clear that they find you attractive, even if that wasn't enough to spur them to try and get to know you better. It's simple, isn't it, despite the way we complicate these things.

And—this is a tiny almost-ignored thought that makes me sigh whenever it presents itself obliquely—Edward's not really pissed off, is he? Why would he be? He seemed pissed off, though. I think again about him glaring at me from across the pub. I don't want him to be annoyed with me, especially after we had such a good time before we went there. Why does he have to be so cross all the time? It's not like . . .

. . .

I'm slightly anxious about going to work in the morning. And irritated with myself for feeling that way. I fiddle about in the car for ages, emptying receipts out of my purse, putting CDs back in their cases. I can't put it off forever, though. I'm sure it'll just be one of those things I've worried about for nothing, I tell myself as I push open the shop door.

Edward's in his usual seat, reading the news on the laptop. He looks up as I walk to the counter.

"Morning," I say. "How are you?"

"I wondered if you'd make it in," he says abruptly.

"You wondered if I'd make it in?" I stare at him. "Why on earth wouldn't I?"

He shrugs. "Late night."

"Good grief. I know I'm ancient"—I lean past him to put my bag under the counter—"but I can just about stay up until half past nine without having to take a sick day."

"Half nine? They were still going at midnight."

"Were they? I didn't stay until midnight."

"Oh." He's turned in his chair to look at me. "Did you go home with that man?"

"Jesus Christ. No, I didn't. Why would you even ask something like that?"

"Oh. I thought you might. He liked you."

I consider this. "Yeah, I think he did, but not enough to make any attempt to . . . Well, anything. Anyway, I've never gone home with a man I just met, it would be wildly out of character. Jesus."

"Huh."

"Huh yourself. *Jesus*." I shake myself.

"You seemed to be getting on well. Laughing and—"

"Yes, he seemed pleasant. Who knows? He lives in Southampton so it's not like I'm going to get to know him."

"He didn't ask to see you again?" He sounds disbelieving, which I suppose is a compliment. Sort of.

"Nope."

"Oh."

"Yes, oh."

"Did you want him to?"

This is the big question, isn't it? "Not really, no."

"Not really? Does that mean yes?"

"No, no, it's not that. I just . . . well, it might be nice, mightn't it, to think someone might like me."

"I didn't think he was all that," he says. "Does that sort of thing appeal to you?"

I just look at him.

"I mean, you know." He does at least look vaguely embarrassed, dropping his gaze as I glare at him.

"Not everyone is lucky enough to be brooding and patrician," I tell him. He looks briefly confused. "I mean, I'm not exactly"—I search my mind—"Cameron Diaz, am I?"

He brushes this aside with a gesture. "If you wonder whether random men might want to fuck you, I imagine the answer is yes," he says.

We stare at each other. I feel unexpected tears pricking. "That's not very . . . that's not exactly what I'm talking about." I'm annoyed by this, his attitude. It's—what? It's rude, is what it is, and I don't understand why he has to be unpleasant. I haven't done anything wrong, have I? What would that even mean, something wrong? The whole thing is irritating. "Or maybe it is. Anyway. Better get on."

I walk away through the shop. I fixed some books yesterday, and I need to unclamp them and take pictures if they look okay and the light's right. It's quite a grey morning. I open the back door and go out into the garden, twirling through my keys and unlocking the door of the workshop. It's messy in there—the floor littered with bits of paper, the scarred surface of the worktable covered in linen and cardboard and pieces of leather. There's a sink, a hot plate for heating the glue pots, and shelves covered in useful things like lunch boxes full of gold leaf and jars of gesso. There's a sofa, demoted from a proper room elsewhere, and a tall workshop chair.

I lean on the table and close my eyes. I don't understand why Edward said that. It might be true, I suppose, or it might not. It doesn't really matter. Once upon a time it might have been troubling to think something like that, but now? Even thinking someone might want . . . that, is a win, after all. Because when the person you've been sleeping with for the last twenty years leaves you, at least one of the implications is that he doesn't want to have sex with you anymore, isn't it? And that's quite depressing. I've never been beautiful or madly sexy, and I got through school assuming no one liked me—that I lacked whatever it takes to be fashionable. I had an inability to conjure a decent haircut, was a bit clever and not very sporty—all of these things coalesce, don't they, into textbook low self-esteem for girls. But once away from school, (and partly thanks to Mark Woodley and the things we did in his bedroom) my confidence, and also my vision of myself as a person who might be attractive—not to everyone, but to enough people—gathered momentum. By the time I got to university I was willing to believe I had something, some spark of—whatever it is. And therefore it seemed to be true.

The people you like don't always like you back the same way, and vice versa, but I knew there were people—boys, and men, even—who might look at me and think, yes, there's something appealing about Thea. Most of that's gone now, worn away, crumpled—the fresh bloom of youth dissipates, but as a grown-up you have other things in recompense. Except those things can be mislaid or broken when someone decides they don't want you anymore. I haven't addressed this side of things, have I? It's definitely true, though, that I'd rather someone "just" wanted to fuck me, however basic that might seem, than have no one ever look at me with desire again.

None of this means I'm going to sleep with anyone anytime soon, however. And I absolutely cannot see what any of it's got to do with my employer.

I look at my hands, nails cut sensibly short, my grandmother's wedding ring, too big for my ring fingers, on the middle finger of my left hand. I stopped wearing my own ring last month, when I finally stopped using my married name. I still feel strange about it; my hand looks naked without the narrow platinum wedding band and the unmatching antique diamond engagement ring we bought in Brighton a lifetime ago. I've put them both away, in a cuff-link box buried at the back of a drawer. I might even sell them, buy myself something new. I try to imagine my hands on someone else. Maybe someone I've never met? Maybe no one, ever.

I unclamp the books and take off the pads that protect the boards from the clamp's biting teeth. They look a hundred times better than they did yesterday, when the covers were entirely separate and in danger of being lost forever. A nice 1950s edition of *Alice's Adventures in Wonderland,* given as a school prize, with a bright and jolly illustrated cover, and a rather battered but fun 1896 *Every Girl's Annual.* Edward didn't think it was worth saving—it came in a box of house clearance stuff—but I was determined.

I put the mended books in a box on the sofa and looked at the to-do pile. There's a knock at the door and here's the man himself, Mr. Maltravers, looking awkward and holding my handbag out toward me. It's a rather frivolous basket covered in exuberant fake flowers, and it looks quite funny dangling from his hand.

"Your phone rang," he says. "And then you got a text. So I brought your bag."

"Suits you. You should get one."

"Ha ha."

I take it from him and slide my phone out of the internal pocket.

"I thought it might be that man," he says, "and I didn't want you to miss it. I was an arse before, and I apologize." He sighs.

"Yeah, well, unless Jilly or Cerys gave him my number—which would seem hugely unlikely—it won't have been him." I roll my eyes. I unlock my phone and look at the message. I laugh.

"As suspected." I hold the phone up. "It's from the bank."

"Oh," says Edward. He looks embarrassed. "Well. Anyway."

"Did you lock up?" I ask him. You can't just abandon the shop, obviously.

"No, I went to Plan B."

Plan B is when you put the till and the laptop in the safe and dig out the emergency notice, which is in a large, curly photo frame and says, THE SHOP IS NOT UNSTAFFED, ALTHOUGH THERE'S NO ONE AT THE DESK AT THE MOMENT. PLEASE RING THE BELL, OR TEXT THIS NUMBER, AND SOMEONE WILL BE WITH YOU SHORTLY. AND REMEMBER, SMILE—YOU'RE ON CCTV.

We use it sometimes if only one person is working and they have to go to the loo or something. The CCTV thing is mainly just to stop people from stealing books. Edward says that often even nice people are tempted to nick stuff, but most people won't if they know (or think) they're being filmed. It seems to work.

"You'd better go back, then," I say. "Did you make any lunch?"

"No. I'll go and get sandwiches from the Old Mill."

"Cool. Prawn please, if they have any."

Edward pulls at his lower lip. "Okay," he says. For a moment I think he's going to say something else, but he changes his mind and leaves me alone in the workshop.

...

Later that afternoon, after eating my prawn sandwiches at the counter, I'm back in the workshop gluing more broken books. I have a terrible headache and matching cramps. I take some painkillers and soldier on, but I feel dreadful. I'm not sure if the headache is a result of being irritated earlier about that stupid conversation with Edward, or whether it's connected to my cramping womb. My cycle has been all over the place since January. I should go to the doctor, as I don't know whether it's been thrown off by the stress of the breakup with Chris, or peri-menopause, or what.

"Stupid womb," I mutter to myself, and stand up, stretching. My back aches and I'm exhausted. I suppose I've had more excitement in the last twenty-four hours than I'm used to. I might go and make a cup of tea. Or I might just sit down on the sofa for a moment.

...

"Thea. Thea. Wake up."

"Not asleep," I mumble. "Resting m'eyes."

"Of course you are, sweetheart. Now come on, wake up, I've made you a nice cup of tea."

"God, have you?" I open my eyes and try to raise my head. I've slumped down onto the arm of the sofa and my neck is as stiff and uncomfortable as it's possible to be.

"All right?" Edward's crouching on the floor beside the sofa, a mug of tea in his hand.

"Urgh."

"Yes, I expect so. Now sit up and drink your tea."

I smile at him. "Thank you. I was going to come and make one."

"I wondered where you were. When it got to half past three I thought you might have died or something."

"I've only been asleep for a moment. Is it really half three?" I take the mug from him. "Oh God." I close my eyes. "Thank you, that's wonderful."

"Are you okay?"

"Yeah, just . . . I'm just tired, and I've got a bit of a dake," I say. "Dake" is a shop word, it means headache. I expect that everyone who works in a very small team has a private language; we're just developing one. If we carry on working together, eventually we'll be impenetrable to outsiders.

"Taken some pills?"

I nod.

"Want me to take you home?"

"Don't be silly."

"It's nearly four now. I'll take you home and come and get you in the morning."

"That's mad."

"No it isn't, you look rough as biscuits."

"Oh, thanks."

He laughs. "Drink your tea. I'll go and cash out."

I bleat feebly, but he's already gone. I lean back against the cushions and close my eyes again. The thought of being driven home is extremely tempting. I could drive, of course, but it's nice not to have to. I sigh and finish my tea and tidy up, checking that the hot plate's turned off, removing my apron, collecting my bag and locking the workshop door behind me.

"All ready?" asks Edward as I come back into the front of the shop.

"Yes. Are you sure you don't mind? I'm perfectly okay to drive. And you'll have to come and get me in the morning. It all seems too tedious."

"It's no problem. Come on." He holds the door open for me. "You're very pale; are you sure you're not coming down with something?"

"No, no, it's just . . . you know."

"No, what?"

"It's time to choose from a colorful variety of euphemisms," I say, yawning.

"What?"

"For the shedding of the lining of one's womb," I say. "Isn't 'womb' a funny word?"

"Oh."

"Yes, isn't it horrid, actually menstruating in your shop? I know you hate that." I laugh.

He tuts. "Is it bad?"

"Quite bad today for some reason. It's a bit random at the moment. Too much information; I do apologize."

He opens the car door for me and I climb up into the seat, closing my eyes once my seatbelt is fastened.

"Very kind," I murmur, but he ignores me.

. . .

I must have been dozing in the car; I jerk awake as we crunch to a halt on the gravel. Opening my eyes, I blink at the front door of the lodge with a feeling of relief. It's nice to be home.

"Keys," says Edward.

"Hm?"

"Keys, give me your keys so I can open the door."

"Oh no, I'm sure I can—"

He holds out his hand, sighing.

I paw meekly through the contents of my handbag, extract the keys and hand them to him. He gets out of the car and comes round to open the passenger door. This isn't down to feebleness on my part, but because there's something wrong with the lock. He releases me and I awkwardly clamber down and follow him as he unlocks the front door.

"Thanks for driving me," I say.

He waves this away irritably, and drops the keys onto the hallstand. "Are you all right? Got pills and so forth? What are you having for your dinner?"

"I've no idea. Did you want a cuppa?" I feel I should ask, although I'd rather just lie on the sofa for a bit and not think about entertaining.

He looks at me, considering. "I'll make it. Stuff's all logical, is it? In the kitchen?"

"Logical?" I wonder if it is. "I think so, yes."

"Go and sit down, then," he says, and puts one finger against my shoulder, pushing me into the sitting room. I don't know why, but this makes me laugh. "All right," I say, "no need to bully me in my own home."

"Just do as you're told for once."

Dropping my bag by the door, I lean against the wall and

take off my shoes. Late-afternoon sunshine puddles on the mossy green carpet and I sink, exhausted, onto the sofa. I can hear various bangs and rattlings from my kitchen as he looks for teaspoons and mugs. I close my eyes for a moment.

"Here you go," he says.

"Thank you. Two cups of tea you've made me today, I could get used to this."

"I make you tea all the time," he objects, frowning. "Honestly."

I bend my head over my cup to hide my smile. "I know you do. Thanks."

He doesn't sit down, instead he's wandering about, looking at the things I've rearranged on the bookshelves, poking at a pile of DVDs and videos. Then he's over by the table.

"What's all this? Are you writing a book?" he asks.

"Oh God, no. No, that's all Andrew's stuff. His memoir, or whatever. Did you know he'd written loads of notes?"

"About what?"

"About his life"—I wave a vague hand—"and so on. Stories about his parents—my great-grandparents. And their parents. You know the kind of thing."

"Oh, right. He did say something about that. Said he had loads of diaries and bits and pieces."

"Yes, there's loads of it. My great-grandmother kept a diary; it's a bit weird really."

"Weird how?"

"Oh, I don't know. I think—I suppose they were reasonably middle-class? Maybe she was a bit of a cut above? I don't know. Anyway it's all morning calls and flower arranging and the Boer War and stuff. Some of it reminded me of— have you ever read any Molly Keane?"

"*Good Behavior*. And"—I see him tracking through the files in his head—"*Devoted Ladies*—"

"I read that one when I was sixteen," I tell him, "and found it appalling and terrifying."

He laughs. "They are a bit, aren't they. Her characters. Horsey. Emotionally abusive—"

"Yes, everyone's horrible and pathetic in a grotesque way. I do like them. The books. But anyway, some of it reminded me of that, although obviously they weren't as . . ." I flap my hand again.

"Posh." He looks at me, a grin lurking.

"Yes, thank you, they weren't as posh as the people in Molly Keane books. It has mostly been quite rubbish," I add, "to be a woman."

"Yes." He pulls out one of the dining room chairs and sits down. "How is it to be a woman right now at this moment?"

"Are you asking me about fourth-wave feminism or my personal womb experience?"

He snorts with laughter. "I meant, how are you feeling?"

"Not too bad."

He's still laughing, shaking his head. He sips his tea and turns to look at the papers on the desk, pushing photographs around in the shoebox lid I'm using to corral them.

"Oh," he says, "is this Fiona?"

"Show me?"

He holds up the photo.

"Yes."

"I've only seen that one." He nods at the framed photograph on the little round table under the window: Fiona aged about nine with her hair in ringlets. The picture he's holding is a school photo, Fiona in a blazer looking distracted.

"Yes. That's her." I rub my fingers against my temples. I wonder. "Did he ever talk to you about her? I meant to ask Jilly's mum ages ago—apparently she knew her. But I forgot. I don't even know what happened. Do you?"

"Oh. Well. Yes, he did talk about her a bit. She liked cycling. They used to cycle about all over the place, her and her pals. There were two of them, anyway, in the accident, if that's what you'd call it. Um—no, can't remember the other girl's name."

I wait while he thinks about the story.

"There were some lads—friends of hers—working on a boat somewhere up beyond Kirkcudbright, I think. Fiona and her friend went up there to see how they were getting on. There was a jetty—a wooden one? It's not there anymore, I don't think. Anyway, it must have been rotten, or maybe she just tripped—I'm not sure. Anyway, they both fell in, and Fiona hit her head on the steps or something. The other girl couldn't swim. The boys went in after them and they got them out, but it was too late for Fiona. There was nowhere to phone from so one of the lads had to cycle for the doctor. Everything took too long. So she died."

"Ah," I say. "Yes, I had in my head that she'd drowned. How awful." I look across at the smiling face of my long-dead second cousin. How unfair everything is, how random. She might have had grandchildren, mightn't she, if she'd lived. One of them might have been sitting here now; maybe even talking to Edward. I shiver.

"Pretty bad," he agrees. "She's buried in the churchyard in town."

"Is she? Do you know where?"

"If you go in the gate, on the Co-op side, it's just along to the left. You'll see from the dates, all the newer stuff is on that side."

"I never even thought to wonder where she was buried. Or any of them." I'm slightly appalled by this.

"Oh, well, they're all there. Left room on her headstone for their names."

We look at each other for a long moment. "God."

"I know. I'd say they're all together now," he says, "if I was that sort of person. And physically it's true." He shrugs.

I sigh. "Yes."

"They used to go to church," he adds, draining his cup, "Mary and Andrew. They stopped after that, more or less."

"I can see how that might happen. I suppose you can go either way, can't you."

"Indeed you can."

Something else occurs to me. "Where's your dad buried?"

"Oh." He grins at me. "We've a tomb. In the church."

Of course they have. "Oh really."

"Yeah, quite fancy. Brass and such like. Only the last three generations, though—you know, glorious war dead and so on. Before that, everyone got slung in the tomb at the house."

"Slung."

He laughs. "Well, I imagine it was all a bit more, you know, elaborate than that. There's a chapel."

"Is there? Whereabouts? I've never noticed that."

"It's only tiny, round the back beyond the stables. A nice bit of exercise for them, walking three hundred yards of a Sunday morning. Anyway, I should get off and leave you alone, you still look—"

"What?"

"I don't know. Fragile?"

"I've literally never been described as 'fragile' in my life," I say drily.

He shakes his head. "No, but you do. You should have an early night. But make sure you eat something."

I roll my eyes. "Thanks, Dad."

He ignores this and gets up. "I'll take your cup, if you've finished. And I'll be back in the morning to collect you. About nine-ish?"

"Thank you. It's very kind of you."

"Whatever," he says, and takes the cups out to the kitchen.

Sixteen

Two weeks later, I'm in the Old Mill, drinking coffee and reading the paper in between emailing various people and fiddling about on Twitter. Cerys comes over and says, "Mind if I sit with you? I'm on my break."

"Feel free."

"So, how are you?"

"Good, yeah, just doing some Twitter stuff for the shop."

"Jilly was admiring your photos on Instagram."

"Yeah, I'm quite pleased with how that's going."

She stirs her coffee. "Never get Ed doing any of that."

She's the only person who calls him Ed. He doesn't seem to mind, but I can't imagine doing it myself. They're reasonably matey, Edward and Cerys—in fact I'd go so far as to say she's his closest friend here. Sometimes they go to the cinema together in Dumfries. I was surprised when I found out about that, but Cerys did a film studies degree and they go to see artsy things that Jilly can't be bothered with.

"What, social media? Shouldn't think so, no. I told him to put it in the job description for his next victim."

"Are you off, then?" She watches me, bright-eyed, bird-like.

"Oh, no. Not at the moment. Not sure what to do. I'm

tempted to stay," I tell her, "but I wonder if that's, you know, cowardly."

"Cowardly?"

"Yeah. Because of how my life fell apart and everything." I drum my fingers on the table. "I had no intention of starting over or anything like that when I came up here. I'd never thought about living somewhere else. But now I'm here . . ."

"Yeah, I know what you mean. I didn't plan on staying. I originally came up on holiday. I did go back home, but only to collect all my stuff." She wrinkles her nose.

"Really?" I'm surprised. I've never thought about where Cerys came from, even though she's clearly not Scottish.

"Mm. That was before I met Jilly. I used to be married, did you know that?"

"What, to a man?"

She laughs at me. "Yeah, I know, imagine that."

"Good heavens."

"Yeah, I was married for nearly ten years. It was okay. Although as you can imagine, I did have some issues. I came up here on a whim, just because there was a last-minute deal on a holiday cottage website. Needed a bit of time to myself. And when I got here, I really liked it. I suppose I'd already decided I was going to leave Ryan. So I thought, hey, sod it, why not just run away? Although I prefer to think of it as running toward," she adds, laughing again.

"What about all your friends? And your family?" I'm secretly impressed by this sort of careless adventuring.

"Don't have any family. And my friends come up here to visit. And I met some people up here—Ed and Jenny and Alistair. And then I met Jilly. And there we are."

"Wow. I suppose I thought you and Jilly had always been together."

"Nope."

"Did you—I'm sorry, this is nosy, and you're welcome to tell me to piss off—did you go out with other women before you were married?"

"Yeah, a bit. Nothing serious. I always thought I was mostly straight. But actually I think I'm mostly not." She laughs some more. "Ah. I'd say it was a waste, but you know it wasn't, not really. I did love Ryan, and I think I wasn't ready for Jilly. If I'd met her when we were twenty, it wouldn't have worked."

"Life's weird, isn't it?"

"Yeah. So I wanted to talk to you," she says, "about Charles."

"Charles?" I look at her blankly.

"Ed's brother?"

"Yes, I know who he is," I say, "but why?"

"He asked me about you."

"Asked you what? He knows about me. I've been to his house. And he's been to mine."

"Yeah, he wasn't asking who you were, you idiot."

"Oh." We both laugh. "What was he asking, then?"

"He wanted to know about your husband. And about you and Ed."

I frown at her. "Really?"

"Yeah. He wanted to know if you were getting divorced. And if I thought you and Ed were . . . you know."

"We're absolutely not." I feel my cheeks burn, annoyingly.

"No shit. After the state he got himself into about that bloke, Jesus Christ."

"What?"

"Your beau at the Arms the other week."

"Oh. Keith. That was weird, wasn't it? Edward was really funny about it." I'm still not sure what I think about that.

She snorts. "Wasn't he? But anyway, yeah. Charles asked, were you divorced, and I said, not quite. But pretty much. And did I think you and Ed were, you know, sleeping together, and I said no, and he said but do you think he likes her, though, and I said, everyone likes Thea—"

"Oh, bless you, how sweet—oh look at me, you've made me well up. Good grief." I dab at my eyes. "What a knob. Me, I mean." I shake my head. It's absurd that I could weep so easily at the thought of anyone saying anything nice about me. Tragic.

"Hm, well, it's true. Anyway, so I said you two seemed to be getting on well and I thought it was good for Ed to have a friend. Of course Charles didn't like that much—I expect he'd like Ed to die a lonely death, but . . . Anyway. Then he asked if Ed was seeing anyone, and I told him I thought Lara was still on the scene. Is she?"

Ugh. I try not to think about Lara. "Yeah, for some reason. Have you met her?"

"Once," says Cerys.

"What did you think?"

"Oh." She shrugs. "They're all the same, aren't they? Posh birds. Do you like her?"

"No. Well, I don't know her. But—"

"But you don't like her."

I can't deny it. "No. And I don't think he does either, which . . . I don't really understand it."

"It's convenient, I suppose."

"Not that convenient. I mean she lives three hours' drive away."

"Yeah, you're right. It's not serious, though, is it? That's more what I meant."

"Hm. But anyway," I say, "what was Charles getting at? I don't understand."

"I don't know. But if he asks you out to dinner or anything—"

I stare at her. "Why on earth would he do that?"

She blinks at me. "He likes you."

"Not like that, though, surely? I mean, I assume his wives have been terribly glossy and elegant and glamorous. In a classy way. Not like me."

Cerys looks thoughtful.

"This might sound rude," she says, "so please don't take it the wrong way, but I think you're right. You're probably not well-bred enough. And maybe too old; you know what men are like. But if Charles thought he could hurt Edward somehow through you, I think he might do it."

"But why would he think sleeping with me would upset Edward?" I frown.

"Thea, you're not stupid, come on. Everyone thinks you're sleeping together, and if you're not, then eventually you will be."

"Oh my God, do they? Surely they don't." I goggle at her, although I do feel quite stupid for not thinking anyone would be interested in us.

"Yes, they do. I'm sorry, it's a small town, everyone's

intrigued. You know he never has women working in the shop. You hang out together, he's never rude to you, yadda yadda."

"He's constantly rude to me, what on earth do you mean?"

"Yeah, hardly."

I sniff. "One of the reasons I liked it up here is because everyone was talking about me at home. I was enjoying the anonymity of Baldochrie."

"Yeah, well, you can forget about being anonymous. Look, it's just that people are nosy, and they like romance and intrigue. You're new and now that people know you're single, they're all wondering who you'll get together with."

"Ugh."

She laughs at me. "And Charles likes you. But he might have a motive beyond 'wouldn't it be fun to take Thea out to dinner.' And I like you too, so I thought I should tell you."

"Bloody hell."

"I mean by all means shag him if you like, it doesn't bother me."

"Yeah, no, you're all right. He's too charming. I don't like charming people."

"You prefer Ed." She laughs. "Not charming."

"Of course I do, I like him a lot. But I don't . . . I'm not going to sleep with him either, you know." I laugh. "Jesus. It's like being at college."

...

I'm in the shop. It's been less than twenty-four hours since Cerys told me all that strange stuff. I don't know what to think about any of it.

My phone rings, a number I don't recognize.

"Hello?"

"Thea. Charles here."

I nearly drop the phone. Jesus flipping Christ. I feel an unexpected bubble of hysteria and have to bite my cheek.

"Can you talk?" he asks.

"I . . . Yeah, hello, hi, I'll just—" I slide off the counter and walk to the back of the shop.

"I shouldn't phone you at work," he says, "but I'll be busy later and I wanted to catch you."

"Well, here I am. Hello. What can I do for you?"

"I wondered if you'd be free for dinner," he says.

I nearly laugh, but I restrain myself. "Dinner? Gosh," I say, "it's suddenly very fashionable to buy me drinks and offer to buy me dinner. How thrilling."

"Why, who's been buying you drinks?"

"Oh, just some guy," I say, laughing at myself. "I met him in the Arms the other week."

"Oh. Did he ask you out?"

"No. Luckily, since I'm not ready to go on dates."

"Oh," says Charles.

"But presumably you're not asking me on a date. Are you?" I'm not sure when making people feel slightly uncomfortable first seemed like fun. Maybe today.

"Well," he says. "It wouldn't *not* be a date."

"You don't want to go on a date with me, though, do you? What's happened to Miranda?" There's a slightly awkward silence. "Is she away or something?"

"Miranda and I are not . . . She's not my girlfriend," he says.

"Isn't she? I kind of thought she was."

"Mm, no, not . . . No."

"Gosh, you Maltravers men with your unconventional relationships." I begin to walk back through the shop toward the front door. "So anyway, where were you thinking?"

He clears his throat. "There's quite a good restaurant at Knockandry."

"The hotel? Hotel dining rooms," I say. "I'm not sure they're ever all that, are they? Sorry, that sounds fussy."

"It's good," he says, "they have a Michelin star. If that helps."

"It does a bit," I say, laughing. "You're probably already regretting this, right?"

"Not at all," he says, polite.

"And when would this be?"

"I thought perhaps Thursday?"

"As in this Thursday?" I lean on the counter.

"Yes, if you're free."

"Oh, well, I generally am. My social life is very limited. Okay, thank you. Shall I meet you there?"

"I'll come and collect you. Half seven suit?"

"Sounds fine," I say. "Thank you."

I slide my phone into the back pocket of my jeans and laugh heartily. Edward is selling a collection of 1970s Thelwell cartoon books to a man in a tweed jacket. Once he's given the man his change and put the books in a bag, he asks, "What's funny?"

"What isn't funny, eh? Good lord. So that was your brother," I tell him. "Guess what he wants."

"My brother? What's he phoning you for?"

"What indeed. Wants to take me out," I say. "We're having dinner."

"You're having dinner with my brother?" Brows beetling, forehead furrowed.

"Apparently so."

"Why the hell are you doing that?"

"Two reasons," I say, "if I'm honest. One is I've never had dinner with a lord." I snort. "And I guess it will be quite fancy, and I like to eat nice food. And the other reason is, oh my God, why on earth would he want to have dinner with me? Do you think he'll get me drunk and try to get me to sign the house over to him or something?"

"If he gets you drunk it won't be the house he's after," says Edward, disapprovingly.

"*Pfft*. Yeah, but seriously, it's weird, isn't it?"

"I'm not sure 'weird' is the right word."

"Oh, come on, of course it is. I asked him if it was a date. He said it 'wouldn't not be a date'!" I chuckle. "That's the sort of thing you'd say."

"If I ask someone out to dinner it's definitely a fucking date," says Edward.

I shake my head. "You bought me dinner the other week and that wasn't a date, was it? Anyway, your brother doesn't fancy me. I'm pretty sure."

"Doesn't he? What makes you say that?"

"What, am I a bit of rough or something? Come on."

He closes his eyes briefly. "Jesus Christ."

"No, I'm not fishing," I say, hoisting myself up onto the counter and banging my heels against the front of it. "I'm being serious. Cerys said something yesterday about this. It doesn't make any sense to me. What about all those glossy women? The house was full of them when I went to that hideous party. I'm not like that."

"Maybe he fancies a change," says Edward. I can't read his expression, which is unusual.

"Yeah, I doubt it."

"What did Cerys say?"

"She said he'd asked about, um . . ." I'm unexpectedly embarrassed. "You know, about us. You and me."

"Ah, well, there you go, then."

"My, that's flattering, isn't it? If he's asked me to have dinner because he thinks for some mad reason that it might annoy you."

"There's probably a bit more to it than that."

"You reckon? I guess I'll find out. I'll ask him."

Edward looks at me, arms folded. "What will you ask?"

I tilt my head to one side. "Hey, Charlie boy, you wanna fuck me or you just wanna fuck with your brother?"

The frown on his face disappears when he laughs. "You're hilarious."

"I know, right?"

"You wouldn't really say that?"

"Why not?"

"I don't know." He shakes his head. "Bloody hell."

"I wouldn't want to find out afterward," I say. "Imagine the hu-mil-i-a-tion."

"It's put you in a good mood, I see."

"Only because it's funny. It's pretty funny, isn't it? I mean, it's a funny way to get at you, if that's what he's doing. I know you don't like him but surely you wouldn't care much if—"

"I wouldn't find it desperately amusing," he says, "if you slept with my brother."

We look at each other.

"No, but it's not much good as revenge, is it? 'Oh yeah, Edward shagged my wife, so I thought I'd cop off with his staff'?"

The frown was back for a moment there, but now he's laughing again. "'Cop off with,' what kind of phrase is that?"

"I dunno, it's Northern I think. One of my housemates at uni used to say it. We'd go sharking, with the hope of copping off. I don't think it meant 'have sex with' actually, just get off with."

"Don't get off with my brother."

"Ha ha, don't worry. Whether or not he fancies me is moot. I definitely don't fancy him."

"That never stopped anyone," he says drily.

"It might not stop you. It would stop me, though. Especially as your brother has all kinds of disadvantages."

"Why go at all, then?"

"I told you. Curiosity."

He shakes his head. "That's why you went to that party. Regretted it, though, didn't you?"

"I did a bit, yeah, but it *was* interesting. And if your brother manages to make me feel common on what isn't 'not a date,' well"—I laugh—"that would be a poor effort. Unless he wants to pull some kind of, you know, *My Fair Lady* shit. Or that other thing, what is it, King Whatsit. Cophetua. Is that right?"

"King Cophetua and the beggar maid?"

"That's the chap. Where's that from? Shakespeare? I only know it because Harriet Vane talks about it when Lord Peter asks her to marry him."

"Don't marry my brother."

This makes me laugh even harder. "Oh my God, can you imagine? I'd flounce home, demanding people call me 'my lady.'" I snort. "I'd be tempted, just to annoy everyone."

He looks at me.

"Not really," I say. "I'm joking." I chuckle to myself. "Oh God, though."

"Thea."

"Yes?"

"I know this will sound . . . it might sound rude. And I don't mean to insinuate that my brother might have an ulterior motive. You're an attractive woman—"

I snort even more loudly.

"But you know I think this might be . . . he might be . . . I think you should be careful."

"Careful? What? D'you think he might try and roofie me?" I pause. "Would that be the verb, do you think? I am roofied, you are roofied, he roofies, she roofies; I don't know, what do you reckon? About the word," I add, "not the chance he'll drug me." I laugh again.

"Jesus Christ." He covers his eyes with his hand.

"What?"

"I'm serious."

"Look. I don't care one way or the other about Charles. Therefore, it's of no consequence if he has an ulterior motive. It's not like I'll be upset. 'Oh, but I thought you liked me, boo hoo.' There was me choosing a trousseau, and then it turns out he only asked me because he wanted to annoy you. And like I say, it's a pretty crappy revenge, isn't it? He'd be better off waiting for you to meet someone you like. You're only forty-seven or whatever, it could still happen."

He turns away. "Unlikely."

"Yeah, maybe, but . . . Or he could, I don't know, buy all the secondhand books in Scotland or tell Lara's husband you're going to elope or something. Mess up your little arrangement."

"I wouldn't care about that. And he probably couldn't buy all the secondhand books in Scotland."

"What would you do if you were him? Since you're Mr. Revenge."

He turns back for a moment. "Yeah," he says, "I'd probably be able to come up with something."

"Go on then, do tell."

"I'll let you know," he says, "if he ever pulls it off."

"Oh, boo."

"Anyway, enough. Haven't you got any work to do?"

...

I'm in the pub with Jenny, Cerys, and Edward the following evening. Although Edward's reading something on his phone, so I wouldn't count him as present exactly. We're talking about my dinner date for tomorrow.

"And I just have no idea what to wear. Something about invitations from Charles make me want to dress like the women from the Human League," I say.

Jenny cackles with laughter. "What the hell?"

"I mean like desperately early eighties but sophisticated. You know. A little hat with a veil. Shoulder pads. Possibly a peplum?" We're all reduced to helpless hysteria by this.

"Oh my God. A peplum?" Cerys wipes her eyes.

"Yes, and maybe patterned tights, you know. Polka dots?"

Jenny grasps my arm. "Oh, oh, or a bow on the ankle."

"Oh my God."

"A clutch?" suggests Cerys.

"Yes, to tone with the hat. I used to cut pictures out of my mum's catalogue of outfits that I thought were particularly elegant," I say. "That little hat with a bird's-eye veil is always tempting."

Jenny nods. "Like Joan Collins."

"Yes, exactly! Joan Collins in *The Bitch,* probably."

"Oh, you should. You could probably get all that in the charity shop."

"What was that woman's name," says Cerys, "the one in the Polo advert?"

"Polos?"

"No, no, you know, the VW Polo. Or Golf? Where she flounces out of the fancy mews flat and throws her fur coat away and she's going to drop the keys down the drain but changes her mind?"

Now I know what she means. "Oh, yes. Paula something. Paula Wilcox."

"No," interjects Edward, "Paula Hamilton. She was a model."

"Yes, that's right. I feel I should channel that." I make vigorous channeling motions with my hands, and Cerys snorts loudly.

"Why, though?" asks Jenny.

"I don't know. It just seems like the right thing."

"You're very silly," says Edward.

"You're just jealous," I say, laughing.

"I am not fucking jealous," he says. He slams his glass on

the table and is out of his seat and across the bar before any of us can say anything. We all stare at the door as it swings shut.

"Christ's sake," says Jenny.

"Don't go after him," says Cerys, but it's too late, I'm outside and looking about for him. There he is, stalking away toward the shop.

"Edward!"

He ignores me, and I run after him. Cerys is right. I should let him stew. But I hate being misunderstood.

"Hey!" I grab at his arm and he shakes me off. I dart ahead of him and spread my arms to stop him walking on. "Hey, what the hell's your problem?"

"I don't have a problem." His face is so thunderous I'm surprised he hasn't actually caused it to rain.

"Right. Just suddenly decided you needed to go home? After swearing at me?" He steps forward, and I step backward. And then again. I look over my shoulder quickly to make sure I'm not going to fall off the curb. We're almost at the shop.

"I wasn't swearing at you," he says. He looks awkward now, rather than angry.

"Yes you were. You said—"

"I know what I said. And it's true. I'm not fucking jealous."

"Jesus Christ. Listen to yourself. Jealous of my *silliness*, is what I meant, because you can't be silly, can you, because you're a"—I wave my arms—"giant flipping *idiot*."

We glare at each other.

"I'd have let you storm off if I thought you knew what I meant. I knew you didn't, though, because you're such a massive arse. And I hate to be misunderstood. So"—I jab my finger at his chest with each word—"don't. You. Dare. Misunderstand. Me."

He steps forward, so I step back again. "You're a—" I continue.

"What am I?"

"A giant—"

"That's just rude," he says. I can see he's trying not to laugh now, and I have to bite my lip. I'm still pissed off with him, though. Making a scene, and making me have to run after him, like he's a teenager, or my—

"What the hell is wrong with you?" I say.

"I think you put your finger on it," he says. "I'm a spectacular cu—"

I interrupt him. "Don't flatter yourself. You have neither the depth nor the warmth," I say, and then he's really laughing. "Or the charm," I add.

"Oh God, Thea Hamilton," he says, "the things you say. You're perfect—" He stumbles slightly over his words. "Perfectly ridiculous."

"It's hardly ridiculous. In fact, it's bang-on."

"This is how you talk to your boss, is it? Shocking."

We're laughing at each other, but it all feels strangely serious, or important, maybe. I'm backed against the door of the shop now, and he ducks his head toward me. For a split second, a tiny moment, I think he's going to kiss me. He doesn't, though. With his lips close enough to my ear I can feel his breath on my cheek, he says, "I think this might be a disciplinary issue."

"Oh my God." I laugh harder. "Are you going to get on to HR? That Mr. Maltravers is a tyrant."

I can't deny I'm totally thrilled by this and if he did kiss me, I'd . . . Well.

He steps back, folding his arms. "Isn't he, though? I'll tell him not to be too harsh on you, don't worry."

"I'm terrified."

"You look it. Now, if you'll get out of the way—"

"Are you going home, then?"

"Cerys has seen me make a dick of myself on numerous occasions," he says, "but I see no reason to give her the opportunity to laugh in my face."

"Oh. Well, okay," I say. I squeeze past him so I'm standing on the street. "Honestly. I can't believe I had to run after you."

"I'm amazed you did," he says. We look at each other for a moment. "I'm not worth the effort, you know."

"Keep going," I say, "you'll convince me eventually. I'll see you tomorrow."

. . .

Back in the pub, Cerys looks surprised to see me. "Oh," she says, "I didn't think you'd be back."

"My bag's here," I say, "and my keys. I wouldn't be able to get home."

They exchange glances.

"You owe me a fiver," says Jenny, and I watch, startled, as Cerys gets her wallet out, sighing, and gives her a five-pound note.

"What's that for?"

"We had a bet," says Jenny.

I pick up my handbag and narrow my eyes at her suspiciously. "What was it?"

"Never you mind. I'll win it eventually," says Cerys. "You off, then?"

"Yeah."

"Catch him, did you?"

"Oh, yeah. What the hell is wrong with him? It's like being friends with a teenager. A stupid teenager."

Jenny laughs. Cerys looks serious. "He just doesn't know how to do this stuff."

"Did he do this to you when you were first friends?"

A loud crack of laughter. "Jesus, no. Although to be fair he did get cranky on occasion."

"I can usually get him to snap out of it," I say. "But it's tiring."

Seventeen

I stand in the hallway and wait for Charles to come and collect me. I'm not nervous because I am not invested in this dinner, even if I did buy a new lipstick, but I am interested to know what he'll say in response to all the questions I'm going to ask him.

When I was leaving work this evening, Edward said, "Without wishing to sound like a prick—please don't sleep with my brother." He wasn't looking at me when he said it, attention focused on the laptop.

"Ha ha. What would you do if I did?"

"I don't know. Let's not find out, eh?"

I blew a loud and childish raspberry, and went home to get ready.

And now I'm dressed in my finery, waiting. No shoulder pads or little hat with a veil, sadly; instead I've had to make do with a sensible black shift dress, a Chinese red silk jacket, lucky finds from the charity shop—that place is just brilliant. I'm wearing my most elegant shoes, and I had to buy hold-ups in the chemist. I'm not impressed with them but hopefully they won't let me down in an embarrassing fashion. I'm dancing in the hallway because I'm in a good mood—I couldn't explain entirely why this should be, because it's not like dinner with Charles is on my bucket list. I wonder whether the staff at the hotel will call him Lord Hollinshaw? If they do, I might laugh.

When the bell rings I have to calm myself. A deep breath, and then I answer the door to a smartly dressed Charles. It's a fine evening, the last pink-gold streaks of sunset lingering in the sky.

"Hello," I say and, feeling that perhaps a handshake is less suitable this evening, I lean forward so he can kiss my cheek.

We make with the polite chitchat while I lock the front door behind me and follow him out to the car. He has more than one car, I think; this evening it's something German in dark blue with pale leather upholstery. I don't care much about cars, but it's certainly comfortable. A Mercedes. Most cars are dark inside, I realize, with black carpet so you can't really see into the footwell. When it's pale, you can see everything; it's quite odd. It's a bit different from Edward's knackered old Defender.

"Have you been across to Knockandry before?" he asks me.

"No, there's nothing much there, is there, except the hotel?"

"Not much, admittedly. There's a beach, and a golf course."

I think about asking if he plays golf, but what if he does? I don't want to talk about golf. Instead, I ask how the building work's going with the barn conversion, and we talk about that, and about the new bathroom I've had put in at the lodge. I've never had a brand-new bathroom, and it's very exciting. I go and look at it quite often, admiring the slate floor and the beauty of the freestanding bath and the fabulous shower. I probably spent more than I should have, but it's great and I love it. Now that it's done, the major inconvenience of having dust everywhere and no loo for a week is easily forgotten.

Talk about builders and plumbing gets us through the half-hour drive to the hotel. It's a very grand building: Victorian, in a rather flamboyant baronial style.

"My grandparents used to come to dances here before the war," he tells me. "And my great-grandparents would go for dinner, you know, before it was a hotel."

"Mm," I say, unimpressed. Then I remember that these people were also Edward's ancestors. I tell myself that doesn't make them any more interesting, but it kind of does. I stand beside the car and look up at the turrets and castellations. It's huge; no wonder it's been a hotel for eighty years. How could anyone ever afford to keep it up?

"Back in those days, of course," he adds, "everyone had a London house as well as somewhere in the Highlands for the shooting."

Jesus. It's not right, is it? I know I find it fascinating, but it's still not right.

We crunch across the gravel and round the corner of the building. A wide sweep of drive, a fountain, formal gardens dropping down to the coast, the darkness of the ocean.

"Can't see much of the view now it's getting dark," he says, "which is a shame. It's very dramatic."

A smartly dressed doorman opens the door for us and we walk through to a vast marble-floored entrance hall. In the center of the room is an enormous display of cut flowers in an urn on a huge shiny table. Dozens of mounted antlers demonstrate the deer-killing expertise of the previous owners. There are tweedy drapes in a subtle tartan and large, comfortable leather sofas arranged in front of an immense fireplace. The front desk is so discreet as to barely be there at all. I don't have much time to look around, though, as we're quickly ushered toward the staircase. The dining room is on the first floor, above the entrance hall, making the most of those views across the gardens and the sea.

"I always sit at the window," Charles says, leading the way between the white-clothed tables. There are a number of other couples here already, and a family party at the far end of the room. The tables are round, there's carpet, everything's hushed and elegant. I'm looking forward to seeing the menu. One waiter takes my jacket, and another pulls my chair out for me, flicking the napkin out and draping it across my lap. They bring the wine list and the menu and I look about me with interest.

"So you come here a lot?"

"Fairly regularly. It's the best place this side of Dumfries. In my opinion."

I nod and return my attention to the menu. I haven't been out to an actual restaurant for dinner for ages. The last time I went somewhere special was with Chris—was that our anniversary? Last September, if so; we went up to London and had dinner at Murano. A year ago, but it seems like fifty. Chris bought me a necklace, which I left behind when I took all my stuff. I'd been wearing it before that, but it seemed, well . . . I left it behind, anyway.

We talk for a bit about food and other places we've had dinner. I'm not sure whether he cares about food or whether he just cares about going to places with a good reputation. I find Charles much harder to read than Edward, but that's probably because I don't make as much effort.

When our starters arrive, I say, "I've been wondering why you wanted to have dinner with me."

He looks surprised. "I thought . . . I thought it would be good to spend an evening together and get to know you better."

"Really?"

"You sound skeptical," he says.

"I am a bit."

He frowns at me and looks quite a lot more like his brother than usual. I find this amusing.

"But why?"

"I can't imagine I'm the sort of person you generally go on things that aren't 'not dates' with," I say, and begin to slice up my smoked trout.

"Why would you say that? I don't ask just anyone out to dinner, you know."

"I'm sure you don't, and this is lovely"—I wave my knife at the dining room—"but it's still true."

"Thea—"

"I shall be blunt," I say. "I hope you don't mind. But the thing is, you see, I can't imagine that I'm suitable material for the next Lady Hollinshaw. And if you want to start something less serious, then Michelin stars seem overenthusiastic." I grin at him. "D'you see?"

"That's . . . I—"

"So you can see why I might be skeptical. I suspect an ulterior motive."

He takes a sip of water. "An ulterior motive."

"Yes. I'm not angry or anything," I add. "I'm just . . . I want to be sure you understand that you have to be honest with me. Until January I spent some time—possibly several years—living with someone who was telling an enormous and fundamental lie. I have no interest in repeating that on any level."

"Your husband. I didn't want to ask what happened," he says. "He lied to you?"

"Yes. He had an affair with a friend of mine. For an unspecified length of time. I know you've been in a similar situation," I say. "And it isn't very nice. And so I wonder, about Miranda, and you, and me, and . . . so on."

"I said before, Miranda and I—"

"Yes, and to be honest I'm not that concerned about Miranda. But what would she think if she knew we were here having dinner?"

There's quite a long pause, which I use to finish my starter. The wine I ordered is good; it's probably lucky I'm not drinking loads of it, though. I wonder how different I might feel if I cared about any of this. But I don't, and it's terribly liberating. I look around the room again. It's almost entirely dark outside now, and I can see the room behind me reflected in the glass of the window. There are a few more people here now; everyone's dressed up. I wonder how many of these couples are staying here. I'll look on the website when I get home, see what the rooms are like. I eat the last piece of bread from the shiny dish on the table and smile at my companion.

"And I suppose I wonder," I say, having just thought of it, "why you're not going out with Miranda in a normal sort of way. She seems suitable."

"Suitable," says Charles. I can't tell if he's annoyed with me or just embarrassed.

"Yes, you know, she's more like you, isn't she? More than I am."

"It's because you're not like Miranda that I wanted to have dinner," he says.

"Oh, okay, is it?" I was right, then, about being a bit of rough. I wonder if there's a way to express that without actually saying it. "Slumming it, are we?"

"Thea." He looks pained. "I'm not sure why you think—"

"Oh, come on. Look—the thing is, Charles, one of the reasons I'm suspicious of your motives is because I'm friends with your brother and I know you hate him." He opens his mouth and I hold up my hand. "I'm not really interested in the ins and outs or whys and wherefores. I know Edward has behaved badly in the past, but I think you have too. I'd like to think that you and I get on well, and I wouldn't like to think that you feel"—here I wait for a moment as the table is cleared by the waiter—"there'd be any mileage in getting, I don't know, closer to me in order to annoy him. I'm not saying it *would* annoy him. But you know, I'm not a bit part or a pawn or anything like that."

"Thea, really, I . . ."

I smile encouragingly.

"I would absolutely never do anything like that," he says.

"Jolly good. Glad to hear it." I lean both elbows on the table. "It would be quite upsetting."

Our main courses arrive and for a moment we're distracted. I wonder, though, what Edward would do if I slept with Charles?

Obviously, I never would.

But if I did?

He'd be angry, I expect, but only because of it being Charles. Having said that, though, he was peculiar about Keith.

I think I'm being odd about Edward. Well, I know I am. I'm trying hard not to think about any of that. I still think the way I feel about Edward—and as I say, I'm refusing to consider how I do feel—is somehow unreal, caused by the situation I find myself in, by the spaces in my life and the amount of time we spend together. He makes me laugh, and he's handsome, and I am an idiot. Even if he's odd about me too, it's meaningless and stupid.

But I'm supposed to be listening to Charles.

"It does . . . It's true I find it awkward that you're friends with my brother," he says. "Because it means I have to try not to say what I think about him, and usually I don't bother guarding my tongue."

"You can say what you like." I shrug. "I mean, I'd take it all with a pinch of salt."

"You like him, though."

"I do like him, yes. I find him entertaining and he's always been nice to me, or fairly nice." I smile at the thought of Edward's reaction to being described as nice.

"It would be impolite of me to be rude about him to you, then. And he's your employer."

"Oh yes, and I'm terribly loyal," I say. "So come on, Charles, why are we here?"

"I just, well, I thought . . ."

I'm eating duck now, and it's delicious. I certainly can't argue with the food here; it's great. Not terribly exciting, maybe, but well constructed and cooked. I suppose they know their audience. It's not somewhere you'd want to be wildly innovative.

"Yes?"

He sighs. "I don't know. Everything you've said is perfectly reasonable. Maybe I should be trying to meet someone I can . . . It's not very romantic, though, is it? I may as well put an ad in the paper: 'wife required.' I've been putting it off. It didn't go well—it hasn't gone well—when I've done it before. And you're . . . I think you're . . ." He sighs again. "I don't know. Maybe you're right to question my motives."

"I'm just a bit suspicious? Sadly, the world doesn't usually offer opportunities like this to women my age, unless the men in question are considerably older. But you're not that much older than I am, are you? And I'm not beautiful, or rich, and I don't just happen to own land adjacent to the park at Hollinshaw; and although I know you want the lodge, you don't need to fuck me to get it."

He chokes on his roast beef. I watch, amused, as he coughs, red-faced, and drinks more water. When his eyes have stopped streaming, I say, "Sorry, that was my fault."

"No, no. Well." He smiles, maybe the first genuinely full-on convincing smile I've seen from him. "It was your fault, but I don't mind. It's . . . That's not what this is about."

"Good."

"I mean, I . . . I'm not trying to acquire the lodge. I want it, yes, but that's not why I asked you to have dinner."

"You see why I might suspect you, though."

"Yes."

"And if I was having dinner with you because I thought you liked me, I might be concerned you have all sorts of motives that aren't really about me."

"Yes. But—"

"But luckily for you, I don't mind," I say. "Because although you're perfectly nice, and very pleasant company, I'm not in the market for boyfriends, or gentlemen companions, or even just sex."

"You're not?"

I laugh. "No."

"That's . . . um."

"What?"

"It's disappointing."

"Is it? After everything I've said?"

"Well," he says, suddenly less awkward, "I'd rather you didn't think those things. But I still find you very . . ." He pauses, choosing his words carefully. "Appealing."

"Appealing. That's nice."

"I've been divorced twice," he says. "I think . . . my second marriage was a mistake. Not just because of what happened. I tried to stop that happening, but I failed. I used to think that was Carolyn's fault, or my brother's—but really I suppose it was mine."

"I'm no expert, but it was probably everyone's."

"You know about all that?"

"Some of it," I admit cautiously.

"And the rest? You know he followed me around, for years, sleeping with my girlfriends?"

"Mostly ex-girlfriends, surely?"

"Just as upsetting, though, if I'm honest." He looks at the tablecloth. "People seemed to think it was funny. And sometimes . . . Well. It isn't pleasant, when people compare you, even if it's supposed to be a joke."

I shrug. "I don't imagine it is. But you can see why I was a bit suspicious about this meal."

"You think I'd do the same. But you said you're not . . . that you haven't . . . with Edward?"

"No. But I was still wary."

They're clearing the plates again and asking if we want to see the dessert menu. I do, of course, even though I hardly ever have dessert.

"I feel as though I've spoiled the evening," he says.

"Oh no, not at all. I'm enjoying myself." I smile at him. "And it's best to get everything out in the open, isn't it?"

Eighteen

I'm late to work this morning, due to a dentist's appointment. I'm proud of myself for proactively booking a checkup even though I don't live here. Because it's not a very big place, I've met the dentist, Louise, and her assistant, Bonnie, before, once at an evening thing at the Old Mill, and once at Jenny and Alistair's. I didn't know my previous dentist socially; it's a bit odd. And they always ask you questions, don't they, when your mouth is open and you can't answer. Fortunately all is well. She bullies me slightly into making a hygienist's appointment and then releases me back into the world. I hurry along the high street, keen to reach the shop before ten. It's about nine-forty, so I expect the shop to be open, but it isn't. I fish through my handbag for the key and unlock the door. Pulling up the blind and looking around, I see the lamps are off and so is the laptop.

"Edward?" I call tentatively. No answer. He must have overslept. First time for everything. I know he's home; his car's outside. I put my bag away and turn on the computer, and then go round the shop switching on the lights. I put the kettle on and stand at the foot of the stairs for a moment, listening. I can hear him moving around upstairs, so he's not dead, at least.

"Hello?"

"Thea?"

"No, I'm a burglar that has broken in. I am stealing everything."

"Oh, okay, carry on," he says, coming down the stairs. He's eating something from a bowl, and his hair is wet. "Sorry. Slept late." He looks exhausted, eyes shadowed.

"Are you okay?"

"Yeah. Bit of a dake."

"Oh, poor you. Is it bad? Have you taken pills? I just put the kettle on; d'you want a cuppa?"

"Go and get a proper coffee, would you? Take some money from the till," he says. "Get yourself one as well."

"Right-oh. Anything else?"

He sighs. "If there's any chance of a bacon sarnie . . ."

"I'll see. It might be a bit late for bacon at the Old Mill."

"Beg Cerys for a favor. She must have a secret stash."

I laugh. "Okay. If they don't have any, I could buy some from the butcher's for you."

"You're an angel."

I roll my eyes. "Flap, flap," I say.

...

"Operation Bacon Sandwich is go," I tell him, putting the greasy bag on the counter. "Also, coffee."

"Oh God, thank you."

"No worries. Hangover?"

"No." He takes the sandwich and turns away.

I hoist myself up onto the counter and take the lid off my coffee. We don't often have coffee from the coffee shop—it seems wasteful when we have a perfectly good kettle here, and it's not like Edward buys shit coffee. We have the fanciest instant money can buy, and a cafetière as well for when he can't face even that. It makes a change to have coffee-shop coffee sometimes, though; it reminds me of my old job, when I bought a giant latte from Costa on the way to work every day.

It's funny how rarely I think of my old work life. Sometimes I think about my colleagues, some of whom I was fond of, but I don't miss anything about it at all; not the journey, which was awkward, involving the worst bits of the one-way system; or the offices, which were badly built and ugly and stuck on a windswept business estate on the outskirts of town with infuriatingly generic "planting" in the car park, four lifts, at least one of which was always broken, and an inconvenient security system, which meant you couldn't spend cash in the canteen but had to put money on your ID card using one of the two machines in the basement, one of which, again, was always broken. And I don't miss the pointless meetings where people wrote things on whiteboards and no one took any minutes and nothing was ever achieved. Looking back, I think when the company that provided the office plants came and took them all away because no one had paid the fee for them to be watered, it was probably a sign that all was not well with Data Tech Solutions.

I sip my coffee and think about my plans for the day. I need to tweet about the books Edward bought last week. I wonder where they are.

"You didn't shelve the new stuff, did you?"

"No, it's all still in the boxes. I put them in Poetry. Some of 'em are heavy; I'll move them for you."

"Okay. Did you have a good weekend?"

"Not really," he says, but I don't get the impression he wants to talk about it. I consider my response. He didn't work Friday or Saturday; I think he was away.

He finishes his sandwich and wipes his fingers with a paper napkin. "What about you? How was your 'not a date' with my brother? Are you engaged?"

I laugh. "Idiot. No, it was okay. Food was nice."

"Is that it?" He raises his eyebrows. "Poor effort on Charles's part if that's all you have to say about it."

I shrug. "I told you it wasn't a significant event."

"Ouch. Did he ask you back for coffee?"

I laugh again. "No he didn't. I told him I wasn't interested, and I didn't think he was interested either, and basically could we not have some complicated thing going on, because I can't be bothered."

"You just came out with all that?" He shakes his head at me.

"Well, I'm paraphrasing. But essentially."

"What did he say?"

"Oh, he got a bit flustered but it turned out okay." I grin at him. "I don't think he's used to people being blunt with him."

"Probably not. Surrounded by sycophants."

"*Pfft.* That seems harsh. Anyway. So what, did you go to Edinburgh?"

"Yes."

I wait to see if he's going to say anything else, but he doesn't. I take the scissors from behind the counter and go through to Poetry to open the boxes. It's very quiet this morning, we haven't had a single customer yet. I slice open the first box and begin to unpack the books. A few minutes later, he comes out to join me. Instead of moving boxes, though, he sits on the sofa and closes his eyes. I regard him sympathetically. I've never seen him look so knackered, almost fragile.

"Should you have stayed in bed?" I ask.

"No, I'll be fine in a minute."

"Sure? You don't look fine."

"Late night. Didn't get home until half four or something."

"Blimey. I'd be dead."

"Yeah, well." He sighs, blinking, and yawns.

"Were you, um . . ." I pause in my unpacking, thinking about what I want to ask. I don't want to be nosy. Or at least, I don't want to *sound* nosy. "How come you got in so late?"

"Massive, spectacular row." He sighs again. "Should have left a lot earlier, but you know how it is."

"Oh. Shouting?"

"Lots of shouting."

"Both of you?"

"Mostly her." He smiles at me. "I don't care enough to shout."

I wince at this. I wonder if this lack of caring is why she shouts at him.

"It's all very boring," he says. "I sometimes wonder . . . But this is not interesting, I'm sorry."

"Sometimes wonder what?"

He sits up and we look at each other. "Oh, nothing. It doesn't matter; it's not important."

"What were you fighting about?"

"Yeah, that's not interesting either. Same old shit."

I turn to the second box and unzip the tape. "Do you have a nice time, though? You and Lara?"

"A nice time?"

"Yeah, you know, like"—I pretend to concentrate on removing books from the box—"does she make you laugh? Or do you make her laugh?"

"I went arse over tit on George Street once in the snow. Thought I'd busted my coccyx. She thought that was hilarious."

"That's not exactly what I meant. I mean, fun. D'you have fun?"

"Fun? Huh. The short answer is no, not really."

"And the long answer?"

"Also no."

"Oh, Edward," I say. "That's . . . well. It's a shame is what it is."

He shrugs. "It doesn't matter. Do you want me to take that last box through, then?"

...

After lunch, he says, "Oh, I forgot. I got you this. For selling all those history books last week."

I look at him, but his face is bland and unreadable. "It's my job to sell books, isn't it? You don't need to buy me things."

"I know, but I don't pay you very much, do I? So think of it as a token." He puts a little brown paper packet on the counter.

I look at it. "I don't think you should buy me things. Unless it's my birthday."

"When *is* your birthday?"

"June."

"Well, I missed it, then, didn't I? Were you in? I mean, did you work?"

I nod. "Yeah, it was a Tuesday."

"You should have said." He frowns at me. "Why didn't you?"

I shrug. "It was fine. We did have cake; I bought you a Belgian bun."

"We'll have to do better for your next birthday." He's still frowning. "D'you think you'll still be here?"

"Who knows? Perhaps."

"Open it, then," he says, nodding at the packet. I pick it up; it weighs hardly anything. I tear off the wrapping and remove the dark blue tissue paper within. A tiny silver spoon, barely the length of my little finger. There isn't room for three initials on the handle, but there's an elegantly curled *A*.

"Oh, that's lovely." I look at him. "What is it? Coke spoon?"

He snorts. "No, it's not a coke spoon. Jesus. It's a salt spoon, I think, or a mustard spoon."

"It's charming. Thank you."

He's turned away, stooping to look for something in one of the desk drawers. "You're welcome."

"Please don't buy me anything else, though; I feel bad."

"You needn't. I wasn't looking for something to buy you; I just spotted it. I spend a lot of time poking about in the sort of places they have that kind of thing. And it didn't cost much."

"That's what you said last time."

"Ha, well, this was even cheaper. And older—it's Georgian. 1801."

"How cheap? Was it less than twenty pounds?"

He nods. "Twelve quid."

"Oh, okay. That seems reasonable. Okay. Thanks. It's lovely. Maybe I should start a spoon collection."

"Prepared to accept it, then, are you?"

"Yes. I've probably bought you twelve quid's worth of buns, so, yes."

"Good."

"But seriously, don't buy me anything else unless it's Christmas, or—"

"Why not?"

"It isn't seemly," I say primly.

He laughs. "I'd hate to be unseemly."

"Well, it isn't, is it? It makes me feel . . ."

He's looking at me intently. "Makes you feel what?"

"I don't know." I'm embarrassed, and stoop to push the spoon into the front pocket of my bag.

"I thought everyone liked presents."

"Yes, but that's not the point."

...

I've been thinking about whether I should go home. I've been here a lot longer than I originally intended, after all, and I've been pretty much ignoring everything that must be going on in Sussex. So maybe I should go back. Not permanently— at least not yet—but to see Chris. I think I'm so far "out of sight out of mind" that he's forgotten he's meant to be remortgaging the house. I'm still paying my share, after all, as well as rent on my empty flat and the fee for my storage unit. I don't want to keep paying for Susanna to live in my house; it's not fair. However childish that sounds. I've been worrying about it, and although I had an email from him yesterday where he reassured me that he's in the process of sorting things out, he's said that before and I still don't have my hundred and fifty grand or whatever. I need to make some plans. Xanthe sent me a link for the developers who are building out on the coast road back home. The flats look good, and I could live in one or rent it out, depending on what I decide to do. It would be good to have some income, even though I'm sure letting agencies are tiresome to deal with. The house is the next step in the process. Once that's sorted, we just have to get divorced, and pretty soon it will only be a year before that can happen without us having to go to court.

Edward's in an unnaturally good mood this morning; he even whistled while he was making coffee. Admittedly, it was "Famous Blue Raincoat" he was whistling, rather than "Sunshine, Lollipops and Rainbows," but nonetheless. It's a week or so since his fight with Lara. He hasn't mentioned it again; but then, why would he?

"You're perky," I say, holding out my mug so he can top it up with milk.

"I doubt I've ever been perky."

I laugh. It does seem unlikely. "Unnaturally chipper."

"Yeah, well, I'm in a good mood." He flashes a grin at me.

"Any particular reason?"

"Yes, actually. I've made some life changes. I think you'll approve."

I take my coffee back toward the front of the shop. "Will I?"

"Mm. I've knocked it on the head. With Lara."

"Oh my God, have you?" I turn back to look at him. "What brought that on?"

"I'd been thinking about what you said. And about the way I haven't had fun with Lara for . . . Well, maybe we never had fun. I can't remember it ever being anything but a god-awful slog."

"Wow. I do approve. Not that it's any of my business. But it did seem a bit pointless. What happened, then?"

"I drove up there last night after work. Told her I couldn't be bothered with it anymore."

I close my eyes briefly. "Bloody hell. I don't like the woman, but could you not have been even slightly tactful?"

He snorts. "Yeah, okay, I didn't say it quite like that. I said it seemed like hard work, and I know it's not working how she wants, and blah blah."

"What a gent. And?"

"And she took it pretty well."

"No shouting?"

"No, remarkably."

"Did you fuck her?"

"Thea, you know sometimes you surprise me," he says, looking pained.

"What?" I take a swig of coffee. "I'm just interested. I mean, people do stuff like that, don't they? Once more for old times' sake and all that." I grin at him. "Even I've done that."

"No, I didn't fuck her."

"Did you want to?"

"No." He sighs. "You know that's been part of the problem."

"What, that you didn't want to—"

"Things have been unsatisfactory on that front for a while. For both of us."

I'm pleased about this, even though it absolutely is none of my business. I'm not going to remotely consider examining my reaction. "I suppose there's no point if you don't like each other and you're not even getting any."

"Quite."

...

I'm on my own in the shop today, as I have been all week. I've been wrestling with pumpkins all morning, sorting out the window display for Halloween: leaves from the Virginia creeper drifting, some battery-operated tea lights in a pair of turnip lanterns that I spent hours carving last night. I have a blister on my palm from hollowing them out; they're much harder to work with than pumpkins, but more traditional. The pumpkins are just going in an autumnal pile. We're going to lean a broomstick against the wall; it's all quite subtle. Becky, the postwoman, breezes in with a parcel, sending the bell clanging.

"Needs signing for," she says.

It isn't very big, about the size of an egg carton, and is addressed to me, which is unusual. I scrawl my name unreadably on her electronic paperwork and look at the package. I haven't ordered anything; I can't think what this could be. I tear open the padded envelope to find an actual egg carton inside. Taped to the lid there's a note.

I'm sending these so you don't have to open them while I'm there. Consider this a late birthday gift. And none of your whinging about how I shouldn't buy you stuff. Not interested. E.

I tut loudly. At the same time, I'm intrigued, and pleased of course. He was right; who doesn't like presents? Even though I'm still a bit uncomfortable accepting gifts from my boss. But anyway. More spoons?

I slice through the tape sealing the egg box shut and open it. Each of the six egg compartments holds a wrapped something. I purse my lips and unwrap one.

It's a napkin ring. Silver and decorated, naturally, with a monogram of my initials. It's beautiful, very plain and stylish. I pause and unwrap two more and see that they are all the same. The hallmarks are on the back, rather than inside. I sit down at the laptop and look them up. These are Glasgow, like my tablespoon. 1857. By the looks of things, even though they're not boxed, they probably cost him the best part of three hundred quid.

"I don't think I can accept these," I say out loud. It doesn't seem right. Even if they'd come on my birthday. Bearing in mind at that point I'd only known him six weeks or something, it would have been extremely odd for him to give me expensive antique napkin rings. But say it was my birthday today—it still seems wrong. I feel very odd about it. As with my tablespoon, I assume he can afford it and doesn't think much about spending three hundred pounds on a random gift. But that doesn't make it okay. No. I can see they won't be much good to him, or as a gift for someone else, but he'll be able to sell them on eBay I expect, or maybe back to the person he bought them off. I rummage in my bag for my phone and send him a message.

> Hey. Thank you for the napkin rings. They're lovely.
> I can't accept them though. Sorry to be a pain, but you spending that much money on me makes me uncomfortable. It would take quite a lot of buns to make it up to you. I'll put them in the safe. I appreciate the sentiment and everything, don't think I'm ungrateful. T.

I put my phone down on the desk and sell some books to a young couple who are up here on their honeymoon. They're both glowing with happiness and make me feel a bit tearful. They've each bought the other one of their favorite books; it's very sweet. I wrap the books up for them. This is a new thing; I've hung a wide roll of lovely brown paper behind the desk, and bought string in a dozen colors. If it's not busy—and it's never that busy—I make beautiful brown-paper parcels. Everyone loves a brown-paper parcel tied up with string. The woman is delighted and has taken a photo for Instagram almost before I've finished.

"Tag the shop," I say, and then we talk about Instagram for ten minutes. I feel it's an extremely successful customer interaction, and one Edward would never have had. I'm an asset, it's true, but not a three-hundred-pound-gift asset.

Next there's an older couple buying some Noddy books in hardback, and one of our regulars, who buys new books here and has come in for the latest Ian Rankin. We don't have a particularly wide selection of new books, but Edward always orders books by Scottish authors and we have two shelves of modern Scottish detective fiction.

I forget about the message I sent and don't look at my phone again until I'm eating my lunch.

Fuck off, is all the response he's sent me, which makes me laugh.

No, seriously.

Not interested.

Edward.

Thea.

Please don't fight with me about this.

The phone rings. "I'm not fighting with you," he says. "Hello."

"Hi, yeah. Look—"

"No, you look. It's my business what I do with my money. I can buy you anything I want."

I laugh at this. "You can't."

"Yes, I can."

"No, you can't. There are loads of things you can't buy me." I empty the remains of a packet of potato chips into my mouth.

"Such as?"

"Love," I say, indistinctly through a mouthful of chips. "Excuse me. Um, happiness. Famously, no one can buy those things. And other stuff that's less"—I wave a hand, not that he can see me—"you know, esoteric. I'd think it bizarre and inappropriate if you bought me underwear, or even outerwear, for instance. I suppose maybe a scarf or something would be okay."

This has thrown him, I think. No response.

"Um, sex toys—that would be wrong. Diet books. Any kind of self-help book, in fact. Pornography. It would be weird if you bought me perfume, or bubble bath, or Class A drugs, or bedsheets."

"You are the strangest woman I've ever met," he says. I'm glad he's not here, because this makes my face burn with embarrassment.

"No I'm not. How rude."

"You are. I hardly think buying you some napkin rings is the equivalent of buying you heroin. Or porn, or a vibrator. Jesus Christ."

"No, but it's inappropriate, is my point. Not the object, in this case, but the cost. Can't you see that?"

"You're boring me now," he says.

I laugh, but it won't change my mind. "Anyway," I say, "I've put them in the safe. And when will you be back?"

"About half an hour."

"Really? You're not driving, are you?"

"No, I'm at the farm shop. Want anything? I suppose you'd accept a cabbage, would you, or some artisanal bread?"

"Oh, yes. If they have the sourdough, can you buy me some? I'll pay you back."

"Jesus." I hear him sigh heavily. "See you later."

Nineteen

It's a perfectly normal Wednesday, or at least, a perfectly normal Wednesday in my strange new perfectly normal life. I've been at work about two hours, we've had our first coffee, Edward's shown me some books on the internet that will be in a sale later in the month and we've talked again about whether we should move Local History to the front of the shop, which I've been arguing for since I started. When my phone pings I don't have a premonition of disaster or anything. I pull it from the pocket of my jeans and look. A message from Xanthe.

I open it. Susanna's pregnant, it says.

I feel the strangest feeling in my belly, from right down at the core of my being. An enormous visceral expulsion of air and pain—like puking, only not. And a strange noise, like a huge dry sob, which I don't at first realize has come from me.

"Are you okay? Thea?"

The phone pings again.

Sorry. Didn't know how to tell you. Phone me, says Xanthe. I put the phone down carefully on the counter.

"Excuse me," I say, and try to walk unhurriedly to the curtain in the hallway that conceals the kitchenette and the loo. There's a customer standing right beside it, though, looking at Children's (Collectible).

"Sorry," I manage, "I need to . . ."

The toilet is at the end of a short corridor, beyond the sink and kettle. It's a narrow windowless room, lit with a horrible low-watt bulb. There's an ancient sink and an old-fashioned loo with a high-level cistern. I manage to close the door and lift the seat before I'm sick.

Objectively, I'm rather surprised at my reaction. I can't think of anything else that I've ever reacted to so physically. And I'd thought of it, after all. I'd wondered that day at the Shed about this happening. I was sort of testing myself, though. I didn't think it really would. Chris has never wanted to have children. Or has he? It seems I've no idea, and the fact that I don't know, that he's as mysterious to me as any-one, when once he was the person I knew best in the world, makes me cry. I pull the clanking chain to flush the loo and wash my hands and face in the tiny sink, drinking water from my cupped hands, but I don't stop crying. I stare at myself in the cracked mirror.

"Look at you," I mutter, "no wonder. No wonder. Jesus Christ."

"Thea? Are you okay? What's happened?" Edward's voice is muffled by the door. Oh shit. Nothing's ever private, is it? Nothing happens in isolation. You're always exposed, forced to explain.

"Nothing, I'm fine," I say, splashing at my face.

"Are you sure?"

I don't know what to say, so I ignore him and continue to cry, trying not to make too much noise. I blow my nose and wash my face again.

Maybe this time I'll never stop crying.

I knew it was over. I've known that since January. I never expected him to change his mind. I've never thought that one day it will all be okay, or at least not for months. I've been . . . getting better, haven't I? Getting over it? Or have I? I can't believe it. Chris is forty-seven. When this child's at university he'll be nearly seventy. It will be the youngest of four and surely its siblings will hate it.

But that's none of my business. I don't need to worry about it, don't need to be concerned for the poor child. It's nothing to do with me. I'll just be "Dad's first wife," if they even ever tell the child about me. I don't know why this makes me cry even harder, but it does.

"Thea? Come out, please."

"I don't want to." I squeeze my eyes shut, as though that might stop the tears.

"There's no one here, or hardly anyone. I'll close up."

"Don't be silly. I'm fine," I tell him through the door.

"Thea, please."

I unbolt the door unwillingly and pull the string, turning the light off. The short piece of corridor is shadowy behind the curtain.

"Sorry," I say, "I must have, um—"

"Are you all right?" He peers at me in the gloom.

"I was sick. Sorry."

"Shit, were you? You should go and lie down."

"No, I'm fine."

"Don't be stupid. Go upstairs and lie on the sofa. I'll lock up."

"You don't need to close the shop, honestly. I'll be all right in a moment. I just . . . I had a bit of a shock."

"Upstairs," he says, "now."

We stare at each other for a moment. I think about arguing. But then I think I'd like to lie down.

"Okay. Sorry."

"Don't apologize, for God's sake. Just go upstairs."

. . .

I climb the wide and elegant stairs and unfasten the gold-
painted childproof gate on the landing, ignoring the notice
that says PRIVATE NO ENTRY. Anyone coming up here to pick
through the Engineering/Naval History section can basically
see into Edward's home—a little way into the sitting room
on the left, the kitchen on the right and up the next flight of
stairs. I've still only been up here alone, to feed Holly Hunter
when Edward's away. I go into the sitting room, which is
bright and sunny and quite unlike my mood. I sit down in
the corner of the sofa and allow myself to cry some more.
Why not, eh? But Jesus, I'm tired of all this. Tired of it. I
don't want to feel like this. I don't want to feel anything.

I wonder when Chris will tell me of this new development. I suppose they'll want to get married, so we'll have to
get divorced, and that means going to court, I think. I haven't
paid much attention, because we'd agreed we'd wait out the
two years of separation and have what is essentially a no-
fault agreement, since I had no desire to stand up and accuse
him of any of the things he's done. It's childish, isn't it? And
it all sounds so old-fashioned, bleating about adultery. Christ.

"Hey," says Edward, coming to find me a few minutes
later. He hands me a glass of water, which I drain, gratefully.
He puts the empty glass on the end table and comes and sits

beside me while I try, unsuccessfully, to stop sobbing. "I brought your phone," he says. "You had some more messages."

I take it from him, but don't look at it. I assume the messages will be from Xanthe, asking if I'm okay, telling me to phone her.

"Is . . . ? Are you . . . ?"

"I'm fine."

"Um. It's none of my business. But you're clearly not fine."

I sniff, shuddering. It's so ridiculous to be crying like this. I feel stupid.

"They're having a baby," I tell him. "Chris and Susanna."

He says nothing. There's nothing to say, is there? We sit on the sofa and I try to control myself, but I can't help the awful noise I'm making. Ugly crying, the worst.

"Hey," he says eventually. He moves closer, turning toward me. "Hey. Don't—you'll make yourself ill."

I do feel like I'm on the edge of hysteria; not a good look.

"Thea."

I blow my nose for the fiftieth time.

"Hey. Look—come here," he says, and puts his arms around me. I wasn't expecting a hug; he's not a huggy person, I don't think. But he hugs me, even though I'm covered in tears and snot. He rubs my back and makes soothing noises. I cry into his shoulder.

"I'm sorry," he says. "That's pretty shit."

"Yeah." I try to reach my face with my sleeve, but I can't. We sit there for ages, Edward stroking my back as I gradually stop crying. I close my eyes and feel myself relaxing. Eventually, I pull away so I can blow my nose.

"I'm sorry. You didn't need to close the shop."

"Don't be stupid. Of course I did. Look at the state of you."

I hang my head. "Yeah, I know, sorry. Thanks."

"Thea. Stop apologizing. Why are you apologizing? You haven't done anything wrong." He puts his hand on mine and rubs his thumb on my knuckles. I find this deeply confusing. But I don't say anything or move my hand.

"I feel stupid. And . . ." But I'm not going to discuss it with him, am I, that would be—

"Why don't you have any children?"

I stare at him. People don't usually just ask. Or at least, I know people do, but no one's ever asked me, not straight out like that.

"I—"

"Did you want to? Or not?"

"I . . . Okay," I say. "Um. I don't work properly, inside. The babies get away."

He looks at me, and I laugh, awkward. "I had a miscarriage when we were first married. We weren't trying to have children. It wasn't awful or anything. It was only, like, six weeks, and I was only twenty-seven. It didn't seem . . . It was fine. I'd been a bit frightened about being pregnant. I didn't feel like I was ready. Anyway, people have m-miscarriages all the time, sometimes they don't even realize."

He's looking at me intently. I feel very exposed. I take a shuddering breath.

"And then I had another one, later. We still weren't trying to have a baby. But I suppose we weren't trying not to either."

I remember the winter morning, the bathroom light, how cold it seemed. It feels like a long time ago, a lifetime. I was a different person then. It's hard to . . . I've always pushed it away, the memory.

"That one was worse. At the hospital they said if we were . . . if we wanted to try, you know—it would probably be okay. But I didn't want it to be something I got obsessed about. Worrying, and counting days, and all that pressure. And he didn't . . . he always said he didn't want children. That's what he said. That he'd never really wanted any. And I've never really been interested. In children. I mean, they're okay." I laugh a watery laugh. "But I could never imagine, you know, being a . . . having any. So we didn't."

I plait my fingers together and look at the veins on the backs of my hands. I'm not sure when they started to show so clearly. Another sign of aging, I suppose. "But maybe he was lying the whole time. Maybe he just said that, because he thought that's what . . . and . . . but I would've. If he'd said. If he'd told me. I just. I'd have done anything." I laugh again. "That makes it sound like having a family is an unusual thing, rather than perfectly normal. But I, um . . . It upsets me," I say, a massive understatement, "to think that perhaps that's what he wanted, and I didn't know, and now—"

"Shit," says Edward. He puts his hand to my face and wipes tears away with his fingers.

"I'm sorry. You don't want to hear all about that."

"Thea."

"It's dull, isn't it? I just . . . I don't want to feel like I've messed everything up."

"You haven't, have you? It was Chris who did that. He slept with your friend."

"I . . . Yes."

"And even if . . . He should have talked to you about it if he wanted to have a family. You're his wife."

"Yes."

"I don't think he did it on purpose," he says. "Or if he did, I bet that wasn't his plan when he started."

"When he started?"

"Sleeping with your friend."

"Oh. No. Probably not."

"Was it from him? The message?"

"No. No, from Xanthe. God knows how she knows about it. Maybe they're telling everyone already." This gives me such a feeling of desolation, I could howl. "I just feel . . . I was feeling better. I mean, still awful. Maybe I've been in denial about it all up here, but I felt like . . . I might get to a point . . . And now I just feel like it must have been my fault. I thought that to start with, but then I thought, no, I didn't do anything wrong. It's just, it's just one of those things, stuff like this happens, it's not . . . But now I—"

"It's pretty shit, yes. But it's not your fault. And you will get through it, and you will be all right."

"Will I? I don't know if I will. I don't know if . . . I feel like he must just think he wasted all that time. All that time we were together, he could have been with someone else, having babies, and . . ."

"Hey. Don't cry. Come on now." He pulls me closer again, but this time he doesn't hug me, he kisses the tears away instead.

And then we're kissing, and that's unexpected, but I—

We kiss for ages. I stop thinking after a while and just feel his lips and tongue and his hand on my face. It's . . . extraordinarily blissful. I didn't expect him to kiss me and anyone would agree it probably isn't the best time for kissing. I guess I'm at quite a low ebb. Vulnerable, even. But I don't want him to stop, because—well, for all kinds of reasons.

When we do stop, though, and pull away and look at each other, I know at once that he's sorry, and that it was accidental.

"Shit," he says. "Oh God. I'm so sorry."

"It doesn't matter." I can't look at him. If I do, I'll just start crying again.

"I didn't mean—"

"I know. It doesn't matter, please don't worry." I pull myself together. Sobbing, puking, spilling my secrets—the whole thing's been a mistake, hasn't it?

His walls have gone up; he drops my hand and stands up. "Tea," he says, "I'll make some tea." Then he's gone, and I pull my legs up, sitting with my face laid on my knees. I'd cry some more but I think I'm actually all cried out. I close my eyes and think of Alison Moyet. How old was I when she sang that? Quite young. Twelve, perhaps. Certainly too young to understand this feeling of emptiness and exhaustion.

What happens when your boss kisses you and then decides he's made a mistake? That's going to be awkward, isn't it? At least we can both claim emotional . . . something. I mean he won't . . . My actions must have been because I was upset, and so I needn't be embarrassed or worry that he'll think I meant it.

Although I did quite mean it.

I wish I was twelve again. Or twenty-five, or forty. Or dead.

He brings two mugs of tea and puts mine on the table

beside the sofa. Then he sits down, but not beside me this time; instead he sits in the armchair by the door.

"Are you all right to drive? I can take you home."

"I don't need to go home. It's not even lunchtime. I'll drink this, and then we can go back and open up."

He frowns at me. "Sure?"

"Yes, I'm sure. Honestly, I'm . . . It was just a shock. I'll get over it, and the best way for that to happen is if I have stuff to think about—you know, keeping busy, like your mum says." I sip my tea. I've never met his mother, of course. "Is that the sort of thing your mum says?"

His expression darkens. "My mother says things like, 'Oh darling, really? A shop?' and, 'I met a lovely girl at a dinner party last week, you'd like her.' "

I laugh, relieved to have something else to think about. "Does she?"

"That sort of thing, yes. I'm a bit of a disappointment, as you can probably imagine."

"She'd rather you were . . . happy, though?"

He looks at me, intense. "She'd rather I followed the rules and didn't cause any trouble."

"Oh."

"I'm not popular with my family. Or at all."

I'm not sure what to say to this. I drink my tea, and we sit in silence.

• • •

At five-thirty, when he's cashing out and I'm getting ready to leave, he says, "How are you feeling?"

"Better than I did." I pick up my bag. "Thanks again, for,

um"—I search for the right word—"for your kindness earlier. I really appreciate it."

He scowls at me. "I'm never kind." He shuffles, awkward. "I'd like to apologize again. For my . . . inappropriate behavior."

I take my keys out of my bag and fiddle with them. "Please just forget about it. It doesn't matter. I know you didn't . . . It doesn't matter."

"I'll be out tomorrow," he says abruptly. "Probably Friday too."

"Oh, okay. Are you going to Fort William, then?"

He nods. "Might go up to Inverness as well. I'll call you if—if I need to."

"Right you are. Thanks again," I say, and leave him in the darkened shop, heading out into the dusk.

I've been here for more than six months, the summer's long gone. It's the middle of October. I should be thinking about going home, but I don't want to. I know that's cowardly. It's not exactly that I want to stay here—or not entirely. I just don't want to go back, less so now than ever. I don't want to see anyone and have them be even more sorry for me than before. The thought of people talking about it—the baby, which they will, and who can blame them—makes me shudder. It would be a lot easier never to go back, except to fetch my stuff. Do I want to stay here, though? I look around at the neat stone houses, lights on, looking cozy in the gathering darkness. I see the lights go off in Alistair's office, teenagers smoking at the bus stop by the Co-op, the impressive Victorian weightiness of the town hall. This is a nice place, I've made the beginnings of a life here. I could stay, easily.

Where else would I go? Anywhere, I suppose, anywhere at all.

...

Edward is away for the rest of the week. He calls each morning to ask shop-related questions. Apart from that he can best be described as "distant." I feed Holly Hunter, but I don't go into any of the rooms of his flat except the kitchen.

I miss him. It's dull when he's away; even bad-mood Edward is company, at least.

I don't think about the kiss, or not much anyway. There's no point, is there? Best ignored and forgotten.

...

On Monday morning I'm running late. I slept badly, and missed my alarm. I rush about, drinking coffee and eating toast while I do my hair. I found a lovely pale cream cashmere twin set among Aunt Mary's clothes, which just about fits because I seem to have lost some weight—which is surprising, but useful—and decide to wear that with a smart pencil skirt that I bought in the charity shop. I don't usually dress up for work, it's not necessary, but today I feel the need to make myself look respectable and together. I am not the woman who collapsed into hysterical sobbing, or kissed someone she shouldn't have.

As I open my front door, I notice an envelope on the mat. The postwoman hasn't been, so it must have been hand-delivered (that's an odd phrase, isn't it; it's not like Becky doesn't use her hands).

It says *Ms. T. Hamilton* on the front but no address. I open it as I walk to the car.

Thea,

I regret to inform you that on consideration I have decided to terminate your employment at Fortescue's Books. Please consider this letter in lieu of notice and find enclosed a check for your month's wages.

I would appreciate it if you could return the keys to me at your earliest convenience.

I would also like to take this opportunity to thank you for the work you have done for the past six months, and to wish you all success for the future.

Yours sincerely,
Edward Maltravers

I stare at the paper. Once again a ball of horrified anguish gathers in my belly. This is because he kissed me, isn't it? Anguish is replaced almost instantly with anger. I'm furious. My hands are shaking. Absolutely fucking livid. In fact, as I get into the car, throwing my bag in the passenger seat, I can't think of a time I've ever been angrier.

• • •

I shove the shop door open so hard it bangs against the back of the bookshelf. The bell jangles loudly. I storm—something I'm sure I've never done before—into the shop, and turn sharply to the counter. There he is, tapping away at the laptop as though everything's normal. He looks up, startled, and is unfolding himself as I begin.

"What the fuck is this?" I shout, brandishing the letter. "What the actual fuck is this?"

He gathers himself, the scowl already firmly in place. "I think it's perfectly clear."

"Yes, it is. Yes, it's perfectly fucking clear. Is this about Wednesday? You fucking arsehole."

I realize there are two customers in the shop, both caught in embarrassment, staring. I don't care, though.

"Thea—"

"I thought we were friends," I say. My voice breaks and I cough, ashamed at sounding upset.

There's a pause, and then he says, "We're not friends."

I step backward, shocked.

"Events . . . events have reminded me of my employment policy," he says. He turns and opens the desk drawer, then holds up the laminated sheet he showed me on that long-ago morning when I came in to ask about the job.

REMEMBER, NO GIRLS

"No girls," I say. "Is that right?" I step toward him and lean on the counter. "Because they fall in love with you? Well, I'm not in love with you," I snap, although whether this is the truth or not, I couldn't tell you. "And you can't seriously expect me to believe that you're in love with me."

He glares at me. "I don't care what you believe."

"Oh really?"

"It's a matter of supreme indifference to me," he says coldly.

"Oh, come on. You're surely not suggesting you'd want to fuck me, are you?"

There's a very long pause.

"Maybe ten years ago," he says, "but no. I wouldn't."

Although I was expecting something like this, I'm still horrified that he'd say it. He could just have said no, it's not like I'd have been surprised. There doesn't have to be a reason, does there?

"Well, that's lucky. Because I wouldn't fuck you if you begged me." I tear up the letter and the check, inefficiently, and throw the resulting, rather chunky confetti in his face.

"Fuck you," I say. "Enjoy the rest of your miserable life."

I pull the shop keys from my bag and throw them on the floor, followed by the Shed keys. Then I stalk out, slamming the shop door behind me. I stand on the pavement, chest heaving, and realize I'm crying at about the same time I realize it's started to rain. I turn randomly and walk blindly away.

We're not friends.

I think that's the cruelest and most hurtful thing anyone's ever said to me, at least since I left school. When Chris told me he was leaving it wasn't cruel. It was tragic and awful, but it wasn't cruel. He tried hard not to say anything hurtful, to make it as civilized as possible. I wipe my face on my sleeve and walk faster. Then I run, wildly and not well in my smart shoes. I turn down side streets without thinking or planning and then I'm not sure where I am. There's a bus shelter, though, and now it's properly raining, so I go and stand under it, sobbing. I feel like I've done nothing but cry for the last nine months and, really, what's worse than the sight of a forty-four-year-old woman crying in public. It's humiliating, or it would be if I gave a toss what anyone thinks.

It's quite a slap in the face, to think you're friends with

someone and find out that you're not. I think of all the time we've spent talking, and the time at the Shed, and all those lunches and drinks after work and the times we've laughed enough to bring tears to my eyes. He bought me a spoon, for God's sake. Two spoons, even. I was pretty confident we were mates. But we weren't. We're not. It's devastating.

I stand there for twenty minutes and I'm crying hard enough that not one but two teenage girls, slender creatures in sportswear with perfect eyebrows, ask me if I'm okay. One of them offers me a cigarette and the other one says, "Aye, they're all bastards, hen." I don't know if they know who I am, they don't look like bookshop regulars, but it's a small town, after all. I don't care, though. I don't care at all.

Twenty

When the bus comes, I get on it. I ask the bus driver where he's going and am pleasantly surprised, through my misery, that he's going to Castle Douglas via the road that passes the turn for the lodge. So I buy a ticket.

When I get off the bus I realize it's a lot farther from my house than I thought. When you drive it's hard to judge. This is also when I realize I've managed to forget I drove to town this morning, and my car's parked by the church. Which is no use to anyone.

It's raining harder, and I'm pretty pissed off with myself for forgetting I've got a bloody car. My shoes are rubbing and I'm soaked. When I catch my heel awkwardly in a pothole and it snaps entirely off, I think quite seriously about sitting in the ditch and waiting to die.

Instead I take off my shoes and limp on in stockinged feet. I've always wondered where those single shoes you see at the side of the road come from. Now I guess I know. It's tempting to fling them away, but maybe it can be fixed, so I carry them. I'm soaking wet, filthy, exhausted from weeping and now holding a broken pair of shoes. Give me strength.

I hear a car behind me and step up onto the verge, which is muddy but cool and strangely soothing to my feet. I must

THE BOOKSHOP OF SECOND CHANCES

be a tragic sight. The car, which is red and shiny, drives past and stops almost immediately. I look up and see Charles climbing out, rather awkwardly (it's a sports car, low slung).

"Thea? Oh my God. I thought it was you. Are you all right? You're drenched."

"Oh, hello, Charles. Yeah, I got the bus, and—"

"Where's your car? Come here, let me drive you home." He opens the passenger door for me and ushers me inside.

I sit, dripping, in the car. It's a Porsche or something, and usually I'd find it interesting to be in a car like this. As it is, I'm shivering and self-conscious about the upholstery.

"What on earth were you doing on the bus? Is there something wrong with your car?"

I suppose Charles has never been on a bus. I can't picture him on one anyway. Maybe when he was at university. My mind drifts and I pull myself back into the moment with some effort.

"I forgot I had it with me."

He turns to look at me, astonished. "You forgot?"

I'm not sure what to tell him. I definitely don't want to talk to him about Edward. "Yes, I . . . It's been . . . I didn't have a very good morning."

"At work?"

I hesitate. "Yes."

"What happened?"

We're at the lodge now, pulling off the drive.

"I had a fight with my boss. Thanks for the lift, it's . . ." But he's out of the car already, coming round to open the door for me. "Thanks."

"You need to get into dry things," he says. "Let me make you a cup of tea."

I'm not sure how to put him off without sounding rude. After all, he gave me a lift and now his passenger seat is wet and there are muddy footprints on the expensive floor mats. I unlock the front door and let him in.

"What happened to your shoes? My God, Thea, you're bleeding."

We both look at the muddy bloodstains on the flagstones.

"Oh. Sorry, I probably bled in your car. I guess I cut myself on the road or something. My shoe broke." I hold it up to show him. "I'm not having the best day." I'm conscious of my extremely torn stockings and the splashes of mud I've kicked up my legs.

He looks horrified. "You ought to wash your feet. Does it hurt?"

I stand on one foot and try to look at the sole of the other. "Not really. A bit. But my feet are like ice; I can't feel anything much. You're right, I should probably wash it."

"You go and do that. I'll put the kettle on."

"You needn't," I say, "I can do that myself—"

"Don't argue," he says sternly. Jesus, maybe he and Edward are more alike than they realize. It's that patrician assumption that people will do as you say, isn't it? When Edward was ordering me upstairs on Wednesday it was fine. I'd probably do all kinds of things if he told me to firmly enough. I'm more resentful of being ordered about by Charles, though.

Mind you, he's right, I should get changed. I'm freezing.

. . .

When I come back in my pajamas and dressing gown—my feet washed and a Band-Aid on the cut, a pair of woolly socks, my stockings thrown away, outfit in the washing basket—Charles is in the sitting room, where he's got the fire going, and there are two cups of tea on the coffee table.

"Oh, that's better," I say, standing by the fireplace, stretching my hands to the flames. I'm surprised he can light a fire. He must have people for that sort of thing, surely. "Ugh. What a grim day. Thanks."

"You're quite welcome. And next time you abandon your car somewhere, Thea, you should ring me."

I laugh. "And you'll come and pick me up? That seems like it might be inconvenient for you. Anyway, I don't plan on doing it again. I can't believe I did it today. Who forgets they have their car with them? I'm an idiot."

I pick up my tea and sit down in the armchair. My hands are still cold, and I'm strangely weary.

He clears his throat. "What were you fighting with Edward about?"

"Oh, just . . . I'd rather not talk about it. If you don't mind. It's not important."

He crosses his legs, and then uncrosses them. He seems uncomfortable, which is unusual; he's one of those supremely "at home" people who always fits in with his surroundings. I assume that's something they teach you at expensive schools.

He puts his cup down on the coffee table. "Are you and he . . . ? I know you said before that you weren't, um . . . but . . ."

Ah, okay, he's unnerved by a personal question. "Are we what?" He can ask me if he wants to know. I'm not going to do the work for him. Anyway, I can't see why he's still interested, not really.

He shifts again, leaning back against the cushions. "Er. People seem to think that—"

"People?"

"It's a small town, Thea, people talk."

"And people are still talking about Edward and me? You'd think they'd have more important things to worry about."

"I know it's none of my business." He reaches for his tea again. "But my brother's a shit."

"Mm. I can see why you'd think that," I agree. "But I've heard the same thing about you."

"From him? Well." He clears his throat again and continues. "I just . . . I'd hate to think you might be involved with someone who—"

"I'm not sleeping with your brother," I say. I'm not sure whether he believes me or not.

"People are bound to talk, aren't they? He's not known for"—his mouth twists—"behaving appropriately. And when you work with someone, just the two of you, and—"

"You needn't concern yourself. Our relationship, such as it is, or was, is entirely platonic."

"So what were you fighting about?"

I consider. I suppose everyone will know soon enough. There were people in the shop, after all, and if I'm not there anymore people will ask where I am.

"He sacked me." I drink my tea calmly.

"He *sacked* you?"

"Mm."

"But—what on earth for?" He's astounded by this, staring at me.

"I'm not entirely sure," I say mendaciously. "He told me

months ago that he doesn't usually employ women. I suppose it was that. I was quite annoyed. So we had a fight."

"And—are you still sacked?"

I nod.

"What an idiot. So you . . . What will you do? Do you—I do beg your pardon for asking—will that be awkward? I mean financially?"

I laugh. "He wasn't paying me an enormous fortune. It will make me focus. Time I decided whether I'm going to stay up here, or go back to Sussex. I suppose I should go home. Don't worry," I add, "if I decide to sell the lodge, I'll let you know."

"Oh, well. Thank you. But you can stay, can't you? There are other places you could work. There are even other bookshops," he says. "Wigtown's full of them. If you want to work in a bookshop. Although surely that's not making full use of your abilities."

Is that a compliment? I suppose it is. I finish my tea. "I haven't decided what I want to do. It was never the plan to stay. So, we shall see. I do like it here, so I might keep the house and let it." I turn to look at him. "I know that's not what you want to hear."

He makes an impatient gesture. "You must do as you wish—you're under no obligation to sell."

"No, that's true." I sigh. "Anyway, I don't know. We'll see." I stand up. I want him to leave, and he's finished his tea. I'm hoping that manners will bring him to his feet. Which they do.

"I'll leave you to it," he says. "Make sure you keep warm. And if you need someone to take you to collect your car, just give me a ring. I'd be happy to help."

"Oh, that's very kind. Thanks. And thanks for the lift and the tea and everything," I say as I lead him out into the hall. I open the front door and shiver, wrapping my arms around myself. There's a cold wind and the rain lashes against the front of the building.

"Oh, you're absolutely welcome, no need to thank me. Right, then."

I think he's about to kiss my cheek, but I put my hand out for him to shake instead, which he does.

"Goodbye," I say, and close the door as he's getting into the car. I hear the roar of the engine as he drives away, and go back to the sitting room, which is now deliciously cozy.

Twenty-one

After Charles leaves, I'm not sure what to do. I sit and stare at the fire. It's a miserably grey day and it's dark, even in my sitting room, which is such a lovely bright space when the sun shines.

I can't believe I've allowed myself to get to a place where someone new can hurt me like this. What the hell was I thinking? Imagining I was making a home, somewhere I could be happy? Stupid. Thinking I'd made friends here? People are curious about new residents in a small town, but that doesn't make them your friends. Probably none of them are my friends. After all, why would they be, if the person I've been spending most of my time with doesn't even like me. You can't blame him, though, can you? I'm not interesting or worthwhile. I'm just a stupid middle-aged woman whose husband left her for someone else, and that's probably not surprising either.

Not entirely sure why you'd kiss someone you don't like. Maybe he finds weeping women a turn-on, although that doesn't seem likely. Then again, he's just spent God knows how long sleeping with someone he didn't like, so who's to say.

As an adult, I have to believe that he meant what he said,

that we're not friends, because what would be the point of saying it unless it was true?

My insides hurt, and so does my brain.

I think I've failed at everything. What am I going to do now? I was angry earlier, and that was kind of a positive feeling, but now I'm drained and empty and cold. I suppose I should leave, shouldn't I? I don't want to be here anymore. I'll run away again. I could just keep doing that forever. Pick a little town at random. Or maybe a city would be better; it's easier to avoid meeting people if you live in a city. I could run away to Inverness or Sheffield and get a job in a supermarket or something, and never speak to anyone except for work.

The phone rings, making me jump. I answer it unwillingly. It's Jenny.

"Are you okay? Cerys just rang and said someone told her you had a massive fight with Edward this morning."

I close my eyes. Jesus Christ, can people not mind their own business? "Yes," I say. "We did."

"What was that about? Are you all right? I tried to call your mobile."

"The signal's shit out here."

"I know, that's why I thought you were probably at home, because I couldn't get through."

"Yes." I know I should say more than this, form a sentence, but really.

"What happened?"

I'm not sure what to say. I don't want to tell her. It's pathetic. Keep it plain and unvarnished. "I'm sacked."

"Bloody hell. It's true, then? That's what Cerys said, but I didn't believe her. Or I thought she must've got hold of the wrong end of the stick or something. She said Micky Doolin was in the shop."

"Oh, he might have been. I don't know. There were some customers. Anyway, yes, it's true."

"What the hell happened?"

I can picture Jenny's face, outraged on my behalf, angry, lips pursed. Perhaps she is my friend. I was just being negative before. I sigh. I suppose I'll have to explain this to a million people. And I really can't be bothered. "I don't know. You'll have to ask Edward."

"I've been in there already, he won't speak to me."

"How mature."

She laughs. "Isn't it? But Jesus he's in a foul mood. He told me to piss off and that was it."

"Yeah, well, I hope he's miserable. I hope it chokes him."

"Well, screw him. The man's a twat, aye. I did tell you not to work for him," she adds.

"Yes. I should have listened."

There's a pause.

"If you want to come over this evening . . ." she says.

"Oh, I can't. Well I could, I suppose. I mean, I left my car in town . . . Anyway, thanks, but I don't feel much like socializing."

"If you're sure. If you want to talk to someone, or anything . . . I can't believe he sacked you."

"No, neither can I. Only I can, really. Actually, thinking about it, it was completely inevitable." I get an image of the bookshop, of the comfort of it, the gentle smell of the books, sunlight on the flagstones. My throat aches. I like the shop as much as I like Edward. Although I don't like him at all, do I?

"Anyway, don't worry, I'm fine. It's probably for the best, and other clichés."

"Hm. Okay. If you're sure. Phone me, though, if you want."

"Thanks."

...

I fetch a blanket from the bedroom, and my book, and go out to the kitchen to make a cup of tea. I think for a moment that I might want something stronger instead; there's half a bottle of Gordon's in the cupboard, although I don't have any lemons or, worse, any tonic. I can't drink utterly raw gin at my age, I think, which is a quote from somewhere. I have a list of things in my head that I'm trying not to think about. It's difficult, though, when you're on your own. I'd better watch a film or something.

I don't want to think about how my husband's having a baby, or how I just lost my job—for the second time this year—or how I might have to move, or how I've managed to lose a friend, or how apparently I didn't even have that friend to lose. I feel like such an unbearable idiot. I'm achingly embarrassed, mortified.

God, it's depressing. I open the cupboard, looking for something to cheer myself up. There's a box of Tunnock's wafers but they remind me of him.

This is shit. How can I be so upset about this? You wouldn't think I'd have room, after everything else that's happened this year, to even care about it.

It's a good thing I haven't allowed myself to think about what it was like to kiss him.

I've fucked this up so badly.

Now I'm crying again. I do quite hate myself.

. . .

When I wake up in the morning there's a split second when I've forgotten everything and I'm thinking about what I might need to do at work. There's a pile of books in the workshop and—oh yeah.

Shit.

Despite all the practice I had during what I no longer have to think of the first quarter of the year, I still don't have a reliable method for dealing with feeling like this. I lie in bed and stare up at the ceiling. It's quite dark; the clock radio tells me it's only half past six, which is much too early to get up when you're unemployed.

I can hear the rain singing in the gutters. Apart from that it's very quiet; the heat doesn't come on until seven. Maybe I should look again at those flats. If I moved back . . . but really, what's the point? What's the point of any of it? If I could choose anywhere in the country to live, where would I choose? This is my chance to move to Brighton or Cornwall or the Outer flipping Hebrides, isn't it?

I should have sold the lodge to Charles as soon as he asked me to; that would have solved a lot of problems. I'd be on my way to a new life somewhere else if I'd done that, or back in Sussex getting on with things.

I put my head under the duvet for a while, but it's no good, I can't go back to sleep. I'll have to get up, and it's cold, and I've nothing to get up for.

I should do one of those tasks I've been meaning to get on

with for months, like photographing Aunt Mary's clothes for eBay. It's hardly an ideal day for photography, though. Maybe I should start boxing up books in the library. At least I know some other book dealers now. I can still sell my books; I don't need Edward for that. Maybe I should open my own bookshop. That would be amusing, wouldn't it?

I'd thought about giving him the Orwell for his birthday. I hadn't decided for sure, because it's worth a lot of money, but I'd thought about it. Giving someone something you already have is not the same as buying a gift, but obviously I wouldn't be buying anyone a gift that costs thousands of pounds; it would be impractical. I feel like a dick for even contemplating this. Luckily the truth came out before his birthday, or else I would have made a complete arse of myself. It makes me shudder to think of it.

Why did he have to kiss me? It's a double whammy, isn't it, because it's made him hate me and it's made me think about things I shouldn't.

Maybe I should be angry about it. How dare he kiss me? Yes, that's better. How dare he and then decide it was all a mistake, a mistake so bad he had to sack me! I should have resigned, shouldn't I? Sexual harassment or something. I mean I didn't ask to be kissed; I wasn't expecting it. I should have pushed him away, told him to fuck off, not melted pathetically like some stupid girl in a romantic novel.

He's really good at kissing, though.

Shut up, what are you, fifteen?

God, I'm so miserable.

I get out of bed and wrap myself in my dressing gown. Time for coffee and lighting the fire.

...

It rains all day. If it stopped, I might go and get the car, but it doesn't stop. Instead, I sit and look out the kitchen window. The plants drip, the leaves are falling. Everything seems extremely symbolic. I haven't done anything today. I had a bath and put on woolly socks and clean pajamas—another pair of Uncle Andrew's. They're probably thirty years old. Blue and white striped flannel old man's pajamas. I love them. There are six pairs and I don't plan on wearing anything else in bed, ever.

Then I lie on the sofa and watch videos. Uncle Andrew had quite the collection of war films and musicals. I've watched *The Longest Day, Ice Cold in Alex, Calamity Jane,* and *Meet Me in St. Louis.* I eat toast for breakfast and again for lunch. I think about phoning Xanthe, but then I decide against it. I'll send her an email tomorrow. I wonder if it will stop raining enough for me to get the bus to town. I know Charles said he'd give me a lift, but I don't want to ask him.

...

At teatime, I look at my phone, and there are two missed calls from the shop.

I look at the number for ages. I wonder why he called. He didn't leave a message. I'm not calling back. If it's important he'll call again.

I spend the rest of the evening determined not to phone and furious with myself for wanting to.

...

On Wednesday, it's still raining. I wonder what would happen if I just never went to get the car. I'd starve to death eventually. This thought makes me laugh; I can't imagine I'd be stubborn enough to die of hunger. Okay, I'll get dressed and go to town.

Walking to the bus stop in a pair of sensible boots is much quicker than trying to do it in heels. I'd been thinking about going home to collect all my winter clothes—and everything else—but now I'm not so sure. Luckily Jenny gave me these wellies, which are surprisingly comfortable, as long as you wear them with two pairs of socks. I wear Uncle Andrews's fishing jacket, which is just the right size, fantastically waterproof and full of pockets. It's only drizzling, and I feel okay, striding along the road and splashing through the puddles. It's cold and grey, but so what?

I forgot to check the bus times, so I have to sit in the shelter for nearly half an hour. You can randomly get a connection up here, though, so I spend my time on Facebook, catching up with what everyone's been doing.

In town, I deliberately walk round the back way, coming out by the Co-op, so I don't have to walk past the shop. I don't look toward it either; I imagine a section of the town square cut out of existence and behave as if there's nothing to look at anyway. I toy with the idea of going into the Old Mill, but I'm not ready for curiosity or sympathy. I'm pretending to be fine, but if Cerys asked me anything I'd get upset, and who can be bothered with that. Instead, I go into the baker's and buy two custard slices and a loaf of bread, and then I collect my car and drive home, carefully avoiding looking at the shop as I drive past.

I hope he's as miserable as I am.

It seems unlikely.

I go home and read Sherlock Holmes in the bath until the water gets cold, and then I put my pajamas back on and make a bacon sandwich for lunch. After that I sit in the corner of the bedroom, which is the only place I can get a signal, and write Xanthe an email.

•••

On Thursday, I go to the beach, even though it's still raining. It's ridiculously wet, but I don't care. I'm pretty well freezing by the time I get home, though, so it's another afternoon bath for me, and another day when I'm in my pajamas again long before bedtime.

•••

At half past three, the doorbell rings. I'm surprised, the only time anyone knocks unexpectedly is when something is delivered. I didn't hear a car, but then I wasn't paying attention. I've been watching *Acorn Antiques* because I suddenly remembered that comedy existed and might be helpful. I bought the DVD for 50p in the charity shop months ago, and I'm grateful to past Thea for this foresight.

I pause the laptop and go to answer the door.

It's Charles, which is unexpected.

"I thought I'd pop round and see how you were," he says.

"Oh! Hello. I'm sorry, I'm not dressed, isn't it shocking? Do you want to come in?" Then I think that sounds rude. "I mean, come in, won't you? Shall I put the kettle on?"

"Thanks. I brought you these." He offers me a wrapped flat box, which I anticipate contains chocolates.

"Oh, how kind, thank you. Come through to the kitchen." I'm glad I bothered to wash up my breakfast things this morning, and last night's pans, even though I didn't want to. The kitchen is suitably tidy and doesn't look too much as though it belongs to someone whose life has collapsed. I put the kettle on, and then open the parcel. My guess about chocolate was correct. Locally made; I've driven past the little factory just outside Dumfries, and they sell them in the farm shop out by Wigtown.

"I dropped Alexa off at her mother's this morning," says Charles, "drove past the shop."

Alexa's his daughter. I've seen her from a distance, but never met her. I've never seen the other one, Duncan, his son.

"That's very kind of you." I open the box. "Ooh. They do look excellent."

We sit down to drink our tea and have two chocolates each. Charles asks me how I am, and I tell him I'm fine.

"You got your car, then?"

"Yeah, went in yesterday."

"You should have called me. I'd have taken you."

I shrug. "Hardly got wet at all, it wasn't a problem."

We sit in slightly awkward silence.

"Have you decided what you're going to do? About work?"

"God, no. No, I've no idea. I should see if I can find something else," I say, "or maybe I should just go home."

"You meant that, then? Back to Sussex?"

"Perhaps."

"Oh. Don't rush into anything," he says. "I'm sure you'd be able to find something."

"Yes, well. We'll see." I clear my throat. I don't know what to say to him, it's not like I didn't see him earlier in the week. I know he wants to ask about Monday, but I'm not going to tell him.

"You know he's not worth being upset about," he says. "I don't know what happened, but—"

"Look, I don't want to talk about it. Thanks. It's not important, I'll be fine, I just need to make a plan. I'd prefer not to have been sacked, but it doesn't matter. I know it looks bad that I'm sitting here in my PJs, but I've been out today and everything. I've just been watching films, you know. It's like being on holiday," I lie, "so I thought I'd make the best of it."

"I saw Jilly at the farm shop. She said—"

"I'm sure everyone's deeply fascinated," I say. "It's a shame there were customers in."

He frowns at me. "Did something happen last week? Between you and Edward? Is that why he sacked you?"

I sigh. "Charles, I don't want to be rude; you've been so kind, and I appreciate that, honestly. But I don't want to talk to anyone about any of this, least of all you."

"Only, you know, he—"

"Charles."

He opens his mouth and then shuts it again.

"Good."

"All right," he says. "Well look, if there's anything I can do, anything at all . . ."

I finish my tea. "Thank you. If I think of anything, I'll let you know." I smile at him. "If you could sort the weather out, that would be great."

"Sadly I can't do much about that." He puts his mug down. "I'd better get going. I've got people coming to dinner."

"Are you cooking?" I can't imagine he is.

"No. No, Lynda's in charge of all that."

"Oh, of course. I always forget about Lynda."

"I'd be completely buggered without her," he says, and stands up. "I hope you feel better anyway."

"Oh God, I'll be fine. Thank you for the chocolates."

In the hallway he hesitates. "Look. You mustn't let him upset you."

"Charles."

Frowning, he says, "He's got no idea about women, he never has."

"Look, it's none of your business, is it? I told you I didn't want to be rude, but I also told you I didn't want to talk about it."

"I wish you would, though," he says.

There's quite a long pause.

"You should get going," I say, "or you'll be late for your dinner." I open the door. "Still raining," I add, peering out into the gathering gloom.

"Yes. All right. Please don't be sad. I don't like to see you so down."

"I'll be fine. I'm a grown-up," I say, but it is quite sweet of him, so I let him kiss my cheek as water drips around us.

"Have a good evening," I say, and wave as he hurries across to his shiny red car.

I've barely sat down when there's a hammering at the door. I'm startled; I live essentially in the middle of nowhere, where it's not like people call round, and now I've had two visitors in one day. Or perhaps Charles has forgotten something? I hurry back into the hallway, retying the belt of my dressing gown, and open the door.

To a furious Edward, face like thunder.

Twenty-two

"What the hell was he doing here?" he snarls. I take a step backward, and he looms over me, dripping raindrops onto the flagstones. He looks at my dressing gown. "And why the hell aren't you dressed?"

"Jesus Christ," I say, "you need to get a grip. What's it to you anyway?" I step backward again. "And who the hell do you think you are, shouting at me in my own home? You've got a bloody nerve."

"Why was he here? Are you sleeping with him?"

"Oh my actual God." I grip the top of my head with both hands. "I suppose that would make me more appealing, would it?"

I surprise myself with this. I guess I'm still angry with him. It's inflammatory, though. He basically growls at me and I retreat further.

"He pretty much asked me if I was sleeping with you as well," I add. "How about I'm not sleeping with either of you and have no fucking wish to? Jesus. He just came round to see if I was okay."

"Why wouldn't you be okay?"

"Jesus Christ. I had a bloody awful day on Monday, didn't I?"

He steps forward again, and I step backward. I'm not frightened, but he's quite wet.

"How does he know that? Did you phone him?"

"I don't think I've ever phoned him. He gave me a lift from the bus stop."

"The bus stop? What?"

"Stop asking me questions!" I glare at him. "I left my car in town." I blink rapidly and press my lips together. I'm sick of weeping. I'm not going to cry. I cried for hours yesterday, and I've done quite well today, hardly any tears at all. No.

"You left it in town?" He's incredulous. "You expect me to believe that? And how come you're in your dressing gown?" He jabs a finger toward me.

"You don't have to get dressed if you don't have a job," I say. "What's the point of getting dressed? And I don't care whether you believe me or not. It doesn't change the facts. I came home on the bus on Monday, and I got very wet walking from the bus stop, and Charles drove past and stopped to pick me up."

"Why on earth did you come home on the bus?" He looks almost as astonished as Charles was. It must be nice to live the sort of life where buses are just like trees or pigeons. They exist, you see them, but they're just part of the scenery.

"I was a bit upset," I say sarcastically. "I got sacked, and someone was really bloody rude to me. So I ran off." I flap my arms, miming someone running pathetically. "And cried in a bus stop, and then I forgot I had a car, so I got on a bus and came home. But I had to walk, like, half a mile with no shoes on, and your brother kindly stopped and gave me a lift. If you must know."

"With no shoes on?"

"I broke a heel." I scowl at him. "Weirdly I wasn't dressed for a hike in the country."

He's calmed down a bit. Now he's just staring at me.

"So what the hell are you doing here anyway? Lurking in the bushes to see who comes to the house? You're soaking."

"No, I . . . No."

"Great, very helpful. Such a way with words."

"No, I . . . Look, Thea—"

"*Look, Thea,*" I mimic. "I don't want to look. I don't know why you're here. I don't want to talk to you." I think of something else. "Who's minding the shop?"

"I closed early. I wanted to see you," he says crossly. "You didn't answer your phone. I was worried—"

"How odd that I didn't want to speak to you. Anyway, what do you care? I thought I was sacked. None of your business, is it?"

"Thea—"

"What? Stop saying 'Thea.'"

"Oh Jesus," he says. He pushes his hands through his hair. "This is all wrong. Look, I'm sorry. I came to apologize—"

I almost laugh. "You came to *apologize*? You've been yelling at me since I opened the door."

He briefly puts his hands over his face, and then looks up at the ceiling. "I know. I'm such a . . . I'm sorry. Can we start again?"

"Good grief, you're very stupid. Go and sit down." I gesture toward the kitchen. "And take your coat off, you're dripping all over the floor."

I watch him, arms folded, as he hangs his coat on the hallstand, and then I follow him down the passage.

He sits at the splay-leg kitchen table. It seems like a long time since he was last here, when he gave me a lift home that time. We sat in the sitting room then, so it's odd to see him here in the neat kitchen with its ice-blue Formica cupboards and speckled countertops, the yellow table with its jolly red vinyl chairs.

The shouting has warmed me up, so I take off my dressing gown and hang it over the back of a chair.

I roll up the sleeves of my old-man pajamas and put the kettle on. Edward watches me gloomily. I get myself a glass of water, make a pot of tea, fetch milk from the fridge. After a moment's thought, I bring out the box of caramel wafers from the cupboard. I'm not sure why I think he deserves one. I shake the remaining five onto a plate—biscuits on a plate is a thing from my youth, and I like to follow this tradition in honor of aunts and old ladies long dead.

I put the plate on the table in front of him and sit down opposite. "Have a biscuit."

He hesitates, probably thinking it seems wrong to have one after the shouting, but is tempted.

"Go on," I say, "I know you want one." Finally, a smile. I shake my head at him. "Okay, then," I say, "so you came to apologize. About something specific, or generally?"

"Oh God. I suppose it should be generally, shouldn't it? I mean, for everything."

I shrug. "Off you go, then." I close my eyes for a moment. "I can't believe you accused me of sleeping with your brother."

He groans and rests his head in his hands. "I'm sorry."

"I don't even *like* your brother. As I keep saying. Although maybe that's harsh. I don't hate him or anything. He was kind to me on Monday. And look, he brought me some chocolates today. They're fancy."

He looks at the box but doesn't rise to it. "I know. I was just . . . I'm sorry."

"I'm not like you, you know. I don't have sex with people for weird convoluted reasons." I take a biscuit myself and unwrap it, taking a bite and chewing thoughtfully. I have no idea what's going to happen. It's . . . What is it? It's fascinating. I'm so surprised he's here, and I can't imagine what he's going to say next. I have butterflies, but I'm not exactly nervous.

"I know. I know. I was just . . . I didn't know what to think, and it's easy, isn't it, to say stupid, horrible things. Easier than saying anything meaningful or true."

"Is it? I don't know, Edward, it seems to me the easiest thing to do is tell the truth or say nothing. I'm not sure why you'd want to hurt people who like you." I feel the tears pricking behind my eyes again, and blink rapidly to ward them off.

"Do you like me?"

"Well, I *did*," I say. Then I laugh. "Why do you think I was so upset? Honestly, you saying we're not friends—" There's the catch in my voice again. I sip my water and clear my throat. "I thought we were. That made me feel stupid." I look at him briefly, and then away. "I've been feeling quite stupid."

"I'm sorry. I didn't mean to. I just . . . I always get this stuff wrong. I never manage to do the right thing, the sensible thing. I always misunderstand or fuck up." He looks miserable and pauses to unwrap his caramel wafer. He folds the wrapper in half lengthways, and then in half again, and again, smoothing the folds with his finger.

I wait.

"If we're not friends, it's my fault," he says.

"Well, yes, it would be."

"Because I do like you."

"That's nice. Usually friendship follows on from that in a pretty straightforward way," I tell him, "especially if you're both adults and everything."

"Yes."

"But?"

"But there's a problem."

"Is it that you're an arse?"

A grin flickers briefly. "No, it's not that. Although it doesn't help."

"Go on then," I say. "I'm prepared."

"I did try to tell you. But I don't think you believed me or wanted to understand what I was saying."

I raise my eyebrows, puzzled.

"We can't be friends because I'm in love with you."

I stare at him for a moment, and then I laugh. Eventually I have to put my head on the table because I go limp, my neck strangely floppy, when I laugh a lot. It doesn't happen often, but at school I spent a lot of time with my head on the desk, weak with laughter.

After what seems like ages, I gradually stop and wipe my eyes. "You idiot," I say. I expect I've upset him. He's scowling again. "You idiot. This is just a thing you do to yourself, isn't it? I think you're just overly suggestible. You spend time with someone and get on with them, and because you've managed to screw up in your head how relationships work, you convince yourself it means something it doesn't. I can see how that's problematic when you're dealing with some . . . teenager. But you don't have to worry about *me*, do you? Or sack me because of it? If we spend enough time together it'll go away, won't it? I mean . . ." I can feel myself starting to get upset again. "I mean, it goes away even if you are in love with someone, in the end. In the end one of you sleeps with someone else, even if you think it will last forever. But honestly. Why would you seriously think that?"

"It doesn't matter," he says and gets up.

"No, it does. I wasn't laughing at you," I add, "just at the notion."

"Why is it funny?"

"Because it's ridiculous. It seems unlikely anyone will ever fall in love with me again. And you especially. I mean, why would you? There are people like Lara for you to fall in love with. Maybe she's not a good example. But you know what I mean. Oh lord." I wipe my eyes. "Sorry, that probably seemed rude, to laugh like that. I didn't mean for it to. Sit down. Finish your tea."

"Thea. It's because I have stupid crushes all the time that I know this is true."

I shake my head. "Oh, right, yeah. How does that work?"

"Because it's completely different."

We look at each other.

"What do you mean?"

"I mean when I . . . I think people are pretty, or whatever, and you know 'what lovely skin' and wonder what it would be like to kiss them—"

"*Pfft.*"

"And even what it would be like to take them to bed, yes,

I admit I do think about that. But I've never thought about what it would be like if they were there all the time and . . . wondered what they'd think about all my favorite places. Or read things and thought, I must speak to them about this, or wondered if they've read that. Or worried or been concerned, because they're sad . . . and I want them to be happy. Wished they were with me when I have to go away."

We look at each other for a long moment.

"A lot of that's being friends, Edward. All of it, really. It's not—"

"And wanted to kiss them every time I see them. I haven't even had a woman in the shop—I mean, given a job to one—for like ten years or something."

"No girls?"

"No, I told you."

"Well, so—"

"But that's how I feel about you."

We stare at each other for ages. I can feel the pulse in my throat.

"But—"

"And I'm sorry I said all those awful things. It's frightening to have these feelings. And I know you don't feel the same way, so probably I should have kept all this to myself. But I didn't . . . I didn't want you to think that we weren't friends because I don't like you. I do, I really like you."

This is so heartfelt I feel tears brimming again. I'm not sure where to look, or what to say. He closes his eyes and continues. "I've known since we went to the Shed. Not that I admitted it then, even to myself. But it was great, being there with you. I thought it would be—that's why I asked you. I've always found your company very . . . relaxing. Almost like being by myself, but better. I like the way you don't need to be looked after all the time. And I like the way you don't get bored."

"I hardly ever get bored," I admit. "And how would I get bored at the Shed? It's brilliant."

He smiles at me. "I know. That's how I feel about it too. But I thought you were married. Although I wondered . . . But then you told me about Chris—I could see how upset you were. And you'd never done anything to make me think you might . . . to make me think you were interested in me. And when you cut your head open—"

I'm uncomfortable, now, thinking of that, his fingers in my hair.

"I forgot where I was, when I was looking at your hair; or who I was, or . . . something."

"Yeah, that was a bit weird. No one had touched me for ages," I say. "It was quite—intense."

"Yes."

I clear my throat, embarrassed.

"That's why I . . . I was worried you'd think I'd manip-ulated the situation. By drinking too much. Trapped you there. And I thought about how . . . if it hadn't mattered," he says, "I might have made a pass at you, I suppose. But I knew it mattered more than that. I had such a nice time."

"I did too. It was lovely. Even though I was slightly anx-ious." Then I see his face, and say, "Um, not because . . . just because I thought it might be . . . awkward. Like when you kissed me on Wednesday. I know you didn't mean to, and it upset me that you—"

"Yeah, well, it wasn't that I didn't *mean* to. But it was

completely the wrong time to kiss you. Not saying there'd be a right time. But I wasn't trying to take advantage of you. Of the way you felt."

"I know."

"I just wanted to make you feel better." He purses his lips, frowning. "And I wanted to kiss you."

"Um."

"So I'm sorry about that. I know you. I know it didn't mean anything. To you." He looks almost anxious as he says this, and I think, not for the first time, how odd it is that we can never know the truth of another's thoughts.

"I'm not sure what makes you think that," I say. "I mean, I'm not completely dead inside."

There's a pause.

"You see the thing is—" I start, as he says, "I wasn't sure if—"

"Go on."

"No, you first."

I gather myself. "You see the thing is, I've been . . . I have been thinking about it. For ages. About you. And I think . . . I think if you like someone, it's much harder to tell if they like you too. Harder than if you were indifferent."

I don't think he's going to help me out here; he's just staring. I soldier on.

"I'm probably not in a very good place. Emotionally. God knows I'll never forget how awful everything was at the beginning of this year. But I felt like I'd been doing okay. Making progress. Because coming up here made it easier for me to forget that any of it was true or real. I'd got used to feeling like it must be my fault, somehow, that he left. Even though

I know logically that's not true. I know I'll get used to being by myself, and I'll bumble along like other divorced people and it will be fine. Because I haven't been as lonely as I might have expected, and that's partly down to you." I pause again, trying to find the right words. For someone who talks a lot I find it hard to get the words right when it matters. "Because while you're quite rude, and obnoxious, and not even always there— Despite all that, having the shop, and someone to talk to about all kinds of things that had nothing to do with Chris or the house or the failure of my life . . . I felt like I was almost me again, in some ways. Properly me, Thea Hamilton. Not Thea Mottram. If I were to go home, I expect it would be awful again, because I'd have to see people and places and all the ordinary everyday things that will never be the same. So maybe it's all been false, this notion of myself as a new version of me, you know. But anyway." I falter, unsure of how to stop. "Sorry, I seem to have been talking for ages."

"You can talk as much as you like," he says. "I don't mind."

"But you were going to say something. Before I started talking—"

"When you say you're not indifferent," he says, then pauses. "Is that what you were saying? At the beginning? I was listening to all of it, but I've rather latched on to that—"

"I wanted you to kiss me, yes. If that's what you're asking." I roll my eyes. "Or at least, it was a surprise, but not . . . not an unpleasant one. And maybe it wasn't the best time. But I thought you might before, you know. When I had to run after you because you were being a twat. I thought you were going to kiss me then."

He looks slightly embarrassed. "In the doorway? Yeah, I—"

"That was the first time I thought you might . . . but then you didn't, and I thought I must have imagined it. But anyway. It's not like I minded, when you kissed me. I really didn't. But you know that, right?"

"I—"

"Right?"

"I didn't. I wasn't sure. I thought . . . I should have asked you if it was okay. I felt bad. But you wanted me to kiss you?" He looks painfully unsure of himself, and it's probably lucky I'm sitting too far away to be able to reach him. I want to reassure him, to soothe and comfort him. I'm not sure if this is a good idea or not.

"Surely you could tell? I mean call me sentimental, or foolish or naïve, but it all seemed quite swoony and . . ." I think back to that moment on the sofa, my hand on his chest, his fingers on my cheek, the hungry way we'd kissed, tongues entwined. "You know." I shrug again. "Sexy."

"Oh God," he says. "It was . . . I don't think I—"

I shuffle my chair a little closer, leaning across the table, and he puts his hands in mine.

"It's difficult to talk about," I say. "Embarrassing and awkward. But it was nice of you to hug me and the kissing was a bonus."

"Okay."

"So please stop worrying about it."

He laughs. "I'll try."

"It's not wrong to find someone attractive," I say. "I'm surprised that you do, but there we are. So now that's all out in the open, can we be friends again?"

He tightens his hold on my hands. "I don't know. Can we? Because I don't imagine I'm going to stop feeling like this."

I can't quite look him in the eye. It's so strange to hear him saying this stuff. His hands are warm, warmer than mine. It's nice to hold hands, even if my arms are stretched farther than is comfortable.

"Yes but . . . you see, I think you're missing the point," I tell him. "It works much better if you're friends. I mean it's more complicated, maybe, but if you're not friends you can't . . . There's nothing to build on. Admittedly it's hard to be friends afterward, if you really throw yourself into it. I suppose we'd have to decide what was more important. It's important to me to have a friend. And I don't know how well I'd cope, at the moment, with someone being in love with me." I frown, because I'm still not convinced that he is, which is probably rude. But I can't see why he would be. Lara was a bad example to give earlier, but it's true there are a million women with good bones who haven't slept with his brother and would be far more suitable. Anyway. "I don't know. Once you sleep with someone everything's different, even if you try for it not to be."

"I've never tried to be friends with anyone I've slept with."

I laugh. "No, I don't suppose you have." I feel like this has all got a bit, I don't know, impersonal almost. I'm not sure what to say now, as I lean here, my chin just above the surface of the table. Holding my head up is making my neck ache. It's tempting to just lay my head on the table. I'm so tired. I put my forehead and my nose against the wood, and close my eyes.

"Thea. Are you all right?"

"I'm just very tired."

"Should I go?"

"We could sit somewhere more comfortable." I look up and he nods. I let go of his hands and get up. He gets up too and I lead him out to the hall. I'd intended to go through to the sitting room, but then I have a better idea. Or a more stupid idea. I've confused myself.

Going to bed would be mad, right? Can I ask him if he wants to? I'm not sure I can. Or what would happen if I did. I don't know if I could do any of the things one does in bed. And taking someone to bed and then finding you can't have sex with them is asking for trouble. I don't think it's a good idea. Even though now that I've thought of it . . .

I know it's a bad idea to sleep with people who are in love with you, if you're not in love with them. I remember that much from my youth. Anyway, I still don't believe he is, not really. It seems so unlikely.

And it's not as though I'm *completely* not in love with him. There may be some . . . grey areas.

I pause for a moment, and perhaps Edward notices my hesitation because he says my name so I turn toward him, and he pulls me closer. "May I kiss you?" he says, which makes me laugh.

"If you like."

"Sure?"

"I'd like it if you did."

I'm glad it's quite dark here in the cold passageway, on this wet Thursday afternoon in late October, because I know my face is red, and my hair has dried oddly, and I am, after all, wearing a pair of old-man pajamas that may well be almost as old as I am. Edward slides an arm round my waist and moves his other hand to my face. I close my eyes and we kiss very slowly. I'm shaking. I am made of lips, conscious of my breasts against his chest, my own hands in his hair, among the curls. I'm breathless when he pulls away. He kisses my forehead, and squeezes me until I squeak. Then we look at each other for ages. Eventually I say, "Did you want to sit on the sofa?" And he laughs. "Shall we?" And we go into the sitting room.

It crosses my mind that it's been a long time since I had sex on a sofa, and this thought makes me blush. I sit down hurriedly. I mean we're not going to . . . there's no need, is there? I have a perfectly serviceable bed hardly any distance away. Not that we're going to have sex. Not yet anyway. Right?

We look at each other. I have no idea what to do.

"Come here," he says, so I move slightly closer. I'm embarrassed for some reason. Edward is entirely familiar to me; I've seen him at least three or four days a week, every week, since May. I spent twenty-four hours with him at the Shed. I've looked at his face more often than anyone else's face since I got here, and yet now he looks quite different, because we've kissed twice and he's told me he . . . My brain shies away from the phrase, stupidly. Come on. He's told me he loves me. These things have changed him forever. I can touch him if I want to, unwind a curl or stroke an eyebrow, put my finger into the crease between his brows.

"You're really staring," he says, and leans closer, his nose against my cheek. I close my eyes and tilt my head slightly, then feel his lips on my jaw, my throat.

Jesus.

It's terrifying, though. He's already made me incredibly miserable, hasn't he? Even if that was all a mistake, a misunderstanding, an error, I was still much more upset than is acceptable. What the hell am I doing?

"Oh God," I say, "is this really stupid?"

He sits back, and we look at each other.

"Probably," he says. "I wouldn't recommend myself to anyone."

"Oh, not because it's you," I say, wanting to reassure him. "It's . . . Whoever it was, would it be stupid? I think I'm broken, and I don't want to—"

"I understand," he says. "And I know I'm not a very good bet. I shouldn't have come."

He goes to get up and I put my hand on his thigh. "No, don't say that. It's not that. I'm glad you did. But I've been . . . I've been very unhappy, this week."

"Yes, me too," he says, and laughs. "I'm not sure I've ever been so miserable."

"Well, I definitely have, but it comes a surprisingly close second."

"I'm sorry I hurt you. I . . . That's the last thing I'd ever want to do. I'm sorry I couldn't tell you how I felt. I was afraid."

"Oh God." I laugh.

"What?"

"Well, you're just fucking adorable, aren't you," I say, and then we're kissing again and it's all quite . . . intense. Everything pulses and throbs in a way that reminds me of other fumblings in long-ago sitting rooms.

Eventually I say, "Okay. Are we going to bed?"

He looks very serious in the half-light. "What, now? Do you want to?"

"Yeah, probably," I say, a bit distracted by wondering if my bedroom's untidy. Pretty sure I made the bed, I usually do. The sheets are clean anyway, changed on Saturday. Not that it matters; I'd be surprised if he cared much about the state of the room or the sheets.

"Probably?"

I laugh at his expression. "Never expect me to say the right thing. I hardly ever do. What I mean is"—I get up and pull him to his feet—"I'd like to go to bed with you, I think, but I don't know if it's a good idea, or if we should. But I do want to, so I'm going to ignore all that."

In the hall, I push open the bedroom door. It's almost dark, the light from the window grey and fading. It's still raining steadily.

Now that we're in here, I think I may have made a mistake. Self-conscious doesn't begin to cover how awkward I feel. I catch sight of myself in the mirror on the dressing table and pull a face.

"What is it?"

I gesture at the mirror. "I just saw my reflection. Reminding me that although I feel exactly like I did when I was nineteen, or twenty-five, on the outside, I sadly don't look like I did then."

"You look pretty good to me," he says. "Those pajamas are—"

"They were Andrew's." I look down at myself, and then grin at him. "There, has that ruined the moment?"

"Jesus. Not at all," he says. "I don't care who bought them or when, it's what's inside that's piqued my interest."

It's pleasing when people say things like that, however hard it is to believe them.

"Have you changed your mind?" He has his hands in his pockets, looking at me across the bed.

"I don't think so." I don't know what to do with my hands, or what I should be doing in general. "I've kind of forgotten how this works." I feel like the light's all wrong, so I pull the curtains, and then it's dark. Too dark? The dressing table mirror glimmers, reflecting light from down the hallway. Edward is a dark figure, large and shadowy. God, this is difficult.

"Candles," I say, "that's what . . . Hang on." I rummage in the drawer of the bedside table. I'm sure there are—yes. Tea lights. And matches. I light one with an unsteady hand. The softer light makes me feel better.

Edward takes his sweater off and lays it over the chair. We stand and look at each other. Taking your clothes off in front of someone for the first time is always difficult. The idea that shortly he'll be naked, in my bed, is . . . hard to imagine. Shit. It's exciting but also scary.

I climb into bed. Still in my pajamas, which are sort of protective. I've got my socks on as well; he'll need to be keen.

"Candles are good," he says. He begins to unbutton his shirt and I pull the duvet up to my nose so he can't see me grinning.

"Flattering," I agree. "Which is a bonus. Um. This is weird. Is it weird? And worse than weird, is it like . . . is it horribly predictable?"

He laughs. "Some people will think so."

"I hate being predictable."

He slides into bed and leans to kiss me. I don't think I

could ever get bored of kissing him. I suppose I'd forgotten what it's like, kissing someone. Kissing someone when it's all still new and thrilling.

He pulls away eventually and we stare at each other. It's different, knowing you can look at someone as much as you like, none of that careful politeness of the outside world. When you're this close, you can really see someone's skin, and the lines on their face, and their stubble. He doesn't shave every day, and his beard grows through much greyer than his hair. The skin on his cheeks above the stubble is smooth, and he's still tanned from the summer. He always looks quite rumpled, uninterested in his appearance to some degree. I imagine he scrubs up well, though, because he's got good bones. And those eyebrows. I put my finger on one, following the way the hair grows, touching the lines between them, his frown lines.

"There were lots of men in paintings at Hollinshaw with these," I say.

"Ah yes, the Maltravers brow."

"Some of them looked a lot like you, your ancestors."

"Poor bastards."

I snort. "Yeah, right. Because firstly, being hideous doesn't matter when you're rich, and secondly, you're not hideous are you?"

"I've got a gloomy sort of face, I always think."

"No, you're just a gloomy sort of person."

"I am not."

"Well, cross, then." I grin at him. "You know what you were saying earlier, about when we went to the Shed? I remember thinking maybe that's what you're really like, how you were that day. The real you. Not so grumpy."

"I am not grumpy." He moves his hand under the covers, warm on my hip.

"You're not grumpy at the moment," I agree. "It makes a nice change. I mean you were terribly grumpy when you got here. And I assume since last week."

He looks away. "Yes, that's fair. I was— I got myself into a bit of a state."

"You could have just talked to me about it. Why on earth didn't you?"

"I didn't think I could. I didn't think . . . Well, bloody hell. I'd never have believed I'd ever be here, in your bed."

"No, it is quite unexpected. I think."

"I'm pleased, though," he says. "It's much better than being upset and by myself."

"No one wants that."

"No. So. What do you want?"

"I don't know."

I think I'm afraid. Not of him, no—of this, of the potential of this moment. I don't know what shows on my face, but he frowns again, and strokes my cheek lightly with one finger.

"If you've changed your mind—"

"No, no, I just . . . it's odd."

"Why is it odd?"

"I'm not sure. Mostly I think it's because I never imagined, truly imagined, that I'd ever be in bed with someone else. So that's odd. And then I never imagined I'd be in bed with you." I laugh. "Ah. That's a massive lie."

"What is?"

"That I've never imagined this. I tried not to. I tried so hard not to."

"Oh yeah," he says, nodding. "I remember, because you wouldn't fuck me if I begged you?"

This makes me laugh a lot. "Ha, oh lord. Well, I might. If you *really* begged. Mind you, that was mean, but what you said was much worse."

"It was. I'm sorry. It was a horrible thing to say. I just wanted to say something awful. I didn't want you to forgive me, so I said the worst thing I could think of." He takes my hand and kisses it. "Because I'm an arsehole, you remember."

"Oh yeah." I think for a moment and put my hand on his chest. "I've just thought of something."

"Always thinking, you."

"I am, yeah."

"And?"

"Well, we can't have sex."

He frowns, then opens his eyes wide. "We can't? That's a blow."

"I know, isn't it? I hadn't thought about the logistics."

He laughs. "The logistics? There's a romantic phrase. What on earth do you mean?"

"I mean I'm not . . . I wasn't expecting to ever have sex again. And certainly not while I'm up here. So I'm not prepared."

"Prepared? Psychologically?"

I think he's teasing me.

"No condoms or diaphragm or pill or anything. No contraception."

"Ah, yeah, fair enough. I'm not prepared either. If we were at mine, it would be okay, but I didn't—I really didn't—expect that this would happen."

"You haven't got a useful wallet full of condoms, then?"

"Sadly not. We'll have to improvise," he says. "But this might mean we have to stop talking. Will that be okay?"

"I suppose so," I say, and then we're kissing again.

...

Sometime later, Edward says, "So here's an idea."

"Mm?"

"We could drive into town. To the flat. There are condoms at my house."

"Oh yeah. You did say."

"And although that was . . . Although I think we did okay without—"

"Yeah, it was all right, wasn't it?"

We grin at each other.

"Not bad. Not bad at all. But you know, we could . . ."

"Properly do it."

He laughs again. "Yeah."

"I admit that's tempting. But it's warm in here, I don't know if I want to get up."

"You don't have to get up immediately. It's only—what time is it?"

I turn so I can see the clock. "Nearly six."

"Hm. So we could stay here a bit longer. And then go to mine. If you wanted."

I think for a moment. "Can I have my job back?"

"Is that what this is about?" He shakes his head. "Mercenary."

I laugh. "Wouldn't it be? Watch me progress my so-called career by sleeping with my boss. Soon I'll take over the company. It's very exciting. So?"

He looks at me long enough for me to think perhaps he'll say no. Then he grins. "All right, then. If you behave yourself."

"I'll be extremely professional, don't worry."

"Not too professional, I hope. I'm going to be flirting with you pretty much constantly."

"*Pfft*. I'm not sure I'll be able to tell that's what you're doing. Does it just involve you not shouting at me?"

Twenty-three

We get dressed and drive into town. We take both cars because I don't want to be trapped with no escape route. He looks at me seriously when I say this. I explain that I don't think I'll need to escape, but I just spent two days without access to my car and it was tedious. I'd prefer we drove in together, but I'm trying to be—what, sensible? I don't feel very sensible. I can hardly concentrate on driving for thinking about what it was like in bed earlier.

I park away from the shop, by the town hall. I couldn't tell you exactly why I do this. It means I get wet, running across the square. Luckily, he's unlocked the door and is waiting for me. We stand in the darkness, surrounded by the books. I realize I genuinely thought I'd never be in here again. I'm full of joy to be back.

He closes the door behind me and locks it, pulling down the blind. Usually when we close the shop, I'm outside. Tonight, though, things are different. I'm not going home later—I'll be locked in for the long haul. It's exciting.

"D'you know what?" he asks.

"Nope, what?"

"I am incredibly, stupidly, madly, absurdly happy." He

grabs me and whirls us round the room in a breathless and hilarious approximation of dancing. Eventually we knock over a stepladder and have to stop because we're laughing so much. Then he kisses me.

"I've never been so happy. I can't believe it."

My eyes fill with tears, and I'm glad it's too dark for him to see. "Oh God. How lovely. If strange."

"Come on, let's go upstairs. Are you hungry?"

I follow him out into the hallway, careful not to bump into the shelves beside the door. "I am a bit. I've barely had anything to eat today, for some reason."

Climbing the stairs in the half dark is a strange feeling. I wonder if I'll do this often. I might. Or not. It's all a mystery, isn't it? You can't know what will happen. The future stretches away into the distance, almost entirely occluded, a series of veils, some thicker than others.

I'm not sure how I feel about this, about earlier, but I recognize that sensation in my belly: lustful, hungry. I'm glad we're going to do it again, and soon. I'm glad I don't have to wait until next week or tomorrow to know it worked okay and that he too is keen to do it some more.

"No, I didn't have any either," he says. "Were you distracted? I know I was." He looks back at me. "Hey, I'll be able to cook for you. I'm looking forward to that."

I suppose it's quite sad, the warm feeling this gives me, like he's hugged me. "Are you?"

He nods. "Hardly ever get to cook for anyone."

"You need more friends." I disapprove of his empty life.

He shrugs at me. "Whatever. Anyway, there isn't time to do anything too exciting this evening." We're in the kitchen now. He flicks on the light and opens the fridge, rummaging.

I lean against the wall. This is only the second time I've been in the flat with him here too; how strange it all is.

"Okay, so, there's cheese and ham and eggs. You could have a *croque monsieur*. Or an omelette. Or a *croque madame*."

"Oooh, I like a *croque madame*. Yes please. Actually, I'm starving."

He grins at me. "Me too. Need to keep your strength up."

"Can I do anything?"

"Put the kettle on? Or you could open some wine. There's some in the fridge if you want white; the red's in the dining room."

Do I want a glass of wine? Maybe I do. Shit. Now I'm nervous again.

I open cupboards, looking for glasses. "You have a lot of kitchen stuff for a man who lives alone."

"I know, I'm a pack rat," he says, beginning to assemble the ingredients for our supper.

I regard the five sets of wineglasses. "Are these for different wines? I'm afraid I don't know about stuff like that."

"It doesn't matter; pick ones you like."

"Will you pity me for drinking white wine out of a red-wine glass?" I look over my shoulder at him.

He snorts. "Hardly."

"Good, I don't wish to be pitied." I smile at him.

"Yeah, I don't pity you. Oh," he adds, coming closer, "except what's going to happen later will be pretty awful."

I don't get what he means, and frown at him. "Why, what's . . ."

He rolls his eyes. "You know. When you have to go to bed with me. Again."

"Oh! That. Yeah well, I'm terribly brave," I tell him, and begin to open drawers, looking for a corkscrew.

"You are. D'you want me to do that?"

"I can open a bottle of wine."

"I know. I'm just offering. To be nice, you know."

"I barely recognize this version of you," I say. We grin at each other. But then I'm serious again. I clear my throat. "I'm a bit worried that suddenly all my eggs are in one basket. And, like, twenty-four hours ago I didn't even have a basket, let alone any eggs."

"What, when this goes tits up, you mean?"

"I'm not saying it will."

"I won't sack you."

"Oh, right." I snort. "You so will. You sacked me once already, remember? I think"—I lean back against the countertop and look at him—"you'd drop me like a shot if you felt it was awkward."

"No, I—"

"Oh, come on. But maybe you'd be right to, I don't know. If this goes pear-shaped I probably wouldn't want to work here. I mean, if you turn out to be a bastard."

"That's not fair, you already know I'm a bastard."

I wrinkle my nose. "Only sort of. You pretend to be worse than you are. Don't you?"

"Jesus," he says, "I think I pretend to be better, not worse. I'm afraid I have huge concealed depths of awfulness."

We were joking before, but I feel like he's not anymore; he believes this. I suppose he'd be insufferable, if he'd grown up with more self-confidence, or whatever it is that's missing. But I think it's sad that he thinks—or seems to think—he's so awful.

"I suppose I'll have to find out about that," I say, "and see what I think." I laugh. "Don't forget whose shoes you're filling. Someone who stood up in front of all their friends and family and made lots of promises and massively failed to keep them."

"I don't suppose I'll ever forget whose shoes I'm filling." He's serious again. "Someone you've known and loved for twenty years."

"Oh, well. I . . . You shouldn't think of it like that. Really."

"Mm. Difficult, though. Because you love him, don't you? Still. You miss him."

"It's not quite as straightforward as that." I frown. "I'm afraid it's more complicated than I'd choose for it to be. I don't want to . . . I don't want to shortchange you, or offer you less than you deserve."

"I shouldn't think that's possible," he says.

It makes my heart ache when he says things like this. And I'm not sure what to say. I put my glass down and step toward him, put my arms round his neck, stand on tiptoe to press a kiss against his cheek.

"Don't say that," I say. "You deserve nice things, don't you? You deserve to have someone give you all the things you've never had."

"Do I? I'm not sure."

"Hey."

He squeezes me and puts his face in my hair. "Mm. You always smell great," he says. "I've thought that before."

We hug for a long time, standing silent in the brightly lit kitchen. Eventually he sighs.

"You said you were hungry."

"I did. I am."

"Better get you fed, then."

...

I'm trying not to feel anxious. It's hard to tell the difference between excitement and anxiety, but I'm trying not to be anxious. That would be silly. After all, we've done the diffi-cult bit, which is being naked. It's a long time since anyone but Chris has seen me naked, but at least Edward didn't run off screaming or anything. And neither did I, which is a bonus.

Is it harder to have actual, penetrative sex with someone than, you know, that other stuff? Only when you're young, surely. I find myself remembering all kinds of things. Scenes from my life. The first time I slept with this person or that person, the first time I went into a boy's bedroom with the intention of . . . I think of damp and sweaty afternoons, deep in the Christmas holidays of my final year at school, nearly but not quite sixteen, doing things with Paul Leverson. A good choice, I felt at the time; he was nice, and although he'd been out with Rachel Palmer it seemed they hadn't got up to much, so it was mostly as new to him as to me. We never had sex, we were much too young and nervous. But we did lots of other stuff. Some of which Edward and I repeated this after-noon. I think of the way I felt then, and the way I feel now. It's not dissimilar, really.

We eat our *croque madames* by candlelight in the kitchen. Holly Hunter has come in, wet from the rain, and crunches biscuits beside us.

"You know," he says, "the first time we met—I know this will sound like hindsight, but—even then, I thought, I don't know. I noticed you, when you first came into the shop."

"Isn't it your job to notice everyone?"

"I don't, though. I ignore them, usually."

"You ignored me, as I recall."

"Faking it," he says, and I laugh. "I liked it when you leaned on the counter to speak to me. I could tell you were . . . amused. And then when you said who you were, I was amazed. And now I feel like . . ."

"Like what?"

"This will sound stupid," he says.

I grin at him, encouraging. "Go on?"

He sighs. "Well. That Andrew sent you."

I blink at him. "That's—that doesn't seem like the sort of thing you'd think."

"I know, it really isn't. I know it's silly. But we were quite good friends. Lots of people don't like me, but he did. He was similar to you, I think. Or you're similar to him. I think he'd have expected us to get along. Be pleased, I hope, that we do."

"He didn't know me, though," I object.

"I know. It is silly."

"It's very sweet, though," I say, slightly doubtful.

"You think I'm an idiot."

I smile at him. "Maybe. But in a nice way."

He snorts. "There's no need to patronize me."

"Whatever you say, boss."

. . .

So then we go to bed. It's nearly midnight somehow. We don't bother to wash up. Edward pushes his chair away from the table and says, "I can't wait any longer, come on."

It makes me feel . . . dizzy, I suppose. I'm not sure what to say, so I get up as well. He holds out his hand and I put mine in it, and then he leads me out to the landing.

"It's upstairs," he says.

"I know. I've been in your bedroom," I remind him.

"Have you? When?" He turns to look at me, startled.

"You asked me to close your window. I wasn't snooping," I add, although that probably makes me sound guilty.

I follow him up the stairs to the second landing. I wonder what he's thinking. I wonder if this is odd, the way I feel. I wonder if I even know how I feel. My heart's banging in my chest, I feel untethered from my normal self.

He pushes open his bedroom door and turns back to look at me. "I feel like there's a lot of . . . Is there a lot of pressure about this? Even though we were in bed together earlier?"

"It has a certain amount of portent," I agree, leaning against the doorframe to watch him as he flicks on the light and goes to close the curtains. I think of something. "Who's Corinne?"

He turns back to look at me. "Corinne?"

"You had a card from her. Edward Hopper."

"Oh, I suppose I did. Nosy. She's a friend. Lives in St Andrews."

"A friend? Like Lara?"

He laughs. "Better than Lara. But I suppose so, yes."

"Are you still seeing her?"

"I don't think I'd count what Corinne and I do as seeing each other."

"No? What do you do?"

He roots through the top drawer of the bedside cabinet nearest the window. "Do you want candles?"

"If you have some. I certainly don't want an overhead light," I say, and he laughs.

He holds up a tin. "Vanilla, I think."

"Perfect. So, Corinne?"

He lights the candle and puts it on the cabinet. "Here okay?"

"I'm sure that's fine. Are you avoiding my question?"

"Turn off the light."

I click the switch and my eyes gradually adjust. "Edward?"

"No, I'm just . . . I hardly ever see her. Maybe once a year, or every eighteen months maybe. We do usually go to bed. But I doubt she'll be heartbroken that won't be happening anymore."

"It won't?"

He looks at me, serious. "I'm all yours now. Aren't I?"

"I don't know. Are you?"

"Thea. I don't know if you've missed something here but I'm absolutely crazy about you."

I grin at him in the dim light. "Are you? That's nice. I mean it sounds so unlikely, but I think I believe you."

"You should."

"How long before you're grumpy with me again?"

"I don't know. A week?"

This makes me laugh. "As long as that?"

"If you're lucky. Are you coming in? Or staying in the doorway?"

"This is the trickiest bit, isn't it?"

"Don't let it be tricky. Come to bed."

I close my eyes. "I'd like you to say that again."

"Thea. Come to bed." He comes closer, his face in shadow. He puts his hand to my cheek, and I close my eyes. I'm shaking. He dips his head to kiss me, and I feel as though I might just melt away, knees weak. He's warm, his arms round me, our bodies pressed together.

"Oh God," he says. "I just . . . I really like you."

"I know. I really like you as well. It's okay." I pat him gently. "You shouldn't worry."

"I do, though. I worry that—"

"We can worry later; give it a couple of days, right?" I slide my fingers between the buttons of his shirt, feel his skin warm against mine.

"Yes." He kisses me again. "I never usually worry about this sort of thing."

"You surprise me. But anyway, try and channel that careless freedom. It's no good both of us being tense."

"Are you tense?"

It takes me a while to answer this. "Less tense now," I say, finally. "Mm. Gosh you're good at kissing."

He rests his forehead against mine. "You say the nicest things."

"I also think you're quite handsome," I say. "And you make me laugh."

"This is all good news."

"Isn't it."

I begin to undo his shirt, kissing his collarbone, his chest. I lay my ear against his heart and hear it beating. I put my finger on his nipple, and then my tongue. He groans, and I lay my hands flat on his belly, his sides, smooth skin, stroking, two fingers pushed into the waistband of his jeans, my other hand pressing against him, my palm against his erection, firm through the denim.

"I think you should take off your clothes," I say, and he hurries to do so, wriggling out of his jeans and abandoning his shirt. Then he's in bed.

"Your turn," he says, so I unzip my dress and let it fall to the floor. I unpin my hair and take off my bra and knickers and climb in beside him, skin on skin.

"Oh God," he says, which makes me smile to myself. He glows golden in the candlelight. I feel powerful, alluring even, full of sexual strength, confident in my ability to please and arouse. I don't always feel like that, and I'm not saying it will last, but that's how I feel now: lustful and filled with desire. It's a long time since I felt like this; I'd almost forgotten what it was like.

"You're so beautiful," he says.

"Especially when I'm not wearing my socks, eh?" I say, which makes him laugh.

...

Later, he says, "Have you spoken to him? Chris, I mean?"

"Not for a long time."

"How often do you talk to him?"

"Oh, hardly ever. We email. Not often. But occasionally. I sent him a birthday card. Which is more than he managed for me." I smile. "That was the last time we spoke, on my birthday."

"In June? That's ages ago. What does he think about you staying up here?"

"I don't know. Probably relieved to have me out of the

way. Makes it easier for them to do couple things with all our friends. I hope that doesn't sound bitter; I don't mean it to."

"But you haven't heard from him since . . . last week?"

"Has he told me himself, do you mean? That he's going to be a father? No. I don't know if he will, or if he'll assume I know, or . . ." I shrug.

"And how do you feel about that now?"

"Oh, well. I think he's mad," I say. "Think how old he'll be when it's twenty. I don't think this can have been his idea. I know I was worried about that last week. But I've thought about it, and I don't believe he . . . I think you were right. That if he'd wanted that, he'd have told me." I frown. "Have you never wanted children?"

"God, no. No. Complicated business, isn't it? Never met anyone, and even if I had, the whole thing's screwed, the inheritance bollocks. I'd hate for my great-grandchildren to be all, 'We could have had a title. That bastard.'" He laughs.

. . .

In the morning, as we eat breakfast in the kitchen, he says, "You should move in here."

I choke on my toast. "What?"

He pours more coffee. "Move in. Here. Live with me."

"You're properly mental. Oh my God."

"Why?"

"What d'you mean, why? Jesus. You don't have sex with someone once"—I hold up my hand—"okay, twice, or whatever, and then move in with them."

"Why not?"

"Because it would be ridiculous. Anyway, you've never done that before, have you? Asked someone to move in."

"No, but that's no reason not to, is it? I think it would be good if you lived here. In fact, I think we should get married." He grins at me.

"You flipping what?"

He laughs. "I don't expect you to agree with me about that."

"No, well, I can't anyway, can I? Even if I thought that was a good idea, instead of thinking you were unbalanced. I'm married to someone else."

"Yes, but you'll be divorced, won't you, in a bit. So you can move in straight away, and then we'll get married later."

I shake my head at him.

"Why not? It's easier, isn't it? I mean what's the point of driving backward and forward? I'd like it if you lived here."

"You barely know me." I frown. It's more tempting than I'm going to admit.

"That's not true, is it? We've been working together for six months. I've never met anyone I've liked even half as much. And I know we've only just started sleeping together, but I'm planning for it to be a long-term thing."

"Are you?"

"Aren't you?"

I look at him, and then look away. "Well, I'm not planning for it not to be," I admit grudgingly.

• • •

We open the shop. It's quite odd to be there doing ordinary shop things. I expect everyone knows he fired me, so there'll be questions when people see me in here. I guess I'll just have to suck it up. Strangely, the idea is not as grim as the thought of telling people why I hadn't been in.

Midway through the morning, while I'm up a ladder dusting shelves, Jenny comes in and bangs her hand on the bell aggressively. Edward looks up.

"Hello," he says, "what can I do for you?"

"As I said yesterday, and the day before, you can bloody well apologize to Thea and give her back her job," she says.

"Oh. Well"—he looks across the room to where I balance, head touching the ceiling, on the highest step of the stepladder—"I don't know if I can do that."

"Why the hell not? I'll be in here shouting at you every day until you do," she says. "That woman's the best thing that's ever happened to this place." This makes me blush. I should get over there before she says anything even more embarrassing.

"She is, yes," Edward agrees, and I climb down the ladder and hurry across toward them.

"What? Why did you sack her, then?"

"It's all right," I say. "I got him to change his mind."

She turns quickly, and grins at me, relieved. "Oh, thank God for that," she says. "You're an idiot," she says to Edward.

"Yes." He nods. "Fair enough."

"Good news anyway," she says to me. "How did you get him to change his mind? He's usually stupidly stubborn."

"Yeah, I guess I was persuasive," I say, avoiding Edward's eye. He laughs.

"She was. Very persuasive."

"Huh. Well. Good. And you're all right?" she asks me.

"I am now, yes."

She frowns at me. "You're sure?"

I nod.

"So, what was that all about?"

"He miscalculated. It's all fine now." I clear my throat. "I hope."

"I hope so too." She shakes her head at him. "Seriously, Edward."

"I know," he says. "I don't deserve her."

Jenny narrows her eyes and looks from him to me and back again. I'm pretty sure I know what she's thinking. I'm not sure I want anyone thinking anything, at least not at the moment. Give it a while, yeah?

"Thanks for coming in to have a go at him," I say. "I'm touched."

"She's been in every day," says Edward.

"I know he can be a dick, aye," says Jenny.

"I don't think he means to be," I say. I glance at Edward, who smiles at me. My heart contracts. Oh my God. Shit. Does he always smile at me like that? Can she see it? Shit.

"Hm," says Jenny. "Okay, good. Don't do it again, Maltravers." She looks at her phone. "I'd better go; I've got someone coming in. I just grabbed five minutes to come over here."

"Thanks," says Edward. "I appreciate it."

She looks at him suspiciously. "You sound almost sincere," she says.

"I am."

"Huh. Well, I'd better run. Don't let him take advantage of you," she says to me, and I'm proud of my straight-faced ability to assure her that I won't.

The bell jangles behind her.

"Good lord," he says. "I suppose you know I've had half the town in here to tell me how brilliant you are."

"*Pfft*. That seems unlikely."

"Not at all. Constant stream of abuse and everyone's best 'we're very disappointed in you' expressions. And fair play to them. I mean, you are brilliant. And I intend to take advantage of you fairly comprehensively."

I frown. There it is again. What's that feeling? It's like . . . Oh my God. We stare at each other, and then I clear my throat and look away.

Twenty-four

It's been so long since I started a relationship, there are things I've forgotten about. I can't remember the protocol. And it's different when you're middle-aged. Or it seems different—I can't just phone all my friends and excitedly scream to them. Although that's more or less what I want to do. I'm not sure what to do, who to tell.

I called Xanthe when I got home, the day after I slept at Edward's the first time. He wanted me to stay again, but I felt like I should be—is "cautious" the right word? I didn't want to just give up my own space, my own home. However much I wanted to be with him.

She was amused, but pleased, I think.

"Ah, there, I expected that to happen. I thought he liked you, when he took you away to his beach house. I was surprised nothing happened then."

"Beach house? You make it sound a lot more glam than it is," I object. "It's just a shed. I don't think you could say he 'took me away' either."

"I think you could say exactly that. And are you seeing him, or what?"

"Well, yes—"

"There you are, then."

There wasn't much I could say to that, annoyingly.

. . .

"Hey, so, tediously," says Edward, leaning on one elbow to look at me, "I have to go to London next week."

"London?" I'm puzzled.

"Yeah, you know—big city, down south?"

"Ha ha. But why? For a sale?" He's never been south of Newcastle since I've known him.

"Yeah, there's a thing at Sotheby's."

"Get you," I say, secretly impressed. "Sotheby's!"

"I thought about canceling, but that seems—"

"Canceling? Why?"

He shrugs, avoiding my eyes. "Oh, you know . . . change in circumstances."

"What, canceling because of . . ." I'm embarrassed. "Me?"

He nods. "But, um—"

"Well, that seems foolish. I'll still be here when you get back, won't I?" We look at each other for long enough that my heart starts thumping. I clear my throat and look away. "How long are you going for?"

"Oh, I usually go for a week or so."

"A week? Really?" I'm shocked, and it must show on my face.

"I do know people in England," he says, amused. "People I don't get to see very often."

"Friends?"

"Yes, I imagine that's what you'd call them."

"Er, friends like Corinne?" I don't want him to think I

care about Corinne—I really don't—but he's called them, these women, "friends" before.

"Not exactly. I've known Corinne a long time, but most of my London friends I've known longer. And they're generally men," he adds, "if that's what you're asking."

"Generally?" I can't really believe it's me saying this, I think I might sound jealous. I'm not, though—at least, I don't think so. Am I? I've really never been jealous of anyone. And I think—I *think*—I'd trust Edward not to sleep with someone else, even if he went to stay with someone he'd slept with before. Would I?

"I usually stay with Alan and his wife. Or Davey. You've seen a picture of Davey," he says. "He's the one with the joint in that photo on the dresser."

"Aw," I say, distracted by the thought of Edward's university pals. "Where do they live?"

"Alan and Trix live in Putney. Davey lives in Wandsworth. If I stay with one, I see the others. And usually some other people."

"From college?"

"And a couple from school."

"I thought you didn't have any friends from school?"

"I've a few."

"You don't talk about them."

He shrugs. "Henry. He's a consultant at the Royal London. He's often too busy to meet. Kirsty, she works for the BBC, she's married to Raj; they live in Peckham. Their house is great, they bought it when houses in Peckham were very cheap. They pretend it's Camberwell," he adds. "Puts three hundred grand on the asking price."

"Blimey."

"Yes. So. Do you want to come with me?"

I'm startled by this invitation. "To London?"

"That's where I'm going, yes."

"But what about the shop?"

"Admittedly, sometimes it seems inconvenient that you work here. By which I mean you could easily come with me if you worked somewhere else."

"Short notice," I say, pretending to consider this.

"Apart from that."

"Well, I—"

"And maybe spending a week in various spare bedrooms having to meet a bunch of strangers when we've only been together ten minutes would be . . ."

"Stressful?"

"Dull, is what I was thinking." He smiles at me.

"Oh, it doesn't sound dull," I say. "It does sound stressful, though. I'd be, er . . . I might feel weird about meeting people, you're right. When it's only been ten minutes."

He leans toward me and puts his hand to my face. "I don't really want to spend a week without you, though."

I laugh. "You can do it."

"I suppose so, grudgingly. But I don't think I can cancel, really."

"You shouldn't anyway, even if you could. I don't want to be a . . . I'm not sure I should be the reason you change your plans."

He looks at me for a long moment. "If anyone would be, it's you."

I'm flustered, again. "Yes, but—"

"But I should probably go."

. . .

He's hired a car because the Land Rover is old and noisy and not ideal for seven hours plus of motorway driving. It's half past six, Friday morning, and we're standing on the pavement outside the shop. He looks strangely more like Charles today; I think that's the car, actually, an unnecessarily large, clean grey Volvo; and he's dressed more smartly than usual. He's selling things too; there's a large box of carefully wrapped books in the trunk, along with his suitcase.

It's cold, and the sun won't rise for another hour. Even though I'm not traveling myself, I slept badly and have an unsettled feeling.

"Right," he says, "better get going. I'll call when I get there." He hesitates. "Will you stay here? Sleep at the flat?"

"What, tonight? I should think so. Hadn't really thought about it. Yes."

"Okay. Speak to you later."

We hug, awkwardly, and kiss, hoping (at least I am) none of the neighbors are unexpectedly looking out their windows. No one knows yet that we're doing this. Not that it's a secret. But I'm being discreet about it until I'm used to the idea myself.

"I love you, Thea," he says, serious. "Please take care."

"Oh God, and you. Drive carefully, won't you? Don't try to drive the length of the country in one go or anything. Look out for other drivers, they're not to be trusted."

He laughs. "I promise to be careful." We kiss again.

"Go on, then," I say, "it's freezing out here." I touch my finger to his nose. "See you soon."

And then he's folding himself into the car, pulling away, looking back to wave. I wave too, vigorously, until he turns the corner and is gone.

I feel very odd, and go back into the shop, locking the door behind me. I'm used to working by myself, of course; he's frequently away. It's not that. I'm not sure what it is. My day is confused, though, because I'm up so early and I've already had my breakfast. It's cold, down here in the gloom, among the books. I'm not sure what to do with myself.

· · ·

It's very quiet in the shop. The weather is grim—icy rain—and we only have three customers all day. There are parcels to post, however, from online sales, and I go to the post office at lunchtime. There are rumors they're going to close the post office, which would be very inconvenient. If I have to go into Newton Stewart, it will be tiresome. I pop in to see Jilly and Cerys, and then go back to the shop.

I sit in Edward's green chair (such luxury!) and read my book as the rain taps against the windows. The wind's getting up too. I wonder what I might have for dinner and I also wonder why I feel so peculiar. He's not even been gone twelve hours, it can't be that. It had better not be, it's dangerous to become too attached to people. I think about Paul McCartney. He and Linda never spent a night apart during their marriage, except for that time he got arrested in Japan. Did that make it easier, I wonder, when she died, or much harder? No one could tell you, could they? I always think it must be worse. I shiver and look at the clock. I had a text at two saying he'd arrived safely, so at least I can stop imagining car accidents. It's nearly six now, so I may as well close the shop and go upstairs.

...

"Hey," says Edward.

"Hello."

"How's your day been?"

"Oh, very quiet. How was the drive?"

"Surprisingly okay, at least until I got to Luton. Traffic was bad from there, but I can't complain really."

"How are your friends?"

"Yeah, they're good. Toby—their son—is enormous. I haven't seen him for ages. Six foot two."

"How old is he?"

"Fourteen."

"Not as tall as you, though."

"Ha, no. I think he was annoyed. He's taller than his dad."

I laugh. "So what are you doing tomorrow?"

"I'm going to Geoff Whitley's, see if I can sell him the Ovid."

"Oh, yeah, you said. Confident?"

"Yep."

I laugh again. "Good."

"Has HH had her dinner?"

"Yes. She's sitting at the other end of the sofa," I say, turning to look at her.

"Not deigned to sit on your lap?"

"Not yet."

We talk briefly about the weather, what I had for my own dinner and other fascinating subjects. I think this is the first time we've had a meandering, pointless chat on the phone. Several times I almost panic, wondering what to say next. It's fine, of course. Eventually, he says, "I'd better go, we're going out to eat."

"Celebrating your arrival?"

"Ha, yeah, I don't think it's that, more like Trix has been at work all day. Anyway, I'll call you tomorrow. Are you going to stay at mine?"

"Oh, I'm not sure," I say. "I'll see how it is tonight."

"Okay. Well. Good night, then. I might text you when I get back."

"I might be asleep," I warn him.

"That's okay."

...

It's odd being alone in Edward's bed. It's very large without him. I mean, it's comfortable, and I've put the electric radiator on a timer so it's cozy enough for Holly Hunter to have ventured in and curled up in the far corner with her back to me. But it feels almost as though I'm here illicitly. I read my book and find my mind slipping away from the words, so several times I have to go back a page and read the same section again. It's a long time before I feel sleepy enough to turn out the light, and then the wind and rain keep me awake for a while.

...

I'm not sure how long I've been asleep, or what wakes me, but the red numbers on the alarm clock tell me it's half past two. Unlike my bedroom at the lodge, it's never properly dark here; the curtains are unlined, and there's a streetlight near enough to push a narrow silver line across the wall. Being in town is noisier too. Although Baldochrie is hardly a bustling metropolis, earlier I could hear music from the pub, and people talking as they walked home, and the occasional car. At the lodge all you can hear is the weather, the wind in the trees, sometimes an owl or the terrifying scream of a fox. I might need to augment the curtains with a blackout blind. Although I haven't had any trouble sleeping here before, so perhaps it's not the noise and light that bother me. I realize I'm straining to listen, although I don't know what for. I'm definitely uncomfortable, though, and the rest of the night is broken sleep and strange dreams.

···

Edward has remembered FaceTime exists. Luckily, I now have broadband at the lodge.

"Where are you?" He frowns, peering at me.

"Oh, I'm at home. I didn't sleep very well last night, I thought maybe I should—"

"Were you cold?"

"No, no. It . . . I just felt a bit weird."

"Weird? Weird how?"

"I don't know. I think—it felt strange without you."

"I didn't sleep very well either. I miss you."

"You're busy, though," I say, turning this aside, uncomfortable.

"Yes, but I wish you were here too. You'd like Geoff. And everyone."

"Have you told them about me?" The thought of this makes me oddly panicky. What's wrong with me?

"Well, not Geoff. I doubt he'd care. But I told Trix and Alan. They were, as you can imagine, delighted."

"Oh, well—"

"Shocked and astounded also," he says.

I'm trying not to look at the very unflattering image of myself in the corner of the screen. Edward looks unusual too from this angle, mostly chin. "Shocked?"

"Well, they'd more or less given me up to a lonely death."

"Oh, really, come on."

"What?" He grins at me. "You know it's true. I think I expounded on your virtues for an hour at least."

"That must have been a thrill for them."

"They seemed quite interested, asked a million questions." He yawns. "Oh, excuse me. God I'm knackered."

"Hopefully you'll sleep better tonight. Are you going out again?"

"No, we're making pizza."

...

I sleep better that night but I'm still awake very early. Something's nagging at me, and I'm not sure what it is. I feel tense somehow, a knot of something in my belly. A vague pre-exam-like feeling. I lie in bed thinking about how, sometimes, it would be useful to be able to turn your brain off. I don't need to think about everything that's spinning through my head. When should I go home to collect my things? Should I even do that? Should I buy a flat down there? What should I do with my things once they're up here, if I fetch them? Should I rent the lodge or continue to live here, even if I decide to spend more time at Edward's? He wants me to live there—or at least, he said he wanted me to live there last week. He's mentioned it several times. He might change his mind, though. And I've grown accustomed to living by myself. I like living at the lodge. I like the garden full of birds, the possibilities of the vegetable patch, the fruit cage.

I realize I could grow vegetables here even if I lived somewhere else. Or I could grow them at Edward's; his garden is big enough. I try to imagine my belongings at his house but can't quite. It seems perfectly well supplied with furniture. He's not lacking anything I could bring with me, although I suppose my pictures would fit in, and my vintage odds and ends. And my books, ha ha, there might be room for them somewhere. My kitchen stuff could all live at the lodge, couldn't it? I'm not massively attached to any of it. I could have one of the spare bedrooms at the flat for my sewing things, perhaps. I'm not sure I can imagine a life there, though. Can I? Actually I can, of course. I like the flat very much, the size of the rooms, the elegance of the space, and Edward doesn't own anything I'd discard, given the choice. He has good taste and has always had the money to buy nice things.

. . .

I talk to Xanthe. She wants to know how it's going, and I tell her he's away, and that I feel weird.

"Weird how?"

"I don't know. I feel anxious."

"Anxious? What do you think is going to happen?"

"I don't know. Nothing. I'm not sure. I just . . ."

"What, though?"

"I think I'm just . . . I don't know."

"Well, this isn't really getting us anywhere, is it? And I don't know him, so I can't really help you. It's very early days, isn't it? And unexpected. And you've only had one partner for like twenty years. I guess he's quite different from Chris."

"Well, yes. Yes, he is. But I don't think . . . I mean, Chris isn't the only boyfriend I've ever had, is he? I don't think it's that. Maybe it's . . ."

"What?"

"I think there are some things I need to speak to him about. And if he were here, I could, but he's not, so my stupid brain is causing me trouble. And then there's this whole thing with his brother," I say. "I mean I can understand why they fell out—it's hard to imagine how they wouldn't have. I get why they hate each other. But how will that work? Charles has always been perfectly nice to me; I'm not going to suddenly stop speaking to him. But that might be really awkward."

There's a long pause, while she considers this. "I suppose so. Can't you get them to sort it out?"

"I don't know. And is it even any of my business?"

Again, a pause as she thinks about it. "Sort of?"

"Yeah. Is that good enough? I don't want to meddle."

"I think you're worrying about things that might not ever be problems."

I have to laugh at this. "But that would be so out of character!"

She laughs too. "Wouldn't it? But this stuff you're worrying over about Edward—"

I don't really want to discuss this with anyone other than Edward, it seems unfair. I change the subject. When the conversation is over, though, I'm thinking about it again. I'm thinking about how different my view of relationships is from Edward's. He's had no practice, and he's been involved in a number of situations that I would never even contemplate. I know he said this thing we're doing is permanent and monogamous, but how does he know that? His last relationship was with a married woman—and as far as I can tell he didn't even remotely care about the circumstances of that. I know he said Lara's husband didn't care either, and I believe him, because why would he lie? But that's not normal, is it? Or is it? Whenever I've said things about posh people and their morals or lack of, he's never disagreed with me. In fact, I know he sort of thinks people only have morals when it comes to judging the behavior of others, and they'll always be able to reconfigure them when considering their own. I don't think that's true, though. Or anyway, it's not true for me. I've never cheated on anyone and I never would, and by that I'd include sleeping with someone who was married, even if I myself were single.

I think about this for ages, and then I remember that when I was first at university, my sixth-form boyfriend Pete slept with a girl on his course, and although I forgave him—or said I had—I felt it had somewhat loosened the agreement between us. That Christmas I got off with—but did not even remotely have sex with, although I certainly thought about it—the flatmate of one of my friends. So my morals aren't exactly perfect. Of course, that was at the end of something. Pete and I should have been brave enough to split up before we went to college at opposite ends of the country because, as I said to Rory many months ago, it was all entirely predictable that we should split up before our third Valentine's Day. You can't expect much different, really; teenagers exposed to loads of fresh new opportunities, arriving at uni without any baggage from home. And I was an absolute goddess at university (I laugh to myself at this thought) so I had plenty of options.

None of this helps.

...

I spend the week at work feeling off-kilter and awkward. It continues to be very quiet at the shop, and the only interesting thing that happens is when the people from the chamber of commerce come to speak to me—well, they came to speak to Edward really, but obviously he's not here—about the Victorian Christmas Shopping Festival. Unsurprisingly, Mr. Maltravers has never engaged in this particular bit of local branding, which is due to happen the week before Jenny and Alistair's wedding, but I'm well up for it and agree at once. I plan the Christmas window display to accompany this event with what can only be described as glee, and I scroll through hundreds of top hats from eBay before it occurs to me that maybe—just maybe—Edward might own one. He seems the type, frankly. He'll have been to a dozen weddings where a silk hat was required, surely. I'm not going to be crinolined, I'm going to drag up. I'm already very excited about fake muttonchop sideburns and an embroidered waistcoat.

I text him.

Have you got a top hat by any chance?
> *Yes, I think so—why?*

Just wondered. Where is it?
> *If it's at the flat, it'll be in the cupboard in the green spare bedroom. In a box.*

Cool, thanks. I mean, is it all right if I look for it and get it out?
> *Of course, help yourself. But what on earth for?*

Victorian Shopping Fest.
> *Oh Jesus Christ no.*

:D:D It's OK, you don't have to do it.
> *I'm not going to.*

No, I didn't think you would. :D

· · ·

You see, it's fine. I speak to him, it's fine. We FaceTime and I look at him and think, *Yes, this is a real thing that's working, it's fine. I'll talk to him when he gets back and . . .* And then I feel sick and nervous and unsure. I know I can't be with someone who would happily cheat.

· · ·

Friday morning, and he's home. He drove through the night despite the weather being awful. At 6:30, he's banging at my front door, to my surprise and astonishment, brandishing a lovely-looking bunch of flowers.

I peer blearily at him and open the door wider. "Those aren't from a convenience store off the motorway. Fancy London flowers?"

"Of course. Hello."

"You should have phoned, I'd have got up."

"You are up." He grins, enfolding me in a bear hug. "Anyway, I wanted to surprise you."

"I am surprised. I thought you wouldn't be back until this evening."

"Yeah, seemed pointless going to bed, so I didn't. God, I've missed you," he says, his face in my hair.

"You smell of the city," I say, nose pressed against his shirt.

"Do I?"

"Well, I assume you do." He seems very solid and real, standing in my hallway, and I wonder exactly how I've managed to create another version of him in my head. Is that what I've done?

He kisses me and I immediately feel less tense and more . . .

"Oh God, Thea," he says. "Darling Thea."

"All right," I say, "calm down. Are you hungry?"

"Famished."

I fiddle with the thermostat and turn up the heat. It begins to clank and thump. I think I should probably get a new boiler, but the rule with boilers is to wait until it's Christmas Eve or another equally annoying day before they go wrong enough to replace, and then live with no hot water for four weeks.

"Did you stop on the way?"

"Had a coffee at Tebay." He yawns, stretching, and follows me into the kitchen.

"Oh," I say, distracted, "are they open all night?"

"A bit of it is. No scones or artisan bread, though, sorry."

"Well, come and have some breakfast. What do you want? Porridge? Bacon and eggs?"

"Is there bacon?"

"There is. Also tomatoes if you like?"

I put the kettle on, and he takes off his jacket and subsides onto a chair.

"God, it's nice to be back," he says.

"But you had a successful trip?"

"Oh yes, very successful. I've spent money but also made money."

"Hurrah." I cut three tomatoes in half and put them under the grill, break eggs into a glass.

"Are you having some?"

"It's a bit early, but I'm up now. So yes." I make two mugs of coffee and place his before him. He slowly stirs a spoonful of sugar into it and closes his eyes. "I'm quite tired," he says.

"I should think so. Are you going to go home to bed?"

"Got to drop off the hire car"—he yawns again—"and pick up the Land Rover."

"Yes, and then?"

"Might have a lie down. We don't need to open, do we?"

"Don't we?"

"Well, I don't know. I'll see how I feel."

"I can run the shop without you, I've been doing it all week."

"Yes, but you'll be needed upstairs," he says, blinking at me.

I laugh. "Oh, right. Stock take?"

"Don't do that until January," he says, pretending to take me seriously, "you know, after the Christmas rush."

"Expecting a Christmas rush?"

"It's usually pretty busy."

"Even though you don't do the Victorian Shopping?"

"I'm open," he says, "just not dressed up."

"Boo. I think you'd look good as a Dickensian shop-keeper."

"It's a ridiculous thing."

"The chamber of commerce seems to think it's very successful." I turn the tomatoes around and lay four slices of bacon in the frying pan. "Toast?"

"Oh, yes please. I'll do it." He gets up and unwraps the bread before cutting four slices. He drops them into the toaster. "They would say that, though, wouldn't they?"

"Well, anyway," I say, "I'm going to dress up. Your top hat fits me perfectly."

"Are you going in drag?"

"Yep."

"Hot," he says, which makes me laugh.

"I'm planning impressive facial hair," I say.

"Even hotter. Muttonchops, or a mustache you can twirl?"

"Oh, actually that sounds appealing. I was going for side-burns, but who wouldn't want a twirly mustache?"

I pour the eggs into the pan, and he takes plates from the cupboard.

"I know two weeks is hardly long enough to get into a domestic routine," he says, fetching the butter from the top of the fridge, "but one of the things I've missed is messing about with you in the kitchen."

I turn to look at him as the toaster pops. He jostles the toast onto a plate and begins buttering it. He catches my eye and winks at me.

My stomach tenses again. This is all very well, isn't it, but I'm supposed to be talking to him about stuff. Admittedly, I wasn't anticipating his arrival before 7:00 A.M. We should at least eat our breakfast. There must be something in my face, though, because he says, "Are you okay?"

"Mm, yes, do you want brown sauce?"

"No. Are you sure? You look . . ."

"What?"

"I don't know, tense?"

"No," I say. I turn the bacon over again, and plate it up with the tomatoes and eggs, then bring the food to the table. I extract cutlery from the drawer and we both sit down to eat.

"Sure?"

"Eat your food," I say, and crunch through half a slice of toast.

...

I'm washed and dressed and driving behind Edward on the way to the shop. He has to go via the car hire place, so I get there before him and open up. I didn't say anything to him while we ate breakfast, or afterward for that matter. I don't know if I'm putting it off or if it's just more sensible to wait until he's rested. I wouldn't want someone landing a big serious conversation on me when I'd been up all night.

I hear the Land Rover outside and notice, with some cynicism, that just the noise of the engine of his car makes me smile.

"Hey hey," he says, pushing the door open and putting his suitcase down by the counter. He turns and goes back outside, returning with two boxes and a carrier bag.

"What did you get, then?" I ask.

"Got this for you—"

"Oh, Edward, really?"

"Yes, and isn't it a thrill to know it won't have to live in the safe for three months like a certain set of napkin rings?" He hands me a slender parcel, almost as long as my forearm.

"Is it a spoon?"

"You'd better open it."

I sigh and carefully unfasten the tape before unrolling the brown paper. Inside is a ladle, rather beautiful, initialed on the handle with a very curly *E & A*. "Oh," I say.

"Yes, sorry, I know it's a bit soppy," he says. "But isn't it handsome?"

"It is, very. Is this older?"

"Eighteenth century. 1750? Or something like that."

"It's lovely."

"To share," says Edward, and my eyes fill with tears.

"Hey, what is it? What's wrong?"

"Ah. Um, look . . ."

"Thea?"

"There's some stuff in my brain," I say.

He looks at me, cautious. "Stuff?"

"Yes, look, I . . . This is where I might say I'm fine," I tell him, "but not really be fine?"

"Please don't say you're fine if you're not. What is it?"

"It's nearly ten," I say. "We should—"

"We don't need to open the shop. What's wrong?"

"You're tired—"

"Not so tired I can't be reasonable. Please, tell me what's wrong?" He goes to the door and locks it. "Let's go and sit down," he says gently, and I follow him slowly through to Poetry/Plays/Lit Crit, where he turns on the lamps and sits down on the smaller sofa.

I perch beside him and try to collect myself.

"So. Tell me about the stuff in your brain."

"I'm not sure if it's really there. At least . . . this week I've been . . . because you weren't here," I say in a rush. "I don't know what I've done, it's like I couldn't remember how you were. Now I see you, I see how you are. I think."

He looks concerned. "Okay? And is that . . . is that bad?"

I laugh. "No. I don't think so. I just . . . Okay, look, I'll just say it. I keep thinking about how . . . Are you the Susanna? In other people's lives? Am I . . . Do you . . . I'm not sure if I can . . . The thing is, what happened with Chris and Susanna hurt me terribly. And I don't think she meant it to. She didn't think about me at all. But you meant to hurt Charles, didn't you, when you and Carolyn . . . And I don't know if—"

"Oh," he says. "This is about what kind of arsehole I am."

I can't tell if he's annoyed. "No, it—"

He waves a hand, dismissive. "Yes, it is. I don't mind. You wonder if it's worse, that I did what I did without caring. At least Susanna cares. She wanted your husband, and she loves him, and she might not have cared about you, but she does care about him, or so we assume. But I hurt two people and broke up their marriage and I didn't even like Carolyn. That's what you mean, isn't it?"

I nod, quite impressed that he should sum this up so effectively without prompting. "Well, I know you said Lara's husband—"

"Oh God, no, he doesn't give a shit. Let's not worry about *him*. But you think I might feel that infidelity is . . . acceptable."

"I'm not sure if I do think that," I say. "But it has been worrying me."

"Yes. I don't, though." He clears his throat. "If I'd been in love with Carolyn, I might not have done it. Is that worse? It might be. But it wasn't about her, it was about Charles. I'm not making excuses. You know I've barely had anything you could call a normal relationship. Some of those people—"

"Charles's exes."

"Charles's exes, yes. Some of them I saw for a while. I never cheated on any of them, though. I've never slept with someone else if anyone's ever thought I was only sleeping with them." He frowns at this rather convoluted sentence.

"Haven't you?"

He shakes his head. "No."

"Corinne—"

"I must take you to meet Corinne," he says. "I think you'd get on. But Lara didn't expect me to be . . . She didn't think I was hers, you know, or anything. It would have been hypocritical, after all. I mean, I'm not saying Lara is particularly thoughtful about moral equivalency or anything"—he makes a face—"but it's not like she doesn't have sex with her husband. If she wanted me to herself, she certainly never said so. I wouldn't think it was acceptable, Thea, is what I'm trying to say. I would never sleep with anyone else. I would never be unfaithful."

"That's what Chris said, though. Saying you wouldn't is meaningless. I mean, you might mean it this second, but—"

"Would you cheat? Not on me, on anyone?"

"No, I . . ." I pause, trying to be honest. "I'd like to think I wouldn't."

"But you can't know that either, can you?" We look at each other, solemn. "I can only tell you how I feel, and promise you that . . . I promise you I'll never let any of your friends persuade me that I ought to fuck them."

I laugh at this. "I don't think I believe in promises anymore."

He pulls at his lower lip, thinking. "I don't want to be put in a position where I can't tell you anything—where I can't tell you the truth about how I feel. Or make you believe me. Because I know you think I'm . . . Well, I don't know exactly what you think. But you think I might do something awful because I've done awful things before?"

I bite my lip, hard, to stop myself from crying.

He sits back. "I don't think I've ever done anything awful except to Charles, or not really. I've been absent and uncommitted and lazy with women—but only because I've never met anyone I really wanted to be with. And you know that's because I didn't try to meet anyone. I know it's pathetic, and I should probably have had loads of therapy a long time ago. But then again, if I had, I'd be married now, I expect, and probably quite content. Because I think I might have an enormous, untapped capacity for contentment." He laughs. "If you'd told me a year ago I'd be saying that, I'd have thought you were mad. But it's true."

"I'm not special, though," I say. "Why is it different?"

"You're special to me. I know what you mean. Probably you're just like loads of people, not unusual. But I think you're great. I can't imagine getting bored with this, with you. I love working with you. I love you. I've missed you so much this week. It's unreasonable. I've fallen hard."

"You have, and that worries me too."

"I think . . . I think perhaps you shouldn't worry. You're right when you say no one knows what will happen next, that we can't predict anything, and you're probably right about promises. But here we both are. I lay my heart at your feet."

I frown at him, troubled by this.

"You needn't pick it up if you don't want to," he says, serious. "If you don't think you can believe me—"

"It's not that. I do believe you."

"You do?"

I take a deep breath. "Yes."

Twenty-five

We've been together nearly a month before I tell anyone other than Xanthe. I come out of the shop after hours, off to the Co-op for milk, when I bump into Alistair walking the dogs. It's about half past seven, and cold, an icy fog making the high street look mysterious. The moisture in the air runs down the windows and drips around us.

"Got you working late tonight," he says.

"Oh, er, not really."

"Not really?"

It's lucky it's dark; I'm hoping he can't see me blushing in the orange light from the streetlights.

"No, I—"

"Thought I saw you yesterday as well," he says. "On a Sunday?"

"Yeah, okay," I say. "I guess it's not a secret."

He grins at me. "Jenny was right, then."

"Why, what did she say?"

"I won't tell you exactly what she said. But she implied that you and Edward had, er, grown closer."

I snort. "Oh, did she?"

"She did. So. You know I'm not Edward's biggest fan . . ."

I sigh. "No one is, are they? Well. Me, I suppose. I am." I shuffle, embarrassed.

He laughs. "But if you like him, good for you. He was in a fantastic mood when I saw him on Saturday. I suppose this explains it."

I'm even more embarrassed. "Was he?"

"Like the morning after a bad storm, all sunshine and clean pavements. Make sure he treats you kindly."

"He has so far. You know I don't mind his . . . the way he is."

"No, Jenny said it doesn't seem to bother you." He shakes his head. "Very odd. But good for everyone if he's more cheerful. So bring him to dinner on Wednesday."

"Are you sure? I didn't want to ask. I know you don't like him."

"I expect I'll like him better now. So bring him. Jilly and Cerys are coming too."

"Okay." I nod. "I'll ask him. I don't know what he thinks about dinner at other people's houses."

In the Co-op, buying milk and looking at the sad remains of the bakery shelf to see if there might be a cake, I try to imagine having dinner at Alistair and Jenny's with Edward. A perfectly normal thing to do, just as though we were a perfectly normal couple, which I suppose we are.

. . .

Jenny says, "Are you bringing Edward, then, tomorrow?"

I nod. "He was thrilled to be asked," I say, and we both laugh, because it's patently untrue.

"You really do like him, then?" she says, curious.

"I do."

"Better than Charles?"

"Oh God, yes. I don't like Charles. Or, that's unfair, he's okay." I wrinkle my nose. "He's always been perfectly nice to me. But I like Edward a lot more. Yes."

"It seems odd to me. But it's none of my business."

"Sadly, there's only one Alistair," I tease her, "and he's already spoken for."

"Oh aye, well. Sorry about that." She hesitates. "He's kind to you, though, is he?"

"Of course." I'm surprised. "I wouldn't bother otherwise. I mean . . ." I pause, unsure of how far to go into this. I like Jenny, she's probably my best friend here. "Chris was kind to me, before he left. I'm not interested in people who are . . . unpleasant."

"Oh, don't be offended. I didn't mean that you were. Sorry."

"No, it's okay. I just . . . I know it doesn't seem like that long since Chris and I split up, and—"

"It was a good while before you came up here, though, wasn't it?"

I nod. "January."

"That's nearly a year. Even after a very long relationship, I don't think you're, you know, on the rebound. Anyway, you seem quite sensible."

"I am, usually," I agree.

She looks at me, thoughtful. "Do you think you're not being sensible about Edward?"

"I think . . . I think I wasn't expecting to meet anyone. So it was unexpected. And he's . . ." I'm not sure what to say, unwilling to expose him too much to the curiosity of his neighbors. "He's very keen."

"Yes." She nods. "He told Cerys he'd never really been in love before."

"Oh my God. Did he?" I'm both horrified and delighted by this.

"Yeah. So. I guess that's quite impressive."

"Well. I have been in love before. More than once. But I like him a lot."

. . .

"Hello, love, how are you?" My mother peers at me from the computer screen. "Still in Scotland?"

I usually Skype from the shop, because I got into the habit before there was broadband at the lodge. I'm upstairs today, though, in Edward's sitting room.

"Yes."

"How's the weather?"

I glance out the window at the grey sky. "Wintery."

"Wet?"

"Not today. Or at least not at the moment."

"It's cold here," she says. "I was surprised." They're in Wyoming now, staying with one of her old school friends, who emigrated to the States before I was born. They're having a marvelous time despite the cold: everyone's friendly, the scenery amazing, mountains and forest and actual buffalo. Snow. Horses and barns and so on. It does sound fabulous.

"Prairies."

"Yes, I thought it would be hot."

"I expect it is, in the summer."

"So where are you? That doesn't look like the shop," she says.

"Oh, no, this is upstairs, in the flat. Look." I pick up my laptop and turn it so she gets a view of the room. "Isn't it lovely? And quite warm, despite the windows, because of the fire."

"Above the shop? Whose flat is that, then? The owner's?"

"Yes. Edward." I clear my throat. I should tell her, shouldn't I? It's not like it's a secret.

"On a Sunday? Are you working?"

"No, I stayed here. Last night."

"Oh," she says. I can see her wondering whether she should ask me about this; I'm famously secretive, or at least, non-forthcoming.

"Yes," I say, feeling sorry for her. "We're . . . Edward and I . . . I suppose we're seeing each other."

She's searching my face, difficult to do at this distance.

From the doorway, Edward says, "You suppose? That doesn't sound very enthusiastic."

"It feels weird saying it," I explain. I turn back to my mum. "He's here, would you like to say hello?"

"Of course! Yes! Let me get Dad—"

"Oh no, no need to—"

I can hear her shouting, though, and then my dad appears, looking confused.

"You don't mind, do you?" I ask Edward. "I know meeting people's parents is the worst thing."

"No, because I'm keener about this than you are," he says, "and would be happy to tell any stranger that you're my lover or even girlfriend."

"Don't say 'lover' to my parents, you freak."

He laughs at me and comes to sit down.

"Er, hello, Dad, how are you?"

"Good, thanks, Thea. Now, what's going on? I can't understand what your mother's on about."

"I just wanted you to meet someone." My parents are squashed together, staring at their screen. "This is Edward, he's . . . he owns the shop. Where I work?"

"Oh yes, the bookshop." Dad nods, adjusting his specs. "Nice to meet you, Edward."

"Hello, Mr. Hamilton. And Mrs. Hamilton."

My mother's beaming at him. "Hello," she says. "I'm Judith. And this is Roy." She nudges my dad, who seems confused.

I clear my throat. "Dad, Edward and I are—"

"Engaged," he interrupts, and I put my hand over my eyes.

"Not engaged," I say, "that would be madness. But we are—"

"Going out," Edward interrupts again. He's grinning at my mum, who looks delighted.

"Seeing each other, yes."

"Well, that's lovely," says Mum. "I'm pleased for you both."

"We're absolutely not engaged, though," I say. "I'd just like to make that clear."

"Yet," says Edward, and yelps as I pinch him.

"No need to rush things," says Mum, smiling happily at me. "Just be kind to each other."

"That's the plan," says Edward.

"So you've known each other awhile," says Mum.

"Yes, since I first arrived, more or less. Of course, I wasn't in any fit state to—"

"No, well, things have been difficult, haven't they? I'm glad you've met someone. I've been worried about you, up there by yourself, not knowing anyone."

"I do know some other people," I object. "I've got friends up here now."

"I know. But all the same. It's good to have someone special."

Edward squeezes my hand. "It is," he agrees. "Good to meet you both. Hopefully, we'll meet in person one day. I'll leave you to it." He pats my leg and gets up.

"Only say nice things about me," he says in a stage whisper, and I roll my eyes at him.

"Idiot. How am I going to be able to do that?"

He laughs, leaving the room. I turn back to the screen.

"So have you been seeing each other long?" My mum's excited. "You've hardly mentioned him."

"Yeah, no. A couple of weeks."

"And that's okay? Working together?"

"It is so far, yes. He's quite easygoing. Er . . ."

"I thought you said he was grumpy?"

"Oh, yeah. He is. I don't mind that, though. He just does it to stop the customers from bothering him. I'm much better with people than he is."

"I find that hard to believe," my dad says. "Never had you down for customer service."

"I know, but we don't get crowds and crowds. It's not like when I worked at HMV. Anyway, we get on well, so far."

I don't like to tempt fate, so I'm cautious when I talk about it. I don't want to jinx it. I want it to be fun for as long as possible.

...

Introducing him to my folks reminded me that I'd wondered about the semi-Bohemian sixties life of his parents, so I look them up. They're almost famous, after all, hovering on the periphery of Swinging London. There are newspaper photographs. His mother getting into a car outside a nightclub, all beehive and false eyelashes. His dad with Brian Jones and Paul McCartney, about 1965, raffishly handsome, his arm round an unseen someone. A set of pictures from a photo shoot, captioned "Mayfair's brightest slumming it." They're sitting on the steps of one of those dilapidated Georgian houses, pre-gentrification Notting Hill or somewhere; empty milk bottles, peeling paint, his mother all kohl eyes and kaftan, his dad in paisley. Another picture of his mother, earlier on, perhaps the late fifties, standing behind Princess Margaret, the flash making his mother's dress blankly white.

They make me slightly uncomfortable, these pictures, a reminder that if things were different, and not much different, he'd be someone else entirely. That fifty years ago our relationship would have been impractical, and eighty years ago more or less impossible. I know he's not a duke or anything, but even so. We'd never have met, would we, unless I was a servant, or perhaps the wife of an employee. I don't want to meet his mother, elegant and well-preserved. I'm certainly not one of the lovely girls she finds at dinner parties and wants to introduce him to.

Twenty-six

It's January. I'm not sure how the last two months have whizzed past in a rush of . . . well: cold beach walks and poetry and love. I'm all aglow with the pleasure of it. We've been out to dinner with various people, been guests at a wedding—where Jenny looked so beautiful I cried throughout the ceremony, which surprised me as much as it embarrassed everyone else—and I had a lovely Christmas, one of the best ever. I admit I was disappointed Edward wouldn't dress up for the town's Victorian shopping festivities. He ended up hiding upstairs while I did it. But now I have lots of photos of me in a top hat, so I guess it's still a win. And then for Christmas Day and Boxing Day we went to the Shed and it was freezing cold but brilliant. We ate loads of food and had lots of sex. I certainly have no complaints.

Finally—at last—I'm shifting Local History to the front of the shop. Sing hallelujah, etcetera. I can't help feeling it's some kind of prize for good behavior, but when I say this Edward laughs and says, "More like bad behavior."

"Meaning what?"

"Pretty sure you know exactly what I mean."

I look at him, hands on hips. "I shall pretend I have literally no idea," I say disapprovingly, and he laughs again.

"No, you've persuaded me," he says. "You're probably right. I can't think of anything you've ever been wrong about."

"Calm down," I tell him. "Won't your brain short-circuit if you're too pleasant?"

He looks at me for ages, then shakes his head. "Why on earth did I not meet you years ago? Why didn't you do your degree in Edinburgh?"

"I didn't want to do a four-year degree," I say seriously. "I did look at the course."

"Oh God. Just think."

"Yes, you'd have looked down your nose at me, I imagine, from the dizzying heights of your final year, and I'd have thought you were a twat, and we might potentially have had sex and never spoken again," I say. "Is that what you mean?"

"Nonsense."

"You'd have missed out on all those girlfriends of Charles's, *quelle horreur*."

"Can't think of a single one I wouldn't swap for the opportunity of having known you for twenty-five years."

I'll never get tired of hearing him say things like this, but I like to pretend to be unaffected by it. "You'd have messed it up, I expect; you don't sound like you were the most emotionally intelligent young man ever to grace the streets of Edinburgh."

He snorts. "Maybe not."

"Anyway, are you going to help me with this?"

He looks at the shelves. I've already put Local History (all eight feet of it) into boxes and shifted those boxes to the front of the shop. I've put Children's (Collectible) and Art

History where the Local History used to be. I've shifted Contemporary Scottish Fiction to where the children's books were, Military History to where that was, and now I have to move Cookery/Craft/Gardening from the front of the shop, and put the Local History in there. I'm a bit dusty, and to be honest, exhausted. I probably should have done all this when the shop was shut, but *meh*.

"I suppose I could take them out of the boxes for you," he says. "Shall I put the kettle on first?"

"Oh, I'll do that. Tea?"

"Yes please."

It's quiet, has been all day—unsurprisingly, since it's a Wednesday in January. The lamps are lit and outside it's raining in a relentless sort of fashion. I go out to the kitchenette and put the kettle on. It's gloomy in there behind the curtain; the window is narrow and looks out (not that you can see through the frosted glass) on an equally narrow piece of outside space that's overshadowed by the wall and the building. To get to it you have to go behind the workshop and shuffle. There's nothing much down there: some random flowerpots, an old gate. Despite this lack of view, and the icy rain, I'm happy. I'm happy every day at the moment and keen to note it. The comparison to this time last year—yesterday was the anniversary of discovering exactly what Chris had been up to—is almost unfathomable.

I wake up in Edward's bed and he brings me coffee and says nice things to me and we look at our phones, as is the modern way, and then we have breakfast and go to work. I am not yet bored of this, despite his fears. I still get time by myself when he goes to sales and, though I miss him, I know this is a good thing. It's all working rather well. I make a pot of tea and try to remember if there are any biscuits left in the tin behind the counter. As I wait for the tea to brew, I hear the shop bell ring and wonder whether we might sell something.

I get the milk out and tap my fingers on the countertop. When Edward puts his head round the curtain, it makes me jump violently.

"Jesus Christ," I say, "you scared me."

"Sorry. Er . . . Thea."

"Yes."

"You'd better come through."

"I'm just waiting for the tea, I won't be a moment."

"I know. But . . ."

I turn to look at him. He sounds peculiar. "Are you okay?"

"Something unexpected," he says.

"Unexpected? What do you mean?"

He screws up his face. "Chris is here."

"What?" I gawk at him.

"Clistopher," he says. This makes me choke with laughter. It's a quote from a Diana Wynne Jones book, *The Lives of Christopher Chant*. It's how the mermaids say Christopher's name, and it's generally how he refers to Chris since we first remembered it, even though I told him not to, because Christopher Chant is much, much cooler than Chris Mottram.

"What are you talking about?" I say.

"He's here. He's just arrived. In the shop."

"By himself?" I have a horrid vision of an enormously pregnant Susanna in my shop.

He nods.

"Are you sure it's him?"

"He told me it was," he says. "I presume he's not making it up. That would be strange, wouldn't it?" He almost laughs at this idea, but then he looks serious again.

"Well, bloody hell." I look around the kitchen, although I'm not sure what for. "What on earth does he want?"

"I don't know, Thea, you'll have to ask him."

I frown. I'm not—I don't exactly know how I feel about this. I gesture at the teapot. "I only made a small pot," I say vaguely.

Edward says nothing. I brush dust from the front of my shirt and try (unsuccessfully) to see my reflection in the window. It's been said—by Jenny, who sees me daily, and by Xanthe, who has to peer at me via FaceTime, that I am looking my best at the moment, glowing with joy. I hope this is true. With luck it will be more noticeable than the dust all over me and the multiple layers I have to wear in the shop during the winter.

It's childish to want to look your best in front of your ex. I know that.

Deep breath, then. "Are you coming?" I ask him.

"Do you want me to?"

I'm not sure. "Yes."

"Okay," he says. "Just let me know if you want me to leave you on your own."

"He's definitely by himself, though?"

He nods.

"Okay. Okay."

I duck round the curtain and turn right into the front

room of the shop. Chris is standing by the fireplace, a vintage detective novel in his hand.

"Thea," he says. "Hello." He pushes the book back into the stack on the mantelpiece and comes toward me. I step backward—not deliberately, I just . . .

I'm surprised by how much he looks like himself. I don't know why this is surprising. Who else would he look like? It's so odd to see him. I haven't seen him for, what, ten months? It seems like forever.

I glance back at Edward. "Er," I say, "hello. So this is Chris—"

"Yes," says Edward, "he introduced himself."

I ignore him. "And this is Edward."

"Yes," says Chris, "hi."

They look at each other, two pairs of eyes steadily regarding each other, weighing each other up. It's almost exactly as awkward as you might imagine introducing your husband and your boyfriend might be. After a pause that lasts a couple of seconds longer than I'm quite comfortable with, I realize that I need to say something else.

"So, hey, this is . . . I wasn't expecting to see you. You should have said you were coming, I'd have taken the day off or something."

"Yeah, I . . . It was a bit spur of the moment."

"A long drive for spur of the moment," I say, frowning at him. "And, well, you didn't drive up today, surely?"

"Yeah, no. Came up yesterday. It's farther than I thought. I've got an Airbnb place in Newton Stewart."

"Right." There's another awkward pause.

"You look well," he says.

Edward, who's gone behind the counter and is pretending

to work, snorts loudly, then turns it unconvincingly into a cough and rattles things.

"Look," I say, "do you want a cup of tea or something? I was just making one when you arrived. Maybe we should . . ." I glance over at Edward again, but he's looking at the computer. "Maybe we should pop over to the Old Mill? Then we could have a drink and sit down." We could go upstairs, but I don't want to invite him up to the flat. "That is . . . Why are you here? That sounds rude, sorry. But—"

"Yeah, I, well, I wanted to talk to you; and you know I hate talking on the phone, and email's not the same, and . . ."

It's all rather odd. He's not good on the phone, it's true, or at least he doesn't like it; and God knows we haven't had a proper conversation since I came up here. But I can't see what we need to have one about, not really. There's the house, I suppose, and the money. And that apparently still-secret baby. I assume it must be about the house. I'm suspicious now that he's going to try somehow to get out of paying me. But that's unfair and based on nothing but paranoia.

"Could we close?" I ask Edward. "It's not busy, is it?"

He looks from me to Chris and back again. "If you like," he says, "or . . . D'you want me to come with you?"

"Yes," I say decisively.

. . .

It's quiet in the Old Mill, which is lucky. I don't particularly wish to be the subject of curiosity, although it's usually unavoidable.

"We'll go out the back," I say, waving at Cerys. They don't usually do table service, but she mimes taking an order at me, head on one side, and I nod. That will be easier than one of us going up to the counter and leaving the other two to make awkward conversation.

The conservatory is empty, raindrops chasing one another down the windows, the winter garden folded in on itself. We have one of those "what about here? yes that's fine" conversations and I slide onto the bench beside Edward. Chris has had a recent haircut, but he hasn't shaved in maybe a week. I don't recognize the top he's wearing, or the jacket he's just taken off. I look down at myself, wondering if I'm wearing something he'd recognize, but it's one of my many generic white linen shirts, and even I can't tell if it's an old one. This cardigan is definitely new, though; Edward gave it to me for Christmas.

Cerys brings us menus and goes away again, consumed, I can tell, with curiosity.

"It's bigger than I imagined," Chris says. "Baldochrie, I mean. How far out is your house? I couldn't remember." He looks from me to Edward and back again. "Do you still live there?"

"It's about five miles away," I say. "Not far. And yes." This isn't exactly a lie, I suppose. I'm not sure why I don't want to just tell him I more or less live at the shop.

"And this is where you're from?" he asks Edward.

"Yep. Well, the family home is about five miles away. Just up the road from the lodge, actually. That's where I was born."

"Were you?" I say, surprised I've never asked about this. "You were born there?"

"Yes, of course. Traditional, isn't it?" He smiles at me. "Charles was born in Dumfries, though, because he has to be different. Although it's always annoyed him that he wasn't born at Hollinshaw."

"You don't sound local, though—I thought you'd have an accent," says Chris.

"It's a disappointment to everyone," agrees Edward.

There's another slightly uncomfortable pause.

"So how are you?" I ask. I think he looks tired, but that's not something you say, is it? I wonder if it's the house full of children and the pregnant girlfriend.

"Yeah, yeah, I'm good, yeah. And you? You look really well," he says again.

"Thanks, yes." I put my hand on Edward's thigh. He puts his hand over mine and squeezes.

Cerys comes back to offer drinks, and we talk about the weather, and Chris's journey north, and the progression of the new development in the town center back home. Chris asks about my parents; I ask about his. He asks about the shop.

"Never imagined you working in a shop," he says.

"I know, it's quite funny," I agree. "But I like it."

"The shop's not how I imagined it either. I thought it would be smaller, for some reason. I don't think Xanthe described it very well."

"You could have looked it up," I say. "There are plenty of photos on the website."

"Yeah, I don't know why I didn't," he says, frowning. "And it's your shop? I mean, you own it?" he says to Edward.

"Yes."

It's clear he can't think of anything else to ask, and we sit for a moment in silence. I keep looking at Chris, poking at my feelings to see how I feel about seeing him. If I'm honest,

I'm slightly irritated. I think his tone when he speaks to Edward is off, and I don't see why it should be. He should be relieved, surely, that I've met someone. Pleased, even. But I don't think he is.

"That's not your name, though, is it? Fortescue?"

"Oh God." I laugh and look at Edward. "No. It's a joke, sort of."

I remember when he explained the shop name to me. It's the most ridiculous inside joke that no one would ever get. His response, when I said that, was, "And anyone who does get it is clearly to be avoided. It's a joke for me."

"A joke?"

"It's not important," I say, dismissive. Cerys is back again with her notebook, and I order coffee and cake, while Chris asks for ham, eggs, and fries, and Edward just has coffee.

I feel the conversation is more or less dependent on my thinking of things to say, which is annoying. I talk a bit about Baldochrie and Christmas and the lodge.

"You're not going to sell it, then?"

"Not at the moment." I don't feel it's necessary to explain my plans. I'm reminded of something I meant to ask before. "Is Susanna going to sell her house?"

"No, she's renting it out at the moment. That seemed the best idea."

I nod. "In case you split up."

"We're not going to split up."

I think I've annoyed him. "Well, I know," I say. "But you might. I mean—"

Edward's phone rings. He peers at it and mutters, "Bugger. I ought to take this." He looks up at me apologetically.

I wave a hand. "That's fine, go on."

He gets up and wanders away. "Hey, Roger, hi . . ." and then I'm on my own with Chris. He watches Edward walk away, and then turns his attention to me.

"Xanthe says his brother's a lord," he says, disbelieving.

"Yeah," I say, distracted. "He is."

"That's weird. He doesn't seem that posh."

"I think he made a lot of effort to be normal, when he was young. That's why he hasn't got an accent, though. A Scottish accent, I mean. Because he really is posh. I think they beat it out of them at school."

"Where did he go to school? Eton?" he says derisively.

"No, they went to Gordonstoun; it sounds terrifying. Prince Charles went there," I add. "And David Bowie's son, but he got expelled."

"Huh."

"I know, mad, isn't it?"

Cerys arrives with Chris's lunch and my cake. "I'll take Ed his coffee," she says. "Shout if you need anything."

Chris thanks her and begins to eat. It's clear the whole gentry thing bothers him, or intrigues him anyway.

"Xanthe said she met his brother."

I nod. "Charles, yes."

"So you're mixing with the aristocracy. What do they call a lord's brother?"

"Mr. Maltravers," I say. "In this case."

"So he's not an 'Honorable' or whatever?"

"No. I mean, he was, when his dad was alive. But that's just for the children of lords, because they don't have titles."

"That must be galling."

I frown at him. "Why?"

"Well, to have your brother be a lord and not be one."

"Oh! No—he's the eldest. He gave it up. Did Xanthe not tell you this bit? He renounced the title."

"Oh. What an odd thing to do." I can tell from his face that he thinks this is both stupid and admirable. I shrug. "I suppose he wouldn't be going out with you if he was a lord," he says, which I think is quite rude.

"Probably not," I say calmly. "Anyway, enough about that. What about your news?"

"My news?"

I roll my eyes. "Do you honestly think I don't know about it?"

"About what?"

"The baby."

"Oh." He looks uncomfortable. "Yeah."

"So congratulations and everything."

"Thanks."

"Are you excited about it?"

"I . . . Yes, of course."

I nod. Maybe I should just ask him, since we're here. I clear my throat. "I didn't know you wanted to have a family. You should have said."

He looks up from his plate, where he's dipping fries into the egg yolk in a desultory fashion. "It's not . . . It wasn't planned," he says.

I'm relieved by this, even though it's none of my business. "Oh. I thought perhaps—"

"No."

He doesn't want to talk about it, but I'm going to make him. "I wondered if, you know. If that was why. Why you left me."

"Thea. No. Please don't think that. It wasn't. You know I didn't exactly plan for any of this to happen."

I nod. "I know. It's okay. I . . . I didn't like to think that perhaps I'd failed you somehow."

"Oh my God. Is that what you think?" He looks appalled.

"I didn't know what to think. Because it's not like we . . . I wondered if you'd wanted to and I hadn't realized." I clear my throat again. "I was more upset than I expected. I know it doesn't make any difference, to me. It's not like . . . But I was upset."

"Oh God. No, no. I know I should have told you myself. I'm sorry. I'm a coward. Honestly, you mustn't . . ." He looks up, behind my shoulder. "Look, there's some stuff I need to talk to you about. It's awkward, with him here. Can I see you by yourself? Before I go home?"

"I . . . Well, I suppose so. Though I don't see why."

"It's just . . . It's weird. No offense," he adds, as Edward sits down.

Edward's not paying attention, though. "That was Roger McBride," he says. "Got a house clearance he wants me to look at."

"Cool," I say. "Look, you don't have to stay. If you want to go back to the shop?"

He looks from one of us to the other. "Sure. Leave you to it?"

I nod. "Won't be long. Will I?"

Chris, who looks pained, shakes his head.

"Okeydoke. See you later." He stands up again, and then leans down to kiss me. "I'll cook for half six, shall I?"

I nod.

"Let me know if you think you'll be later. Good to meet you," he says to Chris, unconvincingly.

We sit for a moment in silence. Surely we won't be here until half six. It's only quarter to four.

I take a breath and try not to panic.

Twenty-seven

"Go on, then, what did you want to say?"

He sighs. "I don't know. Everything's weird."

"Right."

"Christmas was weird, and—"

"Weird how?"

I'm curious. I think again of my own Christmas, and how brilliant it was. Just thinking about it makes me smile.

Chris, however, is not smiling. "I don't know. Noisy. Busy. Different."

"That's all your Christmases from now on," I tell him, amused by his expression. "Anyway, I thought Christmas with children was meant to be magical. Just think, next Christmas you'll have a baby! You can buy one of those outfits with *Baby's First Christmas* on it." I laugh. He doesn't. He just sits there. It's hard work, this. I don't know why I have to make all the effort; I didn't ask him to visit me. I watch two older couples come in, peruse the cake selection, then head out to the conservatory and sit to our left. It seems to take them forever to struggle out of their coats and scarves and settle into their corner. Chris has finished his food and is fiddling with the pepper grinder. I nearly lean over and take it from him, but I know it would be inappropriate.

"Does Susanna know you're here?" I ask with interest. He looks shifty, which is not a thing I'm used to.

"No," he says, "I thought it might be better not to tell her. I told her I was going to see Barney."

Barney lives in Jedburgh. Chris was at university with him; he's quite odd. Odd enough that it would make sense for Chris not to take Susanna to visit him. I nod.

"She'd be upset that you wouldn't want to see her."

I look at him blankly. "Why on earth would I want to see her?"

"She doesn't like to think that you hate her."

I snort. "She should have thought about that before, shouldn't she? Anyway, I don't hate her, particularly. I mean, I did, I suppose, but really." I shrug. "It's . . . I wish it hadn't happened, but it did, and we all have to get on with it, don't we?"

"You're happy?" he asks rather abruptly.

I think about it. I'm not all that happy to be here now, if I'm honest. Mostly I am, though; unexpectedly and delightfully happy, despite the dark thread of sadness that still lingers on the edges of my life. I'm fairly confident that will go away eventually.

"Yes," I say, "I'm happy."

"He's . . . You like him, that . . . Edward."

"I like him a lot, yes. I've been lucky, to meet someone. I didn't expect to."

He's still restless, fiddling with his spoon now, eyes sliding across my face.

"And you? You're happy?" I feel obliged to ask. Cerys, bringing coffees for the old people, has brought me one too. I'm grateful for this, and the unobtrusive way she slides it in front of me and hurries away. "Looking forward to being a . . . to the baby? When will it be born?"

"April. I . . . Yes," he says, but I don't believe him.

"It will be all right once it's born. I expect you're just nervous. It's a big thing, isn't it? You shouldn't worry, though. People fall in love with their children." I smile at him, trying to be reassuring.

That was my job for a long time, to reassure him. You can't just forget something like that. When he was anxious about something at work, or if he had a row with his mum. He hasn't done that for years, but when we were young they used to fight.

I wonder what his parents think about all this. They've been grandparents for ages; his eldest niece is seventeen or eighteen. I feel guilty that I've more or less dropped his family. But I'm sure it's easier for them not to have to think about me. I did send a Christmas card, but I didn't buy gifts, or birthday presents either, for the girls who were my nieces. That's mean; it's not their fault. I shall try to do better.

"I think I'm too old," he says. I see it in his face: he's terrified, the poor bastard.

"Oh, come on, Rod Stewart's a lot older than you," I say, and then, since he looks baffled, I add, "and he's just had a baby. Or quite recently."

"At least he's had loads of children already. He knows what to do. And he probably doesn't have to do anything anyway. Being Rod Stewart."

"Yeah, true. But look, my grandfather was forty-three when my mum was born, and he didn't die until she was nearly forty-three herself. If you're worried about that."

"I'm worried about everything," he says.

"Oh dear. Does Susanna know? That you're worried? You probably should talk to her and not me, ha ha."

"I know, I'm sorry. I just . . . It's hard to talk to her, she's so busy all the time, and the kids are there and . . ."

I sip my coffee, watching him over the rim of the cup. "More fun when you were just shagging?"

"It's not that," he says, but we both know there's some truth in it.

"I suppose you didn't think about that. About the children."

"I had no idea we'd ever move in together," he says, "when it . . . when we were first—"

"Oh yeah," I say, "that reminds me, I was going to ask about that. About when that was. I didn't want to know at first. But now I do. When did you start seeing her?"

"I don't know if . . . Is that helpful?"

"I don't know. But tell me anyway."

He sighs. "It was after . . . D'you remember that bonfire party Deb and Andy had? When you had flu?"

I think of the autumn he's talking about. I hadn't had the flu for years and was shocked at the severity of it. Four years ago last November.

"Yes, I remember." It was a long time ago. Quite shockingly so.

"Well, it was—I suppose it was after that."

"I wondered how it started. I mean, did you kiss her, or say something first, or what?"

"Thea, I don't think it's something we should talk about."

"I don't see why not. I mean I've had to live with the consequences. Had you fancied her for years?"

Four years ago? Flipping heck.

"No, I'd never thought about it. About anyone."

I nod politely. "Oh yeah."

"You do believe me?"

I shrug. "I guess."

"But she . . . I don't know. It was dark, and cold, and there were lots of people and mulled cider—"

"I remember you telling me about all those things," I say, "and baked potatoes and fireworks. But not about Susanna."

"No, well. We were chatting, and she just put her hand through my arm, you know, and . . . I don't know. It was . . . I could easily have ignored her, or pulled away, but I didn't. And afterward, I helped Deb put things away, and everyone had gone, more or less, except Susanna. I asked her how she was getting home, and she said she was walking. So I offered her a lift, and then she asked me in." He pauses. "The children were at their dad's for the weekend."

"And that was that? You weren't terribly late back, or I'd remember. Did you go to bed then?"

"No, no of course not. No," he says, offended. "No. I . . . She gave me her phone number, and told me she—"

I'm not sure I want actual details. I can picture the hallway of Susanna's house, imagine the scene: the cold, the darkness, the two of them in their winter coats, fumbling.

"Did you kiss her?"

He looks at me and then away. "Yes. And she said . . . she . . ."

I can see he's remembering it: the moment, the beginning, the start of "them," the beginning of the end of "us." It's always pleasant to think of the start of something. I could find a smile and some warmth in the thought of the beginning of any of my relationships: the first kiss, the move from potential to actual. But I don't want to see it on his face. I wonder what she said. Did she tell him she liked him? Or that it was wrong? Or that she was up for it? I think of a summer evening long ago, Chris putting his arm round my shoulders for the first time as we sat slumped on the sofa in his rather grim flat, the taste of cheap lager and cigarettes. Tragic, isn't it? It seems like five minutes ago and five hundred years.

He's talking again, and I should listen.

"I wasn't going to do anything about it. I felt bad just for kissing her."

"Just." It's not nothing, is it? An illicit kiss, a secret snog, then back to your house, your bed, your wife.

I drain my cup, wait for him to go on.

"I didn't text her for ages." He wants me to believe him, and then forgive him. And maybe he didn't text her right away. I bet he thought about it, though. I wonder if he thought about it when we were together, in bed; did he imagine how it would be? Susanna with her mass of curls, her skin darker than mine, her enormous breasts? I wouldn't say she was fat, plump maybe, and she does have big tits. A comfortable body. She's had three kids, after all. And she's sexy, I suppose, if you like that sort of thing. I said before: earthmotherish. She's got a tattoo on her shoulder, a sunflower, and smells of coconut oil. I can almost smell it now; perhaps I can. He might smell of her. After all, she's always there, isn't she, in his house, buying shampoo for him and shower gel, possibly ironing his shirts.

It's interesting to think these things and watch myself for a reaction.

"But then you started texting her? Is it weird that I want to know?" I laugh. "I don't know why I do, really."

"I told myself I was texting to tell her it . . . that I wasn't going to . . . that I couldn't get involved."

"Oh, right. But that's not what happened."

"No. I was . . . it was . . . and then it seemed like just texting wouldn't hurt. Although I knew it was wrong."

"And it escalated."

He closes his eyes. "Yes."

"Okay. And when did you start sleeping together? That year?"

He doesn't want to tell me, does he? He doesn't like to think about it, or not as it might seem to me. Being in the wrong is problematic.

"Not until the spring."

"Gosh. How restrained."

He opens his eyes. He looks pained, but that's not my problem, is it? I think I'm being very calm. I don't even want to make him feel bad, but he's a decent enough bloke, so I assume he is feeling bad. And then probably resentful, because guilt makes you irritable. I bet he can think of a hundred reasons why all of this happened, and none of them will be "because I couldn't keep it in my fucking pants."

"Thea—"

"And then you fell in love. When was that?"

"I don't know. Not for a while, it was maybe that summer. I thought for ages it didn't matter, that it didn't make any difference to us. You and me."

"It didn't seem to," I say. "I mean, I didn't notice. That made it worse, I think. I had no idea. I didn't even think you were being distant, or that you were absent more than usual. That's what made it so odd for me. So difficult to process. It was a total shock."

I think about that text he sent, the picture. Thinking about yesterday was what he'd written. I don't think I'll ever forget it, how I felt when I saw it, her hands on him. Is that what he's thinking about too? He looks embarrassed. As he should. I wonder if it was deliberate. Subconscious, maybe. If he was in love with her, and they wanted to be together. It was an easy way to do it. He never had to sit me down and say, "Thea, I've got something to tell you."

I remember sitting at the kitchen table, waiting for him to come home from work, my brain full of static, unable to think straight. I didn't shout or even cry, not to begin with. When he got in, I just waited until he came into the kitchen.

"What are you doing?" he asked me, and I pushed my phone across the table toward him and said, "I'm thinking this might be important."

His face as he realized what had happened. I could almost hear it: the collapse of everything in my life.

I thought he'd beg me to forgive him. He didn't, though, he just said, "Shit." And looked at me and said, "It's exactly what it looks like, I'm so sorry."

I believe that too—he was sorry. Sorry I found out, but also sorry to hurt me. I know he wouldn't have chosen to do that, but it's not like he chose not to, is it? It's not a foregone conclusion, cheating on your spouse. You have to make decisions, a series of decisions, before you end up in a situation where your wife's looking at a photograph of your dick in someone else's mouth.

"I know," he says, "I know. I'd been . . . relieved that you didn't suspect anything." He closes his eyes again. "All the words for this are so shitty," he says.

I laugh. "Yes. You could say that." I know what he means; it's like I said to Edward months ago. All such a cliché.

"It seemed for ages as though . . . I don't know. I suppose I thought it would go on for a while and then stop. I didn't think we'd end up here. Like this. I used to sit in the car sometimes and say it out loud. 'I'm having an affair.' But it never seemed . . . Oh, I don't know. I'm sorry, Thea."

I sigh. "I know. Anyway. Never mind all that. What did you want to talk to me about?"

"Oh. Yes. Okay. The thing is. You'll laugh," he says, "and who can blame you. But . . ."

There's quite a long pause. I raise my eyebrows, waiting.

"I think . . . Have I made a massive mistake? I think I might have."

He's right, I do laugh: an explosive "HA." It reminds me of my reaction to the news about the baby, that sob pushed up and out from my diaphragm in exactly the same unexpected fashion, loud enough for the old people in the corner to turn and look across.

"I know. What sort of . . . I can't even believe I'm saying it."

"To me as well. Of all people."

"Yes."

"You shouldn't be saying it to me, should you? What would you do if I said, oh yes, but don't worry, we can fix it?"

He says nothing. I almost think that's what he wants.

"I'd be mad to, Chris, you can see that, can't you? I mean you're having a fucking baby."

"I know."

"Jesus."

"I know."

I shake my head. "You don't know at all. You're a . . . I don't even know what you are." I sigh. "But it's just cold feet, isn't it? You don't mean it. If I said, 'Okay, let's fix it,' you'd be in as much trouble, or worse."

"I just . . . I don't know if I can do it." He does look frightened: scared and exhausted. Not for the first time, I wonder what it's like at home for him. Very different from how it used to be.

"Bloody hell. So it's not even like you're saying, 'Thea, I love you'?" I shake my head at him. "You must think I'm a complete mug. Oh yeah, great, come on, let's try again because you're frightened by what you've done? I mean you've been shagging her for four years, Chris. That's bloody ages."

He doesn't say anything.

"Oh my God. I can't believe it. I'm outraged."

"I do love you," he says.

"Yeah, right."

"No, I do, of course I do. It's the hardest thing about it all, isn't it? If I didn't, it would be easy."

"Pardon me for not seeing which bits were hard for you. I seem to remember you told me our marriage was dead; that seemed fairly final, don't you think? I don't see how you come back from that. 'Oh no hang on—not dead, just sleeping'? I hardly think so."

"There's no need to be—"

I close my eyes and make a placating motion with both hands. "Look. I don't want to fall out with you. I'll always have . . . I should think I'll always . . . I don't want to hate you, do I? I've loved you so hard and for so long. But try and see it from my point of view for two seconds. I'm not here to help you or offer support or succor. You decided you wanted to get that stuff elsewhere. Extracurricular everything. And I haven't made a fuss, have I? Or not much of one. I could see in your face it was pointless. If I'd thought I could change your mind, I'd have tried. I'd have done anything."

I hear my voice break, my words trembling. I will not cry. I won't.

"But that was then, and things are different now. Everything's changed, hasn't it? And the most significant change is little Mottram junior. Babies need fathers, and they don't always get them, but you've no get-out, no excuse. We'll get divorced, and you can marry Susanna, and I hope you'll be happy. I'd like you to be happy, because if I thought you'd messed up my whole life, and brought everything I'd worked to create for decades, crashing down round my ears for nothing, I'd be absolutely bloody furious."

I sit back in my chair, exhausted.

"You're right, of course," he says after a moment.

"You're damn right I am. Honestly. You should be ashamed." I look at him and relent slightly. "It will be fine; you know it will. I expect you'll love it, being a dad. You'll be good at it, won't you? You're patient and loving and that's all anyone can ask for in a parent."

"I dunno."

I don't know what else to say; it's not my job to perk him up.

"And Susanna's excited about it?"

"I think so. Yes. No, she is—planning stuff. We'll have to build an extension probably."

"Oh. I suppose you will."

"Yeah, there's not room for all of them."

"I suppose not." The eldest, Ruby, is fourteen, then there's Alfie, who's ten or thereabouts, and the youngest is seven, maybe. I can't remember his name. Joe? I'm not sure. Anyway, none of it works if they have to share, I guess. Not my problem, though.

"Anyway, so I'll have to remortgage for that. And then you'll get your money. I'm sorry it's taken so long to sort out."

"That's okay. You're lucky there was some money from Uncle Andrew."

"Yeah, I know. You'd have told me, though, if you needed the money? I'd have found it somehow. I wouldn't want—"

"I guess. Anyway, it'll be good to have it. I thought I might buy one of those flats on the coast road, you know, the new ones."

He looks surprised. "What, back home? Are you moving back, then? I thought—"

"Oh, no. Not at the moment, no. But house prices down there—it seems like a good investment, doesn't it? I'm trying to be sensible."

"Are you going to sell your house? You'll live together, you and . . . him?"

"No, I shall keep it. Holiday rental maybe. Not sure. We don't live together at the moment, or not exactly, but we might. Since he lives over the shop and I work there it seems quite practical. The flat is lovely," I add, "but it's sensible to have somewhere of my own as well, I think. Because you never know, do you?" I glance at him. "I'll never feel entirely safe. I don't want to . . . I need to make sure I'm okay."

"Yes."

"Anyway. So is that . . . was that what you wanted to talk about?"

He nods. "Yeah, I . . . Don't tell anyone, will you?"

Oh right, now he's concerned that this might escape into the world, that people might think badly of him. I sigh. "Who would I tell? Come on, Chris."

"Xanthe."

"Everyone tells Xanthe stuff, don't they? But I won't if you don't want me to." I look at him. "You'll be fine. Don't worry about it. Seriously."

"I hope so."

"You will. Right. I should go; we've been here for hours." I stand up and put on my coat. "I'm sure Edward's been terribly busy." I laugh.

"Yeah. Thanks for listening. I appreciate it."

"That's okay. I look forward to getting an enormous check or whatever. Money transfer?"

"Probably easiest, isn't it? I'll be in touch. And about the divorce."

"Okay, just let me know what I need to do. Do I have to divorce you? I'm afraid I haven't looked into it; I didn't think there'd be any, you know, rush."

"There isn't really. I mean we can't get married before the baby's born now anyway. She doesn't, you know . . . She doesn't want to be a pregnant bride."

"Oh yeah, once was enough," I say, and laugh again. "No. Okay. I don't mind if you want to leave it until it's two years or whatever. It's better if it's like a no-fault thing, isn't it. Even though, it's obviously all your fault."

He doesn't look amused, so I point at my face. "See me smiling. A joke. Admittedly not a very funny one, but still." I pick up my bag. "Goodbye, then," I say. "Take care."

"Yes," he says, "and you."

I head for the door, but he calls after me.

I turn back. "What?"

"I . . . Nothing. Goodbye."

I raise my hand in farewell and walk to the front of the shop, leaning against the counter. I close my eyes for a moment.

"You okay?" asks Cerys.

"Oh, yeah. Yeah. Can I pay you? And thanks for that extra coffee. I very much needed that."

"Thought you might. You've been here for hours. Paying for all of it?"

"Yeah." I can buy Chris's lunch; it won't kill me. She rings it up and I search for my purse.

"That your ex?" she whispers. "Sorry. None of my business."

I laugh. "No, it isn't, and yes, he is."

"Everything all right?"

"Yeah. Stuff to arrange, you know. He owes me half a house."

"Oh, of course. Did he give you a massive check?"

I laugh. "Wish he had. But no, not quite." I look over my shoulder to where Chris still sits in the conservatory, staring out at the rain. "Right, thanks, see you tomorrow."

I push out into the cold afternoon air, stop for a moment, and breathe out. Bloody hell. It's not easy, is it? Any of it. I'm not sure how to think about any of what just happened. I hope . . . I hope he'll be all right. I don't want him to be miserable, even if he does deserve it. I look across at the bookshop and smile. Lucky me. My new life is fun, isn't it, and surprisingly not at all stressful. Isn't it an odd thing? I cross the road, avoiding the enormous puddle by the bus stop. Isn't it funny to think that I might be in a better place than Chris is? Not that I'd gloat about it. Or not much anyway. I push open the shop door and the bell jangles above me.

"Oh hey," says Edward. "All right? You were ages."

"I know. Jesus. What time is it?"

"Nearly half five. May as well close?"

"May as well."

. . .

Upstairs, as I peel potatoes and Edward makes pastry, he says, "So, that was Chris."

"Yeah, weird, right? God."

"Mm."

"What did you think? He was a bit off with you, wasn't he? I thought. Which is odd, when you've taken me off his hands, as it were. Or at least, you know . . ."

"Mm."

I turn to look at him. "Mm? Is that all you've got?"

He screws his face up. "I thought he'd be taller," he says. I laugh. "He seemed . . . What did he want?"

"Oh, I dunno. I'm not sure he knew himself. It's all getting a bit real and he's freaked out."

"I suppose that's understandable. It is quite old to start being a parent. I wouldn't fancy it much myself."

"No, me neither."

After a while, he says, "Did he ask you to go back to him?"

I'm astonished and turn again to stare at him.

He nods. "Thought so."

"No, he . . . How the hell did you guess that?"

He shrugs. "It's a long way to come to talk about mortgages."

"Well, but—"

"What did you say?"

"I told him to fuck off, obviously."

"Did you?"

"Oh, come on. What do you reckon?"

He shakes his head. "I don't know. Maybe you're thinking about it?"

"Edward."

"You might want your old life back."

"Wouldn't matter if I did, would it? That's not what I'd be getting."

"Near enough."

"Edward."

He opens the drawer and rattles about, looking for the rolling pin.

"That's not . . . You don't really think—"

"I don't know."

"Yes you do. Don't be stupid." I empty peelings into the compost bin. "Seriously."

"Well, but—"

"You're not, like, my second choice, you idiot," I say. "Jesus."

"Am I not?"

"Fuck's sake."

This makes him grin, but then he's serious again. "I'd understand if I was. Sort of understand. I mean, he did seem to be a twat, so . . ."

I look at him. He has a noble expression on his face, which is how I know he doesn't quite mean it.

"He's all right, mostly, usually for about, um, fifteen years, and then he starts shagging your mate," I say.

Edward opens the cupboard beside the oven and crashes through a selection of roasting pans and cake tins, retrieving a fluted flan dish. We're having quiche.

"Did you ask him about that, then?"

"Yeah. Four years they've been seeing each other."

"Shit, really?"

"Mm."

"That's . . . that's ages."

"Isn't it?"

"Are you okay?"

I shrug. "Makes no difference, does it?"

"No, but—"

"Anyway, he didn't exactly ask me. Or he didn't exactly mean it, anyway. He'd have been terrified if I'd said yes." I sigh. "I don't know what I'd have done if he'd asked me, I don't know, nine months ago."

"You'd have thought about it?"

"No, no . . . I don't think I would have. I'm not a total idiot. But it would have upset me."

"But you're not upset now?" He flips the pastry neatly over the flan tin, pushing the rolling pin across the top, and then pauses, looking at me.

Wrinkling my nose, thoughtful, I say, "I feel a bit smug, actually."

He laughs. "Do you?"

"Well, my life's quite . . . It's . . . I don't like to say it's brilliant, because that's asking for trouble." I plant my hands firmly on the chopping board, touching wood for all I'm worth. "But you know. It's pretty, er, great."

"Is it? Earning minimum wage in a dusty bookshop in the back of beyond?"

"Yeah, and sleeping with my boss, because who else would I sleep with?" I grin at him.

"You could probably find someone."

"Maybe." We look at each other. An intense moment. I smile and lean to kiss him. "Ah. I'm pretty happy with what I've got, to be honest. Suits me fine."

. . .

Time to go home. To Sussex, I mean. I've given notice to my landlord and I need to fetch my things. I'm going down on the train, so I can hire a van when I get there rather than driving down in an empty van, which would be annoying. I've shifted things round at the lodge to make room, and been up in the loft space to see how suitable it is for storing anything I don't need for the moment.

Edward is still saying I should properly move in with him, but I'm not certain. I'm at the flat more than I'm at home, because it's convenient. It's not just that, though. I like being there, with him. Sometimes we go to the lodge, and occasionally I sleep there on my own, but he doesn't really like it. I mean, I do as I please, but if I'm honest, I don't like it either. It seems wasteful, when we could be together. He says he's waited a long time for me, and so he wants to make the most of it. And fair enough; I doubt anyone ever lay on their deathbed and wished they'd had less sex.

Finally, I have the money for the house from Chris. I'm not paying the mortgage anymore, and now that I won't be paying rent on the flat, I'll be quite a lot better off. I'm hoping that if I buy a flat in the new development, the mortgage will be barely noticeable.

I'm looking forward to seeing Xanthe and Rob, and the kids, and Angela. I'm not going to see Chris, though. I got Xanthe to go and pick up the box of photographs, the ones we couldn't sort out last year. I have no idea if he's kept any of them. I don't care much.

I don't imagine Edward will want to come with me, and I'm surprised when he says he does.

"I'd like to see where you're from," he says.

"But we'll have to go on the train."

"I can handle that."

"And it will be tedious. Moving furniture."

"I can handle that as well. Unless you don't want me to come with you?"

"No, I . . . It just—it didn't occur to me, that you'd want to."

"Why wouldn't I?"

"The shop—"

"I do go on holiday sometimes, you know. I can close. It's February; not busy, are we?"

"I suppose not. Are you sure you want to come? The flat's horrible."

"Does it have a bed?"

"Yes."

"And will you be there?"

"Yes."

"Then I want to be there."

"Okay. Thanks. It will be better," I say, "if you're there."

"At last she admits it," he says, and we smile at each other.

...

It's funny being back home with Edward. I show him various places—my schools, the flat I lived in when I came back from university, the flat Chris and I lived in when we first got together. We drive past Mum and Dad's, and, cautiously, past Chris's house; Susanna's old Renault Espace parked (badly) outside it. There's a tricycle upside down in one of the flower beds, which is odd—none of her children are young enough for a tricycle. I don't feel much when I look at the house, except that it seems smaller than I remember.

We go to Chichester for the day, and to look at the new flats, which are a bit small and cramped, if I'm honest; but I don't plan on living there myself, so I guess that doesn't matter. We discuss at some length whether it's worth paying extra for the sea view. (It's a pretty distant view.) We have lunch with Angela and Jeff, and dinner with Xanthe and Rob. I'm relieved that Edward is at his most charming, and they all seem to like him. Angela is wide-eyed when I help her fetch dessert, whispering, "Jesus, Thea, you didn't say he was . . ."

"Was what?"

"Well, you know. Really good-looking."

"Oh, that. Didn't I?" I'm amused.

"No, you didn't. Jesus."

"Lucky he's a grumpy sod, or he'd have been snapped up years ago."

"He absolutely doesn't seem to be grumpy," she says, handing me a stack of dishes.

"Yeah, I've cheered him up a bit, I think." I grin at her.

"Bloody hell. Time I stopped feeling sorry for you."

This makes me laugh. "I definitely don't need your sympathy."

"I should think not."

Twenty-eight

It's nearly April. In a fortnight, it will be the anniversary of my arrival.

I've had an idea, and it's time to discuss it with Edward. I wait until breakfast on Sunday, when we're lounging in the sitting room drinking coffee, with the spring sunshine falling all round us.

"I thought maybe we should have a party," I say cautiously.

He looks up from reading the paper on his phone. "A party? Good grief, are you mad?"

"I know. Not a massive one. Just a few people. You know. We've been to dinner with some people, and—"

"Yes, and if I'd realized having a girlfriend would mean being polite to my neighbors—"

I tilt my head at him. "Yeah? You'd what?"

"I'd have accepted it grudgingly."

I look at his irritable expression until he can't hold it any longer and grins at me. "You've ruined my life," he says. "I used to be miserable all the time and now I'm forced to be happy."

"I'm going to ignore all that. Anyway, I thought, I've been up here a year, nearly. I'd like to do something to celebrate that. We could have some people round for drinks, and make party food, and . . . it needn't be too awful."

"Hm."

"Otherwise it's a series of dinner parties."

"No."

"That's what I thought. Even though you're a great cook and it's a shame. But we could get through everyone if we had drinks. All at once, I mean."

"Who would you invite?"

I begin listing people. After about fifteen or so, I say, "And I thought perhaps—only perhaps, so hear me out—maybe we could invite your brother?"

"Why the hell would we do that?"

"Because I get on okay with him, and it would be easier for everyone if you two could be in a room together."

"It's not my fault we can't be."

This causes me to choke. "Oh my God. Yes it is. Jesus Christ. You slept with his *wife*."

"Oh yeah."

I laugh so much I go limp, sliding down the sofa cushions and hiccupping. He watches me, smiling, until eventually I manage to open my eyes properly and wipe away the tears. "Oh God. Well, now that I've reminded you of that tiny fact . . . I don't suppose he'd come, but if we invite him, we're making a gesture, aren't we, and maybe next time—"

"You mean we'll have to do this more than once?"

"Edward Maltravers. However much I might like to sit up here and barely speak to anyone, that's not how things work. It's good to have friends, and it's useful, and I'm not giving up my tiny social life just because I live with Mr. Misanthrope."

"Huh."

"Huh yourself. Can I invite him? And whoever he's seeing if he's seeing someone?"

"He won't come."

"No, so there's no risk, is there?"

He looks at me, considering. "What if he does?"

"It's not like you'd have a fight, would you? Wouldn't that be a bit rude? I mean, to me. Would he bring it up? I can't imagine he would."

"Hm."

"No, but he wouldn't, would he? When I told him we were seeing each other he didn't really comment."

"What could he say? 'Don't'?"

"He more or less said that once before. After you sacked me. He told me you were a shit."

"*Pfft.* He's not wrong."

"Yeah, and I told him you said he was one."

"Ha."

"Anyway. What do you think?"

He looks thoughtful. "I think you're right, he won't come. Invite him if you like. If he does come, I can handle it."

"When was the last time you spoke?"

"God knows. Possibly when he shouted, 'Are you sleeping with Carolyn?' at me." He laughs and then tries to look serious. "Sorry. I know that's not funny."

"Jesus."

...

The flat is full of candlelight and the smell of canapés. We've been busy: everything's polished and shining warmly, music plays, the dining room and sitting room are tidy and beautiful, full of people chatting, laughter. I feel very grown-up. I found a lovely dress on the internet and Edward looks . . . I know he's my boyfriend, so obviously I find him attractive, but I keep looking at him in astonishment. He looks fantastic. He grumbled about ironing a shirt and polishing his shoes and said, "Why does it have to be formal?"

"It's not really formal, is it? It's only people we know. You don't have to dress up."

"You're dressing up."

"I just have a nice frock."

"You've had your hair cut."

"Yes, but—"

"And you look gorgeous."

"Thanks—"

"I don't want to let you down."

I smile. "As if you could. You always look great."

He doesn't always look *this* good, though. Whenever I catch his eye he winks at me exaggeratedly, because I told him he looks hot.

We've not had anyone round since we've been together. Not that either of us ever had people round before. I admit I'm not that sociable, but I've always tried to fight my desire to sit in and read all the time. I have to work harder up here too—these aren't people I've known for twenty years plus, after all; they could easily drop me if I don't make an effort. No one turned us down—all intrigued, I should think, to visit the flat and see us together. Even Charles accepted, much to my surprise and Edward's irritation.

"You don't have to talk to him," I said.

"Huh."

"Well, you don't. He knows everyone else, doesn't he? Just say hello. Be charming. I know you can do it."

"*Pah*."

"It's only for a couple of hours," I coaxed. "Then they'll all be gone and I can make it up to you."

"Oh yeah. And how are you going to do that?"

"I don't know. You see if you can think of anything."

...

"He's very drunk," I say. "I've never seen him like this."

"Me neither," says Jenny.

"I shouldn't have invited him. I feel pretty stupid."

"Don't be ridiculous."

"And Edward's furious." I wring my hands.

"He'll get over it. Do you want me to talk to Charles?"

"No, I'll . . . You go and make sure everyone's happy, got enough to eat. I suppose I should call a cab or something; he can't drive home in this state, can he?"

"You'll be lucky to get one."

"Bloody hell. Honestly, I hate drama," I say. "I'd better go up and make sure he's not passed out or . . ."

I hurry up the stairs. It's nearly twenty minutes since Edward and Charles had an angry, muttered conversation, the details of which I was too far away to grasp. Charles went upstairs, and I could hear him thumping about, which made me anxious. I couldn't decide whether to follow him or not. There was some sinister crashing from the bathroom, but it's stopped, now, thank God. I'm worried he's trashed it, though, or been into the bedroom or something. I'm not sure how we got to this point; everything seemed to be going so well.

"Fucking idiots," I mutter. Edward stomped off downstairs after his brother went upstairs and if there weren't guests here I'd have gone after him. Not that he should need going after, for God's sake; he's an adult. Allegedly.

I tap on the bathroom door. "Charles? Charles, are you okay?"

Silence.

I rattle the handle, and the door, surprisingly, opens. No sign of him. "Oh," I say. "Where are you?"

Don't be in the study, I think, a sudden image of Charles tearing up Edward's notes or breaking his records. But he's not in there either, or in our bedroom. I open the door of the larger of the spare bedrooms cautiously. "Charles?"

It's very dark—which makes me think he must be in here, because someone must have drawn the blind. I reach for the light switch.

"Don't put the light on," he says.

"Come on now, you can't hide up here in the dark. Or do you need to lie down? You can if you like. Or I can see if I can get you a cab, or call Lynda?"

"She'll be in bed. I can drive myself."

"I don't think you can," I say, peering into the gloom. "Or at least, you shouldn't." I can't tell where he is, but I sort of assume he's sitting on the bed. He isn't, though, because when I step farther into the room, he shuts the door behind me. I turn round quickly, but I still can't see him. He must be standing in front of the door; the narrow line of light from the landing is obscured on one side, where the hinges are.

I'm suddenly rather nervous, although at the same time that seems silly. Doesn't it? He's practically my brother-in-law, after all.

For some reason this doesn't reassure me even slightly.

"Now I can't see anything," I complain, trying to sound calm. "What are you doing up here anyway?"

"I hoped you'd come to look for me." He doesn't sound as drunk as he did earlier.

"Well, here I am, looking—or trying to look—and I wish you'd open the door." I peer into the gloom, the darkness pressing like felt against my eyeballs.

"I don't want to."

"I can't stay up here in the dark with you, Charles. There are other people here, you know."

"You should be doing your hostess thing."

"Yes, I should."

We stand in silence for a moment.

"Nice for Edward," he says.

"What is?"

"That he's got you and I've got nothing."

"Oh bloody hell," I say. "Come on, don't be—"

"Don't be what? Don't be fucking furious? Too late."

"Charles—"

"He ruined my life," he says. "What about if I ruin his?"

"Charles. You know he felt like you already had, that's why he . . . You know all that stuff didn't come from no-where."

"I don't care about that. I want to know what he'll think about you being up here with me."

"Yes, I expect he'll be annoyed," I say, trying to remember where the furniture is in here, and whether there's anything I could maybe hit him with. Of course I would be in one of the only two rooms in the house with no flipping books.

"If I told him we'd had sex," he says conversationally, "do you think he'd believe me?"

I do something that can only be described as a full-body eye roll. "Oh my God. No."

"Why not?"

"Because . . . he'd believe me," I say, "wouldn't he? And I'd tell him we hadn't."

"What if we did?"

"Can you stop talking like this? And let me out? There's no point in any of this. I'm sorry I invited you," I add. "I hoped you'd be able to get past all the—"

"You think I'll be able to get past my brother sleeping with my wife?"

I roll my eyes again, not that he can see me.

"It's a long time ago. I know you were upset, and who can blame you? It was an awful thing to do. But he's right when he says she can't have cared that much. It's easy to avoid having an affair with your brother-in-law, you know. It isn't only Edward's fault."

"And what about the others?"

"None of them would have slept with him if they didn't want to, would they? Come on, try to be objective about it. I'm sure it's very . . . I'm sure it's horrible to think about, but seriously."

"And how's that supposed to make me feel? That anyone I care for would cheat on me with my brother?"

I sigh. "It's supposed to make you feel like shit. I'm not defending his actions."

"But that's . . . You don't care. It doesn't bother you that he could do something like that?"

"I was shocked when he told me," I say, "but it's not like he's proud of himself. Your relationship with him was messed up before he ever slept with"—I search for the name of the first one—"Tasha, or whoever. Wasn't it? He says he did it out of revenge and so you should probably think about why he wanted to be avenged. I mean, I think it's awful, and melodramatic, but it's also a long time ago. How long have you and Carolyn been divorced? Eight years?"

"I . . . Yes."

"You need to stop fixating on it. It's difficult for me," I complain, "trying to be friends with you as well as being Edward's girlfriend." It still feels odd saying this. I'm much too old to be someone's girlfriend.

"You'll have to choose, then, won't you?"

"I don't know what you want me to say. And you know if I had to choose, I'd choose Edward, because I . . ." Again, I pause, feeling awkward. "Because I love him."

"I know you do. And he loves you. It's all very cozy."

It's odd having this conversation in the dark. I bet if he could see me he wouldn't be able to say any of this. I sigh, irritated. "For God's sake. What's that supposed to mean? No one did any of this deliberately. None of this has been like some great mysterious plan or anything."

"But you still chose him."

"That makes it sound like I had to pick between you, and we all know that's not true."

"Yes it is."

"Jesus Christ. You took me out to dinner, and I told you I didn't believe you had any real interest in me. I still don't. This is about you and Edward, and it's just unfortunate for me that I'm the one in the middle, when it could easily have been . . . I don't know, Lara or someone."

"He didn't care about Lara."

"No, that's . . . that's not my *point*. My point is—"

This is where the hammering on the door begins.

"Thea? Thea, are you in there?"

"Oh and now look," I say. "Now there's going to be a ridiculous scene and you've spoiled my evening."

"Go away," Charles yells, "we're busy."

"Oh, for Christ's sake." I move closer to the sound of his voice and push at him. "Get out of the way. Edward!"

"Thea—what the hell's going on?"

"I suppose you think you're clever," I say, kicking at Charles's shins. "Charles won't let me out," I say louder. "And it's dark."

"Open the door," says Edward.

"Leave us alone. I told you, we're busy. Ow, stop kicking me," he hisses.

"I shan't. Get away from the door." We tussle in the darkness. I'm pretty angry, to be honest. I'm worried about Edward's temper, and about being stuck in here in the dark with Charles, and . . . I manage to thump my fist on the light switch and we stand blinking at each other.

"Now get away from the door," I say, and pull at his arm. He steps toward me and the door opens.

"What the fuck—" says Edward.

"Oh thank God. Look, I don't know what to do with him," I say, "he's—"

But now they're glaring at each other, toe to toe.

"What the hell's going on in here?"

"Yes," says Charles, "it's not pleasant to catch your girl-friend in a bedroom with your brother, is it?"

"Oh, for GOD's sake," I say. "You two are—"

It's a bit late, though, because Edward punches Charles, who staggers backward and sits down rather unexpectedly on the bed. He looks surprised and puts his palm to his nose.

"Jesus Christ," he says, slightly muffled.

"Yeah, well don't shut yourself into bedrooms with my girlfriend," says Edward. He looks at me. "Are you okay?"

"Yes, I'm fine. Just quite angry, because this has nothing to do with me." I jab my finger at Charles. "I don't wish to spend the rest of my life wondering if you're going to try and sexually assault me—"

"Jesus Christ," says Edward. "He'd better not have laid a fucking finger on you—"

I grab for his arm. "No, he didn't, and I don't really think he was going to. But that's not the point. You can't carry on like this. I'm sorry I tried to get you to behave like grown-ups when it's clearly beyond you."

Edward puts his hands on his hips and snorts derisively. We all glare at one another for a long moment. Then he says, "All right, I wish I hadn't done it. I know it was a shit thing to do. It only made me feel better for ten minutes."

"What?" says Charles.

"Sleeping with Carolyn. I fucked that up for you. I shouldn't have." He glances at me. "There," he says.

"Okay, good," I say. "Charles, did you hear that?"

"Of course I heard it."

"No. Did you *hear* it?" I bang my hand on my chest. "Did you feel and believe it?"

"I . . . no."

"Again," I say, imperious.

Edward sighs heavily. "It's true, though. I mean it. I did it on purpose, and I was glad I'd done it at the time. I wanted to hurt you and I was glad I'd managed something so . . . spectacular. But it didn't last long, that feeling. Because it was . . . it wasn't any way to fix the stuff that was broken."

"You were sleeping together for months," says Charles.

"We were, yeah, but that doesn't make what I'm saying less true. It was wrong."

"And what about the others? Maddy and Therese? And Poppy and—"

"Yes, all of them," says Edward. I'm not sure even I completely believe him, and I notice he hasn't actually said he's sorry, but even this is a huge step, surely.

"And you," I say. "What about you, Charles? Are you sorry about . . . what was her name?" I ask Edward. "I don't think you ever told me her name. The one when you were a teenager."

"Cleo."

"Oh my God," says Charles. He's staring at Edward, a trickle of blood dribbling slowly down his lip. "Cleo Robertson? Is that . . . ? Oh my God."

"You broke my fucking heart," says Edward, "the pair of you."

"Oh my God. Jesus."

"You didn't think it was completely random, did you? You see the problem is, Charles, you've no self-awareness."

"But that was a *joke*," says Charles.

"Yes, a joke to you. But very serious to me."

"But—"

"Charles," I say, "there's no point 'butting.' You did something childish and hurtful. And although you were obviously a child, more or less, at the time and I think Edward could have dealt with it in a . . . healthier fashion—"

"Thanks, doll," says Edward, and I have to concentrate in order not to laugh.

"No one's saying that sleeping with all your girlfriends was a good idea—but can you at least see what might have put the idea into his mind?"

"Shit," says Charles. "But I . . . That was . . . It was a joke."

"I really liked her," says Edward. "Yes, it all sounds pathetic now, doesn't it, thirty fucking years later, but at the time I was devastated. And because I spent the next twenty years arsing about and failing to meet anyone, it's still one of the worst things that's ever happened to me. I suppose if we'd ever been friends it wouldn't have happened. But we haven't, have we?"

Charles, frowning, doesn't say anything.

"Try not to bleed on the bed," I say. "If you can help it. I'll get you some tissues." I look at Edward. "No fighting while I'm gone."

"Okay, boss," he says. He shakes his head at me. "Was this in your plan?"

"No, it bloody wasn't."

. . .

I fetch a wet facecloth and a towel from the bathroom, as well as tissues, and take it all back to the bedroom. Charles dabs at his face. I sigh heavily.

"I have to go back downstairs," I say. "I can't just leave everyone on their own. How do you feel?"

"My face hurts," Charles says indistinctly.

"I should think it does." I glance at Edward. "Are you coming back downstairs?"

"In a moment."

"No fighting."

He shakes his head. "I promise."

I shut the door on them and hurry back down to the sitting room.

...

"What's going on up there?" asks Alistair.

"Some kind of sibling nightmare."

"Are they fighting?"

"Not now."

Jenny laughs. "But they were? We could hear Edward shouting."

"I'm so embarrassed," I say. "I'd never have thought getting involved with the minor aristocracy would be so much like a soap opera."

She laughs. "Are they talking now?"

"God knows. As long as no one's getting punched, I don't care."

Louise, the dentist, comes over. "We should probably be getting back for the babysitter," she says. "Is everything okay?"

"It's fine, don't worry." I glance from her to Simon, her husband. "Must you go? I feel bad for abandoning you all."

"Oh no, don't feel bad." She smiles at me. "Entertaining is a tricky business. I can't believe you even got them both in the same room."

"Beginning to wish I hadn't," I say gloomily.

"Don't say that. It's quite a coup. And I'm sure it will all work out. Anyway, thank you so much for inviting us. Maybe you'll be able to get Edward out for Si's fiftieth? It's in May; I'll send you an invitation."

The chat becomes general and several other people mutter about making a move. Soon they're gathering coats and beginning to descend the staircase.

"Do you need us to help you tidy up?" asks Cerys. "You know we're trained in this sort of thing."

"Catering queens," agrees Jilly. "I can carry five full dinner plates at a time."

"No, no there's not much to do, is there? Just collecting glasses." I look around. It's true, mostly glasses on end tables and bookshelves.

"If you're sure. I hope you don't have to spend any more of your evening listening to the pair of them talking shit to each other." Cerys chuckles.

I snort. "Here's hoping."

"D'you want us to take Charles home, aye?" That's Gavin, the bathroom supplier. "He's more or less on the way for us."

I hesitate. "I don't know. He can't drive, that's for sure. But he can stay here; we're well supplied with bedrooms."

The final guests collect their belongings and I follow them down the stairs and into the shop.

"It was lovely," says Jenny, "please don't think it wasn't. Don't give up having people round because of this. It was great to spend an evening with you both, and the food was amazing."

I smile at her gratefully. "It was, wasn't it? All Edward. He's a wasted talent."

I watch them all go out into the street, waving and calling goodbye to one another, and then I lock the front door behind them and go back upstairs. The sitting room seems strangely empty. I pick up some glasses and plates and take them through to the kitchen, and go into the dining room to see what, if anything, is left of the food. I eat two spoonfuls of guacamole and some miniature crab cakes, and then, sighing, ascend the second flight of stairs to see what's going on.

In the spare bedroom, Charles has taken his shoes off and is propped up on the pillows, a wad of tissues held to his face. Edward is in the armchair by the window and he must have slipped downstairs while I was seeing everyone out because there's a bottle of Talisker and two glasses on the bedside table. I shake my head.

"Is more booze really what's required?"

"Medicinal," says Charles rather thickly, like someone with a bad cold.

"Are you still bleeding?"

"I don't think so." He pulls the tissues away and looks at them. "Hardly at all."

"Good. You'd better stay here," I say, "if you think Lynda will have gone to bed."

He looks at Edward, who shrugs.

"Thanks."

"Okay, well. I'd better go and load the dishwasher," I say. "It would be good to get at least one—"

"I'm sorry about before," says Charles. He looks up at the

ceiling, unwilling to meet my eyes. "I was being a . . . I behaved very badly."

"Yes," agrees Edward.

I wave a hand. "Just don't do it again."

"I apologize, though."

"Yes, yes, I forgive you. If the pair of you could agree to
attempt some kind of civil behavior in the future, that would
be enough."

They look at each other.

"Can't promise much more than very basic civility," says
Edward.

"Willing to make the attempt," says Charles.

"I suppose that will do. Well done, welcome to being an
adult even when you don't want to be." I look at my boyfriend. "Are you going to help me with the plates and stuff?"

Edward gets up. "Don't drink all that whisky," he tells his
brother. "Is there any food left?"

"Not much. A few crumbs. They've pretty much picked
the carcass clean," I tell him as we head back downstairs. On
the landing he puts his hand on my arm.

"Thea."

"What?"

"You know you're brilliant, don't you?"

I laugh at him. "What do you mean? In what sense, particularly?"

"Everything you do is brilliant, and wonderful, and I love
you."

I look at him suspiciously. "Are you drunk as well?"

He laughs. "No. Or not very. Come here." He hugs me.
"He's an arse, my brother, but I'm going to try not to tell him
that to his face."

"Noble."

"Isn't it? I'm sorry he was awful earlier. I know it's my fault. Thank you for being so perfect about it."

"Perfect? I kicked him." I snort. "And I was quite harsh, even before that."

"I know. It's good for him."

I lean back so I can see him better. "D'you reckon? Did he tell you I kicked him?"

"He did. He told me I was lucky and I said"—he pulls me closer again and kisses me—"that I'm well aware of that."

"*Pah.*"

"Anyway, I'm not so keen on the idea of clearing up, now. Why don't we go straight to bed?"

"That's a terrible—" but then we're kissing again, this time for ages. Even though I know I'll be sorry in the morning, it's hard not to be persuaded. "Okay, not terrible; I meant great . . . idea."

"There. I said you were brilliant," he says, and we go back upstairs to bed.

Twenty-nine

Today, we're at the lodge, painting the sitting room. I've had the hideous fireplace taken out. Edward was right about there being something larger and more pleasing behind it. There's a new, more elegantly Georgian surround and a high mantelpiece. It looks a hundred times better, but it did make quite a mess. Finally, though, the plaster is dry enough to paint over. The furniture is all pushed to the middle of the room, and the blanket-covered table is stacked with paintings. I've washed the curtains, which hang drying on the line, just visible from the recently cleaned windows. I washed all the knickknacks and ornaments too, and they're in a big plastic tub in the kitchen, waiting for everything to be put back so they can be rearranged on shelves and end tables.

It's the beginning of May, and next week there are people—friends of Xanthe and Rob's—coming to stay here for two weeks. My first holiday booking. It's all family and friends this year so I can make sure I've got it right.

The library is a bedroom once again, the books boxed up and taken to the shop, divided between keepers—upstairs, in the flat—and sellers. There's a complex spreadsheet to keep track of the money, although I think I'm going to use it as an investment in the business. I need to have a chat with Alistair about the legal issues. Anyway, we've moved beds around—my bed from home is in the master bedroom here now. Andrew's bed is in the library, and there are new twin beds in what was once Fiona's room. All the rooms have been repainted, and we took a cupboard out of the kitchen to get a dishwasher in there. I didn't replace anything else, although there is new cookware direct from Glasgow IKEA, and have described the feel as "retro" to my guests. There are new mugs and plates and dishes to replace Uncle Andrew's china, my favorite bits of which have joined the mismatched, teetering piles in Edward's kitchen cupboards.

It's been an absolutely beautiful day, and I'm very happy with how efficient we've been. It's only taken a couple of weeks, working on our days off and in the evenings. Edward is surprisingly keen on doing things properly, with masking tape and drop cloths, and although my face and arms are freckled with pale paint spots, we've managed not to tread emulsion across the carpet or flagstones, spill anything, or shout at each other. Now we're tidying up, and I stand at the sink, running the cold tap to clean the brushes. There's always a lot more paint in a paintbrush than you'd think possible.

"So anyway," I say, "I'm going to ring Charles in a minute."

"Are you? Whatever for?" He's looking in the cupboard to see if there's anything to eat. There really isn't, though, unless he wants to make soup from stock cubes and ketchup. The only food in the house is potential homemade pizza. Edward did the dough this morning, and we brought it with us, along with a big jar of sauce and Tupperware containers of various toppings.

"Thought I might ask him if he wants to come over."

"Over here?" From his look of horror you'd think I'd suggested something truly outrageous.

"Yeah. I mean what does he even get up to in the evening? Scrabble with Lynda?"

He opens his mouth to say something but decides against it. "Hm."

"Well, anyway. I thought I'd ask him if he fancies beer and pizza. He might not."

"Hm."

"Noncommittal."

"As always," he says inaccurately.

"Yeah, right. What do you think?" I stuff the brushes into a jam jar full of water and begin to rinse the rollers.

"Rather have you to myself," he says, which is his standard response to any hint of sociability.

"You have me to yourself all the time. And I'm not going to invite him to stay over, am I? He lives literally five minutes away. So if you think you can manage not to punch him . . ."

"Yes, yes," he says. "I hardly ever punch anyone." He laughs. "I've really only ever punched Charles, and let's face it, there were pretty much thirty years between the last two occasions."

"Considering there were about thirty years when you barely saw him or spoke to him—"

"That's not quite true. Maybe ten years."

"I feel my point stands. Anyway." I dry my hands on a very elderly tea towel, earmarked for end-of-life tasks. "But what do you think? Would that be okay? You don't mind?"

He regards me thoughtfully. "I'm not filled with enthusiasm."

I open my eyes wide. "You don't say. *Tsk.* Luckily, I do not require enthusiasm." I pull my phone from my pocket, scroll through the numbers, and call Charles.

"Thea! Hello."

"Hey, Charles, how are you?"

"Oh," he says, "I'm good, yes. And you? To what do I owe?"

"We're at the lodge," I tell him, "wondered if you'd had your dinner?"

A pause. "No, I—no."

"Got anything planned? I thought you might like to pop around. We're having pizza. Homemade. And there's beer."

"You and—Edward?"

"Yep," I say, "Edward Maltravers as ever is. We've been decorating. Just finished."

"Oh, right. Right, well."

"Be nice to see you," I say, trying not to laugh at Edward, who is looking lugubrious, and about as keen as Charles sounds. "If you fancy it." I look at the kitchen clock. "In about half an hour?"

There's quite a long pause while he thinks about it. "Yes, all right," he says eventually. "That would be— I'll walk down, shall I?"

"Up to you. But if you might drink more than one beer, yes."

"Okay," he says. "See you shortly. Er, thanks."

"You're welcome." I hang up and turn to Edward. "We could sit outside," I say, "if there aren't too many bugs."

"No need to go mad," he says.

. . .

Forty minutes later, the three of us are sitting at the kitchen table eating pizza. We decided not to risk the garden, despite the lovely evening sun.

It's quite funny. They're both being cautious and trying not to say anything controversial. In fact, we've mostly been talking about DIY.

"You should come and look at the barn," Charles says, "now that it's finished."

"Is it finished? That's taken ages." I don't really like beer, so I've got a glass of wine. Rosé, the wine of summer. I take a mouthful. It's funny how things can taste pink.

"It has. Twice as long as they thought." He sighs. "I don't know why I thought it would be quicker, it's not like I've never worked with builders before."

"Why?" asks Edward. "I mean, why has it taken so long?"

"Oh, I don't know. The usual. There was more wrong with the roof than we thought. Then the builders were doing something else, then it was winter . . . I'm glad it's finished."

"Is that the last one, then?" I've been to look at the barn, but not for months. Last time I saw it, it was still covered in scaffolding and partly open to the weather. There are other outbuildings there, at the home farm, some of them converted already.

"I'm not sure. The stables are a possibility. Might get two one-bedrooms out of that. Or even three."

"Who's done the inside?" I ask. Julia did the other ones, I think. Presumably she doesn't still do them, although you never know.

"Oh, a friend of Miranda's. She's not a pro but"—he clears his throat—"she's very good. Looks great."

"How is Miranda?" I ask carelessly. They both look at me.

"She's, er . . ." says Charles. "She's well, yes."

"Saw you out riding," I say, "last week." I concentrate on my pizza, not looking at him.

"Yes, we—"

Edward grins at him. "What Thea's trying to ask is whether you're—"

"I know she is," says Charles. "Not for the first time either."

I laugh. "Well, I'm interested. She seems okay. You know."

"I like her," says Edward. He stands up and goes to the fridge.

I turn to watch him. "Even though she calls you Eddie?"

Charles laughs, and then looks as though he thinks Edward might not find it funny. He glances quickly at his brother.

"She doesn't do it to my face," says Edward. "'Nother beer, Charles?"

"Oh, er—thanks."

"And you've never slept with her, have you?" I ask Edward.

Once again, they're both looking at me. Edward hands a bottle of beer to his brother, and rubs a hand over his face, shaking his head, pretending to be appalled at my manners.

"What?" I open my eyes wide, innocent.

"It's—" Edward's trying to look stern.

"No, but have you?"

"No," says Edward. He looks at Charles, who's opening his beer. "No, I never have."

"So that would be—" I go on.

"Thea," says Edward, "I don't think—"

"Oh, come on. Surely that's the ideal scenario?" I laugh at them. "Either that or someone Edward's never met and wouldn't fancy."

They both look at me. I laugh again. "Just to be on the safe side. *Pfft*."

"You told me once you thought she was suitable," says Charles.

"Oh yeah, when we had dinner? Well, she is. Or seems like it. More suitable than some people I could mention. Ha ha."

"She split up with that guy, didn't she," says Edward, as he sits back down at the table. "The hedge fund bloke."

"Hamish? God, yes," says Charles. "That was years ago. Before—years ago, anyway."

"He was a tit," says Edward.

"He was," agrees Charles. He cuts his last piece of pizza into three, and then adds, "He married one of the Mortimer-Jones girls."

"Gels," I say, in my most affected accent, and laugh. They both frown at me. When they do this, they're startlingly alike.

"Which one?"

"The middle one. Clarissa."

"Clarissa Mortimer-Jones," I say rapturously. "What's she like? Don't tell me. Excellent hair. Sophisticated. Never says the wrong thing."

They exchange glances.

"Dark hair," says Charles.

"Kind of irritating," says Edward, and Charles smothers a laugh. "I wouldn't call her sophisticated either."

"Says the wrong thing practically all the time," adds Charles. They both laugh at this.

"But anyway," I say, dragging them back. "Miranda?"

Charles puts his cutlery down and picks up his beer. "What about her?"

"You're being cagey."

"Am I?"

They both laugh again. I'm enjoying myself. Look at them, sitting at my kitchen table, almost conspiring against me. I've made this happen. I don't need them to be best mates—and really, I don't think they have it in them—but I like this. I can make all of it less serious. If I make all of the past—all those lovely exes of Charles's, so willing to jump into bed with Edward—a joke, a comical thing, then the power of it all, the anger and jealousy, all of that might just dissipate. That's my ideal scenario. I'd like Charles to be happy, for him to have someone special, someone who likes him. I'd like us to be able to have informal unimportant insignificant meetings like this one. It might be silly—and probably is a bit ambitious, perhaps—but wouldn't it be pleasant?

I look at Edward. "Isn't he? What do you think?"

He tries again to look stern. "I think it's really none of our business."

"Oh, well. I mean, it's not. Obviously. It's totally not. And yet I am strangely fascinated."

Charles sighs. "Miranda and I have been going riding together for years," he says.

"Yes? And?"

"She's very tenacious, isn't she?" he says to Edward.

"You have no idea."

"Just either tell me," I say, "or tell me to bugger off and never mention it again."

"Well. That would be rude," says Charles. He's definitely teasing. "We do sometimes have dinner."

"Yes?"

"And while, you know, I can have dinner with people who don't want to sleep with me and are happy to say so—"

"Is he talking about you?" says Edward. I kick him under the table.

"It's better for me if they're more amenable."

"Amenable? Oh lordy." I'm really laughing now.

"Anyway," he says, "she's coming to Alexa's birthday party. So you can ask her about it."

"I would never dare. When's Alexa's party, then? Are we invited?"

He looks from one of us to the other. "If you think— Would you like to come? The invitations are going out next week."

"Well, that would be lovely," I say.

Edward makes a face. "Will Mum be there?"

"I don't think I can get out of that one." He looks at me. "Have you met our dear mama?"

"No, I'm terrified."

"Oh God, you needn't worry. Julia will be there, so Mum will just spend all afternoon bleating to her about what a shame it is that we got divorced."

"Poor Julia," says Edward.

"How old is Alexa going to be?"

"Sixteen, if you can believe it. She's got some friends coming from school, so in the evening they're watching films, and then God knows what."

"Drinking peach wine and smoking menthol cigarettes?" I ask.

"I hope not." Charles looks pained. "Is that what you did on your sixteenth birthday?"

"I might not have discovered peach wine at that point. And I didn't start smoking until I left school. So I probably drank cider. I did have a party; my parents sat upstairs in their bedroom. Netty Wilson was sick all down the stairs."

"Jesus," says Edward.

"I know. And I didn't even like her very much. Angela and I had to clear it up, it was surprisingly tricky and quite unpleasant." I grin at his look of disgust.

"I was at school for mine," says Charles. "No party for me."

"So was I," says his brother. "I did get very drunk, though. Peter Lovatt gave me a bottle of whisky, and we drank it on the beach. Stayed out all night."

"Did you get caught?"

He shakes his head. "We were extremely cunning."

"Peter Lovatt," says Charles. "I'd forgotten all about him. D'you ever see him?"

"No. He lives in Australia, I think. Or Canada, possibly."

"Hm."

They sit in silence for a moment, thinking about school, I presume.

"Is Duncan coming too?" I ask.

"Oh, yes, and he's bringing a friend as well. Julia's fetching the lot of them."

"Lucky Julia. She gets all the treats, then."

"Yes, well—she lives closer to the school. But anyway, you know, that's why we're having an afternoon party. So there can be cake and bunting and"—he waves a hand—"floral decorations and cousins and grandparents and so on. Before they do their own thing in the evening."

"No offense," says Edward, "but it sounds like a nightmare."

Charles laughs at this. "I've had to go to dozens of children's parties," he says, "you've got off very lightly."

"I suppose I have. Well. I guess we should go," he says, looking at me.

"Of course we should. Just think, if it wasn't for me you'd never have been invited." I chuckle. "See how I improve your life in every way?"

"Yeah, well, I'll try not to resent you too much."

Charles laughs, and looks at his brother. "It won't be too bad," he says. "They're old enough now that they don't need you to play games with them, and no one will cry or be sick. With luck."

"A whole new bunch of people to meet," I say. "To whom I am practically related. I'd be excited if relatives weren't so tiresome."

"They're mostly okay," says Charles. "I mean, mostly."

"I don't really care anyway, I'm old enough and ugly enough to look after myself. Although I am scared to meet your mum."

"If it's just for a couple of hours it won't be too bad," says Edward. "And it's not like you'll ever have to see much of her."

"She's long since given up on Edward doing anything she might approve of," says Charles, "so you'll be a welcome respite."

I laugh. "I doubt that."

"Oh, no, I think she's pleased. She asked me what I thought of you. I said you were great."

"Aw. Well. Thanks." I'm almost embarrassed.

"He's right, though, isn't he?" Edward grins at me.

"Shucks. You guys." I roll my eyes.

Charles looks at his phone. "I should get going," he says. "It's getting on for eight, and I'm expecting a call."

"Is it really as late as that?"

He nods.

"Who's calling? Miranda?"

"Thea," says Edward, "leave the poor fellow alone."

Charles manages a respectable poker face and doesn't answer my question. We all stand up, chairs scraping on the lino.

"Thanks for having me," says Charles. "The pizza was excellent." He turns to Edward. "I can't believe you made it yourself."

"He's good at that sort of thing," I say as we proceed down the passageway toward the front door. "Anyway, you're welcome."

"I'll send the invitation to the shop?"

"Yes please. Cheers for coming over, it's good to see you." I offer my cheek and he kisses me, looks over my shoulder at his brother. "Yes. Good to see you too. Both of you."

"Good night," says Edward. "See you later."

I close the door behind him and head back to the kitchen.

"Well done," I say. "That was okay, wasn't it?"

"Yes, it was fine. I suppose you're awfully proud of yourself."

"Ha ha." I turn to smile at him, and he moves closer to put his arms round me. "I am quite. Witness the détente that I have wrangled."

"Good wrangling," he says into my hair.

...

Later, as we're puttering about getting ready for bed—sleeping at the lodge for the last time for what might be a long while—I stand in the shadowy hallway and watch him tidying the kitchen. What a wonderful thing, to be here, alive, now, in this moment. I think of what he said last year, about having an untapped capacity for contentment. I really don't think I'm special, but I've definitely helped him find a way to be happier. That's a good feeling. I'm happy too, pleasantly tired from our productive day, full of pizza, a tiny bit smug about the evening's family gathering.

Edward looks around. "Oh, there you are. What on earth are you doing lurking out there?"

"Just feeling lucky."

"Lucky?"

"Yeah, you know. Lucky to know you. Lucky you're here."

His look of revulsion makes me laugh.

"I'm having such a nice time, Edward. You're great, and I love you."

Now he's smiling. "I'm the lucky one, aren't I? Even if having you in my life means I have to be nice to Charles and go to children's parties."

"I imagine Alexa would be outraged to hear you describe her party like that."

"Don't much care what she thinks."

"You astonish me."

He holds out his hand and I take it. "Is it right to be this happy?"

"Of course it is, you idiot."

He laughs and pulls me closer. "That's good to know."

"I'm so grateful," I say. "My whole life leading me here. All the awful, terrible things seem almost worth it."

"Only almost?"

We're kissing, then, greedy kisses. I pull away for a moment so I can look at him. "Okay, then. Entirely."

"Glad to hear it," he says, and we're kissing again.

Acknowledgments

I love reading acknowledgments and writing them is even more fun.

My parents are better than anyone else's and always have been, so thanks to Pam and Vic for all their support and encouragement, and their willingness to believe that this might actually happen, without adding any pressure. Thanks to Stewart and Tess too, for their support and excitement about this project in what has to have been the most intense and weirdest year ever.

I met lots of writers on the now-defunct Authonomy writers' forum, many of whom have been a great help to me, and some of whom, as members of the Facebook Women's Fiction Critique Group, read an early draft of *The Bookshop* (as it was called then) and made useful comments. I'd particularly like to thank Ann Warner, Kate Murdoch, Gail Cleare, Margaret Johnson, and Katie O'Rourke, all of whom have been incredibly supportive and all of whom have their own books that you should check out. Angela Elliott gave Fortescue's its name, and Carla Burgess, Tamsin McDonald, Mick Jones, and Leonie Roberts have encouraged me to "just get on with it" on a number of occasions.

I'd also like to thank friends and erstwhile colleagues Liz

Haynes, Donna Wood, and Clare Ashton, who've all read previous work of mine and have been enthusiastic cheerleaders for my writing for the last eight years, and Denise Laing, who encouraged me to submit my first novel to an agent, more years ago than I care to remember.

Sarah Albiston, Katie McCallion, and Mat Winser have been available to talk about books and writing (and everything else in the world) for more than thirty years and I am eternally thankful to all of them. Mark Manson definitely wouldn't buy a book like this but he's an excellent beta reader and his feedback is always appreciated. And thanks to Stephen McConnachie for holding my hand before a Very Important Meeting, and Jimmy Martin for joining me in a celebratory drink afterward.

I'm extremely grateful to Sara-Jade Virtue at Simon & Schuster UK, who read my sample chapter and liked it enough to ask to see the rest. She and my editor, Alice Rodgers, have been brilliant, and the rest of the team of designers, editors, marketers, and the people in the rights department have all done loads of stuff I don't even know about. Thank you.

I could never have imagined the book would be published in the United States, so I am both astonished and grateful for this opportunity. Thank you to Shauna Summers, Lexi Batsides, and everyone else at Ballantine for their kindness and enthusiasm.

Last but not least, all my love and thanks to Ollie, for shopping, cooking, and driving me about, and without whom it would all be pointless.

The Bookshop
of
Second Chances

JACKIE FRASER

A Book Club Guide

Questions for Discussion

1. Compare and contrast the two Maltravers brothers and their relationships with Thea. How did your opinions of them shift as the novel progressed?

2. On page 44, following Xanthe's departure, Thea muses: "For all intents and purposes, I'm alone. No one to please but myself. No one to talk to, unless I make an effort. I'm both thrilled and terrified by this feeling." Upon finishing the novel, what do you make of this? How did you see Thea's character grow and change as a result of her time in Scotland?

3. Though Thea was never close with her uncle Andrew, upon spending more time in Baldochrie, she realizes that her inheritance and a change of scenery were exactly what she'd needed to overcome the chaos and dissatisfaction with her life in Sussex. Have you ever experienced something you later came to view as a blessing in disguise?

4. As Thea and Edward spend time together at the beach and begin to open up to each other, their relationship evolves into something more. What about their characters makes them a good match?

5. Fortescue's proves to be a savior for Thea in many ways; in time, the bookshop becomes something of a second home. Is there a place that provides the same sense of solace or retreat for you? What do you find so comforting about it?

6. Xanthe's loyalty and welcome sense of humor make her Thea's closest, most treasured friend. When you think of their friendship, does a specific person from your own life come to mind? Why do you value him or her in this way?

7. When Edward fires Thea, she struggles to understand his reasoning. How do the revelations about Edward's past, his romantic history, and his relationship with his brother inform his behavior throughout the novel?

8. Between Rory, Alistair and Jenny, and Jilly and Cerys, Thea meets a number of vibrant, interesting individuals as she settles into her new life, all of whom welcome her with open arms and become dear friends. Did you relate to or favor any of these characters in particular? Why or why not?

9. When Chris shows up at the shop unexpectedly, Thea decides to confront him about his infidelity and is faced with some harsh truths. What about Thea's experiences leading up to this encounter have prepared her to face him? Discuss how you feel her character might have responded had he shown up earlier on.

10. Share your opinions about the final chapter. How do you picture Thea and Edward's life together after the events of the novel, and what do you think is in store for their future?

ABOUT THE AUTHOR

JACKIE FRASER is a freelance editor and writer. She's worked for AA Publishing, Watkins, the *Good Food Guide,* and various self-published writers of fiction, travel and food guides, recipe books, and self-help books since 2012. Prior to that, she worked as an editor of food and accommodation guides for the AA, including the *B&B Guide, Restaurant Guide,* and *Pub Guide* for nearly twenty years, eventually running the Lifestyle Guides department. She's interested in all kinds of things, particularly history (and prehistory), art, food, popular culture, and music. She reads a lot, (no, really) in multiple genres, and is fascinated by the Bronze Age. She used to be a bit of a Goth. She likes vintage clothes, antiques fairs, photography, and cats.